LA BÊTE HUMAINE

ÉMILE ZOLA was born in Paris in 1840, the son of a Venetian engineer and his French wife. He grew up in Aix-en-Provence where he made friends with Paul Cézanne. After an undistinguished school career and a brief period of dire poverty in Paris, Zola joined the newly founded publishing firm of Hachette which he left in 1866 to live by his pen. He had already published a novel and his first collection of short stories. Other novels and stories followed until in 1871 Zola published the first volume of his Rougon-Macquart series with the subtitle *Histoire naturelle et sociale d'une famille sous le Second Empire*, in which he sets out to illustrate the influence of heredity and environment on a wide range of characters and milieux. However, it was not until 1877 that his novel *L'Assommoir*, a study of alcoholism in the working classes, brought him wealth and fame. The last of the Rougon-Macquart series appeared in 1893 and his subsequent writing was far less successful, although he achieved fame of a different sort in his vigorous and influential intervention in the Dreyfus case. His marriage in 1870 had remained childless but his extremely happy liaison in later life with Jeanne Rozerot, initially one of his domestic servants, gave him a son and a daughter. He died in 1902.

ROGER PEARSON is Professor of French in the University of Oxford and Fellow and Praelector in French at The Queen's College, Oxford. He is the author of *Stendhal's Violin: A Novelist and his Reader* (1988), *The Fables of Reason: A Study of Voltaire's 'Contes philosophiques'* (1993), *Unfolding Mallarmé: The Development of a Poetic Art* (1996), *Mallarmé and Circumstance: The Translation of Silence* (2004), and *Voltaire Almighty: A Life in Pursuit of Freedom* (2005). For Oxford World's Classics he has revised and edited Zola's *The Masterpiece* and translated Voltaire, *Candide and Other Stories* and Maupassant, *A Life*.

OXFORD WORLD'S CLASSICS

*For over 100 years Oxford World's Classics have brought
readers closer to the world's great literature. Now with over 700
titles—from the 4,000-year-old myths of Mesopotamia to the
twentieth century's greatest novels—the series makes available
lesser-known as well as celebrated writing.*

*The pocket-sized hardbacks of the early years contained
introductions by Virginia Woolf, T. S. Eliot, Graham Greene,
and other literary figures which enriched the experience of reading.
Today the series is recognized for its fine scholarship and
reliability in texts that span world literature, drama and poetry,
religion, philosophy and politics. Each edition includes perceptive
commentary and essential background information to meet the
changing needs of readers.*

OXFORD WORLD'S CLASSICS

ÉMILE ZOLA

La Bête humaine

Translated, with an Introduction and Notes, by
ROGER PEARSON

OXFORD
UNIVERSITY PRESS

OXFORD

UNIVERSITY PRESS

Great Clarendon Street, Oxford OX2 6DP

Oxford University Press is a department of the University of Oxford.
It furthers the University's objective of excellence in research, scholarship,
and education by publishing worldwide in

Oxford New York

Auckland Bangkok Buenos Aires Cape Town Chennai
Dar es Salaam Delhi Hong Kong Istanbul Karachi Kolkata
Kuala Lumpur Madrid Melbourne Mexico City Mumbai Nairobi
São Paulo Shanghai Taipei Tokyo Toronto

Oxford is a registered trade mark of Oxford University Press
in the UK and in certain other countries

Published in the United States
by Oxford University Press Inc., New York

First published as a World's Classics paperback 1996
Reissued as an Oxford World's Classics paperback 1999
Reissued 2009

British Library Cataloguing in Publication Data

Data available

Library of Congress Cataloging in Publication Data
Zola, Émile, 1840–1902.
[Bête humaine, English]
La bête humaine / Émile Zola : translated, with an introduction
and notes by Roger Pearson.
(Oxford world's classics)
Includes bibliographical references.
I. Pearson, Roger. II. Title. III. Series.
PQ2498.A36 1996 843'.8—dc20 95–47332

ISBN 978–0–19–953866–9

17

Printed in Great Britain by
Clays Ltd, Elcograf S.p.A.

CONTENTS

INTRODUCTION

> 'Our civilization is still in a middle stage—scarcely beast,
> in that it is no longer wholly guided by instinct; scarcely
> human, in that it is not yet wholly guided by reason.'
>
> Theodore Dreiser, *Sister Carrie* (1900)

'TOO many trains, and too many crimes', complained Augustin Filon in *La Revue bleue* on 22 March 1890, a fortnight after the publication of *La Bête humaine*. ' "Murder" should have been the title of M. Zola's new book', commented *The Athenaeum* that same day: 'In the first fifty-six pages we find preparations going on for no fewer than three brutal assassinations, two by the knife and one by poison, committed for three different reasons by three distinct sets of persons.' 'M. Zola', Augustin Filon continued from his side of the Channel, 'does not deny that human beings are half angel and half beast, but he never shows us more than one side at a time'. 'What we have described', concluded *The Athenaeum*, 'is not art and is not nature. It is not true to life'. Two years later the North American reading public was informed by Sir Edwin Arnold that 'the whole volume seems to be written in blood, so full are its red pages of the shadow of evil passions, assassinations, envies, hatreds, malice, and all uncharitableness';[1] while, several generations later, Joanna Richardson greeted Alec Brown's English translation of the novel with the observation that 'there is no beauty in *La Bête humaine*: there is not a passage in it that could have been written by a Gautier or a Flaubert.'[2]

Other commentators, however, were quick to recognize the latest Zola as having the potential status of a World's Classic. Reviewing the novel for *Le Temps* on 9 March 1890, Anatole France was moved to compare the author of *La Bête humaine* with no less a precursor than Homer. Far from being a 'puerile vulgarizer' of technological achievements, the creator of La

---

[1] *The North American Review*, 154 (Jan.–June 1892), 85–93.
[2] *Time and Tide*, 39 (24 May 1958), 650–1.

Lison (the locomotive which plays a key role in the novel) was for this reviewer nothing less than a 'poet': 'It is his genius, which is large and uncomplicated, to produce symbols. He is able to create fresh myths . . . He is the great lyric writer of our time.' The previous day in *Le Figaro*, Jules Lemaître had used similar language in describing Zola as 'the poet of man's darker side' and considered that 'his whole work ought to bear this title: *La Bête humaine*'.

And indeed, more than any other early reviewer of the novel, Lemaître had understood its point: 'In his latest novel M. Zola examines the most frightening and most mysterious of all primordial instincts: the instinct for destruction and slaughter, and the obscure connection between this instinct and the erotic instinct'. The protagonists are not so much 'characters' as 'instincts which speak, and walk, and move about', and the effect of such 'simplification' is at once 'awesome and beautiful'. Rather than dwell on those aspects of the novel which may be (misleadingly) reminiscent of second-rate contemporary crime fiction, Lemaître alerts potential readers of *La Bête humaine* to its grandeur, to the way in which it seeks to remind us all of our distant origins:

There are brutes among us, countless brutes. Christian though we be, and civilized, and literate, and artistic, we also experience feelings of hatred or love, of concupiscence or anger, feelings which come to us, as it were, from beyond ourselves; and we do not always know what makes us respond as we do. We paltry, transient persons are but the infinitely tiny waves upon an ocean of blind, eternal, and impersonal forces; and beneath the waves there lies always an abyss. This, in short, is what—with a wild and melancholic majesty—*La Bête humaine* expresses. It is a prehistoric epic in the guise of a modern-day story.[3]

Sensationalist claptrap, or the epic grandeur of a classic? More than a century later the reader of *La Bête humaine* may well be torn between these two responses. On the face of it the novel is pure tabloid press: sex aplenty, child abuse, political corruption, murder to suit every taste, even a treasure hunt. At the same time this compassionate story of an amiable psychopath epitomizes the Naturalist vision of the human condition; for it demonstrates

---

[3] *Le Figaro*, 8 Mar. 1890.

how easily human beings may be—and few critics have resisted the pun—'derailed' by atavistic forces which defy all reason and defeat the will. And not only the individual human being but society at large. The final chapter of *La Bête humaine* displays the inability of the dominant moral order to recognize and deal with the irrational, while its unforgettable final image (which it would be a crime indeed to reveal in advance) suggests that society itself can lose its grip: warfare is the psychopathy of the collective.

Seen from the vantage-point of the present, this novel which juxtaposes the marvels of technology with the depradations of the human beast seems to stand prophetically on the threshold of a century which has witnessed both the magic of the aeroplane and the massacres of the Somme, the wonder of a lunar landing and the abyss of the Holocaust. But perhaps all centuries have exhibited such contrasts ever since the first wheel was smashed across a human skull. Does human nature evolve (as Theodore Dreiser implies in the epigraph to this Introduction)? Or does the unbridgeable and ineradicable divide within the human beast simply grow ever wider? For all its violence and the aura of fateful, tragic inevitability which here raises the Naturalist vision to the level of a Racinian tragedy, *La Bête humaine* offers an essentially optimistic answer to this question. The essential focus of the book is not so much on the inevitability of defeat as on the drama of resistance: yes, the beast will out—for now; but what Zola calls the 'strength derived from education' is increasing with every generation, and the overriding value of *La Bête humaine* lies in its contribution to that education.

La Bête humaine first appeared in serial instalments in the illustrated weekly *La Vie populaire* between 14 November 1889 and 2 March 1890. It was then immediately published in book form, of which 60,000 copies had been printed by the end of that month. As the seventeenth of the twenty novels that comprise the Rougon-Macquart cycle—which Zola famously subtitled 'The Natural and Social History of a Family under the Second Empire'—its central protagonist is Jacques Lantier. Descended from the doomed, illegitimate Macquart branch of this family, he is the son of Gervaise, the tragic laundrywoman of

L'Assommoir (1877), and thus the brother of Claude, who appears as a young artist in *Le Ventre de Paris* (*The Belly of Paris*: 1873) and becomes the suicidal hero of *L'Œuvre* (*The Masterpiece*: 1886), of Étienne, the leader of the striking miners in *Germinal* (1885), and of the eponymous heroine of *Nana* (1880). But such links to the rest of the Rougon-Macquart series are essentially superficial: while *La Bête humaine* continues to treat the theme of heredity, it is nevertheless a self-contained and independent work of literature which can be read quite satisfactorily in isolation from Zola's other novels.

The preparatory notes for the novel run to 677 pages, seven of which contain a list of some 130 possible titles which Zola contemplated for his novel and from which he chose *La Bête humaine*. The phrase itself crops up several times in the works of Victor Hugo, though Zola preferred to think he owed it to his intellectual mentor Hippolyte Taine. He uses the phrase on a number of occasions from the 1860s onwards, both of himself (as when recounting how Manet painted his portrait as he might have painted the portrait of 'any old human beast') and of humanity in general: 'The human beast is the same the world over', he wrote in *Le Roman expérimental* (1880); 'only the clothing is different.' The phrase came to enjoy a certain vogue in the 1880s, and Jules Lemaître had already used it in 1885 as a summary of the central subject of Zola's work. On 6 June 1889, having just completed the first chapter of the novel, Zola wrote to the Dutch journalist Van Santen Kolff that the choice of title had caused him considerable difficulty, but that in the end he had plumped for *La Bête humaine* because he wanted to convey the idea of 'the caveman that still lives on inside nineteenth-century man, of that part of us which derives from our distant ancestor'. And he confidently predicted that the title would 'catch on when people have read the book'.

While Zola fixed on the title only at the last minute, the basic idea for the novel dates back to the late 1860s when he was drawing up his masterplan for the Rougon-Macquart cycle. At that stage there were to be ten novels, in which he intended

to study the ambitions and appetites of a family launched upon the modern world, making superhuman efforts but always failing because of

their own nature and the influences upon it, almost getting there only to
fall back again, and ending up by producing veritable moral monsters,
the priest, the murderer, the artist. The times are in turmoil, and it is
this turmoil of the moment which I shall depict.[4]

The 'murderer' was to have figured in the last of the ten, a
'courtroom novel as I understand the genre (which has been
rather left to the mercy of patented suppliers of serial novels) and
which could have the makings of something at once highly literary and profoundly moving'. Such a book would allow him to
include the legal world in his panorama of France under the
Second Empire (1852–70), while its hero (then envisaged as
Étienne Lantier) would illustrate 'one of those strange cases of
the hereditary criminal who is not mad but one day kills in a
moment of mental imbalance (*crise morbide*) at the prompting of
some bestial instinct'. Claude Lantier, the artist, will inherit
'genius' from his flawed parents, while Étienne's legacy will be
'murder'. In this way Zola sought to go beyond the account of
murder which he had recently provided in *Thérèse Raquin*
(1867), where the lovers Thérèse and Laurent kill Thérèse's
husband Camille simply because he is in the way and not because
of any hereditary impulse. On the other hand, when Zola finally
came to write *La Bête humaine*, the hereditary impulse which
drives Jacques to murder stems not so much from his parents as
from all his (male) ancestors since the dawn of time.

    The idea for a novel about the railway came much later,
perhaps ten years later when Zola bought his house at Médan on
the Seine, some forty kilometres west of Paris. The Paris–Rouen
line ran past the bottom of his garden, and the commuting writer
soon became familiar with its Parisian terminus, the Gare Saint-
Lazare. According to the memoirs of the Italian critic Edmondo
de Amicis who visited him at this time, the author of the fast-
expanding Rougon-Macquart now envisaged 'the most original'
novel of them all,

which will have a railway network as its setting: there will be a large
station in which ten separate lines converge, with each line having its
own plot and all of them linked to the main station; and the whole novel

---

[4] *Les Rougon-Macquart*, v (Paris: Gallimard, Bibliothèque de la Pléiade,
1966), 1738–9.

will be imbued with the colour of the locale, and you will be able to hear, like background music, the rattle and roll of this hectic life, and witness love on a train, a tunnel accident, the toil of the locomotive, collisions both head on and from behind, disasters, fleeing passengers, the whole dark, smoke-filled, noisy world which he [Zola] has been mentally inhabiting for so long.[5]

Not only personal experience of the railway but a certain spirit of rivalry may also have motivated Zola at this period. In 1877 Jules Claretie had published a novel entitled *Le Train 17*, which provides a detailed account of the life of an engine-driver; and in 1879 Zola's Naturalist 'disciple' Karl-Joris Huysmans had included in his novel *Les Sœurs Vatard* a number of atmospheric, 'Impressionist' descriptions of the Gare Montparnasse which themselves owe much to the inspiration of Claude Monet, who had recently painted several canvases of the Gare Saint-Lazare.

Railway transport had, of course, already been evolving for over half a century, during which time the maximum speed of a locomotive rose from 9 to more than 80 kilometres per hour. The first passenger steam railway in the world opened in England between Stockton and Darlington in 1825. In France the steam railway was demonstrated the following year between Saint-Étienne and Lyon, although the first regular passenger service did not begin until 1837 and ran between Paris and Saint-Germain. The early development of public railways was marked by passionate debate concerning the relative merits of state funding and private enterprise, and the French Assembly finally passed a law on 9 July 1836 which authorized private companies to build new railways but under strict public control—which no doubt explains why so many companies subsequently appointed prominent politicians and other public servants (like President Grandmorin in *La Bête humaine*) to their boards. While Belgium, Prussia, and the rest of what later became Germany pressed ahead efficiently with the expansion of a state-run railway, and the British and American railways for their part flourished rapidly under private enterprise, the French option of a 'mixed economy' led to delay, and French politicians continued to debate at length not only the relative priority of com-

---

[5] Quoted in the Pléiade edition, p. 1710.

mercial and military criteria, but also the place of Paris in a new national network. It was not until 1838 that three private companies were authorized to begin work on lines linking Paris and Le Havre (via Rouen), Paris and Orléans, and Strasbourg and Basle. But it proved impossible to raise sufficient capital from private sources, and it required a state loan of 12 million francs (at 4 per cent interest) in 1840 for the Paris–Le Havre project to proceed.

The Gare Saint-Lazare, the first railway station in Paris, had already opened in 1837 to serve the Paris–Saint-Germain line. Trains arrived and departed by passing through a tunnel under the Place de l'Europe; and soon afterwards a further tunnel was built to the north under what was then the village of Batignolles (where the Impressionists would later congregate). The star-shaped Pont de l'Europe which figures in the opening paragraphs of *La Bête humaine* was built only in 1867, to replace the Place de l'Europe. As for the station itself, it was successively enlarged and rebuilt by the Compagnie de l'Ouest as the railway extended its reach: the Paris–Rouen line opening in 1842, Paris–Le Havre in 1847, and Paris–Auteuil in 1854. The celebrated (and still extant) train-shed designed by Eugène Flachat was built between 1851 and 1853. This was the Gare Saint-Lazare which is described in *La Bête humaine* (set in 1869–70), and which Monet was to paint in 1877.

The idea of a novel about the railways continued to develop in Zola's mind throughout the 1880s, and he began to collect newspaper cuttings describing various train accidents and crimes connected with the railways. At this point there were plans once more to enlarge the Gare Saint-Lazare, this time to cope with the large number of visitors expected for the Exposition Universelle (or World Fair), some of whom would be coming from overseas to see Paris (and the newly erected Eiffel Tower) via the port of Le Havre. The work was entrusted to the architect Juste Lisch and carried out between 1885 and 1889: it was nearing completion when, in February 1889, Zola finally began his research into the railways in preparation for *La Bête humaine*, which he started to write on 5 May.

His first and principal source of information was Pol Lefèvre, who worked for the Compagnie de l'Ouest and had co-written a book about railway technology. Zola met him on a number of occasions between February and April and visited the Gare Saint-Lazare in his company, learning what railwaymen did and storing away their anecdotes for possible use. He made the journey to Le Havre, where he questioned an elderly railwayman about how the station would have looked back in 1869. On 15 April he took his famous trip to Mantes aboard a locomotive, standing on the footplate alongside the driver and fireman to experience directly how it felt: he arrived back in Paris exhausted, his legs still trembling from the constant vibration of the locomotive and his memory filled with all the sensory detail which make the descriptions of Jacques's train-driving so compelling in *La Bête humaine*.

During Zola's journey of exploration to Le Havre, he had also stopped off at Rouen to visit the Palais de Justice, for he had now decided to use the railways as the setting for the 'legal novel' (*roman judiciaire*) which he had been intending for so long to write. He had intended that the Rougon-Macquart cycle should comprise no more than twenty novels; and having already decided to devote separate novels to the subjects of money, war, and science (as he subsequently did in *L'Argent* (*Money*: 1891), *La Débâcle* (1892), and *Le Docteur Pascal* (1893)), he was in a sense running out of opportunities to treat the criminal mind and the world of the railways separately. But in any case the two subjects were strongly associated in the public imagination, both in France and England. Already in the 1860s there had been much urgent debate about the dangers of travelling by train, which, as *The Globe* reported in 1863, offered the criminal new and heaven-sent opportunities:

The loudest screams are swallowed up by the roar of the rapidly revolving wheels, and murder, or violence worse than murder, may go on to the accompaniment of a train flying along at sixty miles an hour. When it stops in due course, and not till then, the ticket collector coming up may find a second-class carriage converted into a 'shambles'. We are not romancing.[6]

_____

[6] Quoted in Ivor Smullen, *Taken for a Ride* (London, 1968), 131; and in Wolfgang Schivelbusch, *The Railway Journey: The Industrialization of Time and Space in the Nineteenth Century* (Leamington Spa, Hamburg, and New York, 1986), 79.

And nor was Zola. The first murder in *La Bête humaine* is based on the Poinsot affair, which began on 6 December 1860 when a senior judge was murdered in a first-class compartment on his way home to Paris from Troyes. He was found shot dead, and his watch and banknotes were missing: the passengers in the next compartment had heard nothing. A certain Charles Jud was suspected, but the police never caught him; and rumours circulated that Jud was a police invention designed to conceal the real motive for the crime, namely vengeance on the part of the brother of a girl whom the judge had seduced. Following the Briggs murder in England four years later, also committed in a first-class carriage, the problems of travelling alone in a compartment were again highlighted, and eventually footboards (of the kind which play a crucial role in the plot of *La Bête humaine*) were fitted to the outside of carriages to allow railway personnel to reach each compartment. (Corridor trains only entered regular service in the 1890s.) These murders were brought to the public's attention again when, on 14 January 1886, newspapers reported how the Prefect of the Département de l'Eure, a man called Barrême, had been murdered in a train on his way back from Cherbourg to Paris: once more the murderer was never caught.

Other murders or attempted murders in *La Bête humaine* not directly related to the railway also have their basis in fact. The crime committed at the beginning of the novel and the homicidal plan which Jacques and Séverine conceive towards the end both owe something to the Fenayrou case. Gabrielle Fenayrou, a pharmacist's wife, was discovered by her husband to be having an affair with one of his employees; and he agreed to forgive her if she helped him to kill the lover. Having lured the man to a deserted house on 18 May 1882, they murdered him and disposed of his body by throwing it into the Seine. But most important of all to the plot of *La Bête humaine* was the notorious case of Jack the Ripper. For several months from September 1888 onwards the press on both sides of the Channel regaled its readership with the gruesome exploits of this serial killer who murdered a succession of prostitutes in Whitechapel in the East End of London in the manner suggested by his nickname. He, too, was never caught. In his preparatory notes for the novel,

Zola describes Jacques Lantier as suffering from 'the maniacal need . . . to kill and to kill a woman'; and in a newspaper interview published in Rome in November 1889 he explicitly compares Jacques with his namesake. And the favoured murder weapon in *La Bête humaine* is, of course, not a gun but a knife.

Zola was particularly drawn to the case of Jack the Ripper because the nature of his interest in the criminal mind had evolved considerably since he had first drawn up his masterplan for the Rougon-Macquart novels some twenty years earlier. Then he had focused on the possibility of a Lantier inheriting murderous tendencies from his parents; now he was more intrigued by the question of atavism, or what human beings might owe not to their immediate forebears but to their most distant and primitive ancestors. This question was the subject of lively public controversy among criminologists during the 1880s, when particular attention had focused on the work of Cesare Lombroso (1836–1909). Lombroso's *L'Uomo delinquente* (*The Criminal Man*), published in Italian in 1876 and again in 1878 in a version three times as long, appeared in French translation in 1887. Its principal thesis is that some two-thirds of criminals are 'born criminals', and that these 'born criminals' display a range of physical deformities explicable in terms of a hereditary regression to the appearance and behaviour of a primitive human ancestral type (and, Lombroso further claimed, as the morbid consequence of epilepsy). While studying the skull of a notorious brigand, he later recalled, it suddenly came to him that the criminal is 'an atavistic being who reproduces in his person the ferocious instincts of primitive humanity and the inferior animals'.[7] His book contains among other things, therefore, a series of face portraits exhibiting a range of features from enormous jaws to large eye-sockets and handle-shaped ears which demonstrate the criminal's reversion to a savage or ape-like state, with each group of portraits being supposedly illustrative of a particular brand of delinquent ('burglars', 'purse snatchers', 'German murderers', etc.).

[7] Quoted in Robert Nye, *Crime, Madness, and Politics in Modern France: The Medical Concept of National Decline* (Princeton, 1984), 99.

Lombroso's theory was but one contribution to an age-old debate: are criminals born or made? should we blame nature or nurture? Such a debate quickly becomes political, as it did in the 1880s. Then the Lombrosan theory upset the Catholic Church because it seemed to deny human free will and thus to remove all moral justification for punishment; but at the same time it appealed to reactionary members of the Establishment who preferred to see crime as in some way inevitable and requiring firm, repressive measures. Others, such as Alexandre Lacassagne (1843–1924) and Gabriel Tarde (1843–1904), regarded Lombroso's views with considerable suspicion and distaste and were concerned that society should not be absolved of its share of the blame. At the First International Congress of Criminal Anthropology in Rome in 1885, Lacassagne denounced the absurdity of linking apparently primitive anatomical features with a pathological predisposition to crime and stressed that the 'important thing is the social milieu'. 'The social milieu', he argued, borrowing the up-to-date terminology of Louis Pasteur, 'is the mother culture of criminality; the microbe is the criminal, an element that gains significance only at the moment it finds the broth that makes it ferment.' In short, he concluded aphoristically: 'societies get the criminals they deserve.'[8]

Gabriel Tarde, who was a judge at Sarlat in the Dordogne before becoming a professor at the Collège de France, had read Lombroso in Italian and, beginning with his *Comparative Criminology*, published in 1886, he wrote a series of works on crime and punishment in which he sought to combat anatomical studies of the 'born criminal' by providing the theoretical structure for a social interpretation of crime. For Tarde 'the born criminal is not a savage, no more than he is a madman. He is a monster, and, like many monsters, he exhibits regressive traits relating to the past history of his race or species, which are differently combined in him than in other people.'[9] That 'combination' may depend on the social environment; and contemporary society would therefore do well to remember, in Tarde's view, that while the human race has made considerable intellec-

---

[8] Nye, *Crime, Madness, and Politics*, 103.
[9] Quoted in the Pléiade edition, pp. 1714–15.

tual and technological progress, the process of moral improve-
ment which we call 'civilization' has been much slower and
much less sure. Modern civilization may appear to have led us
out of the cave but, far from disappearing, atavistic urges have
simply adapted to the changed circumstances.

The 1880s and early 1890s marked a turning-point in the
history of criminology and, thanks particularly to French doctors and jurists, people began to question any penal code based
exclusively on traditional notions of free will. Instead there was
a move to include measures which would allow the state to make
the punishment fit the criminal as well as the crime. So where
does Zola stand? On a superficial level the influence of Lombroso
is clear in the somewhat formulaic manner in which the physical
appearance of the characters is presented in *La Bête humaine*. In
Chapter I, we find Roubaud gazing in the mirror at 'his rather
squat head, with its low forehead, thick neck, and round, ruddy
face'; his hair is red and curly, and his eyebrows meet in the
middle, 'lending his forehead the bushy mark of the jealous
man'. Jacques Lantier is 'a handsome fellow with a round face
and regular features spoilt only by too heavy a jaw'; while
Pecqueux, his fireman, has 'a low forehead' and a 'full mouth
with its jutting jaw'. But Zola was not simply trying to illustrate
the Italian's theories. Indeed Lombroso himself went to the
trouble of writing an article about the novel in which he points
out that while Jacques Lantier exhibits the physical character-
istics of a 'born criminal', his temporary enjoyment of normal
sexual relations with Séverine and his overwhelming sense of
compassion after her death are completely atypical.[10]

Neither, also, was Zola trying to make a statement about the
social causes of crime. This may come as a surprise to readers of
L'Assommoir and *Germinal*, where the appalling living conditions
of urban slum dwellers and slave-like miners are so powerfully
evoked. Violent crime in *La Bête humaine* knows no class
boundaries. Misard, illiterate and almost mindless, is a murderer, as is the ill-educated Pecqueux; but so too are Roubaud,
an assistant station-manager, and Jacques, a highly qualified

[10] '*La Bête humaine* et l'anthropologie criminelle', *La Revue des revues*, 5
(1892).

engine-driver. And so also, to all intents and purposes, are President Grandmorin, in that his assault on Louisette leads rapidly to her death, and the Emperor himself, who despatches young soldiers to the front. None of the killings in the novel can be attributed to social deprivation. Apart from the murder for which Cabuche has spent five years in prison and which seems to have been a case of over-energetic self-defence, the remainder all appear to have their origins in sex. While Misard's slow destruction of Phasie by poison is apparently motivated by his desire to lay his hands on her thousand francs (representing half an assistant station-manager's annual salary and a quarter of an engine-driver's[11]), his avarice may nevertheless constitute a sublimation or perversion of the sex drive ('No, no, he never cared much for that side of things. All he really does care about is money'(p. 39)); and his struggle with his wife is repeatedly presented as a pathological, rat-like effort to gnaw away at female vitality (Phasie's former physical power and active sex-life are likewise repeatedly stressed). Grandmorin's destruction of Louisette is an act of patriarchal lust; while the murders carried out by Roubaud, Flore, and Pecqueux are crimes of passion in that they spring from jealous (and, in Pecqueux's case, drunken) rage.

In its bizarre, atavistic way Jacques's murder of Séverine is also sexual in origin. From the beginning his fear of women is the fear that he may carry out an act of vengeance for some primordial female betrayal:

For each time it was like a sudden attack of blind rage, some unquenchable thirst to avenge wrongs suffered in the distant past and yet which he could not precisely remember. Did it all go back so far, to the evil which women had perpetrated upon his sex, to the sense of grievance accumulated from male to male ever since that first betrayal in the depths of some cave? And he could feel, too, in the midst of his attacks, the need to do battle with the female, to conquer her, to subjugate her, the perverted need to sling her dead body over his shoulder, like a prey snatched away from others, ever his. (p. 54)

The reader will see that when he finally grabs the knife to murder Séverine, the same language is used once more.

---

[11] See below, the explanatory note to p. 13.

For Jacques, murder comes to represent the extreme form of
sexual 'possession', a word which recurs frequently in this novel
where only Misard and the Lachesnayes seem to care about
material possessions yet where many of the characters are 'possessed' by obsession, be it Misard's quest for his wife's thousand
francs or Madame Lebleu's determination to catch Monsieur
Dabadie and Mademoiselle Guichon 'in the act'. For as long as
Jacques is confident that his relationship with Séverine has cured
him of his 'awful hereditary disorder', he is ready to believe that
sexual possession adequately sublimates his murderous 'thirst':
'Was it that physical possession satisfied this thirst for death?
Did possessing and killing amount to the same thing deep within
the dark recesses of the human beast?' But as he lies in bed with
Séverine for the last time, he realizes that sex is no substitute for
murder but rather what leads to it: 'Was it that the more she
loved him, the more there rose within him, from out of the
terrible shadows of male egotism, the desire to possess her, and
to possess her to the point of destroying her? To have her even
as the earth itself might have her: dead!' And when finally he
murders her, the 'gates of horror' open 'on to the black chasm of
sexuality, of love unto death, of destruction as the most complete
possession'. And yet who or what is 'possessing' whom? Is not
Jacques the one who is most truly 'possessed'?

This 'black chasm of sexuality' is evoked repeatedly throughout the novel: sometimes incidentally, as when Séverine recalls
how on one occasion the sight of Roubaud's 'red, convulsed face'
as he made love to her recalled the 'face of the murderer'; and
sometimes more fundamentally, as when Séverine tells Jacques
the story of Grandmorin's murder between frantic bouts of
love-making in the pivotal scene depicted in Chapter VIII. Here,
as later in Chapter XI when Jacques and Séverine are in bed
together planning Roubaud's murder, sexual satisfaction seems
to be enhanced by the memory or prospect of bloody slaughter;
and the repeated motif of the knife being plunged into a neck
and gouging out a gaping wound needs no knowledge of Freud
to be interpreted as a displacement of the sexual act.

For Zola, then, the murderer is a pathological individual in
whom the sex drive has become perverted by some hereditary
flaw (as in Jacques) or by the violent emotion aroused by a

particular circumstance and which causes temporary regression to a brutish state. Thus, at the beginning of the novel, Roubaud's frustrated sexual appetite (when Séverine resists his advances) turns to bestial rage after the revelation of Grandmorin's abuse of Séverine, and he is overtaken by 'the one, single need to appease the beast that howled within him'. As with Jacques later, sexual longing seeks an outlet in murderous destruction: 'in the turbid darkness of his flesh, from the depths of his sullied, wounded desire, abruptly there rose a need for death.' Similarly with Flore, the 'warrior virgin', whose frustrated yearning for Jacques is transformed into an instinctive resolve to murder both him and Séverine, even if that means murdering innumerable train passengers as well: 'She didn't reason it out logically, she was simply following the primitive instinct to destroy'; 'Here was the irrevocable moment, the cuff of the she-wolf's paw as it breaks the back of a passing prey. In the egotism of her vengeance she still saw only two mutilated bodies, and gave no thought to the crowd . . .'. In all these cases the murderer acts out of instinct, and hence knows no remorse—unlike Cabuche, who has killed accidentally in self-defence and feels great shame.

The one exception to this presentation of murder as the result of irresistible instinct threatens to be the calmly calculated murder of Roubaud by Jacques and Séverine, but this precisely is the one murder which proves impossible to carry out (a failure which is seen as analogous with sexual impotence). In this aspect of his plot Zola was consciously writing 'against' the portrayal of murder in the novels of Dostoevsky, which had recently appeared for the first time in French translation (*Devils* or *The Possessed* in 1884, *Crime and Punishment* in 1885, and *The Brothers Karamazov* in 1888). In *Crime and Punishment* the impecunious student Raskolnikov persuades himself that he would be morally justified in killing a grasping old woman for her money and sees a certain Napoleonic valour in doing so. In *The Brothers Karamazov* Ivan Karamazov reflects that if there is no God, then moral principles and the notion of 'conscience' have no divine sanction and 'everything is permitted', including the right to murder in certain circumstances. Or as Raskolnikov puts it at the end of Part I, Chapter 2 of *Crime and Punishment*:

What if man isn't really a beast—man in general, I mean, the whole human race, that is; for if he is not, then all the rest is just prejudice, just imagined fears, and there is nothing to stop you from doing anything you like, and that's as it should be!

But for Zola it is the beast that murders, not the human, not the rational, conscious self who carefully weighs up the pros and cons. Jacques's shamefaced belief that he would be 'foolish and cowardly' not to kill Roubaud 'rationally, out of self-interest, with logic' recalls Raskolnikov's aspiration to emulate the bravery of generals, and he tries desperately to persuade himself that 'he had the right to murder, the right of the strong who find the weak in their way, and who devour them'. But, try as he may, an 'inner protest' rouses 'his whole being' against such a notion:

No, no, he would not strike! It seemed a monstrous, unfeasible, impossible thing to do. Within him the civilized human being was fighting back, with the strength derived from education, from the slowly erected and indestructible edifice of inherited ideas. One should not kill, he had been suckled on that idea by the milk of generations: and his brain, thus refined and furnished with scruples, rejected murder with horror as soon as he began to rationalize it. To kill from need, in a flash of instinct, yes! But to kill with intent, from calculation and self-interest, no, never, that he could never do! (p. 264)

Urged on by Séverine, he once more rehearses 'the arguments which would make of this murder a wise and legitimate action which had been logically considered and decided upon (. . .) he was exercising a right, the right to life itself, since this blood that belonged to another was indispensable to his own very survival'. But as Roubaud passes within inches of him in the station yard, he realizes finally that such a philosophy is false:

Murder would never be done by reasoning; it needed the instinct that makes the jaw snap, the leap that launches you on to the prey, and the hunger or the fury which tears it to pieces. What did it matter if conscience was but a set of ideas handed down from one generation to the next, the gradually accumulated, inherited notion of what is just! He simply did not feel that he had the right to kill, and despite his efforts he was unable to persuade himself that he could give himself this right. (pp. 268–9)

The central drama of *La Bête humaine* is thus the battle which takes place within Jacques Lantier between the atavistic instinct to destroy and the scruples, or conscience, born of centuries of education. There is no nobility in having the 'courage' to murder; indeed the final picture of France's headlong rush into war with Prussia suggests that any military parallel reinforces the view of murder as a form of pathological alienation. Rather, perhaps, there is a certain nobility in the desperate efforts Jacques makes to withstand the tragic 'malady' by which he is possessed. While so many characters in the novel, including Séverine, seem only too ready to dispose of their fellow, Jacques is paradoxically the one central figure in whom humanity can be seen to put up the greatest fight. Which is why there is such pathos in the penultimate chapter when, with Roubaud's arrival imminent, the engine-driver gazes down at the bleeding corpse of the woman he loved:

He had not been able to wait for the man whose life he had been sparing for months because of the scruples born of education, and all the humane notions which had gradually been acquired and transmitted from one generation to another; and against his own interests he had just been carried away by the heritage of violence, by that need to kill which, in primordial forests, had once set beast upon beast. As if one killed by calculation! A person kills only from an impulse that springs from his blood and sinews, from the vestiges of ancient struggles, from the need to live and the joy of being strong. (p. 332)

Whatever the criminological or psychiatric merits of Zola's attempts to establish an exclusive link between the urge to murder and sexual desire, it is notable that without exception he presents the violent criminal in *La Bête humaine* as someone to be pitied rather than despised. These people are sick, not wanton enemies of bourgeois stability and prosperity, but powerless victims of internal forces beyond their control. Jacques genuinely loves Séverine, and the paradisal life in America beckons alluringly; but his 'malady' leaves him an eternal fugitive in the 'black night of limitless despair'. Though Séverine herself wants rid of Roubaud, her murderous intent seems permissible in the light of her experiences at the hands of both Grandmorin and her husband; and there is considerable poignancy as the two lovers seek comfort in each other's arms:

They held each other close, merging the awful sadness of their plights. For theirs was a suffering unto eternity, without prospect of oblivion or

forgiveness. They wept together and felt the blind forces of life weighing upon them, a life of struggle and death. (p. 239)

Even Misard, for all his rodent lack of charm, gets his come-
uppance in the shape of La Ducloux, the ex-barmaid with a
shady past, and is last seen returning home to continue his
everlasting search as though punished like Sisyphus to spend the
remainder of his days repeating the same endless, futile task.
Pecqueux, the jovial workmate, is finally destroyed by drink and
jealousy, while Roubaud, who murdered out of genuine revulsion at the defilement of the woman he worshipped, is eaten away
by 'moral gangrene'. And Flore's onward march to her death
leaves behind an image of strength and courage, of personal
qualities which in other circumstances might so easily have led to
greatness.

Zola's case for the defence—of these powerless victims of a
pathological condition—is much strengthened by the nature of
the prosecution in *La Bête humaine* and by the way in which the
truth which Zola alone has 'revealed' is concealed and manipu-
lated by the state. The key figure in Zola's *roman judiciaire* is, of
course, Monsieur Denizet—who is expressly intended by his
creator partly as an ironic retort to the sage figure of Porfiry in
Dostoevsky's *Crime and Punishment* and partly as a spoof on the
(already) hackneyed figure of the clever crime-solver of popular
fiction. As we read in the final chapter, at the moment of his
supposed great triumph:

The magistrate continued to probe the psychology of the case with true
professional zeal. Never, he said, had he delved so deep into human nature, it was more like divination than observation; for he flattered himself on belonging to that all-seeing school of magistrates who can weave
a spell over a man and expose him with a single glance. (pp. 348–9)

Monsieur Denizet is a *juge d'instruction* or examining magistrate, a function which may require some explanation for readers
unfamiliar with the French legal system. Under this system, the
essentials of which date back to Napoleon's root-and-branch
reforms at the beginning of the nineteenth century, a criminal
case opens with a prolonged investigation, the purpose of which
is to assure that a *prima facie* case is prepared for subsequent
presentation in court by a public prosecutor. This investigation

is entrusted to a sort of trainee judge who has the power to detain the accused, whom he interrogates, and to hear and question witnesses (with whom the accused is finally confronted). If the *juge d'instruction* finds a case against the accused, he forwards the dossier to the public prosecutor for trial. It has often been argued that this system is unfairly weighted against the accused. First, while the examining magistrate is supposed to be impartial, he may find himself being unduly influenced by the police and by the public prosecutors. Second, his powers to detain and interrogate may be intimidatory; and it is only since 1897 (i.e. nearly thirty years after the period in which *La Bête humaine* is set) that the accused has had the right to refuse to speak except in the presence of his counsel. Which leads to the third problem, namely that the investigation in a sense constitutes a private trial which may prejudice the accused before his public trial. While the principle of an accused person being presumed innocent until found guilty by a proper court is proclaimed as proudly in France as in Britain or the United States, the fact remains that the case presented by a public prosecutor in a French court already carries with it the 'weight' of the *juge d'instruction*'s considered opinion.

French court procedures differ greatly from those in Britain in that they are based on an 'inquisitorial' rather than an 'accusatorial' system. Rather than acting as a kind of referee who 'hears' a case as it is presented before him by counsel for the prosecution and the defence, the French presiding judge or magistrate is expected to take the lead, to seek out the truth as well as simply weighing the arguments and evidence before him. Thus, as we see in the last chapter of the novel, it is the President, or presiding judge, who interrogates the accused and the witnesses. There is no cross-examination. The public prosecutor can ask questions, but defence counsel are obliged to direct theirs through the presiding judge, who may refuse to put them. At the same time the rules of evidence are distinctly looser than in Britain or the United States.

The dangers of such a system are great when the examining magistrate is as intellectually complacent and professionally self-seeking as Denizet (and doubtless, in Zola's view, many others in his position). From the start he is presented as one who has learnt not to get 'carried away by his love of the truth' but rather to proceed 'with extreme caution, at every stage discerning pitfalls in which his future prospects might be swallowed up'. Given the 'great qualities of perspicacity and energy which he considered himself to possess', he is much given to following his 'nose'; yet each time he hears the truth, he discounts it because it does not match up with his expectations of a 'properly conducted judicial enquiry'. By the end of the novel, so closed has his mind become and so attached is he to his own 'explanation' of the two murders that he simply smiles at Roubaud's confession: 'and a wave of irrepressible incredulity, the incredulity of the professional, twisted his lips into a moue of mocking disbelief'. But, of course, his whole 'explanation' is based on the motive of money rather than sex: namely, that Roubaud wishes to get his hands on the house at La Croix-de-Maufras and has used Cabuche to do the dirty work. In this he demonstrates the limitations of a criminal investigator who believes all crime to be logical rather than instinctual.

But *La Bête humaine* is more than a critique of the French judicial system and a lampoon of the forerunners of Sherlock Holmes. For the miscarriage of justice depicted in the novel is part of a much broader social and political canvas, in which the Secretary General at the Ministry of Justice, Monsieur Camy-Lamotte, occupies a central position. Akin to a Permanent Secretary in the British system but without the permanence or (usually) the control over an entire Ministry, the Secretary General is head of a division within a Ministry—in Camy-Lamotte's case, that which administers the courts and their staff. As 'a figure of some importance in charge of appointments, with the power to promote', he is able—in Zola's reading of the situation—to exercise considerable influence over the conduct of individual cases by using career prospects to manipulate his judges. Accordingly he is summoned almost daily to the Tuileries, the palace of the Emperor Louis-Napoléon (Napoléon III), and is used by the Emperor to deal with 'more intimate matters' than it is politic for the Head of State to delegate to his Minister. In acting as the Emperor's agent in this way his one overriding ambition is not so much justice as the interests of the state, particularly as the political temperature rises (in Chapter

V) with the approach of the elections in May 1869: 'All that concerned him was the public face of the régime he served.'

La Bête humaine is set in the years when, two decades before he came to write this particular novel, Zola had first elaborated his masterplan for the Rougon-Macquart cycle and commented that 'the times are in turmoil, and it is this turmoil of the moment which I shall depict.' The considerable economic progress which had been achieved in the first decade of the Second Empire was beginning to wane, and there were crises in the cotton, silk, and wine trades. As the fear of war increased, so credit became more difficult to find; and when the leading finance house, the Crédit Mobilier, overextended itself with unorthodox financial dealings, the other leading banks (notably Rothschilds) refused to bail out what Berryer, a contemporary lawyer, had called 'the greatest gambling house in the world'. At the same time the rise of Prussia and the relative decline of the Austrian Empire led to calls for France to rearm. But a programme of public works had been set in train to combat the unemployment resulting from the recession, and the state purse could ill afford rearmament in addition. Attempts to make military service less easy to avoid brought the Army Law of January 1868, which provoked widespread protest from left-wing republicans. The atmosphere of crisis was further exacerbated that same year when Baron Haussmann, the Prefect of the Seine region who had been financing the rebuilding of the city by raising credit in a manner no less unorthodox than the dealings of the Crédit Mobilier, had to ask the state for retrospective sanction for a loan amounting to approximately one quarter of the entire French budget.

La Bête humaine opens in mid-February 1869 and ends in July 1870, and its account of the individual disintegrations of Roubaud and Jacques Lantier thus unfolds against the backdrop of the dying days of the Second Empire. As the elections of May 1869 approach, so the opposition press is keen to exploit the Grandmorin affair in order to discredit both the judiciary and the capitalist railways. In the event the opposition won some 3,300,000 votes (a million and a half more than in 1863), against approximately 4,400,000 for the government's own candidates. The increasingly unpopular leader of the government, Eugène

Rouher (1814–84), was finally forced to resign, as the Emperor
(now in increasingly poor health) bowed to opposition demands
for a more strongly parliamentary form of government. At the
beginning of 1870 the non-aligned politician Émile Ollivier was
appointed head of the first and last parliamentary government of
the Second Empire, the so-called 'Liberal Empire'. A new constitution was drawn up in April 1870, which established government by a cabinet accountable to parliament; and these liberal
reforms were submitted to a plebiscite on 8 May and overwhelm-
ingly approved by some 7,358,000 voters (almost three-quarters
of the electorate).

The Emperor's position was much strengthened in consequence, but was almost immediately threatened by the international developments which led to the Franco-Prussian War.
Bismarck, seeking to extend Prussian influence, had secured
the offer of the Spanish throne to a prince of the Hohenzollern
line, and the offer was accepted in June 1870. After some ten
years in which the French had felt themselves to be continually
outmanœuvred and humiliated by Prussia, this was seen as
the moment to call a halt to Prussian expansionism. With war
threatening, the acceptance of the offer of the Spanish throne
was subsequently withdrawn, but the French desire to teach
Prussia a lesson led them (at the particular behest of the sick
Emperor's Spanish wife, the Empress Eugénie) to insist that the
king of Prussia guarantee this withdrawal personally. However,
in the so-called Ems telegram (on the provocative date of 14
July), Bismarck presented the king's quite reasonable refusal
in brusque terms; and on the resulting wave of French anger,
war was declared on 19 July. *La Bête humaine* ends at this point,
with the departure of soldiers to the front. As every reader in
1890 knew, the subsequent war proved disastrous for France
and its ill-equipped armies and, after a rapid series of calamitous defeats, the Emperor himself surrendered at Sedan on
1 September. In the battle of Sedan alone some 20,000 French
soldiers lost their lives. The Second Empire was at an end,
Louis-Napoléon went into exile in England, and the Third
Republic was proclaimed.

In the context of *La Bête humaine* the lives of Roubaud and
Jacques Lantier seem almost to present an allegorical reflection

of the Second Empire. On the one hand, Roubaud's gambling and his gradual moral decline into spinelessness and 'conjugal complaisance' seem to evoke the 'gambling house' mentality of the boom years of the 1850s followed by the weak government of Rouher and the ineffectual French responses to Prussian expansionism; while his progressive accumulation of sallow fat perhaps offers a veiled comment on the state of France after fifteen years of the Second Empire and bourgeois prosperity. On the other hand, there seems to be a clear parallel between Jacques's irresistible descent into homicidal mania and the underlying national bellicosity which proved no less irresistible as France plunged, needlessly and irrationally, into war with Prussia.

At the same time one cannot help wondering if the evocation of the contemporary political scene in *La Bête humaine* refers only to the France of the late 1860s. Clearly many of the aspects which Zola highlights—the political partiality of the judiciary, the role of the press, the idiocy of war—are not particular to that period (or that country); and it may be that he intends some oblique commentary also on the France of 1889–90. The mid 1880s, no less than the 1860s, had been a period of financial crisis and industrial slump in France, and dissatisfaction with the republican government had found a rallying-point in the figure of General Boulanger, a charismatic military figure who seemed to offer the prospect of restoring French military pride after the disasters of the Franco-Prussian War. Having been Minister of War from 1886 until 1888, he attracted such popular support that it seemed in January 1889 that he might launch a *coup d'état*. When he failed to do so and subsequently left the country, his support fell dramatically, and in the elections of 1889 republicans gained a solid majority. But perhaps Zola, with his own left-wing sympathies, was reminding his readers at the end of *La Bête humaine* of the reality of war that may be forgotten by those who fall victim to the lure of patriotic oratory and jingoistic pride. In *La Débâcle* (1892), his novel about the Franco-Prussian War, the reminder would be altogether more forceful.

Within the social and political context which Zola depicts, the one major casualty is the truth: the Emperor, until the triumph of the plebiscite, fears it; Camy-Lamotte suppresses it; the press distorts it; the examining magistrate cannot believe it. And the

overarching authorial strategy in *La Bête humaine* is to suggest
that this novel reveals a truth beside which all official versions
are themselves but fictions. Nowhere is this more explicitly
suggested than in the final chapter when Denizet rejoices in the
coherence of the case which he has constructed against Roubaud
and Cabuche: 'the sureness of the logic and the strength of the
evidence lent such irrefragable solidity to the case he had constructed that the truth itself would have seemed less true, sullied
by fantasy and illogicality.' But all along we readers have known
the truth and been persuaded by the novelist's art that
this 'fantasy and illogicality' constitutes a higher form of truth,
while Denizet's version is indeed 'quite a creation'—or as
Philomène puts it: 'quite a saga, you could write a book
about it'.

And Zola has. But *La Bête humaine* is a 'whydunnit', not a
'whodunnit'. Indeed it may be said to provide an answer to the
very question 'pinned' to Séverine's throat by Jacques's knife:
'But why? My God, why?', a question which, on the last occasion
we encounter her in the novel, is etched indelibly in 'those blue
eyes, opened so immeasurably wide, which were still asking
"Why?"' From the beginning we know who the (first) murderers
are, even if Zola makes a concession to our delight in suspense by
deferring the 'howdunnit' until Chapter VIII. We are thus constantly privy to the truth while we witness other people being
blind to it—whether from prejudice, professional incompetence,
or political intent. Denizet's whole case about Roubaud and
Cabuche is itself a poor novel, based on stereotype and hackneyed material motives; and Camy-Lamotte possesses the one
piece of evidence—Séverine's brief letter to Grandmorin—
which would reveal its falsity. This 'purloined letter', which he
burns at the end, comes to symbolize the truth itself:

Who else could possibly know the secret which [Séverine] must have
taken with her to the grave? Oh yes, most assuredly: truth, justice, all an
illusion! . . . And as he brought the letter over the flame and it began to
burn, he was filled with enormous sadness, a foreboding of misfortune:
why destroy this piece of evidence, why burden his conscience with
such an act, if it was the Empire's fate to be swept away, like the pinch
of black ash which had now fallen from his fingers? (p. 352)

The function of *La Bête humaine* is thus, in a manner of speaking, to replace this 'purloined letter' and to say the unsayable. In the courtroom at the end, as Jacques gazes at Roubaud and Cabuche, there is a brief moment of revelation: 'There was deathly silence in the courtroom, and the members of the jury felt a lump in their throats at this sudden wave of emotion which seemed to have sprung from nowhere: they were witnessing the silent passage of the truth'; and it is later suggested that the jury accepts the plea of extenuating circumstances because they had 'yielded to the uncomfortable feeling of doubt which had momentarily run through the courtroom during that silent passage of the melancholy truth'. Like some eloquent courtroom orator, the author of *La Bête humaine* is seeking to undermine our ready notions about the causes of crime and to sow the seeds of doubt so that we, as reader and jury, shall also accept his plea of extenuating circumstances.

Zola's 'eloquence', or novelistic art, is manifold in *La Bête humaine*. First, he seeks to persuade us by his very absence from the novel, by the absolute dispassion with which he apparently narrates his tale. His narratorial omniscience is disguised by extensive use of point-of-view technique whereby, for example, a description of the Gare Saint-Lazare is seemingly provided only because Roubaud is at that moment looking down on to it. The narrator withholds all commentary, save on the rare occasion when the hypocrisy of the examining magistrate tempts him into sarcasm: 'Jealous of this unlimited power, especially now that he was on the point of abusing it . . .'. Furthermore, through his recurrent use of the pluperfect tense, the narrator manages to give the impression that the events which he is recounting are continuing quite independently of him and sometimes even that he is having difficulty in keeping up with them. In Chapter I, for example, during the time it takes the narrator to describe the scene which Roubaud and Séverine are watching out of the window, Roubaud has become sexually aroused: 'Gradually, without a word, he had tightened his embrace'; and his subsequent attack on her is so sudden and so violent that the narrator is momentarily overtaken: 'By the time they finally drew breath . . . they had returned to the bed.' Similarly, in Chapter VI, the storm continues as the narrator dwells on Pecqueux's hungry interest in Jacques's food-basket; and only when this has been dealt with are we told that 'another clap of thunder had just shaken the engine-shed'.

Second, Zola prepares each major event in the novel so carefully that when it eventually takes place it seems fated to have happened, rather than being merely the product of his imagination and what the plot demanded. Denizet can claim to have known, with a complacency born of retrospect, that 'the first murder would lead mathematically to a second', but the links in his story lack all the precision of Zola's own 'masterly piece of work'. Having completed the first chapter, the author of *La Bête humaine* wrote to Van Santen Kolff on 6 June 1889 to say that he considered 'the construction of the plan . . . perhaps the most finely worked I have ever produced, I mean the one in which the different parts hang together with the greatest degree of intricacy and logic': and, as he already knew by then, Chapter I foreshadows the rest of the novel in many ways. Indeed there is a peculiar insistence on how, as in classical tragedy, a whole sequence of fateful consequences are going to hinge on one crucial moment, in this case on a chance remark: 'One little, miserable, insignificant detail, one forgotten lie about this ring, had just brought everything to light in a single, brief exchange of words. And it had taken no more than a moment.' The fact that the ring in question figures a serpent seems to connote some original 'sin' or disaster from which all suffering will follow. Similarly, the shortest of letters (summoning Grandmorin) may entail all manner of consequence, and Séverine trembles with fear 'at the unknown prospects opened up by these two simple lines'—the lines of a text, but the lines also perhaps of the symbolic railway of destiny leading into a mysterious future.

More specifically, Roubaud's threatened attack on Séverine with a knife anticipates Jacques's murder of her, while the reference to 'extenuating circumstances' as she narrates her sad past prepares for the courtroom verdict at the end. The red triangle which remains as the final image of the departing train (and which Jacques will see again just after witnessing the murder in Chapter II) seems like a foretaste of the large number of triangular relationships in the novel, which have such bloody or murderous consequences: Grandmorin–Séverine–Roubaud; Roubaud–Séverine–Jacques; Pecqueux–Philomène–Jacques; Jacques–La Lison–Pecqueux; Séverine–Jacques–Flore; Grandmorin–Louisette–Cabuche. The novel begins with an image of the over-heated room and the stove which has been stoked to excess, while the dénouement will hinge on a similarly excessive stoking of an engine's firebox; and the departing train at the end of the first chapter itself foreshadows the final image of the novel: 'It was racing away, and nothing now would stop this train as it hurtled forwards at full steam.'

At the same time this chapter introduces a contrast between child's play and adult violence which recurs throughout the novel as a symbolic echo of the central presentation of crime as a reversion to some original state in the history of civilization during the 'childhood' of man. At first Roubaud sets the table 'as if he were playing at dolls' tea-parties' and listens to the young Dauvergne girls laughing and singing down below; then Séverine brings him a gift of a knife, teasing him like a child and requiring him to say 'a little present all for me': within the hour Roubaud has almost murdered Séverine with this knife to the accompaniment of Claire Dauvergne singing nursery songs. The image of the doll is recalled in the following chapter in the comparison of Grandmorin's corpse to a 'broken puppet', which Jacques inspects 'like a nervous child'; while the singing and dancing recur in Chapter VIII as an accompaniment to Séverine's account of Grandmorin's murder. At the end of the novel, the soldiers depart for war in a state of intoxicated merriment, singing. The theme of the nursery rhyme will recur later in the implicit parallel between the story of Cabuche and Louisette (later Cabuche and Séverine) and the tale of Beauty and the Beast. Throughout the novel Séverine's persona as 'a passive grown-up child' is maintained, despite the sexual awakening which she undergoes with Jacques; and this woman who had wanted to murder her husband remains childlike until the moment of her violent death: 'a person whom life had steeped in filth and now in blood without her being really aware of it, so that she remained none the less loving and innocent, never having understood'—a child as innocent as the one in the Square des

Batignolles playing in the sand with his bucket and spade as she implicitly confesses her guilt to Jacques. And in death she, too, will become no more than a 'broken puppet'.

Such preparations for future events in the novel are not restricted to Chapter I. In Chapter II the cartload of stones from the quarry and Flore's urging of the horses to prevent the cart from remaining stuck on the line anticipate the disaster related in Chapter X; while Jacques's assault on Flore and his subsequent flight into the countryside prepare for his eventual murder of Séverine and his desperate departure into the darkness of the night and his own despair. In Chapter VI the visit to Philomène by Jacques and Pecqueux, after which she is beaten by her brother as the two men return to sleep side by side in the Rue François-Mazeline, exactly parallels a similar visit in Chapter XII, while the quarrel between the two men at the end of the novel is prepared by the quarrel avoided at the beginning of Chapter VII. The passengers boarding the train like 'a routed army' after the hold-up in the snow discreetly foreshadow the transport of soldiers on the last page of the novel.

Certain chapters are endowed with their own symmetry, imposing a rhythm of departure and return which apes the central motif of the railway journey. Chapter II begins and ends with Jacques shying away from Flore, Chapter III with the wind blowing in from the sea at Le Havre, and Chapter V with Séverine coming up to speak to Jacques aboard his locomotive. Chapter VII begins and ends with a train departure, while at the start it is Roubaud who notes 'the look of anxious affection' exchanged between Jacques and Séverine, while at the end it is Flore who 'paled once again to see this tranquil exchange of affection pass between them'.

Or symmetrical patterns are established between chapters, and with suggestive implications. In Chapter I Séverine rejects Roubaud's advances, while in Chapter II Flore initially rejects Jacques's. In Chapter VIII, set in Mère Victoire's room overlooking the Gare Saint-Lazare, Séverine waits for Jacques as Roubaud waited for her at the beginning of the novel; and, of course, there are many parallels between this scene in which she confesses to Jacques her part in Grandmorin's murder and the earlier scene in which she confesses to Roubaud how she had slept with Grandmorin. Some parallels and repetitions offer tacit, ironic commentary. As an illustration of the hierarchy of power, Camy-Lamotte keeps Denizet waiting in an adjacent room while receiving Séverine just as Denizet himself keeps his witnesses 'readily available' next door to his chambers. Moreover, while the blinkered Denizet fondly believes himself to be a 'moral anatomist, endowed with second sight, and extremely sharp-witted', it is in fact Camy-Lamotte who sees through people, in this case Séverine: 'He observed her, saw the corners of her mouth quiver. It was her. From that moment his conviction was total.'

Other echoes seem rather to serve a mnemonic purpose (particularly for the novel's first readers who read the book in serial instalments). Séverine's 'periwinkle' eyes and pile of black hair recur like a leitmotif throughout the narrative, while other formulae similarily fulfil the function of identity tags. Madame Bonnehon twice has the 'strong, opulent beauty of an ageing goddess', while Monsieur Desbazeilles, Madame Bonnehon's admirer, now suffers so badly from rheumatism that this former Lothario is left with 'naught but fond memories'. Flore's recurrent 'helmet of blond hair' contrasts with Séverine's 'helmet of black hair', and she is repeatedly presented as a warrior virgin, a kind of latter-day Amazon, a mannish woman in this novel where otherwise only men are physically capable of murder. These 'identity tags' may irritate some readers, but they serve also as quasi-Homeric epithets, raising the characters from the level of the real to the level of myth.

Third, Zola persuades us to his central thesis by subjecting us to the rhythms which characterize the ongoing struggle between the human and the beast, by making us empathize with the central psychological tension between calm and fury, clarity and confusion, order and chaos. For the human criminal, in Zola's analysis, life is an alternation between a 'normal' state of self-control and aberrant moments during which this normal self is ousted by 'the rabid beast within' and departs the body through the hereditary 'crack'. But the whole world of *La Bête humaine* is marked by this alternation in such a way that we come to see and experience it as a universal norm.

At a fundamental level such empathy with the characters and events of the novel is encouraged by the way in which our essential experience as readers is mirrored within it. Indeed, according to his friend and biographer Paul Alexis, Zola consciously envisaged such a parallel: 'You're perhaps going to think me an old Romantic, but I would like my work to be itself like some great train journey, departing from a terminus and arriving at a final destination, with periods of reduced speed and stops at every station, that is to say, at each chapter.'[12] Accordingly, as we begin to read the narrative, we learn of someone entering a room and preparing to eat a meal, of a train making ready to depart, or (in Chapter II) of a ship about to be launched. Our own progression through the successive chapters of the novel is a series of departures and arrivals, which are themselves the events with which many of the chapters begin and/or end. At the beginning of Chapter II we may identify with Jacques 'the traveller', for whom physical access to the crossing-keeper's house at La Croix-de-Maufras is no less arduous than it may intellectually be for us (in terms of the distance between its strange, illiterate inhabitants and our own mental world of the literate). Conversely, as the novel approaches its end, the number of deaths increases rapidly, including the 'death' of La Lison, while incarceration figures in the dénouement as a scarcely less terminal fate. Such new beginnings as the novel presents towards the end are ironic: the prospect of Denizet's triumph leading to his promotion to the Legion of Honour and an appointment in Paris, and the runaway train bound for the Franco-Prussian War ('an image of France itself', as Zola wrote in his notes).

At a more complex level this empathy is achieved by breaking down conventional distinctions between the 'psychological' and the physical so that we can look at human experience afresh. To this end the normally discrete domains of the human, the animal, and the mechanical are fused by an insistent and insidious use of metaphorical equivalence. This collapse of conventional distinctions is most evident in the constant comparison of human beings with animals. Roubaud is like a wolf, Flore a wolf or a goat; Pecqueux, Cabuche, and Denizet are intermittently canine,

---

[12] Quoted in the Pléiade edition, p. 1712.

while Philomène's 'scrawny' physique is variously that of a mare or a cat on heat. Even Séverine, who is the least 'bestial' of the main characters, clings to the outside of the train after the murder of Grandmorin, 'by sheer force of instinct, like an animal that has dug its claws in and simply refuses to let go'.

But we find also, for example, that a runaway goods wagon is like 'a crazed beast', that a quarrel may be stoked as intently as a firebox, that an admission can come 'oozing out . . . from every pore' like sweat. 'Psychological' experiences such as excitement and fear become events of temperature–change or meteorological variation: witness the 'red mist' which 'clouds' Jacques's eyes when his mania threatens and which is mirrored (in a Naturalist version of the Romantic fallacy) by the actual 'reddish glow' cast by the moon submerged beneath 'milky-white cloud' or analogous with a 'freezing fog at dawn in which everything merges into everything else'. And such mists and clouds are, of course, closely related to the whorls of steam and smoke which fill the world of the railway. Indeed physiological events are frequently suggestive of adjacent mechanical processes, as with the oral and anal poisoning of Phasie, from above and below, as if she were a railway with its up line and its down. Similarly, the administrative structure of the Compagnie de l'Ouest is likened to a complex machine, while for Camy-Lamotte 'the affairs of this world' have been reduced to 'a simple question of mechanics'. La Lison lies 'dying', an 'iron beast' giving up the ghost from the 'crack' in her belly, while a maimed cart-horse whinnies desperately in its death agony by her side. In the wreckage of the crash, severed limbs, both animal and human, lie strewn about with broken axles and connecting-rods.

Here are fine examples of what Michel Serres first called the 'epic of entropy', and what David Baguley has dubbed the 'entropic vision' of Naturalism, presenting us with 'the passage from order to disorder, from mental stability to hysteria and madness, from sobriety to intemperance, from integrity to corruption':

At the heart of the naturalist Vision . . . there is a poetics of disintegration, dissipation, death, with its endless repository of wasted lives, of destructive forces, of spent energies, of crumbling moral and social structures, with its promiscuity, humiliations, degradation, its decomposing bodies, its invasive materialism, its scenes of mania, excess, destruction.[13]

And this poetics of 'disintegration' is further effected throughout the novel by the blurring interpenetration of the literal and the metaphorical. In Chapter I Roubaud experiences jealousy like an iron blade sinking into his chest, which will lead to his planting an actual blade in Grandmorin's throat. Similarly, having sated his appetite for food, he 'hungers' for vengeance—and satisfies this hunger not by cutting bread but human flesh. When a train whistle shrieks like a woman being ravished, it is as though the railway outside is re-enacting the story which Séverine has just told Roubaud. Later in the novel similar examples may be found, as in Chapter X when Flore feels her jealousy as 'wheels . . . cutting her heart in two'; soon her body will be similarly lacerated in her suicide. And when, during their last conversation, Séverine asks Jacques to 'devour' her so that 'there's nothing left of me that's not inside you', her metaphorical sense equates with Jacques's own physical sensation of being a ravening beast intent on stealing a prey from the claws of others. Indeed the metaphor of 'devouring' pervades every characterization and every plot and sub-plot in the novel, right up until the soldiers vanish into the night as 'cannon-fodder' to be devoured by the Prussians.

As is apparent from several of the foregoing examples, in persuading us of the emotional and imaginative truth of his explanation of the sexual origins of crime Zola uses the imagery of the railway to particular effect. On one level, of course, he is trying to achieve literary equivalents of Impressionist paintings, as he had already in *L'Œuvre*. In *La Bête humaine* he has Monet's 1877 paintings of the Gare Saint-Lazare particularly in mind, and from the fourth paragraph of the novel his pen strives to emulate the painter's brush:

Then, before the locomotive moved forward, there was a silence, the steam-cocks opened, and steam hissed across the ground in a deafening spurt. And presently he saw its swarming whiteness billow out from

[13] *Naturalist Fiction: The Entropic Vision* (Cambridge, 1990), 208, 222.

under the bridge, swirling like snowy down before flitting away, up through the iron girders It turned an entire corner of the open space white, while the gathering clouds of smoke from the other locomotive spread their veil of blackness wider and wider.

On another level, the world of the railways comes to symbolize certain fundamental aspects of the human condition. The locomotive requires coal and water as human beings require food and drink; like human beings it may become overfed, or over-heated, eating up the track at a furious rate, capable of going out of control. Or it devours grease like a glutton with the same insouciance as Séverine may spend her winter savings in a department store. Usually it seems to be fixed on a pre-ordained path, following the track that leads to the future, traversing tunnels of darkness and madness, but emerging into the light. Yet sometimes, at moments of crisis (such as a blizzard), it appears to have no railway line to follow—or its path is blocked by snow, or a cartload of stones. Then again it is like a woman, the beloved mistress of its driver and fireman. A new engine, such as the 608, is a virgin who has to be deflowered or a young filly that has to be broken in; while the terms in which La Lison's virtues are described ('the rare qualities of a good woman . . . gentle, obedient, easy to start, regular and unflagging in her action') are suggestive of the most crudely male chauvinist ideal of the domestically efficient and sexually co-operative female.

But the train is also a phallic symbol, entering a tunnel soon after Jacques has failed to 'enter' Flore or arriving at Le Havre station, 'rumbling and whistling, making the ground shake' just as Jacques first makes love to Séverine. At the same time it is a symbol of mortality, the crushing engine of destiny mowing fragile mortals down in its path. Thus Phasie, Louisette, and Flore are 'three wretched creatures, of the kind who fall by the wayside and are crushed, and now departed as though swept away by the terrible gust of wind created by the passing trains!'; while Séverine, killed at the very moment that the Paris express tears past the window, is 'crushed and borne away in the fateful path of murder'. A symbol of sexual desire and of ineluctable mortality, the train is likewise a symbol of the unstoppable urge that even a highly competent and conscious 'driver' like Jacques is unable to control. Nowhere is the symbol more powerfully employed in this way than in the parallel between the train crash and Jacques's murder of Séverine. In the first case, Jacques emerges from the Barentin tunnel and rounds the bend in the cutting before coming face to face with an unavoidable obstacle: 'Here was the inevitable'; in the second case, the murder constitutes a moment of pre-ordained arrival, and the quasi-organic progress of Jacques's mental illness a railway line from which it is impossible to diverge: 'for a year now every hour that passed had brought him closer to the inevitable.' The red circle of light reflected from the stove on to the ceiling in Chapter VIII resembles 'the large red signal' which figures in the first description of the Gare Saint-Lazare; and it serves almost as a warning to Jacques as he listens to Séverine's confession, a warning not to listen further in case his malady should return. But he ignores the signal with fatal consequences. In these ways the train brings together in symbolic union the triple strands of sex, mortality, and mania. Like the runaway train at the end of the novel, each of these might be described as a 'prodigious, irresistible force that nothing now could stop'.

At the same time the train symbolizes the unstoppable progress of 'civilization', apparently a force for good but yet also an emblem of the potentially destructive nature of capitalism and of the uncaring, heedless anonymity of the crowd. In this respect the crossing at La Croix-de-Maufras is the eye in the middle of the storm, the place where Misard the watchman (in French a *stationnaire*) must remain constantly in the same place to safeguard the passage of others, and Phasie in her loneliness watches as all these people go by and not one of them stops to talk or listen:

the whole world passed by here, and not only French people, foreigners too, people from the furthest lands, since nowadays nobody seemed able to stay put at home any more . . . And what saddened her was the sense that in their constant breathless rush, amidst all the continuous to-ing and fro-ing, amidst all this money and well-to-do prosperity on the move, the crowds of people had no idea that she was there, in danger of her life . . . (p. 41)

International capitalism and technological wizardry: this is where the 'track' of destiny is apparently leading, but at the expense of humanity:

And past it went, past it went, mechanical, triumphant, hurtling towards the future with mathematical rigour, determinedly oblivious to the rest of human life on either side, life unseen and yet perennial, with its eternal passions and its eternal crimes. (p. 44).

Phasie (connoting the Greek *phasis* or speech) is a prophet crying in the wilderness of La Croix-de-Maufras, and it is the function of *La Bête humaine* to bring her voice to this wider public, indeed perhaps to these very people who buy 'railway novels' at station bookstalls and peruse them on their journey. In the course of the novel it is only the snow and then Flore's savage act of vengeance which succeed in arresting this 'mechanical torrent' outside Phasie's door: in the first instance, the passengers are reduced to a band of shipwreck victims, 'pushing and shoving, letting themselves go completely and without a thought for their personal appearance'; in the second, they end up on 'the field of slaughter', either dead, injured, or fleeing the scene in panic to seek cover in the nearby woods.

Like La Croix-de-Maufras (etymologically, the cross of evil fracture), the novel provides an arresting nexus of themes and images through which Zola seeks to bear 'phatic' witness to 'the passage of progress on its way towards the twentieth century, and in the midst of a dreadful and mysterious drama to which all are blind—the human beast beneath civilization' (as he wrote to Van Santen Kolff on 6 June 1889). Or as Phasie herself says of the steam-engine:

'Ah, yes, it's a fine invention, there's no denying. People go fast now, they know more . . . But wild beasts are still wild beasts, and they can go on inventing bigger and better machines for as long as they like, there'll still be wild beasts underneath there somewhere.' (p. 41)

Like the snow, or the dray loaded with stone, the novel seeks to stop us in our tracks and to bring us face to face with this unpleasant truth. Indeed Zola at one stage thought that such was the value of criminal trials, as he commented in an article in *La Tribune* on 13 December 1868 concerning the case of three women being tried for poisoning: 'Such debate offers a painful spectacle, but one which is both useful and necessary. It is good that human muck should be raked like this from time to time in full view of the public.' Given Phasie's opinion that 'with everyone so busy, it was no wonder they could step in the muck and not notice a thing', it would seem that a novel like *La Bête humaine* has precisely this object in view, to make us notice. 'A violent drama to give the whole of Paris nightmares' is how Zola puts it at the beginning of his preparatory notes, but in the course of composition the end result for the reader became more subtle than a nightmare. In taking the world of the railways, Zola has chosen the perfect symbol for the human experience of time. Always moving forward, learning new things and discovering new places, we undergo the onward march of so-called progress or civilization; and yet the prospect of a return journey is always there, be it a return to (second) childhood or mindless submission to our baser instincts. Our world of routine has the regularity of a railway timetable, but there are breakdowns, delays, cancellations, the wrong sort of leaf on the line, the worst sort of snow. The future beckons as a safe haven: be it Le Havre itself, or the idyllic world of opportunity across the Atlantic. But such horizons are distant, to be gazed at by Roubaud perched on his gable-end smoking a pipe, yet never to be reached: reality is an endless shuttle between two termini, birth and death, hope and defeat, love and hate, bestial need and human consciousness. And the faster we travel, the less we see and understand.

But *La Bête humaine* offers us pause. A serial novel about a (potentially) serial killer and a 'railway novel' which takes a novel look at railways, it bids us read between the lines. For Séverine, novels are a useful source of information about how to commit a murder; for us, this novel may offer a reminder of the frailty of human life, the pathology of crime, and the need to stop—in the midst of the incessant onrush of modern civilization—and think. Is Jacques Lantier's murder of Séverine any less of a 'crime of passion' than Roubaud's murder of Grandmorin? Within the courtroom of fiction we are presented with the evidence and asked to decide. Shall we perhaps—like the 'twelve men of Rouen, trussed in black frock-coats, stout and solemn'—yield 'to the uncomfortable feeling of doubt which had momentarily run through the courtroom during that silent passage of the melancholy truth' and ourselves accept Zola's eloquent plea of 'extenuating circumstances'?

Eighteen years later, during the Dreyfus Affair, Zola was to write his famous article 'J'accuse' and be found guilty of libelling the Minister of War. Among the 130 or so further titles which he considered for *La Bête humaine*, there is one in particular which stands out thematically from all the rest and which the novel might well have borne: *L'Excuse*. We may mourn for Séverine, but who shall cast the first stone at a man who will not—cannot—kill in cold blood and whose desperate mental handicap has been made so powerfully plain? When you, reader, have read *La Bête humaine*, whom shall you accuse and whom excuse?

NOTE ON THE TRANSLATION

THIS translation is based on the text of *La Bête humaine* edited by Henri Mitterand and published in vol. iv of Émile Zola, *Les Rougon-Macquart* (Paris: Gallimard, Bibliothèque de la Pléiade, 1966) and as a separate volume (Gallimard, Folio, 1977).

La Bête humaine first appeared in English as *Human Brutes*, published in Chicago in 1890 as 'a realistic novel by Émile Zola, tr. from the French by Count Edgar de V. Vermont'. The first translation to be published in Britain was that of Edward Vizetelly (Hutchinson, 1901) and entitled *The Monomaniac*. Vizetelly & Co., the company founded by Edward's father, Henry, had been publishing translations of the Rougon-Macquart novels since 1884; but following the publication of *Earth* (*La Terre*) in 1888, Henry Vizetelly was twice tried for purveying pornography, and on the second occasion found guilty and sentenced to three months in prison and a hefty fine. No publishing house dared touch a Zola novel for the next three years; and then only the heavily bowdlerized versions prepared by Edward's brother, Ernest, were sufficient to tempt Chatto & Windus into production (Vizetelly & Co. having gone bankrupt).

The Monomaniac was reprinted in 1902, and first appeared in paperback in the same year: two further reprints were made in 1915 and 1920. In 1956 Alec Brown's translation, *The Beast in Man*, was published by Elek Books. A third translation, by R. G. Goodyear and P. J. R. Wright appeared in 1968 (New English Library/Times Mirror), and a fourth, by Leonard Tancock, in Penguin Classics in 1977.

La Bête humaine poses none of the problems of colloquial usage which Margaret Mauldon has handled so skilfully in her translation of *L'Assommoir* (World's Classics, 1995). Apart from the occasional expletive at moments of great anger, or the slightly more 'popular' syntax sometimes employed by the less educated (Pecqueux, Philomène, Phasie, Flore), Zola's characters here employ perfectly 'respectable' French. Indeed in her account of Grandmorin's murder in Chapter VIII, Séverine's narrative and descriptive language is implausibly indistinguishable from that of her creator. Zola's use of technical vocabulary is similarly sparing, and the incidence of 'steam-cock', 'regulator', 'slide-valve', and 'connecting-rod' is sufficiently low for the translator to be able to avoid any impression of playing the linguistic train-spotter.

The ambition of the present translation is readable accuracy. Particular efforts have been made to preserve Zola's considerable economy of expression, as well as his carefully modulated use of tense and his knowingly arranged word-order. 'Le Président Grandmorin' has been translated as 'President Grandmorin' rather than 'Judge Grandmorin' throughout in order to preserve his symbolic value as an authority figure and the political connotations which are an important aspect of Zola's novel. The title has been the most difficult phrase of all to translate. Alec Brown's *The Beast in Man* can now be considered inaccurate on the grounds of gender, while *The Human Beast* demonstrates the inadequacy of literal translation. Perhaps *The Beast Within* could have provided a more idiomatic alternative, but in the end it has seemed best to retain the original French: for, thanks partly to Renoir's celebrated film starring Jean Gabin and Simone Simon (1938), this is the title by which Zola's tale of murder on the railways has come to be best known by successive generations of English speakers.

In the preparation of the Introduction and Explanatory Notes to this translation, I am indebted to the scholarship of Henri Mitterand and Philippe Hamon. I should also like to express particular gratitude to my wife Vivienne for her attentive and morale-boosting scrutiny of the typescript; to I. P. Foote for his many acute observations, especially in respect of linguistic register; and to Virginia Llewellyn Smith for the professional competence with which she has endeavoured to save me from inaccuracy, inelegance, and prolixity.

SELECT BIBLIOGRAPHY

In English

All twenty novels in the Rougon-Macquart cycle have been translated into English. In particular *L'Assommoir, Nana, Germinal,* and *The Masterpiece* are available in World's Classics in new or recently revised translations, with up-to-date introductions and bibliographies, as are *The Attack on the Mill and Other Stories* and the early success *Thérèse Raquin.*

For an account of Zola's life the reader may wish to supplement the Chronology which follows with F. W. J. Hemmings, *The Life and Times of Émile Zola* (London, 1977). Also available are Alan Schom's *Émile Zola: A Bourgeois Rebel* (London, 1987); and Philip Walker's *Zola* (London, 1985), which includes plot-summaries. Graham King's *Garden of Zola* (London, 1978) is specifically subtitled 'Émile Zola and his Novels for English Readers' and ends with an informative section on English translations of Zola's novels.

The best literary critical introduction to Zola's work is still F. W. J. Hemmings, *Émile Zola* (2nd edn., Oxford, 1966; reprinted with corrections, 1970). Elliot Grant's *Émile Zola* (New York, 1966) may also be relied upon. Of further interest is Angus Wilson's *Émile Zola: An Introductory Study of His Novels* (New York, 1952). David Baguley's edition of *Critical Essays on Émile Zola* (Boston, 1986) presents a useful cross-section of essays and articles (in English or English translation) by leading writers and critics from Swinburne to the present day. Valuable contributions by leading Zola specialists of today have been edited by Robert Lethbridge and Terry Keefe in *Zola and the Craft of Fiction (Essays in Honour of F. W. J. Hemmings)* (Leicester, 1990; paperback reprint 1993).

Among more closely focused studies, Brian Nelson's *Zola and the Bourgeoisie* (London, 1983) and Naomi Schor's *Zola's Crowds* (Baltimore, 1978) can be recommended. As a comprehensive and perceptive overview of Naturalist literature and of Zola's place within it, David Baguley's *Naturalist Fiction: The Entropic Vision* (Cambridge, 1990) is outstanding. Of specific relevance to *La Bête humaine* is Martin Kanes, *Zola's 'La Bête humaine': A Study in Literary Creation* (Berkeley and Los Angeles, 1962), while those interested in Jean Renoir's film treatment of the novel may consult Michèle Lagny's article 'The Fleeing Gaze: Jean Renoir's *La Bête humaine* (1938)', in S. Hayward and G. Vincendeau (eds.), *French Film: Texts and Contexts* (New York, 1990).

In French

The standard edition of *La Bête humaine* appears in vol. iv of *Les Rougon-Macquart* in the Bibliothèque de la Pléiade (Paris, 1966), where Henri Mitterand provides useful documentation and a scholarly account of the novel's genesis and composition. An abbreviated version of this apparatus is supplied in the Folio edition (Paris: Gallimard, 1977), which also includes an introductory essay by Gilles Deleuze. By far the best single study of the novel in any language is Philippe Hamon's *Émile Zola, 'La Bête humaine'* (Paris: Gallimard (Foliothèque), 1994), which contains a helpful bibliography and other supplementary material.

Valuable general studies of Zola's work include Michel Serres, *Feux et signaux de brume: Zola* (Paris, 1975), Auguste Dezalay, *L'Opéra des Rougon-Macquart* (Paris, 1983), and Philippe Hamon, *Le Personnel du roman: Le système des personnages dans les 'Rougon-Macquart' d'Émile Zola* (Geneva, 1983). Henri Mitterand has published three volumes of essays on Zola: *Le Discours du roman* (1985), *Le Regard et le signe* (1987), and *Zola: L'Histoire et la fiction* (1990). (All published Paris: Presses Universitaires de France.)

A number of excellent conference papers on *La Bête humaine* in both English and French are brought together in Geoff Woollen (ed.), *'La Bête humaine': texte et explications. Actes du colloque de Glasgow, 1990* (Glasgow, 1990), which also includes extensive excerpts from Zola's preparatory notes for the novel.

Concerning the background to *La Bête humaine*, a thorough account of criminology in the late nineteenth century is to be found in Robert Nye, *Crime, Madness, and Politics in Modern France: The Medical Concept of National Decline* (Princeton, 1984). The political and legal context is authoritatively analysed in F. Ridley and J. Blondel, *Public Administration in France* (2nd edn., London, 1969). As for the world of the railways, there is a whole literature in English devoted to the subject, ranging from the affectionate and anecdotal in the works of C. Hamilton Ellis (for example, *Rapidly Round the Bend* (London, 1960)) to the definitive studies of Gordon Biddle (for example, *Great Railway Stations of Britain: Their Architecture, Growth and Development* (Newton Abbot, London, and North Pomfret, Vt., 1986)). On the Gare Saint-Lazare and the development of the French railway system during the nineteenth century, Karen Bowie (ed.), *Les Grandes Gares parisiennes au XIXe siècle* (Paris, 1987) contains much useful information and invaluable illustrations. On the place of railway transport in French literature, see Marc Baroli, *Le Train dans la littérature française* (Paris, 1964; on *La Bête humaine* see pp. 215–74).

CHRONOLOGY

1825   First passenger service by steam railway opens between Stockton and Darlington in England

1837   First passenger service by steam railway in France opens between Paris and Saint-Germain. Gare Saint-Lazare opens

1840   (2 April) Birth of Émile Zola in Paris, the only child of Francesco Zola (b. 1795), an Italian engineer, and Émilie, née Aubert (b. 1819), the daughter of a glazier. The Naturalist novelist was later proud that 'zolla' in Italian means 'clod of earth'

1842   First major French train disaster: the Paris–Versailles train crashes and catches fire; 150 people killed. The Paris–Rouen line opens

1843   Family moves to Aix-en-Provence

1847   (27 March) Death of father from pneumonia following a chill caught while supervising work on his scheme to supply Aix-en-Provence with drinking water. The Paris–Le Havre line opens

1852–   Becomes a boarder at the Collège Bourbon at Aix. Friendship with Baptistin Baille and Paul Cézanne. Zola, not Cézanne, wins the school prize for drawing

1853   Eugène Flachat's two-year renovation of the Gare Saint-Lazare completed

1858   (February) Leaves Aix to settle in Paris with his mother (who had preceded him in December). Offered a place and bursary at the Lycée Saint-Louis. (November) Falls ill with 'brain fever' (typhoid) and convalescence is slow

1859   Fails his *baccalauréat* twice

1860   (Spring) Is found employment as a copy-clerk but abandons it after two months, preferring to eke out an existence as an impecunious writer in the Latin Quarter of Paris. (6 December) Beginning of Poinsot affair, following murder of judge on Mulhouse–Paris line.

1862   (February) Taken on by Hachette, the well-known publishing house, at first in the despatch office and subsequently as head of the publicity department. (31 October) Naturalized as a French citizen

1863   (31 January) First literary article published

1864   (9 July) Beginning of Briggs case, following murder of bank clerk on local Hackney line in London. (October) *Tales for Ninon*

1865   *Claude's Confession*. A *succès de scandale* thanks to its bedroom scenes. Meets future wife Alexandrine-Gabrielle Meley (b. 1839), the illegitimate daughter of teenage parents who soon separated, and whose mother died in September 1849

1866   Forced to resign his position at Hachette (salary: 200 francs a month) and becomes a literary critic on the recently launched daily *L'Événement* (salary: 500 francs a month). Self-styled 'humble disciple' of Hippolyte Taine. Writes a series of provocative articles condemning the official Salon Selection Committee, expressing reservations about Courbet, and praising Manet and Monet. Begins to frequent the Café Guerbois in the Batignolles quarter of Paris, the meeting-place of the future Impressionists. Taken to visit Manet by Antoine Guillemet. Summer months spent with Cézanne at Bennecourt on the Seine. (15 November) *L'Événement* suppressed by the authorities

1867   (November) *Thérèse Raquin*. Construction of the Pont de l'Europe

1868   (April) Preface to second edition of *Thérèse Raquin*. (May) Manet's portrait of Zola exhibited at the Salon. (December) *Madeleine Férat*. Begins to plan for the Rougon-Macquart cycle of novels

1868–70 Working as journalist for a number of different newspapers

1869   (23–24 May) Legislative elections

1870   (January) Émile Ollivier appointed head of parliamentary government. (April) New constitution drawn up. (8 May) Plebiscite on new constitution. (31 May) Marries Alexandrine in a registry office. (June) Offer of Spanish throne to prince of Hohenzollern line accepted. (14 July) Ems telegram. (19 July) France declares war on Prussia. (1 September) Emperor Napoléon III surrenders at Sedan. End of Second Empire: Third Republic proclaimed. Moves temporarily to Marseilles as Prussians advance on Paris

1871   Political reporter for *La Cloche* (in Paris) and *Le Sémaphore de Marseille*. (28 January) Armistice with Prussia. (March)

Returns to Paris. (28 March) Election of the Commune. (28 May) End of the Commune. (October) Publishes *The Fortune of the Rougons*, the first of the twenty novels making up the Rougon-Macquart cycle

1872   (January) *The Kill*

1873   (April) *The Belly of Paris*

1874   (May) *The Conquest of Plassans*. (November) *Further Tales for Ninon*

1875   (April) *The Sin of the Abbé Mouret*

1876   (February) *His Excellency Eugène Rougon*

1877   (February) *L'Assommoir*. Claude Monet paints a series of canvases of the Gare Saint-Lazare

1878   Buys a house at Médan on the Seine, forty kilometres west of Paris. (June) *A Page of Love*

1880   (March) *Nana*. (May) *Les Soirées de Médan* (an anthology of short stories by Zola and some of his Naturalist 'disciples', including Maupassant). (8 May) Death of Flaubert. (September) First of a series of articles for *Le Figaro*. (17 October) Death of his mother. (December) *The Experimental Novel*

1882   (April) *Pot-bouille*. (15 May) Fenayrou case begins

1883   (March) *The Ladies' Paradise* (*Au bonheur des dames*). (30 April) Death of Manet. The Orient Express between London and Venice enters service

1884   (March) *La Joie de vivre*. Preface to catalogue of Manet exhibition

1885   (March) *Germinal*. First International Congress of Criminal Anthropology held in Rome

1886   (January) General Boulanger appointed Minister of War. (14 January) Beginning of Barrême case, following murder of the Prefect of the Département de l'Eure on the Cherbourg–Paris line. (April) *The Masterpiece*. Publication of Gabriel Tarde's *La Criminalité comparée*

1887   Denounced as an onanistic pornographer in the *Manifesto of the Five* in *Le Figaro*. Cesare Lombroso's *L'Uomo delinquente* (2nd edn.) published in French translation. (May) General Boulanger forced to resign as Minister of War. (November) *Earth*

1888   (September) First of Jack the Ripper murders in the East End of London. (October) *The Dream*. Jeanne Rozerot becomes his mistress. Foundation of Institut Pasteur

1889   (February) Begins research for *La Bête humaine*. (5 May) Begins writing. (6 June) First chapter completed. (September) Republican success in national elections. (20 September) Birth of Denise, daughter of Zola and Jeanne. Juste Lisch's five-year enlargement of the Gare Saint-Lazare completed in time for the Exposition Universelle. (14 November) First instalment of *La Bête humaine* appears in *La Vie populaire*

1890   (2 March) Last instalment of *La Bête humaine* in *La Vie populaire*, and publication in book form

1891   (March) *Money*. (April) Elected President of the Société des gens de lettres. (25 September) Birth of Jacques, son of Zola and Jeanne

1892   (June) *The Débâcle*

1893   (July) *Doctor Pascal*, the last of the Rougon-Macquart novels. Fêted on a visit to London

1894   (August) *Lourdes*, the first novel of the trilogy *Three Cities*. (22 December) Dreyfus found guilty by a court martial

1896   (May) *Rome*

1898   (13 January) 'J'accuse', his article in defence of Dreyfus, published in *L'Aurore*. (21 February) Found guilty of libelling the Minister of War and given the maximum sentence of one year's imprisonment and a fine of 3,000 francs. Appeal for a retrial granted on a technicality. (March) *Paris*. (23 May) Retrial delayed. (18 July) Leaves for England instead of attending court

1899   (4 June) Returns to France. (October) *Fecundity*, the first of his 'Four Gospels'

1900   Electricity replaces steam on Paris suburban railways

1901   (May) *Toil*, the second 'Gospel'

1902   (29 September) Dies of fumes from his bedroom fire, the chimney having been capped either by accident or by anti-Dreyfusard design. Wife survives. (5 October) Public funeral in Paris, attended by some 50,000 people

1903   (March) *Truth*, the third 'Gospel', published posthumously. *Justice* was to be the fourth.

1908   (4 June) Remains transferred to the Pantheon

1938   Nationalization of the French railway service and creation of
        the Société nationale des chemins de fer français (SNCF)

1972   Steam locomotives cease to be used on the French national
        railways

La Bête humaine

CHAPTER I

Upon entering the room, Roubaud set the loaf of bread, pâté, and bottle of white wine down on the table. But Mère Victoire must have banked the fire in her stove with so much slack before going down to work that morning that by now the heat was stifling. And so the assistant station-master opened a window and leant his elbows on the sill.

This was in the Impasse d'Amsterdam, in the last house on the right, a tall building in which the Compagnie de l'Ouest* housed some of its employees. The window, located on the fifth floor just beneath the sloping mansard roof, looked out over the station, its broad swathe breaching the Quartier de l'Europe* in a sudden unfurling of the horizon, which seemed to be extended still further, that afternoon, by a mid-February sky of wet, warm grey shot through with sunlight.

Opposite him, beneath the powdery rays of the sun, the houses in the Rue de Rome blurred into nothing, mere insubstantial shapes. To his left, the glass roofs spanned the station concourses like giant porches, their panes blackened by smoke, and the eye plunged into the huge mainline shed that was separated by the buildings of the mail and the foot-warmer depots* from the other, smaller sheds of the Argenteuil, Versailles, and Ceinture lines;* while, to the right, the iron star that was the Pont de l'Europe cut across the open space, which reappeared beyond it only to vanish into the distance in the direction of the Batignolles tunnel. And directly beneath the window itself, occupying the whole vast area, the three pairs of railway lines emerging from under the bridge fanned out and multiplied into innumerable metal branches which disappeared beneath the station roofs. By the three pointsman's huts, just in front of the bridge-arches, could be seen tiny patches of denuded garden. Amidst the indeterminate blur of carriages and engines cluttering the tracks, a large red signal stained the pale light of day.

For a moment Roubaud gazed with interest, comparing, thinking of his own station at Le Havre. Each time he came to spend a day in Paris like this and put up at Mère Victoire's, the job took hold of him again. Beneath the roof of the mainline station the arrival of a train from Mantes had brought the platforms to life; and his eyes followed the shunting-engine, a small six-coupled tank engine with low wheels, as it began to disconnect the train, a brisk little busybody taking the carriages out and backing them into the sidings. Another engine, a powerful one this, a four-coupled express locomotive with great, devouring wheels, stood on its own, its chimney giving out thick black smoke that rose, very slowly, straight up into the breathless air. But his whole attention was caught by the 3.25 for Caen, which was already full of passengers and awaiting its engine. He could not actually see the latter, halted beyond the Pont de l'Europe; he could only hear it as it asked for permission to proceed with short, urgent blows on its whistle, like someone gradually being overtaken by impatience. An order was shouted, it answered with a brief whistle that it had understood. Then, before the locomotive moved forward, there was a silence, the steam-cocks opened, and steam hissed across the ground in a deafening spurt. And presently he saw its swarming whiteness billow out from under the bridge, swirling like snowy down before flitting away, up through the iron girders. It turned an entire corner of the open space white, while the gathering clouds of smoke from the other locomotive spread their veil of blackness wider and wider. From behind came the long, muffled sounds of insistent hooters, the barking of orders, the jolting of turntables. A gap appeared, and in the distance he made out a Versailles train and an Auteuil train as they crossed, the one on the up line, the other on the down.

Just as Roubaud was about to turn away from the window, a voice calling his name made him lean out. And below him, on the fourth-floor balcony, he recognized a young man of about thirty, Henri Dauvergne: a chief guard, he lived there with his father (who was responsible for the mainline service) and his sisters, Claire and Sophie, two adorable fair-haired girls of eighteen and twenty, who, on the six thousand francs brought in by the two men, kept house amidst one constant round of merriment. The elder was to be heard laughing, while the younger sang and a cage of exotic birds strove to match her trills.

'Hello, Monsieur Roubaud, what on earth are you doing in Paris? . . . Oh yes, of course, I forgot, that business of yours with the Sub-Prefect!'

Once more leaning on the window-sill, the assistant station-master explained that he had had to leave Le Havre that same morning by the 6.40 express. An order from the operations manager had summoned him to Paris, and he'd just been given a severe dressing-down. Very lucky, in fact, that he hadn't lost his job.

'And Madame?' enquired Henri.

Madame had wanted to come too, to do some shopping. Roubaud was waiting for his wife here in this room to which Mère Victoire gave them the key every time they came to Paris and where they liked to have a quiet lunch together on their own while the good woman was detained below at her post of lavatory attendant. This particular day they'd had a bread roll in Mantes, wanting to get their chores over with first. But it was now gone three, and he was dying of hunger.

Henri, to be friendly, enquired further:

'And are you staying over in Paris?'

No, no, they were both returning to Le Havre that evening, on the 6.30 express. Oh indeed, yes, some holiday! They brought you all this way just to give you a talking-to, and then it was straight back to the kennel!

For a moment the two railwaymen looked at each other, shaking their heads. But they could no longer hear what the other was saying, as a crazed piano had that minute burst forth into a stream of loud notes. The two sisters must have been hammering away on it together, laughing even more loudly and driving the songbirds wild. Whereupon the young man, caught up in the fun, waved and went back inside; and the assistant station-master, left on his own, remained for a brief instant staring down at the balcony where all the youthful gaiety was coming from. Then, on looking up, he caught sight of the engine, which had closed its steam-cocks and which the pointsman was now sending down the line to join the Caen train. The last flaky remnants of white steam were vanishing into the great whorls of black smoke that blotted the sky. And he, too, turned back indoors.

Seeing the cuckoo-clock standing at twenty past three, Roubaud gestured despairingly. What on earth could be making Séverine so late? Once she'd gone into a shop, there was simply no getting her out again. To take his mind off the hunger gnawing at his stomach, he decided to lay the table. The huge room with its two windows was familiar to him, a combined bedroom, dining-room, and kitchen, and familiar too was its walnut furniture, the bed covered in a red cotton bedspread, the dresser, the round dining-table, and the Norman wardrobe. From the dresser he fetched napkins, plates, knives and forks, and two glasses. They were all spotlessly clean, and he took pleasure in these household tasks, as if he were playing at dolls' tea-parties, delighting in the whiteness of the linen, a man very much in love with his wife, and laughing with that same hearty, fresh laughter into which she would burst the moment she came through the door. But having put the pâté out on a plate and set the bottle of white wine beside it, he became anxious and looked about him. Then, briskly, he drew two forgotten packages from his pockets, a small tin of sardines and some gruyère cheese.

The half-hour struck. Roubaud paced up and down, cocking an ear at the slightest sound from the stairs. As the idle waiting continued, he stopped to gaze at himself in the mirror. He showed no signs of ageing, and although he was nearing forty, his curly hair was as bright red as ever. His beard, which he wore full, still grew thickly also, the colour of sunshine. And as a man of medium height but of exceptional vigour he found his person pleasing, and drew satisfaction from his rather squat head, with its low forehead, thick neck, and round, ruddy face, lit by two large, keen eyes. His eyebrows joined in the middle, lending his forehead the bushy mark of the jealous man. As he had married a woman fifteen years younger than himself, these frequent glances at the mirror brought him reassurance.

At the sound of footsteps Roubaud ran and opened the door slightly. But it was the woman who worked on the station newsstand returning home to the neighbouring flat. He came back, and inspected a box of shells lying on the dresser. He knew it well, this box, it had been a present from Séverine to Mère Victoire, her nurse. And this small object was all it required for the whole story of his marriage to come flooding back to him.

Nearly three years now, already. Originally from the South, from Plassans, where his father had been a carter, he had left the army a sergeant and worked for a long time as a porter at Mantes station, before being promoted to head porter at Barentin; and that's where he had first met her, his beloved wife, when she used to come from Doinville to take the train with Mademoiselle Berthe, the daughter of President Grandmorin.* Séverine Aubry was no better than the youngest daughter of a gardener who had died while in service with the Grandmorin family; but the President, her godfather and guardian, used to spoil her so, making her his own daughter's companion and sending them both to the same boarding-school at Rouen, and she herself had such natural good breeding, that for a long while Roubaud had been content to desire her from afar, with the passion of a no longer wholly unscrubbed worker for a delicate jewel which he judged to be of great price. Such was the one and only love of his life. He would have married her without a penny, simply for the joy of having her for himself, and when he eventually plucked up the courage, the reality had exceeded his wildest dreams: as well as giving him Séverine and a dowry of ten thousand francs, the President, now retired and a director on the board of the Compagnie de l'Ouest, had also taken him under his wing. The day after the wedding he had been promoted to assistant station-master at Le Havre. Yes, no doubt, he had had a good work record: he was dependable, punctual, honest, of limited but sound intelligence, all sterling qualities which might explain the prompt response to his application and the rapidity of his promotion. But he preferred to believe that he owed everything to his wife. He adored her.

When he had opened the tin of sardines, Roubaud finally lost patience. They had agreed to meet at three. Where could she possibly be? She wasn't going to tell him that it took all day to buy six chemises and a pair of ankle-boots. And as he passed once more in front of the mirror, he noticed his bristling eyebrows, the forehead traversed by that single, hard line. Never once had he suspected her in Le Havre: in Paris he imagined all manner of danger, deception, and misdeed. The blood rushed to his head, and the fists of this former station-worker curled tight, the way they used to when he was shunting rolling-stock. He was

turning back into the unthinking, brutish instrument of his own
strength, he could have crushed her to a pulp in a fit of blind
fury.

Séverine pushed open the door, looking all fresh-faced and
pleased with herself.

'It's me . . . You must have thought I'd got lost, eh?'

In the full bloom of her twenty-five years she appeared
tall, slim, very lithe, yet also fleshy and small-boned. She was not
obviously pretty, with her long face and a strong mouth that
gleamed with good teeth. But on closer inspection she came to
seem attractive because of the magical charm and strangeness of
her large blue eyes under the pile of thick black hair.

And then, as her husband said nothing but continued to exam-
ine her with that veiled, doubtful look she knew so well, she
added:

'Oh, have I been running . . . Can you imagine, not a single
bus to be had. So, rather than spend money on a cab I ran all the
way . . . Just look how hot I am.'

'See here,' he said violently, 'you're not going to have me
believe you've just come from the Bon Marché.'

But at once, with the sweetness of a child, she threw her arms
round his neck and placed her soft, pretty little hand over his
mouth:

'That's enough, you horrible man, you . . . You know perfectly well I love you.'

Her whole being exuded sincerity of this sort, he felt how
candid, how honest she had remained and hugged her madly for
it. His moments of suspicion always ended in this way: she,
abandoning herself, delighting in making him have to coax her;
he, covering her with kisses, kisses she did not return. And
indeed this was what made him vaguely uneasy about her, this
passive grown-up child with her filial affection but in whom the
lover had not yet stirred.

'So you bought up the shop then?'

'Yes, yes. I'll tell you all about it . . . But first let's eat. Am I
starving! . . . Oh, wait, I've got you a little present. Come on, say
it: "A little present all for me". '

She was laughing in his face, close up. She had thrust her right
hand into her pocket where she was holding something which
she refused to take out.

'Quick, come on: "A little present all for me".'

He, too, was laughing, good-naturedly. He gave in.

'A little present all for me.'

It was a knife she had bought for him, to replace one he had lost and been lamenting for the past fortnight. He exclaimed in surprise, and said how superb it was, this handsome new knife, with its ivory handle and gleaming blade. He was going to use it right this minute. She was delighted at how pleased he looked; and, jokingly, she made him give her a coin so that their relationship should not be severed.

'Let's eat, let's eat,' she repeated. 'No, no, please, don't close it yet. I'm so hot!'

She had joined him at the window, and stood there for a few seconds, leaning against his shoulder, looking out over the vast expanse of the railway station. For the moment the trails of smoke had gone, and the copper disc of the sun was sinking through the haze, behind the houses in the Rue de Rome. Below, a shunting-engine was bringing in the Mantes train, fully made up and due to leave at 4.25. Having shunted it the length of the platform, under the roof, the engine was then uncoupled. Beyond, in the Ceinture train-shed, the sound of buffer on buffer indicated the unscheduled coupling of extra carriages. And there, on its own in the middle of the tracks, its driver and fireman all black with the dirt from their journey, the heavy locomotive of a stopping train stood motionless, as though tired and winded, with just a thin trickle of steam coming from one of its valves. It was waiting for the line to be opened so that it could return to the Batignolles depot. A red signal-arm clicked and disappeared. The engine left.

'They don't half lark about, those young Dauvergne girls!,' Roubaud said, turning away from the window. 'Can you hear them banging away on their piano? . . . I saw Henri just now, he said to send you his regards.'

'Food, food,' cried Séverine.

And she attacked the sardines, gorging herself. Oh, it was a long time since she had had that roll at Mantes! She found it intoxicating coming to Paris. She throbbed with the pleasure of having dashed about the streets, and was still in a fever from her shopping at the Bon Marché. Every spring, at one fell swoop, she would go there and spend her winter savings, preferring to buy

everything in the one place and maintaining that the money she
saved paid for her ticket. And so, without pausing between
mouthfuls, she poured out the whole story. Finally, and with
some embarrassment, she blushingly divulged the total sum she
had spent, more than three hundred francs.

'Blimey!' said Roubaud, shocked. 'You do yourself pretty
proud for the wife of an assistant station-master! ... But you
only went for six chemises and a pair of ankle-boots, didn't you?'

'Oh, but my love, there were special offers, never to be
repeated! ... A small piece of silk with these delicious stripes!
And this terribly smart hat, an absolute dream it is, and ready-
made petticoats, with embroidered flounces! And all of it going
for next to nothing. I'd have paid twice as much in Le
Havre ... They're sending them on, you'll soon see!'

He had decided to take it in good part, so pretty was she in her
joy and with her look of embarrassed pleading. And anyway it
was so charming, this improvised picnic of theirs, and being
tucked away together like this in a room where they could be on
their own, much nicer than being in a restaurant. Normally she
only drank water, but now she was letting herself go, and she
drained her glass of white wine without a moment's thought.
The tin of sardines was empty, so they started on the pâté using
the splendid new knife. It was a great success, it cut so well.

'But wait, what about you? That business of yours?' she enquired. 'Here you are making me chatter away like this, and you
haven't told me how things went, you know, about the Sub-
Prefect.'

So he gave her a detailed account of how the operations manager had received him. Oh, a right dressing-down that had been!
He had defended himself, told him the real truth, about how that
little peacock of a Sub-Prefect had insisted on entering first class
with his dog when there was a second-class carriage reserved for
gundogs and their masters, and then the row that had followed,
and the things that had been said. Essentially the manager told
him he had been right to try and enforce the regulations; but the
tricky bit was what he himself admitted to having said: 'You
won't always be the masters!' He was suspected of republican
sympathies. The debates which had just marked the opening of
the 1869 parliamentary session and the government's own un-

spoken dread of the forthcoming general election* were making it nervous. So he would certainly have been transferred if it hadn't been for the good word put in by President Grandmorin. Even then he had been required to sign the letter of apology which the President had suggested and indeed drafted.

Séverine burst in:

'Well, there you are then, wasn't it a good idea of mine to write to him and go and visit him with you this morning before you went to face the music . . . I knew he would help us out.'

'Yes, he cares a great deal for you,' Roubaud went on, 'and he has a lot of influence in the Company . . . But look where it gets me being a good employee. Oh, of course, they didn't spare the praises: not much initiative perhaps, but handles himself well, obeys orders, doesn't shrink from carrying out his duty, you name it! Well, I can tell you, my dear, if you hadn't been my wife and if Grandmorin hadn't spoken up for me, out of affection for you, I'd have been done for, sent off in disgrace to some little station or other.'

She was staring blankly into space, and muttered as if to herself:

'Oh, yes, he has a lot of influence all right.'

There was a silence, and she sat there, wide-eyed, gazing into the distance, no longer eating. No doubt she was recalling the days of her childhood, back at the château at Doinville, fourteen miles outside Rouen. She had never known her mother. When her father, the gardener Aubry, had died, she was just entering her thirteenth year; and it was at this point that the President, already a widower, had taken her in and arranged for her to be looked after with his daughter Berthe by Madame Bonnehon, the wife of a factory-owner, herself now similarly a widow and the present owner of the château. Berthe, who was two years older, and a bride six months after her, had married Monsieur de Lachesnaye, a shrivelled, sallow little man who was a judge in the Rouen courts. Up until the previous year the President had still been presiding at these courts, for his own district, when he had then retired after a distinguished career: born in 1804, appointed deputy public prosecutor at Digne following the 1830 Revolution, then at Fontainebleau, then Paris, subsequently public prosecutor at Troyes, advocate general at Rennes, and finally chief presiding judge at Rouen. Worth several million francs, he had been a member of the General Council since 1855,* and he had been made a commander in the Legion of Honour on the very day of his retirement. And as far back as she could remember, she could see him as he still was, stocky and heavily built, his hair cut short and prematurely white, though tinged with the golden blondness of younger days, a fringe of beard closely clipped, no moustache, and a squarish face rendered severe by piercing blue eyes and a large nose. He had an abrupt manner, and everyone around him went in fear and trembling.

Roubaud had to raise his voice, twice asking:

'Well, what are you thinking about?'

She jumped, shivering a little as though startled and gripped by fear.

'Oh, nothing.'

'Aren't you going to eat anything else? Aren't you hungry any more?'

'What? Oh, but of course . . . Just you watch me.'

Emptying her glass of wine, Séverine polished off the slice of pâté remaining on her plate. But then, disaster! They had finished the bread, and not a crumb was left for the cheese. There was much shouting, and then laughter when, on turning everything upside down, they discovered the stale end of a loaf at the back of Mère Victoire's dresser. Although the window was open, the room remained warm, and the young woman, sitting with the stove behind her, had scarcely had the chance to cool down, indeed had grown still more flushed with the excitement of their makeshift meal and so much talking. Prompted by the thought of Mère Victoire, Roubaud had returned to the subject of Grandmorin: now *there* was another woman who owed him a thing or two. Originally an unmarried mother whose child had subsequently died, then a wet-nurse for Séverine whose own mother had just died giving birth to her, and subsequently married to one of the Company firemen, Mère Victoire had been eking out a living in Paris as a seamstress (while her husband squandered everything they had), when a chance meeting with her former nurseling had restored her previous connection and brought her, too, under the wing of the President; and today he had secured her a position in the lavatories, in charge of the first-class conveniences, the ladies', which were the best of all. The Company paid her only one hundred francs a year, but she made nearly fourteen hundred from the tips, and not to mention the accommodation, this room, where even her heating was free. All in all, she did very nicely. And Roubaud calculated that if Pecqueux, her husband, had really brought home the two thousand eight hundred francs he earned as a fireman, bonuses included, then instead of being on the breadline their household could have had a joint income of more than four thousand francs, double what he, as an assistant station-master, was earning in Le Havre.*

'No doubt,' he concluded, 'not every woman wants to be a lavatory attendant. But there's no such thing as a lousy job.'

Meanwhile their ravenous hunger had abated, and they were now eating in a merely desultory manner, cutting off small pieces of cheese simply to prolong the feast. Their conversation, too, was becoming less animated.

'Talking of which,' he exclaimed, 'I forgot to ask you . . . Why did you refuse when the President invited you to go and spend a few days at Doinville?'

Contentedly digesting his meal, he had been reflecting on the visit they had made that morning to the grand house in the Rue du Rocher, close by the station; and he had been imagining himself back once more in the large, forbidding study, and could still hear the President telling them that he was returning to Doinville on the following day. Then, as if on the spur of the moment, he had suggested accompanying them on the 6.30 express that very evening and then taking his god-daughter on to his sister's at Doinville: she had been wanting to see her for ages. But the young woman had given all sorts of reasons which, she claimed, prevented her.

'You know, as far as I was concerned,' Roubaud went on, 'I would have been quite happy for you to go off on a little trip like that. You could have stayed there till Thursday, I would have managed somehow . . . I mean, in our position, we need them, don't we? It's not a very good idea to go refusing their kind offers, especially as he seemed really hurt that you had. That's why I only stopped pressing you to accept when you tugged me by the coat. After that I just said whatever you said, but without really understanding why . . . Eh? Why didn't you want to go?'

Séverine, her eyes shifting uncertainly, gestured with impatience:

'How can I possibly leave you all on your own?'

'That's no reason . . . In the three years since we've been married, you've actually been to Doinville twice like that, for a week. Nothing was stopping you going a third time.'

The young woman's discomfort was growing, and she had turned her face away.

'Well, I just didn't fancy it, that's all. You're not going to force me to do things I don't want to, are you?'

Roubaud spread his arms out as if to say that he was not forcing her to do anything. Nevertheless he pursued the matter:

'Look here, you're hiding something . . . That last time, did Madame Bonnehon make you feel unwelcome or something?'

Oh, no, Madame Bonnehon had always made her feel extremely welcome. She was such a nice woman, so tall, so strong, with that magnificent blond hair, and still a beauty despite her fifty-five years! Since she had been a widow, and indeed even while her husband was still alive, people used to say how she was always losing her heart to someone or other. They adored her at Doinville, she made the château such a delightful, special place, the whole of Rouen society came to visit, especially the legal people. Madame Bonnehon had had a particular number of gentlemen friends among the legal profession.

'Well, come on, admit it then, it was the Lachesnayes, they snubbed you.'

To be sure, since her marriage to Monsieur de Lachesnaye, things were no longer as they had been between Berthe and herself. She had not exactly become kind-hearted, poor Berthe, and how plain she was, with that red nose of hers. In Rouen the ladies spoke highly of her distinction. What is more, a husband like hers, ugly, hard, tight-fisted, seemed if anything just the sort whose character rubs off on his wife and makes her ill-natured. But no, Berthe had behaved perfectly well towards her former companion, who could think of nothing in particular with which to reproach her.

'So it's the President you don't like there?'

Séverine, who until then had been replying in slow, even tones, was again seized with impatience:

'Him? Don't be ridiculous!'

And she went on, in short, tense bursts. They hardly ever saw him. He had set aside a summer-house in the grounds just for his own use, with a door that gave on to a deserted lane. He would come and go unobserved. Indeed his sister never even quite knew which day he would be arriving. He would take a carriage at Barentin, have himself driven out to Doinville in the dark, and spend whole days in his summer-house, quite unbeknown to everyone. Oh, he wasn't the one to bother you there.

'I only mentioned it because you've told me twenty times or more about how he used to scare the living daylights out of you when you were a child.'

'Oh, the living daylights, come on, you're exaggerating again, as usual . . . Certainly he hardly ever laughed. He used to stare at you so hard, with those big eyes, that you had to look down at once. I've seen people get all flustered and be quite unable to say a single word to him because they were so much in awe of him, with his great reputation for being severe and wise . . . But he's never scolded *me*, in fact I've always felt that he had rather a soft spot for me.'

Once more her speech was slowing, her eyes drifting off into the distance.

'I remember . . . when I was little and used to play with other girls, along the paths, if he happened to appear, all the others used to hide, even Berthe his own daughter, because she was always afraid she'd done something wrong. But me, I used to wait for him, all calm and collected. He would pass by and see me there, smiling, looking up, and he would give me a little tap on the cheek . . . Later, when I was sixteen and if Berthe ever wanted something from him, it was always me she got to do the asking. I would speak up and look him full in the face, and I could feel those eyes of his boring into my skin. But what did I care? I was so sure he would grant me whatever I asked! . . . Oh, yes, I can remember, I can remember! There isn't a clump of bushes in those grounds, not one corridor, not one room in the château, that I can't picture if I shut my eyes.'

She fell silent, her eyelids closed; and across her flushed, bloated features there seemed to pass the trembling shadow of these things of bygone days, these things of which she did not speak. For a moment she remained thus, her lips gently quivering, as if some involuntary tic were plucking painfully at the corner of her mouth.

'He's certainly been very good to you,' Roubaud continued, after lighting his pipe. 'Not only did he bring you up as a young lady, but he looked after your few francs pretty well, *and* rounded the figure up very handsomely when we got married . . . Not to mention that he's bound to leave you something, in fact he said so in front of me.'

'Yes,' murmured Séverine, 'that house at La Croix-de-Maufras, the property the railway cuts across. We used to go and spend the odd week there. Oh, I'm not counting on it, the Lachesnayes must be working on him to make sure he leaves me nothing. And anyway, I'd rather he did leave me nothing, nothing at all.'

She had spoken these last few words so sharply that he was startled, taking his pipe out of his mouth and looking at her with wide eyes:

'Aren't you the funny one! They say the President's worth millions. Where'd be the harm in his naming his god-daughter in his will? It would be no surprise to anyone, and it would certainly help our finances nicely.'

Then a sudden thought occurred to him, and he laughed:

'You're not worried about people thinking you're his daughter, are you? . . . 'Cos you know, for all his cold looks, people don't half tell some stories on his account. Apparently, even when his wife was alive, he had every single one of the maids. Altogether a man who likes his fun and even now grabs his bit of skirt before you can say Jack Robinson . . . Anyway, what the hell, what would it matter even if you were his daughter!'

Séverine had stood up from the table, in sudden violence, her face blazing and her blue eyes darting anxiously beneath the heavy mane of black hair.

'His daughter, his daughter! . . . I don't want you making jokes about that, do you hear! How can I be his daughter? Do I even look like him? . . . Anyway, that's quite enough on that score, let's talk about something else. I don't want to go to Doinville because I don't, because I'd rather go back to Le Havre with you.'

He nodded, gestured to her to be calm. Fine, fine! if she was going to get all upset about it. He smiled, he'd never seen her so worked up before. The white wine, no doubt. Wanting to be forgiven, he took hold of the knife once more, saying again how splendid it was, wiping it carefully; and to demonstrate that it was as sharp as a razor, he sat there cutting his nails.

'Quarter to four already,' Séverine mumbled, standing in front of the cuckoo-clock. 'I've still got some things to get . . . There's our train to catch.'

But as if to regain her composure before tidying the room, she went back to lean on the window-sill. Putting his knife down and leaving his pipe, he too rose from the table and walked towards her; and standing there behind her, he gently took her in his arms. And he held her thus, entwined, his chin on her shoulder, his head leaning against hers. Neither of them stirred as they looked out.

Beneath them, still, the little shunting-engines moved ceaselessly back and forth; and the muffled sound of their wheels and the occasional, discreet whistle-blast were scarcely audible as they went about their business like tidy housekeepers. One of them passed by and disappeared beneath the Pont de l'Europe, taking the carriages of a Trouville train off to the shed after uncoupling. And there, beyond the bridge, it brushed past a solitary engine coming in light from the depot, with gleaming brass and steel, all fresh and sprightly, ready for its journey. This engine had halted, tooting twice to the pointsman for a line; and he, almost immediately, sent it down to its train which was standing at its platform, fully made up, beneath the mainline station roof. It was the 4.25 to Dieppe. A stream of passengers was hurrying forward, the barrows laden with luggage could be heard clattering along, and men were pushing the foot-warmers one by one into the carriages. But the engine and its tender had come up to the van at the front of the train, striking it with a dull thud, and the foreman was to be seen tightening the screw himself on the draw-bar. The sky had grown dark over the Batignolles district: an ashen twilight engulfed the house-fronts and seemed already to be falling on the broad fan of railway lines; while away in the murky distance the trains on the suburban and Ceinture lines crossed endlessly in arrival and departure. Beyond the shadowy expanses of the great train-sheds, over darkening Paris, shreds of russet smoke vanished into the air.

'No, not now,' murmured Séverine.

Gradually, without a word, he had tightened his embrace, excited by the warmth of the young body he was holding thus, wrapped within his arms. His head was light with the smell of her, and she only quickened his desire as she arched her back in attempted escape. In a single movement he wrenched her from the window, shutting both sides of it with his elbow. His mouth had found hers, he was crushing her lips and bearing her off towards the bed.

'No, no, this isn't our own place,' she repeated. 'Please, I beg you, not in this room!'

For her part, she felt almost drunk, giddy from the food and wine, and still throbbing from her feverish dash across Paris. The over-heated room, the table littered with the remains of their meal, the unexpectedness of this day-trip that had turned into a lunch-party, it all stirred her blood and made her body tremble. And yet she would not give herself, but rather stood there, with her back pressed against the wooden bedstead, resisting in an act of frightened defiance that she would have been hard put to explain.

'No, no, I don't want to.'

His face flushed, he tried to control his big, brutal hands. He was shaking, and could have broken her into little pieces.

'But nobody'll know, silly. We can remake the bed.'

Usually she would abandon herself in docile compliance when they were at home in Le Havre, after lunch, when he was working nights. She seemed to take no pleasure in it herself, and yet exhibited a contented softness, a kind of affectionate consent that he should have his pleasure of her. And what drove him wild at this particular moment was to sense her now as he had never had her, burning, shuddering with sensual passion. The black reflection of her hair cast a dark shadow over her calm, periwinkle eyes, and her strong mouth stood out blood-red in the gentle oval of her face. Here was a woman he did not know. Why was she refusing to give herself?

'Tell me, why not? We have all the time in the world.'

Then, from the depths of an inexplicable anguish, in the midst of some inner debate in which she did not seem able to judge things clearly, as if she too did not know herself, she let out a cry of real pain, which made him be still.

'No, no, I beg you, leave me be! . . . I don't know why, it sickens me, the very idea, just now . . . It wouldn't be right.'

They had both slumped down on to the edge of the bed. He passed his hand over her face, as if to remove the heat that was burning it up. Seeing that he was himself again, she leant over tenderly and planted a big kiss on his cheek, wanting to show that she loved him all the same. For a moment they remained like this, without a word, recovering. He had taken hold of her left hand again and was playing with an old gold ring, a gold serpent with a small ruby head, which she wore on the same finger as her wedding-ring. It had been there since he had known her.

'My little serpent,' said Séverine in a dreamy, automatic tone, thinking that he was looking at the ring and feeling the urgent need to speak. 'He gave me that at La Croix-de-Maufras, for my sixteenth birthday.'

Roubaud looked up in surprise.

'Who? The President?'

When her husband's eyes had met hers, she had started suddenly from her daydream. She felt a sudden chill cool her cheeks. She wanted to reply, and found nothing to say, strangled by a kind of paralysis which had taken hold of her.

'But,' he went on, 'you always told me it was your mother's, that she'd left you the ring.'

Even now she could take back what she had said, what she had let slip in a completely absent moment. She only needed to laugh it off, to play the scatterbrain. But she refused to, she was out of control, heedless.

'Never, my darling, I have never told you that my mother left me this ring.'

Roubaud shot her a look, as he too turned pale.

'What do you mean, you never told me that? You must have told me that twenty times or more! . . . There's no harm in the President having given you a ring. He's given you plenty of other things . . . But why hide the fact from me? Why lie to me, and about your mother?'

'I never mentioned my mother, darling, you're quite wrong.'

It was idiotic, insisting like this. She could see that she was getting in deeper, that he could read her thoughts, and she wished she could have started all over again, taken back her words. But it was too late, she could feel her every feature disintegrating, could feel the admission oozing out of her, despite herself, from every pore. The chill on her cheeks had spread to the rest of her face, a nervous tic was tugging at her lips. And he, terrifyingly, suddenly red in the face again as if the blood were about to burst his veins, had grabbed her by the wrists and was staring into the distraught terror of her eyes, trying desperately to discover what it was that she would not say out loud.

'Dear God!' he spluttered, 'dear God in heaven!'

She was afraid now, and ducked her head behind her arm to shield it from the blow of the fist she could sense coming. One little, miserable, insignificant detail, one forgotten lie about this ring, had just brought everything to light in a single brief exchange of words. And it had taken no more than a moment. He shoved her back across the bed, and attacked her with both fists, at random. In three years he hadn't so much as clicked his fingers at her, and here he was murdering her, blindly, drunkenly, in the brutish rage of a man who had once shunted wagons with his own bare hands.

'You whoring bitch! You slept with him! . . . slept with him! . . . slept with him!'

He was growing more and more furious as he repeated this, bringing his fists down on her with each word as if to brand them in her flesh.

'An old man's cast-off, you whoring, fucking bitch! You slept with him! . . . You slept with him!'

Anger choked his voice to a whistle, and stopped the words from coming. Only then did he hear that she, cowering beneath his fists, was saying no. She could think of no other way of defending herself, she was denying it to stop him from killing her. And this appeal, this obstinacy in deceit, sufficed to push him over the edge.

'Admit that you slept with him.'

'No! No!'

He had picked her up off the bed and was holding her in his arms to prevent her falling face down on the covers, like some poor creature trying to hide. He was forcing her to look at him.

'Admit you slept with him.'

But she slid from his arms and tried to run for the door. In one bound he was on her once more, his fist raised; and, infuriated, with a single blow, next to the table, he struck her down. In a trice he had flung himself down beside her and grabbed her by the hair, to pin her to the ground. For a moment they lay like that on the floor, face to face, motionless. And in the terrifying silence the sound of singing and laughing could be heard coming up from the Dauvergne girls, whose piano fortunately was going full tilt, blotting out the noise of the fight taking place above. It was Claire singing nursery songs, while Sophie accompanied her for all she was worth.

'Admit you slept with him.'

She did not dare say no again and offered no reply.

'Admit you slept with him, for Christ's sake, or I'll slit you open.'

He would have killed her there and then, she could tell it clearly from the way he looked at her. As she fell, she had caught sight of the knife, lying open on the table; and she could see once more the gleam of its blade, she thought he was stretching out his arm. Now she just wanted to give in, to abandon herself, to abandon everything, she needed to be done with it.

'All right, then, yes, it's true. Now let me go.'

An appalling scene ensued. This admission that he had been demanding so violently had struck him full in the face, like an impossibility, like something monstrous. It was as if he could never have conceived of such an infamy. He seized her head and banged it against a leg of the table. She struggled, and he dragged her across the floor by the hair, knocking the chairs aside. Each time she tried to get up, he knocked her back down on to the floor with his fist—and all the while panting, teeth clenched, with savage, imbecilic tenacity. The table, thrust aside, nearly knocked over the stove. Hair and blood stuck to a corner of the dresser. When they finally drew breath, dazed and gasping with the horror of the scene, tired of punching, of being punched, they had returned to the bed, she still sprawled on the ground, he

crouching, now holding her by the shoulders. And they recovered their breath. Down below the music continued, and
there rose in snatches the very audible and very youthful sound
of laughter.

Roubaud jerked Séverine up and propped her back against the
end of the bed. Then, still on his knees, leaning on her, he was at
last able to speak. He had stopped hitting her now and was
torturing her with his questions, with his burning need to know.

'So, then, you did sleep with him, you bitch! . . . Come on, say
it again, say you slept with that old man . . . And what age were
you, eh? only just a girl, weren't you, a young girl?'

All of a sudden she had burst into tears, and her sobs were
preventing her from answering.

'For Christ's sake, will you tell me or won't you? . . . Eh? you
weren't even ten, were you, when you gave the old man the bit of
fun he wanted? That's why he took you under his wing, wasn't
it, so he could have his filthy way with you. Say it, for Christ's
sake, or I'll start all over again!'

She was crying, she couldn't get a single word out, and he
raised his hand, stunned her with another slap on the face. Three
times, not getting any response, he struck her, repeating his
question.

'What age were you, tell me, you bitch, tell me?'

Why go on? Her very being was ebbing away. He could have
pulled the heart out of her, with his stiff, clumsy working-man's
fingers. And the interrogation continued, she was telling him
everything, so prostrated by shame and fear that her words,
barely whispered, could scarcely be heard. And he, devoured by
his excruciating jealousy, grew more and more enraged at the
suffering which was tearing him apart as he listened to the scenes
she evoked: he could not find out enough, he kept making her go
back over the details, be more precise. With his ear pressed
towards the lips of the poor woman, he was in agony as he
listened to this confession, his threatening fist still raised, ready
to strike anew if she should stop.

Once again her whole Doinville past paraded itself before him,
her childhood, her youth. Had it been in the bushes of the great
park? Or in some forgotten corner of a corridor inside the
château? So the President already had an eye on her when he

kept her with him after his gardener died and had her brought up with his own daughter? Of course, it must all have started those times when the other young girls used to run away if he chanced by while they were playing, when she waited with a smile, chin up, for him to tap her on the cheek as he passed. And later, if she was brave enough to speak to him in person, to get anything she wanted from him, wasn't that because she felt she was in control, while all the time, respectable and severe with the others, he was buying her with the kind of favours he employed to make short work of the maids? Oh, how filthy can you get, that old man playing the grandfather who wants his little kiss-kiss, watching the young girl grow, testing her with his hands, every now and then starting in on his feast, not having the patience to wait till she was fully ripe!

Roubaud was panting.

'Well, what age were you . . . just tell me, what age?'

'Sixteen and a half.'

'You're lying!'

Lying? My God, why? She shrugged in immense exhaustion and surrender.

'And the first time, where was that?'

'At La Croix-de-Maufras.'

He hesitated for a second, his lips quivering, and a yellow gleam came over his eyes.

'And—I want you to tell me this—what did he do to you?'

She remained silent. Then, when he brandished his fist:

'You wouldn't believe me.'

'Tell me anyway . . . He couldn't manage it, is that it?'

She nodded. That was exactly it. And then he insisted on trying to picture the scene, wanting to know every single detail, and resorting to dirty words, revolting questions. She wouldn't open her mouth, and continued simply to indicate yes or no. Perhaps it would ease things for both of them when she had finished confessing. But he was finding the detailed circumstances—the extenuating circumstances as she saw it—even more painful to bear. Full, normal sexual relations would have haunted him with a less torturing vision. This debauchery defiled everything, it was like plunging the poisoned blades of jealousy back into the depths of his own flesh. And now, it was all over, he would never again be able to live a normal life, he would always be able to call up that execrable vision.

A sob ripped from his throat.

'Oh, God . . . oh, God! . . . it can't be, no, no, it's too much, it can't be!'

Then, suddenly, he shook her.

'But why did you marry me then, you bitch? . . . Don't you know it's a vile thing to have done, deceiving me like that? There are thieving women in prison with less on their conscience than that . . . So you despised me, you didn't love me? . . . Eh? Just why *did* you marry me?'

She gestured vaguely. How did she know, now? She had been happy to marry him, hoping to have done with the other man. There are so many things one doesn't want to do and yet which one does do, because in fact they're the wisest thing one can do. No, she didn't love him; and what she was avoiding telling him was that, if it hadn't been for all this, she would never ever have consented to be his wife.

'But him, eh, he wanted to put a roof over your head, didn't he? He had found a willing beast . . . Hadn't he? He wanted to put a roof over your head so that things could continue. And you did continue, didn't you, those two times you stayed there? That's why he took you there, isn't it?'

Once more she nodded.

'And that's why he was inviting you again this time? . . . So, to the bitter end, then, it would have continued, this filth? And if I don't choke the life out of you now, it's going to start all over again!'

His writhing hands reached forward to take hold of her throat once more. But this time she argued back.

'But you're just not being fair. Seeing as it was me who refused to go. You were all ready to pack me off, I had to get angry, remember . . . You can see I didn't want to any more. It was all finished with. I wouldn't ever have wanted to, never ever again.'

He sensed that she was telling the truth, and it brought him no relief. The terrible pain, the iron blade stuck in his chest, was the fact that what had happened between her and that man could never be undone. The horror of his suffering was simply that he was powerless to make everything as if that had never been. Not yet letting go, he came up close to her face, apparently spellbound, magnetically drawn there, as if he were looking into the blood of her tiny blue veins in search of everything she had just told him. And he muttered, obsessed, hallucinating:

'At La Croix-de-Maufras, in the red bedroom . . . I know the one, the window looks out on to the railway line, the bed's opposite it. And it was there, in that room . . . I can see now why he talks about leaving you the house. You've certainly earned it. And well might he look after your few francs for you and give you a dowry, it was certainly worth that much . . . A judge, a man with millions to his name, so respected, so learned, so high up! It makes your head spin, it does . . . and just think, what if he were your father?'

Séverine struggled to her feet. She had shoved him back with a degree of force that was extraordinary from the poor, weak creature who had lain there vanquished. Now violent herself, she was protesting.

'No, no, not that! Anything, whatever you say as far as the rest's concerned. Beat me, kill me . . . But don't say that, it's a lie!'

Roubaud still had hold of one of her hands.

'What do you know? It's only because you have doubts yourself that you get so worked up about it.'

And, as she was taking her hand away, he felt the ring, the little gold serpent with its ruby head, there on her finger, temporarily forgotten. He tore it off and ground it into the floor with his heel in renewed rage. Then he paced up and down the room, speechless, distraught. She, having collapsed on to the edge of the bed, was sitting looking at him with her large, staring eyes. And the terrible silence dragged on and on.

Roubaud's fury did not abate. As soon as it seemed to slacken at all, back it came at once, like drunkenness, in great, redoubled waves that bore him away in their tumult. He was no longer in control of himself, flailing in the void, tossed hither and thither by every shift in the wind of violence that lashed him, sinking back into the one, single need to appease the beast that howled within him. This need was physical, pressing, like a hunger for vengeance, it contorted his body, and would grant him no rest until he had given it satisfaction.

Still pacing up and down, he drummed his fists against his temples and, in a voice of anguish, he stuttered out:

'What am I going to do?'

Since he hadn't killed the woman there and then, he wasn't going to kill her now. His cowardice at letting her live made him even angrier. For it *was* cowardly, it was because he still wanted the bitch that he hadn't strangled her. And yet as things stood, he couldn't keep her. So, then, was he going to get rid of her, kick her out on to the streets, never to be seen again? A renewed surge of pain bore him up once more, and a hideous wave of nausea passed right over him as he sensed that he wouldn't do even that. What then? All he could do was to accept the abomination of it and take this woman back to Le Havre, continue to live with her, resume normal life just as if nothing had happened. No! No! Rather die, rather they should both die, here, now! By this time he was filled with such distress that he cried out even more loudly, wildly:

'What am I going to do?'

From the bed where she still sat, Séverine's wide eyes continued to follow his movements. The calm affection which she had been used to feel for him, as for a good friend, meant that already she pitied him for the excess of pain she could see him suffering. The bad language, the punches, she would have forgiven it all if this mad frenzy had not left her so surprised, so surprised indeed that she had not yet got over it. She who was passive and docile, who as a young girl had fallen in with an old man's desires and later simply let marriage happen to her, as a way of straightening things out, she could not begin to understand an outburst of jealousy such as this, and all because of wrongs committed in the past and which she repented. As someone in whom there was no badness, whose flesh had scarcely yet been aroused and remained that of a sweet, gentle girl still only half-aware and, despite everything, still chaste, she now watched her husband, pacing up and down and turning on his heels in fury, as she might have watched a wolf, or some creature from another species. What had got into him? So many of them were without anger! What terrified her was to sense the animal in him, the animal which she had half been conscious of these past three years from his dark growls, and which was today unleashed, frothing at the mouth, ready to bite. What could she say to him, to prevent something terrible happening?

With each turn of his heels, he found himself once more beside the bed, in front of her. And she was waiting for him, she dared to speak.

'Dearest, listen to me . . .'

But he didn't hear her, he was off again to the other end of the room like a straw buffeted by a storm.

'What am I going to do? What am I going to do?'

Finally she grabbed him by the wrist, held him there a minute.

'Dearest, please, look, since I was the one who refused to go . . . I would never have gone there again, never, never. It's you I love.'

Now she was acting all affectionate, enticing him, raising her lips for him to kiss. But, having slumped down beside her, he pushed her away in disgust.

'Oh, you bitch you, now you'd like to . . . Before, though, you didn't feel like it then, did you, you didn't want me then. And now you'd like to, to get me back, eh? When you get a hold on a man that way, oh yes, it's a firm hold . . . But it would burn me up to go with you now. It would. I can just feel my blood burning with the poison.'

He shuddered. The thought of having her, the picture of their two bodies falling upon the bed, had just shot through him like a tongue of flame. And in the turbid darkness of his flesh, from the depths of his sullied, wounded desire, abruptly there rose a need for death.

'If it's not to kill me, going with you again, you see, I'll have to kill *him* first . . . Kill *him*, kill *him*!'

His voice was rising, and he repeated the words standing up, taller, as if the words themselves by resolving things had calmed him. He said no more, but walked slowly over to the table and looked at the knife where it lay, its blade wide open, gleaming. He shut it automatically and put it in his pocket. And there he remained, his arms dangling by his side, his eyes gazing into the distance, thinking. The obstacles before him made two deep furrows across his brow. Still in search of a solution he walked over and opened the window again, installing himself there, his face to the cold evening air. Behind him his wife had risen to her feet, once more afraid; and, not daring to question him, trying to guess what was going on inside that hard skull, she too stood waiting before the broad sky.

With night beginning to fall, the distant buildings loomed, black shapes against the sky, and the vast station yard was filling with a purplish haze. Over in the direction of the Batignolles district especially, the deep cutting lay as though buried under a coating of ash, and beneath it the girders of the Pont de l'Europe were also starting to fade from view. Towards Paris, the glass panes in the great train-sheds paled with the final gleam of daylight, while underneath them the gathering darkness fell like rain. Sparks shone out, the gas-lamps were being lit along the platforms. A large white light appeared too, the headlamp on the engine of the Dieppe train, which, packed with passengers, its doors already closed, stood waiting for the station foreman to give the order to depart. There had been a hold-up, the points-man's red signal was barring the way while a tiny shunting-engine came and recovered a number of carriages left behind on the line after some poor marshalling. Trains moved about unceasingly in the deepening shadows, amidst the inextricable tangle of rails, between the rows of stationary carriages parked in the sidings. One left for Argenteuil, and one for Saint-Germain; another arrived from Cherbourg, a very long one. There was signal after signal, whistles blew, hooters sounded; from all directions, one by one, there appeared red lights, and green, and yellow, and white; it was all a jumble at that murky twilight hour, when it seemed as though everything should collide, and yet everything passed, and slid by, and emerged, all at the same gentle crawl, vaguely, in the depths of the dusk. But the pointsman's red light faded, and the Dieppe train whistled and began to move forward. From the pallid sky came the first few drops of a scudding rain. It was going to be a very wet night.

When Roubaud turned round, his face looked thick and stubbornly set, as though filled with the shadows of this falling night. He had made up his mind, and his plan was clear. In the fading light of day he looked at the time on the cuckoo-clock and said out loud:

'Twenty past five.'

And he was surprised: one hour, one short hour, and so many things! He could have believed that they had been devouring each other here like this for weeks.

'Twenty past five, we've still got time.'

Séverine, not daring to question him, continued to follow his movements with anxious eyes. She saw him rummage in the cupboard and take out some paper, a small bottle of ink, and a pen.

'Here, you're going to write a letter.'

'Who to?'

'To him . . . Sit down.'

And, as she instinctively shied away from the chair, not yet knowing what he was going to demand of her, he dragged her back and sat her down in front of the table with such a heavy hand that there she remained.

'Write . . . "Leave this evening on the 6.30 express, and don't let anyone see you before Rouen."'

She was holding the pen, but her hand was trembling, her fears growing at the unknown prospects opened up by these two simple lines. So she found the courage to look up at him, imploringly.

'My dear, what are you going to do? . . . Tell me, I beg you . . .'

He repeated in his loud, inexorable voice:

'Go on, write.'

Then, his eyes staring into hers, without anger, without coarse language, but with a weight of determination which she could feel crushing her, destroying her:

'You'll soon see what I'm going to do . . . And understand this, what I'm going to do, I want you to do with me . . . That way we'll stick together, there'll be something solid between us.'

He was terrifying her, and once more she recoiled.

'No, no, I want to know . . . I won't write before I know.'

Then, without another word, he took her hand, a frail, childish hand, and pressed it in his iron grip, squeezing it steadily like a vice, till it was crushed. It was his own will that he was thus inserting into her flesh, at the same time as the pain. She screamed, and everything broke within her, everything yielded.

The innocent girl she still was, sweet, gentle, passive, could only but obey. An instrument of love, an instrument of death.

'Go on, write.'

And she wrote, with her poor sore hand, painfully.

'That will do fine. Thank you,' he said, when he had the finished letter. 'Now, tidy up here a little, get things straight . . . I'll come back for you later.'

He was very calm. He retied his tie in the mirror, put on his hat, and left. She heard him double-lock the door and remove the key. It was getting even darker now. For a moment she remained seated, listening to all the noises outside. From next door, where the woman who sold newspapers lived, came the sound of a soft, steady moan: a dog, probably, left on its own. Below, in the Dauvergnes', the piano was silent. Now instead there was the merry clatter of crockery and saucepans, as the two young housekeepers busied themselves in their kitchen, Claire with making a mutton stew, Sophie preparing a salad. And feeling utterly drained, she listened as they laughed, in the calamitous misery of the oncoming night.

At a quarter past six the engine for the Le Havre express emerged from under the Pont de l'Europe and was despatched down the line to its train and connected. Congestion had made it impossible to accommodate the train in the main concourse, and it was waiting outside where the platform extended in a kind of narrow jetty out into the darkness of an inky sky, and where the row of occasional gas-lamps placed along its length seemed no more than a string of smoky stars. A shower of rain had just fallen, leaving cold, damp air to spread across the huge open space that seemed still more immense in the mist, stretching as far as the small, pale lights in the buildings along the Rue de Rome. It was a vast, dreary, watery expanse, pricked here and there by a blood-red fire, and dimly inhabited by opaque masses, engines, carriages, standing on their own, the odd remnants of half-disconnected trains slumbering in sidings; and from the depths of this pool of shadows came noises, sounds as of giant lungs filling with air, a fevered panting, whistle-blows like the piercing shrieks of women being ravished, distant hooter-blasts echoing sorrowfully in the rumble from the neighbouring streets. Loud orders were given for a carriage to be added.

Standing there motionless, the express's locomotive released a great jet of steam from its valve, and up it rose into all this blackness, fraying into wispy tatters and strewing tears of white across the limitless mourning that draped the sky.

At twenty past six Roubaud and Séverine appeared. She had just returned the key to Mère Victoire on their way past the lavatories next to the waiting-rooms; and Roubaud was urging her forward with the air of a husband in a rush who's being delayed by his wife—he, impatient and brusque, his hat tilted back, and she, her veil clutched tight to her face, faltering, as if she could walk no further. A stream of passengers was making its way along the platform, they merged with it and moved along the line of carriages, looking for an empty compartment in first class. The platform had come to life, porters were pushing their barrows of luggage along to the van at the front of the train, an inspector was helping a large family to find seats, the assistant foreman was checking the couplings, signal-lamp in hand, making sure that all had been properly fastened tight. And Roubaud had finally found an empty compartment into which he was on the point of ushering Séverine when he was spotted by the station-master, Monsieur Vandorpe, who was walking by with his assistant, Monsieur Dauvergne, the person in charge of the main lines, both with their hands behind their backs, watching as the extra carriage was connected. Greetings were exchanged, they had to stop and have a word.

First they discussed the business with the Sub-Prefect, which had ended to everybody's satisfaction. Then it was about some accident which had happened that morning at Le Havre, news of it having come through by telegraph: the connecting-rod had gone on one of the engines, La Lison, the one that hauled the 6.30 express on Thursdays and Saturdays, just as it was entering the station, which meant that its driver, Jacques Lantier—who came from the same part of the world as Roubaud—and his fireman, Pecqueux (Mère Victoire's man), would both have to stay put for two days while it was repaired. Standing by the door of the compartment, Séverine was waiting to board the train; her husband, meanwhile, was busy being expansive, talking loudly, laughing. But there was a jolt, and the train moved two or three metres backwards; it was the engine backing the front carriages on to the one they had just added, the 293, a private coupé.* And Henri, the younger Dauvergne, who was travelling on the train as chief guard, had recognized Séverine beneath her veil and just saved her from being hit by the open compartment door by pushing it smartly to one side. Then, apologizing, smiling, most amiable, he explained to her that the coupé was for one of the Company directors, who had just requested it half an hour before the train was due to depart. She gave a short, nervous laugh, for no apparent reason, and he hurried off to his duties in delight, because he had often said to himself that she would make a very agreeable mistress.

The clock was showing 6.27. Three minutes to go. Abruptly Roubaud, who had been keeping an eye on the waiting-room doors while he chatted, left the station-master's side and returned to Séverine. But the carriage had moved, and they had to retrace their steps a short way in order to find the empty compartment; and, turning his back, he hustled his wife along and handed her roughly aboard, while she, anxiously compliant, instinctively glanced back to have a look. It was a passenger arriving late, carrying nothing but a rug, with the collar on his heavy blue greatcoat turned up so high and the rim of his bowler hat pulled down so low over his eyes that all that could be seen of his face in the flickering light of the gas-lamps was a small patch of white beard. Nevertheless Monsieur Vandorpe and Monsieur Dauvergne had both walked forward, despite the passenger's evident desire not to be seen. They followed him, and he did not acknowledge them till some three carriages further on, in front of the private coupé into which he hurriedly climbed. It was him. Séverine had slumped, trembling, on to the seat. Her husband was crushing her arm in a tight squeeze, as if taking possession of her for the last time, exulting, now that he was certain to do it.

In a minute's time the half-hour would strike. A vendor was stubbornly proffering evening newspapers, one or two passengers were walking about on the platform, finishing their cigarettes. But all of them climbed aboard: the inspectors could be heard approaching from each end of the train, shutting the doors. And Roubaud, who had been unpleasantly surprised to find the compartment he had believed empty now occupied by a dark form, no doubt some woman in mourning, sitting silently and perfectly still in the corner, could not contain an exclamation of real anger when the door opened again and an inspector propelled a couple inside, one large man, one large woman, who subsided into their seats gasping for breath. They were about to depart. It had started to rain again, a fine drizzle, enveloping the huge, dark, expanse of track and its ceaseless passage of trains: and of these only the lighted windows were visible, a row of tiny mobile panes. Green lights had appeared, one or two lamps were bobbing about just above the ground. And otherwise nothing, nothing but an immense blackness, in which all that could be seen were the glass roofs over the mainline platforms, pallid with dim, reflected gaslight. Everything had vanished into darkness, and even the sounds were becoming muffled, leaving only the thunderous roar of the locomotive, opening its steam-cocks and releasing great billowing whorls of white steam. A cloud was rising into the air, unfurling like a ghostly shroud, and through it passed great puffs of black smoke issuing from heaven knew where. It blotted out the sky once more, and a cloud of soot moved off over the lights of Paris, which burned like a brazier in the night.

Then the station foreman raised his lamp, a signal to the driver to ask for the road. The whistle went twice, and over by the pointsman's hut the red light faded, to be replaced by a white one. Standing at the door of his van the chief guard was waiting for the order to depart, which he then passed on. The driver gave another whistle, a long one, and opened his regulator to start the engine on its way. They were off. At first the movement was imperceptible, then the train began to roll. It slid beneath the Pont de l'Europe and made towards the Batignolles tunnel. All that remained visible were its three rear lights, bloody like open wounds, the red triangle. For a few seconds longer it could still be seen in the quivering blackness of the night. It was racing away, and nothing now would stop this train as it hurtled forwards at full steam. It vanished from sight.

CHAPTER II

AT La Croix-de-Maufras, in a garden traversed by the railway, the house is placed at an angle, so close to the line that it shakes with every train that passes; and a single journey is enough to fix it in the memory: the whole world hurtling by knows it to be just there, yet knows nothing else about it, standing there permanently shut up, as though abandoned in distress, its grey shutters turning green from the rain that drives in from the west. It is a wilderness, and the house seems to add still further to the isolated feeling of this lonely spot, cut off from every living soul for miles around.

The only thing there is the house of the level-crossing keeper, at the corner of the road which crosses the line and goes to Doinville, five kilometres away. With its cracked walls and its roof-tiles nibbled by moss, it squats with the crushed air of a penniless waif in the middle of the garden which surrounds it, a garden planted with vegetables and enclosed by a hedge, in which stands a large well as high as the house itself. The level-crossing is situated between the stations at Malaunay and Barentin, exactly in the middle, four kilometres from each. Indeed it is very rarely used, and the old, half-rotten gate is seldom rolled back except for the drays from the Bécourt quarries, half a league away, in the forest. It would be hard to imagine anywhere more remote, nor a place more cut off from living people, for on the Malaunay side the long tunnel blocks every approach, and one can only reach Barentin by an overgrown path that runs beside the railway line. So visitors are scarce.

On this particular evening, at dusk, with the weather grey and very mild, a traveller who had just stepped off a train from Le Havre at Barentin was striding along the path to La Croix-de-Maufras. The countryside hereabouts is one long succession of valleys and ridges, as though the land were a choppy sea, and the railway crosses it alternately on embankments or through cuttings. On either side of the railway line the uneven terrain, with its constant ups and downs, makes the going difficult. As a result, the place seems all the more isolated: the land, with its poor, whitish soil, has remained uncultivated; trees crown the hillocks with small copses, while along the narrow valleys run streams overhung by willow. Some of the chalky ridges are completely bare, and their barren slopes follow one upon the other, in silent, deathly dereliction. And the traveller, young and vigorous, hurried along, as though anxious to flee the sad spectacle of so gentle a dusk falling upon this desolate landscape.

In the keeper's garden a girl was drawing water from the well, a tall, well-built girl of eighteen, with fair hair, a full mouth, large, greenish eyes, and a low forehead beneath a heavy mane of hair. She was not pretty, she had heavy hips and the firm arms of a young man. As soon as she caught sight of the traveller coming along the path, she let go of the bucket and ran to take up position by the hedge-gate.

'Jacques! Hello!' she shouted.

He had raised his head. Just turned twenty-six, he was tall also, very swarthy, a handsome fellow with a round face and regular features spoilt only by too heavy a jaw. His hair, thick and wiry, curled, as did a moustache so full and black that it accentuated the pallor of his complexion. He might have been taken for a gentleman with his smooth skin and well-shaven cheeks, had it not been for the indelible mark of his trade, the grease that was already turning his train-driver's hands yellow, hands that were nevertheless still small and supple.

'Evening, Flore,' he said simply.

But his eyes, which were large and black and dotted with gold, had clouded over as though with a reddish mist, turning them pale. The eyelids quivered, and the eyes looked away in sudden embarrassment, discomfited, almost pained. And for an instant his whole body had instinctively recoiled.

She, standing there motionless, her gaze directly upon him, had noticed this involuntary shudder, which he always tried to control whenever he came near a woman. It seemed to have left her thoroughly pensive and downcast. Then, as he sought to cover his confusion by asking if her mother were in, even though he knew her perfectly well to be ill and unable to go out, she merely nodded, standing aside so that he might enter without touching her, and walked back to the well without a word, erect and proud.

With his brisk stride Jacques crossed the narrow garden and entered the house. There, in the middle of the front room, a vast kitchen where they ate and lived, he found Aunt Phasie—as he had called her since childhood—sitting alone by the table on a wicker chair, her legs wrapped in an old shawl. She was a cousin of his father's, a Lantier,* who had been his godmother; and she had taken him in at the age of six, when his parents had disappeared off to Paris, leaving him behind in Plassans, where he had later attended the Technical College. He still felt warmly grateful to her, saying that he owed it all to her that he had been able to make his way in the world. When he had become a driver first class with the Compagnie de l'Ouest, after two years of service on the Paris–Orléans line,* he had found his godmother remarried to a level-crossing keeper called Misard and buried away in this backwater of La Croix-de-Maufras together with her two daughters from her first marriage. Today, though scarcely forty-five, the beautiful Aunt Phasie of former days, so tall and ample of figure, seemed nearer sixty, shrivelled and yellowed, and shaken by continual tremors.

She exclaimed with joy.

'Jacques! It's you! Well . . . Ah, my big boy, what a surprise!'

He kissed her on both cheeks and explained that he had just been given two days' enforced leave: his locomotive, La Lison, had broken her connecting-rod that morning, just as they were coming in to Le Havre, and since they couldn't repair it within the day, he would only be on duty again the following evening, to drive the 6.40 express. So, he had wanted to come and say hello. He would stay over, he wouldn't have to leave from Barentin till the 7.26 next morning. And he held her poor, limp hands in his, telling her how much her last letter had worried him.

'Ah, yes, my dear boy, things are not good, not good at all . . . You are kind to have guessed I wanted to see you! But I know how busy you are, I didn't dare ask you to come. Well, and here you are, and I've ever so much to tell you!'

She broke off to glance apprehensively out of the window. In the fading daylight, on the other side of the track, her husband Misard could be seen in a block-section box, one of those wooden huts set up every five or six kilometres along the line and linked by telegraph in order to ensure the proper running of the trains.* When his wife, and later Flore, became responsible for the level-crossing gate, Misard had been given watchman's duties.

Almost as if he could have heard them, she lowered her voice to a trembling whisper:

'I really think he's trying to poison me!'

Jacques started in surprise at this revelation, and as his eyes now turned also towards the window, they were again dulled by a peculiar blurring, that little cloud of reddish mist that turned their gleaming, gold-flecked blackness pale.

'Oh, Aunt Phasie, what a notion!' he muttered. 'He looks so gentle, so weak.'

A train had just gone past on its way to Le Havre, and Misard had left his hut to close the line after it. As he raised the signal-arm, changing the signal to red, Jacques was watching him. A short, puny man, with a few, colourless hairs on his head and chin, and a lined, emaciated face. And silent with it, self-effacing, even-tempered, obsequiously polite to his superiors. But now he had gone back into his hut to record the passage of the train in his time-book, and to press the two electric buttons, the one which told the up-line box that the track was clear, and the one which offered the train to the next watchman along the line.

'Oh, you don't know what he's like,' Aunt Phasie continued. 'I tell you, he must be slipping me something nasty . . . Me! who used to be so strong, who could have had him for breakfast, and here he is, this runt of a man, this nothing-at-all, devouring me!'

She was beginning to seethe with sullen, timid rancour, as she poured out her heart, delighted at last to have a captive audience. What had she been thinking of, getting married again to a sly one like that, not a button to his name, and tight-fisted, and she five years older than him, with two daughters already, one of six, one of eight? It would soon be ten years since she'd brought off this marvellous *coup*, and not an hour had past when she hadn't regretted it: a life of misery it was, being buried away up here in the frozen North, always shivering with the cold, bored to death, with never a soul to talk to, not so much as a woman next door. Him, he had previously been a plate-layer and now earned twelve hundred francs as a watchman; and from the start she had got fifty francs for doing the gate, which Flore now looked after: such was her present and her future, with nothing else to hope for, just the certain knowledge of always living here in this hole where one day she would give up the ghost, a thousand miles from any soul that breathed. What she omitted to mention were the consolations she used to have, before she was ill, when her husband was doing the ballast* and she would remain behind on her own with her daughters to look after the gate; for then, such was her reputation as a beauty, from Rouen to Le Havre and all the way down the line, that the line-inspectors would pay her a visit on their way past; there had even been some rivalries, and foremen plate-layers from another section were always making tours of inspection, absolute models of vigilance. The husband was no obstacle, so deferential with everyone, slipping in and out of the house, coming and going and never seeing a thing. But these distractions had ceased, and here she remained, for weeks, months, on end, upon this chair, in this lonely solitude, feeling her body waste away, little by little with every hour that passed.

'I tell you,' she repeated by way of conclusion, 'he's after me, and he'll finish me off, he will, runt or no runt.'

The sudden tinkling of a bell made her dart another anxious look outside. It was the previous box offering Misard a train for Paris, and the needle on the section indicator in front of the window was now pointing in that direction. He stopped the bell and came out to signal the train's approach with two blasts on the hooter. At that moment Flore arrived to shut the crossing gate and then took her position, holding the flag up straight by its leather sheath. The train could be heard now, an express, still hidden by the bend in the track, coming closer and closer, its thunderous roar gradually growing louder. It passed like a thunderbolt, making everything rattle and shake and threatening to sweep the tiny house away in a tempest of rushing wind. Already Flore was on her way back to her vegetables; while Misard, having closed the up line behind the train, was about to reopen the down, pulling the lever to obliterate the red signal; for the further sound of a bell, accompanied by the other needle rising, had just informed him that the train which had passed five minutes earlier had now also passed the next section-box on the line. He went in to his hut again, signalled to the two boxes, recorded the time of the train's passage, and then waited. Always the same routine, which he carried out for twelve hours at a stretch, living there, eating there, never reading so much as three lines of a newspaper, never even seeming to think a thought, beneath that slanting skull of his.

Jacques, who used to tease his godmother about breaking the hearts of so many line-inspectors, could not help smiling as he said:

'Perhaps he's jealous.'

But Phasie shrugged pityingly, though she too could not help a twinkle coming into her poor pale eyes.

'Oh, my boy, what are you saying? . . . Him, jealous! He never gave a damn, just so long as it didn't cost him any money.'

Then, beginning to tremble again:

'No, no, he never cared much for that side of things. All he really does care about is money . . . The reason we're on bad terms, you see, is that I refused to give him Father's thousand francs, last year, when I came into it. So, just as he threatened me it would, it's brought me bad luck, I've become ill . . . And the illness has never left me since then, no, not since that very moment.'

The young man understood, but as he believed it to be simply a case of an ailing woman's dark thoughts, he tried once more to convince her otherwise. But she would not be dissuaded, shaking her head with the air of someone whose mind is firmly made up. So in the end he said:

'Well, it's quite simple then, if you want to stop feeling ill . . . give him your thousand francs.'

An extraordinary physical effort brought her to her feet. And now, revived, violent:

'My thousand francs?! Never! I'd rather die . . . Oh, they're well hidden, they are, very well hidden. They can turn the house inside out if they like, but I can tell you, they'll never find them . . . And he hasn't half tried turning it inside out, the cunning old devil! I've heard him at night tapping all the walls. Keep looking, keep looking! Just seeing his face get longer and longer would be enough to keep me going . . . Wonder who'll give in first, him or me. I keep my eyes open now, I don't swallow anything he's been touching. And if I did give up the ghost, well, too bad, he still wouldn't get my thousand francs! I'd rather leave them to the ground itself.'

She fell back on to her chair, exhausted, jolted by another blast on the hooter. This time Misard was standing at the entrance to his hut, signalling the approach of a train from Le Havre. Despite shutting herself away inside this obstinate refusal to part with her inheritance, she was still secretly afraid of him, and her fear was growing, as a giant fears an insect that is eating it alive. And in the distance the train just signalled, the 12.45 slow train from Paris, was coming nearer, with a dull rumble. It could be heard leaving the tunnel, puffing louder still in the surrounding countryside. Then it passed, its carriages huge, its wheels thundering, with the invincible force of a hurricane.

Looking out, Jacques had seen the little square windows go by, each framing the profile of a passenger. He wanted to take Phasie's mind off these dark thoughts, so he continued jokingly:

'You know, Auntie, you're always complaining you never see a soul in this godforsaken hole of yours, but there you are, there's people for you!'

She did not understand at first, looking nonplussed.

'Where, what people? . . . Oh, them, you mean the people that go by. A fat lot of use they are, I'm sure. We don't know them, we can't have a chat with them.'

He was still laughing.

'But you know me, you see me going by often enough!'

'Yes, I know you, it's true, and I know the time of your train, I look out for you, up there on your engine. Only you're going ever so fast! Yesterday you went like that with your hand. I don't even get a chance to do the same back . . . No, no, that's no way to be seeing people.'

And yet this idea of crowds of people being transported up and down the line every day by the trains, amidst the great silence of her solitude, gave her pause and left her gazing at the track, on which night was now falling. When she had been well and able to get about, standing there at the crossing gate with the flag in her fist, she had never thought of such things. But now, since she had been spending her days just sitting in this chair, having nothing to think about but her mute struggle with her man, her mind would fill with a muddle of confused, barely coherent imaginings. It struck her as funny, her living here like this, lost in the wilderness, without a soul to unburden herself to, while all the time, day and night, so many men and women were passing in the sudden squalls brought by the trains, which shook the house and vanished away at full speed. But that was right, the whole world passed by here, and not only French people, foreigners too, people from the furthest lands, since nowadays nobody seemed able to stay put at home any more, and soon anyway, so they said, all peoples would be one. That was progress for you, all brothers, all travelling off together to a land of Cockaigne. She was trying to count them, on average, so many per carriage: but there were too many, she couldn't manage it. Often she thought she could recognize some of the faces, a gentleman with a blond beard, an Englishman no doubt, who made the journey to Paris every week, and a little dark-haired lady, who went past regularly every Wednesday and Saturday. But they were borne away in a flash, she was never very sure she had seen them, all the faces blurred together, merged into one another as if they were the same, the one vanishing into the next. The torrent flowed by, leaving nothing of itself behind. And what saddened her was the sense that in their constant breathless rush, amidst all the continuous to-ing and fro-ing, amidst all this money and well-to-do prosperity on the move, the crowds of people had no idea that she was there, in danger of her life, so much so that if her fellow were to finish her off one evening, the trains would continue to come and go past her corpse, without the least suspicion that a crime had taken place, there, in that lonely house.

Phasie had been sitting staring at the window, and she summed up how she felt, a feeling so indefinite that she could not explain it at length:

'Ah, yes, it's a fine invention, there's no denying. People go fast now, they know more . . . But wild beasts are still wild beasts, and they can go on inventing bigger and bettter machines for as long as they like, there'll still be wild beasts underneath there somewhere.'

Jacques nodded once more in agreement. For a moment he had been watching Flore reopening the crossing gate for a cart from the quarry which was carrying two enormous blocks of stone. The road led only to the Bécourt quarries, so that at night the gate was padlocked and it was very rare for anyone to rouse the girl from her bed. Seeing her chatting easily with the quarryman, a short, dark-skinned young man, he exclaimed:

'Cabuche must be ill, then, if his cousin Louis's driving the horses? . . . Poor old Cabuche. Do you see much of him, Auntie?'

She raised her hands without a word, and heaved a heavy sigh. There had been quite a drama, last autumn, the last thing she needed in her condition: her daughter Louisette, the younger one, who had been in service as a chambermaid to Madame Bonnehon at Doinville, had run away one evening in terror, covered in bruises, off to her sweetheart Cabuche's place, where she had died, right in the middle of the forest. There had been rumours, something about President Grandmorin being guilty of assault; but no one dared repeat them openly. And she, her mother, though she knew perfectly well what had gone on, also preferred to avoid the subject. Nevertheless she said finally:

'No, he doesn't come in any more, he's become a proper lone wolf these days . . . My poor Louisette, so lovely she was, such fair skin, so sweet! She loved me all right, she would have looked after me, she would, but Flore, my God! I'm not complaining, but she's simply not all there, just does whatever comes into her head, disappearing for hours on end, and proud with it, and wild! . . . Ah, it's all very sad, very sad.'

As he listened, Jacques continued to watch the cart, which was now crossing the track. But its wheels got caught in the rails, and the driver had to crack his whip while Flore herself shouted, urging the horses on.

'Christ!' exclaimed the young man, 'there'd better not be a train coming . . . A fine mess there'd be then!'

'Oh, no danger of that,' Aunt Phasie replied. 'Flore may be a bit odd from time to time, but she knows her job, she keeps her eyes open . . . We haven't had an accident here for five years now, thank God. Once, before, a man was run over, cut in two. In our time we've just had the one cow, it nearly derailed a train. Ah, the poor beast! They found the carcass here and the head over there, near the tunnel . . . With Flore about, you can sleep sound.'

The cart had made its way across, and one could hear the heavy jolting of its wheels in the ruts beyond. Then she returned to her one constant preoccupation, the subject of health, other people's as well as her own.

'And you, are you completely better now? You remember, when you were with me, that business you suffered from, that the doctor could make no sense of?'

His eyes shifted in their usual uneasy way.

'I'm perfectly fine, Auntie.'

'Really! All gone, that pain you said used to bore a hole in your skull, behind your ears, and those sudden high temperatures, and those times you were so miserable you used to hide yourself away like an animal, in some dark corner?'

As she spoke, he became more and more uncomfortable, and finally so upset that he interrupted her curtly:

'I'm perfectly well, I assure you . . . There's nothing wrong with me any more, nothing at all.'

'All right, all right, so much the better, my boy! . . . It's not as though you being ill would help cure me any. And anyway, at your age, you should be healthy. Ah! Good health, there's nothing like it . . . Well, it was very good of you all the same, to come and see me like this when you could have been off somewhere else enjoying yourself. You will have supper with us, won't you? And then you can sleep up there in the attic, next to Flore's room.'

But once more the sound of the hooter interrupted her. Night had fallen, and as they both turned towards the window, they could only barely see Misard, who was talking to another man. It had just gone six, and he was handing over to his replacement, the night-watchman. He would be free at last, after his twelve hours spent in that hut, its only furniture the small table beneath the instrument panel, a stool, and a stove which gave out such excessive heat that he had to leave the door open almost the entire time.

'Ah, there he is, he'll be coming in now,' murmured Aunt Phasie, once more afraid.

The train which had been signalled was coming closer, a very heavy, very long train, its rumble growing louder and louder. And the young man had to bend down to make himself heard by the sick woman, moved by the miserable state she was getting herself into and wanting to ease her distress.

'Listen, Auntie, if he really is up to no good, perhaps it'll make him stop if he thinks I'm involved . . . It'd be as well if you let me look after your thousand francs for you.'

She managed one last surge of resistance.

'My thousand francs! Not to you, not to him! . . . I've told you, I'd rather die!'

At that moment the train was passing, in all its stormy violence, as if it might sweep away everything that lay in its path. The house shook with it, engulfed by a blast of air. This particular train, on its way to Le Havre, was very crowded, for there were to be celebrations the following day, a Sunday, to mark the launching of a ship. Despite its speed they glimpsed the full compartments through the lighted windows, and the tidy rows of serried heads, each with its own individual profile. One after another they came, then disappeared. So many people! Still that crowd, that limitless crowd, amidst all the rolling of the carriages, the whistling of the engines, the tinkling of the telegraph, the ringing of the bells! It was like some huge body, a giant creature laid out on the ground with its head in Paris, its vertebrae the length of the track, its limbs stretching out with every branch-line, and its hands and feet in Le Havre and other destinations. And past it went, past it went, mechanical, triumphant, hurtling towards the future with mathematical rigour, determinedly oblivious to the rest of human life on either side, life unseen and yet perennial, with its eternal passions and its eternal crimes.

It was Flore who came in first. She lit the lamp, a little paraffin-lamp, without a shade, and set the table. Not a word was exchanged, she hardly even glanced at Jacques, who stood by the window facing away from her by the window. On the stove there was cabbage soup keeping hot. She was serving it when Misard appeared in his turn. He exhibited no surprise at finding the young man there. Perhaps he had seen him arrive, but he did not ask him anything, showed no interest. A shake of the hand, three brief words, and that was that. Jacques was obliged to volunteer the story of the locomotive's breakdown and how he'd thought of coming to say hello to his aunt and stay the night. Gently, Misard simply nodded his head, as if to say he found all this perfectly in order, and then they all sat down and calmly ate their meal, at first in silence. Phasie, who since that morning had not taken her eyes off the saucepan in which the cabbage soup was cooking, accepted a bowl of it. But when her husband got up to give her her iron-water, which Flore had forgotten, a carafe with nails steeping in it, she refused to touch it. He, meek and puny, and coughing his nasty little cough, seemed not to notice the anxious look on her face as she followed his every movement. When she asked for some salt, of which there was none on the table, he told her she'd be sorry she'd always taken so much of it, that was what was making her ill; and he got up again to go and fetch her some and brought her a pinch in a teaspoon, which she accepted—since salt purified everything, she would say. Then they talked about the particularly mild weather they'd been having for the last few days, and about a derailment at Maromme. Jacques was coming to the conclusion that his aunt was imagining things, for he could detect nothing untoward about this little man, obliging as he was, and with that vacant expression in his eyes. They were an hour at table. Twice, when the hooter went, Flore had disappeared for a moment. The trains passed, the glasses on the table shook; but none of them paid the slightest attention.

A further blast on the hooter was heard, and this time Flore, who had just cleared the table, did not return, leaving her mother and the two men to a bottle of apple brandy. The three sat on for a further half-hour. Then Misard, whose darting eyes had come to rest on one corner of the room, grabbed his cap and left, with a simple 'goodnight'. It was his habit to poach in the little streams nearby, which contained superb eel, and he never once went to bed without having gone to check his lines.

As soon as he was gone, Phasie looked hard at her godson.

'Well, do you believe me now? Did you see the way he was peering over there, into the corner? . . . It's because he's got it into his head that I might have hidden my little hoard behind the butter-jar . . . Ah, I know him all right, I bet you tonight he'll go and move the jar, to see if it's true.'

But the sweats were beginning again, and her limbs started to tremble.

'There you are, you see, here we go again! He must have drugged me, my mouth tastes all bitter as if I'd just swallowed some old coins. God knows, I didn't eat anything he'd had his hands on. It's enough to make a person go and throw himself in the lake . . . Well, I'm all in this evening, time I went to bed. Goodbye then, my boy, because if you're leaving on the 7.26, I'll not be up. And come back, mind? And let's just hope I'm still here.'

He had to help her to her bedroom, where she lay down and fell asleep, exhausted. Left alone, he wondered if he, too, shouldn't go upstairs and lie down on the makeshift bed which awaited him in the attic. But it was only ten to eight, there would be time enough for sleep later. And so he in turn left the room, leaving on the small paraffin-lamp in the empty, slumbering house which was shaken from time to time by the sudden thunder of a train.

Outside Jacques was surprised by the mildness of the air. Doubtless more rain was on its way. Milky-white unbroken cloud had spread across the sky, and the full moon, submerged and invisible behind it, illuminated its vast reaches with a reddish glow. Thus he could make out the countryside quite clearly, with the surrounding land, the hillsides and the trees, silhouetted in black against the uniform flat glow that shone peacefully, like a nightlight. He took a stroll round the small vegetable-patch. Then he thought of walking towards Doinville, the road being less steep in that direction. But, drawn by the spectacle of the lonely house standing at an angle on the other side of the track, he crossed the railway line via the side-gate, the main barrier having already been locked for the night. He knew it well, this house, he always looked at it as he went past on his trips, amidst the rattle and roar of his engine. It haunted him without his knowing quite why, leaving him with the curious feeling that somehow it mattered in his life. On each occasion he would experience, first, a kind of dread that it might not be there any more, and then a sort of uneasiness that it was. Not once had he seen it with its doors or windows open. All he had ever been told was that it belonged to President Grandmorin; and that evening he was seized with an irresistible desire to have a look round, to find out more about it.

Jacques remained standing out in the road for a long time, opposite the entrance gate. He kept stepping back a pace or two and standing on tiptoe, trying to get the lie of the land. In cutting across the garden the railway had in fact left only narrow flowerbeds enclosed by a wall to the front of the main steps, while at the back there were fairly extensive grounds surrounded by a hedge. The house looked sad and lugubrious in its abandoned state, beneath the ruddy glow of the misty night; and, with a shiver, he was about to leave when he noticed a gap in the hedge. The thought that it would be cowardly not to enter was sufficient to see him through the gap. His heart was beating fast. But immediately, as he was moving along the side of a small dilapidated glass-house, the sight of a shadow crouching in the doorway brought him up short.

'What, you?' he burst out in astonishment, as he recognized Flore. 'What on earth are you doing here?'

She, too, had been startled. Then, calmly:

'You can see what I'm doing, I'm helping myself to these ropes . . . They've left a whole pile of them here, just rotting away, they're no use to anyone. So, seeing as I'm always needing rope, I come and help myself.'

Squatting on the ground with a stout pair of scissors in her hand, she was indeed unravelling bits of rope and cutting the knots when they refused to give.

'Doesn't the owner come here any more, then?' asked the young man.

She began to laugh.

'Oh, since that business with Louisette, there's not much chance of the President showing his face again at La Croix-de-Maufras. I can have his rope all right, don't you worry.'

He remained silent for a moment, apparently troubled at the memory of the tragic story to which she was referring.

'What about you, do you believe what Louisette said, do you think he tried to have her and that she got hurt trying to fight him off?'

Her laughter ceased, and with sudden violence she cried:

'Louisette never lied, never, nor Cabuche neither . . . He's my friend, Cabuche.'

'Your lover, perhaps, now?'

'Him? Cor, you'd have to be a real slut! . . . No, no, he's my friend just. I don't have lovers, me, and I don't want any either.'

She had raised her powerful head, with its thick mass of blond hair that came down low over her eyes; and with every firm and supple fibre of her being she displayed the savage energy of her will. Already a legend had begun to spring up about her, throughout the district. There were stories, tales of rescue: a cart dragged free with one single tug just seconds before a train went past; a runaway goods wagon rolling down the incline at Barentin and halted in its path, like a crazed beast, as it careered madly towards an express. Such displays of strength were a source of wonder, and made men desire her, especially as she was thought at first to be of easy virtue, always off across the fields the moment she had any free time, searching for secret places, lying about in dark corners, silent and perfectly still, her eyes gazing into space. But the first ones to try their luck had been left with no wish to try again. As she liked to bathe for hours on end, naked, in a nearby stream, lads of her own age had made it a sport to go and watch her; and she had once grabbed one of them, not even bothering to put her chemise back on, and dealt with him so satisfactorily that no one ever watched her again. Finally, there was that story going round about her and a pointsman on the Dieppe branch-line, at the other end of the tunnel: a certain fellow called Ozil, about thirty or so, a very decent sort, whom she seemed to encourage for a while and whom then, when he tried to take her one evening, thinking she was giving herself, she almost killed with a single blow of a stick. She was a virgin and a warrior, disdainful of the male, which was what eventually convinced people that she really must be off her head.

Hearing her declare that she wanted no lover, Jacques continued teasing:

'So, it's all over then, no marriage to Ozil? The way I heard it, you were off up the tunnel every day to see him.'

She shrugged.

'Oh, sure, me get married . . . I just like the tunnel. Running along in the dark, for two and a half kilometres, thinking you could be cut in two by a train if you don't keep your eyes open. You should hear those trains under there, bellowing away! . . . But he bored me, Ozil. He's not the right one for me.'

'So you do want someone else?'

'Oh, I don't know . . . Hell, no, I don't.'

She had begun to laugh again, while a slight sense of embarrassment made her turn her attention back to a knot in the ropes which she was unable to undo. Then, without looking up, as if very absorbed in what she was doing:

'And you, what about you, don't you have a sweetheart?'

It was his turn to become serious once more. His eyes shifted away and gazed unsteadily into the distance, into the darkness. He answered curtly:

'No.'

'So it's true then,' she went on. 'They told me you didn't like women. Mind you, it's not as though I didn't know you well enough already, you're not the sort who'd say something nice to any of us . . . But why not, eh?'

He still said nothing, and she decided to abandon the knot and look at him.

'Is it because you only love your engine? People make jokes about that, you know. They say you're always rubbing it, and polishing it till it gleams, as if it were all you ever did stroke . . . I'm only saying it, you know, 'cos I'm your friend.'

He too was now looking at her, under the pale light of the misty sky. And he remembered her when she was little, already wild and wilful, but always throwing her arms round him the moment he walked in, with the passion of an unruly young girl. Then, since it was often quite a while before he saw her again, he would each time find her taller than ever, yet still greeting him with that same violent embrace, disturbing him more and more with the fire in her big bright eyes. Now she had become a fine, desirable woman, and probably she had loved him, at a distance, from the very depths of her childhood. His heart began to beat faster, and he had the sudden feeling that he was the one she was waiting for. He felt a great tumult welling in his skull as the blood rose in his veins, and his first impulse in this mounting panic was to run away. Desire had always driven him crazy, it made him see red.

'What are you doing standing there?' she continued. 'Sit down, for goodness' sake.'

Once more he hesitated. Then, his legs grown suddenly very weary, and overwhelmed by the urge to try, once more, to love, he slumped down beside her, on top of the pile of ropes. He could no longer speak, his throat all dry. It was she now, the proud, silent one, who was chattering away breathlessly, all gay and light-hearted, talking herself dizzy.

'You see, where Maman went wrong was to marry Misard. It'll turn out badly for her ... But what do I care? I mean, anybody's got enough to do just looking after themselves, haven't they? And anyway, Maman always packs me off to bed the minute I try to interfere ... So, let her get on with it, I say! I live out of doors, me. I think about things, for later on ... Oh, incidentally, I saw you go past this morning, you know, on your engine, from those bushes over there in fact. That's where I was sitting. But you, you never look at me ... And I'll tell you what they are, these things I think about, but not now, later, when we're proper friends.'

She had let go of the scissors, and he, still silent, had taken hold of her two hands. Thrilled, she let them rest in his. Yet, when he raised them to his burning lips, she jumped, startled in her virginity. The warrior in her was aroused, bridling, ready for battle, at this first approach of the male.

'No, no, leave me alone, I don't want to ... Stop it, let's just talk ... You men, it's all you ever think about. Oh, if I were to tell you what Louisette told me, the day she died at Cabuche's ... Anyway, I knew all about the President already, because I'd seen the dirty things that used to go on, here, when he brought young girls to this place ... And there's one that nobody knows about, one he married off ...'

He wasn't listening, didn't hear what she was saying. He had grabbed her in a brutal embrace and was crushing his mouth against hers. She gave a slight cry, or rather moan, so deep and soft, in which could be heard the avowal of a love that had long lain concealed. But still she struggled, refusing none the less to yield, instinctively resisting. She wanted him and yet she would not give herself without a struggle, needing to be conquered. Wordlessly, chest against chest, each strove, panting, to push the other back. For a moment she seemed likely to prove the stronger, indeed might well have held him down beneath her, so weak had he become, if he had not then seized her by the throat. Her blouse ripped open and her breasts burst forth, hard and swollen from the battle, milky white in the bright shadows. And back she fell, ready to give herself, vanquished.

Then he, gasping for breath, stopped, stared at her instead of taking her. A sudden fury seemed to grab hold of him, some ferocious urge that had him casting about for a weapon, a stone, anything at all with which to kill her. His eyes lit on the scissors, gleaming amidst the lengths of rope; and he grabbed them in a single movement, and would have driven them into her naked bosom, between the two white breasts with their pink flowers. But a sensation of icy coldness was already bringing him to his senses, and he threw them away, and fled, distraught; while she, her eyelids closed, thought that he was rejecting her because she had resisted him.

Jacques ran away into the melancholy night. He sped up the path over one ridge and down again into a narrow valley. The pebbles rolling beneath his feet startled him, and he veered left into the bushes, making a detour that brought him out on the right, on to an empty plateau. He raced down the hillside only to find his way blocked by the fence that ran alongside the railway line: there was a train coming, roaring, flaming; and at first he didn't understand what was going on, and stood there petrified. Oh, yes, of course, all those people going past, the endless stream, while here was he suffering agonies! Off he set once more, and climbed, and descended. He kept finding himself back at the railway line now, way down at the bottom of cuttings as deep as chasms, or along the top of embankments that shut out the horizon like giant barricades. Criss-crossed by ridge upon ridge, this wilderness was like a labyrinth without an exit, in which his madness turned and turned upon itself amid the dreary desolation of this uncultivated land. And he had been racing up and down the slopes for a long while when in front of him he saw the round opening of the tunnel, its black gaping mouth. An up-line train was disappearing into its depths,

howling and whistling, and as it vanished, as though quaffed by
the earth, it left behind one long shudder with which the
ground continued to shake.

Then Jacques, his legs exhausted, collapsed beside the line
and began to sob convulsively, spreadeagled on his stomach, his
face buried in the grass. My God! so it had come back, the
terrible affliction he had thought himself cured of? He had
wanted to kill that girl back there! Kill a woman, kill a woman! It
reverberated in his ears, from out of the depths of his younger
days, along with the growing, maddening fever of desire. As
other men awake to puberty and dream of possessing a woman,
he had been driven by the idea of killing one. For there was no
denying it, he had grabbed those scissors to plunge them into her
flesh, the minute he had seen it, the warm, white flesh of her
breasts. And it wasn't because she had resisted, oh no! It was for
the pleasure of it, because he wanted to, because he wanted to so
much that if he wasn't clinging on to the grass with both hands,
he'd have gone straight back there now and throttled her. My
God! the Flore he had known since she was a child, that wild
young thing who, as he had just discovered, was deeply in love
with him. His twisting fingers sank into the earth, and sobs tore
at his throat, in rasps of terrible despair.

But he made every effort to calm himself, he wanted to understand. How was he any different from the others? Back there, in
Plassans, in his youth, he had often asked himself this question.
True, his mother Gervaise had had him when she was very
young, when she was fifteen and a half; but even then he was her
second-born, she was scarcely into her fourteenth year when
she had given birth to her first child, Claude; and neither of his
two brothers, neither Claude nor Étienne, born later, seemed to
suffer any ill effects from being sons of such a young mother and
an equally young father, the handsome Lantier, whose bad character was to cost Gervaise so many tears.* Perhaps each of his
brothers had his own secret affliction, the elder one especially,
who was devoured by ambition to become a painter, and so
wildly obsessed, it was said, that his genius bordered on insanity.
The family was hardly what you might call all there, many of
them were half cracked. He could feel it well enough sometimes,
this hereditary crack; not that he suffered from bad health, for it

was only the apprehension and the shame brought on by his attacks that had used to make him thin; but rather it was those sudden losses of control, deep in his being, like fractures, holes, from which his self would escape, in the midst of a kind of thick haze that bent everything out of shape. At such moments he was no longer his own master but rather the obedient servant of his muscles, of the rabid beast within. Yet he did not drink, and would not even allow himself the occasional nip, having discovered that the merest drop of alcohol sent him crazy. And he was beginning to think that he was paying for the others, for the fathers and the grandfathers who had drunk, for the generations of drunkards of whose blood he was the corrupt issue, that he was paying the price of a gradual poisoning, of a relapse into primitive savagery that was dragging him back into the forest, among the wolves, among the wolves that ate women.

Jacques had raised himself on one elbow, thinking, gazing at the black entrance to the tunnel; a further sobbing convulsion travelled up his spine from the small of his back to the nape of his neck, and he fell forward again, rolling his head on the ground and screaming with anguish. That girl, he had wanted to kill that girl! It kept coming back to him, sharp, ghastly, as if the scissors had pierced his own flesh. However he thought of the matter, he could find no peace: he had wanted to kill her, he would kill her if she were there now, with her bodice undone, her bosom naked. He could well remember, he was scarcely sixteen, that first time when the affliction had taken hold of him, one evening while he was fooling about with a young girl, two years younger than him, the daughter of a relative: she had fallen on the ground, he had seen her legs, and he had lunged. The following year he remembered sharpening a knife to plunge it into the neck of another girl, a little blonde he used to see walking past his door every morning. That one had had a very plump, pink neck, on which he had already selected the place, a brown mark underneath her ear. There had been others after that, and yet others, a nightmare procession, all those women who had been the fleeting objects of his sudden, murderous desire, women he had bumped into in the street, women whom chance meetings had turned into brief, proximate acquaintances; one woman especially, newly married, sitting next to him in the theatre, who laughed very loudly and whom he'd had to escape from, in the middle of the perform-ance, so as not to slit her stomach open. Since he didn't know them, what possible furious grievance could he possibly have against them? For each time it was like a sudden attack of blind rage, some unquenchable thirst to avenge wrongs suffered in the distant past and yet which he could not precisely remember. Did it all go back so far, to the evil which women had perpetrated upon his sex, to the sense of grievance accumulated from male to male ever since that first betrayal in the depths of some cave? And he could feel, too, in the midst of his attacks, the need to do battle with the female, to conquer her, subjugate her, the per-verted need to sling her dead body over his shoulder, like a prey snatched away from others, ever his. His skull was bursting with the effort, and he was unable to provide answers to his own questions, he was too ignorant, he thought, and his brain too numb with the anguish of a man driven to acts in which his will counted for nothing and for which the cause deep within him had vanished from view.

Another train passed in a flash of lights, and disappeared into the tunnel like a clap of thunder rumbling and fading; and, as if this anonymous, indifferent crowd of people in a hurry might have heard him, Jacques had risen to his feet, stifling his sobs and adopting the look of an innocent man. How many times, follow-ing one of his attacks, had he started guiltily like that, at the slightest noise! He was only ever at peace, happy and cut off from the world, when he was on his engine. When it was carrying him along, amidst the clatter of its wheels, at top speed, when he had his hand on the regulator, completely absorbed in his attention to the track, watching for signals, then he no longer thought any-thing, he simply imbibed great lungfuls of the fresh air that was always roaring in a storm around him. And that was why he loved his engine so much: it was like a soothing mistress from whom he expected nothing but contentment. When he had left the Technical College, despite his keen intelligence, he had cho-sen the job of train-driver for the solitude and mental vacancy in which it allowed him to live—and to live without ambition, moreover, since he had reached the level of driver first class in four years and was already earning 2,800 francs (which, with his bonuses for stoking and greasing, put him on over 4,000), but without aspiring to more. He watched his fellow-workers—less qualified drivers of the third and second classes, and the men whom the Company trained itself, the fitters it took on as apprentices—he watched almost all of them marry other railway workers, faceless women who were only ever to be glimpsed, occasionally, at departure time, when they brought along their little baskets of provisions; while those of his fellow-workers who had ambitions, especially the ones who had been to college, were waiting to be made depot managers before they married, in the hope of finding themselves someone well-to-do, the type of woman who wore a hat. For his part he shunned the company of women, what were they to him? He would never ever marry, and all he had to look forward to was rolling along on his engine, alone, on and on, without respite. Accordingly all his supervisors spoke of him as a quite exceptional driver, a man who neither drank nor chased women, who was merely teased by some of his more fast-living workmates on account of his excessively sober behaviour, and whom others found vaguely worrying when he had his fits of depression and fell silent, his eyes pale and his complexion ashen-grey. How many hours he remembered spending in his little room on the Rue Cardinet, from which one could see the Batignolles depot where his engine was kept, all his free time spent cooped up like a monk in his cell, wearing out the vigour of his desires by sleeping and sleeping, flat out on his front!

Jacques endeavoured to drag himself to his feet. What was he doing here, in the grass, on this mild, misty winter's evening? The surrounding countryside was bathed in shadow, and the only light came from the sky, where the thin fog, like a vast dome of frosted glass, was lit from behind by an invisible moon which cast a pale, yellowy gleam; and the dark horizon lay slumbering in the immobility of death. Come on, it must be nearly nine o'clock, the best thing for it was to get home and go to bed. But in his dazed state he saw himself once more back at the Misards' house, climbing the stairs to the loft, stretching out on the hay, next to Flore's room, against a simple wood partition. She would be there, he would be able to hear her breathing; indeed he knew she never shut her door, he could join her. The trembling took

hold of him again, and the thought of the girl lying there undressed, her arms and legs spreadeagled, warm with sleep, shook
him once more with a sob so violent that he fell forward on to the
ground. He had wanted to kill her, wanted to kill her, for God's
sake! He was choking for breath, tortured by the thought that he
would be going to her room to kill her as she lay in bed, now, in
a short while, if he went back. It would be no good having no
weapon, or clutching his head in his arms to blot himself out; he
could feel that the male within him, beyond his control, would
push the door open and strangle the girl, whipped on by the
instinct to assault and driven by the need to avenge some ancient
wrong. No! no! Better to spend the night wandering round the
countryside than to go back there! Already he had leapt to his
feet, and away he fled once more.

And so, again, for half an hour or so, he careered across the
dark landscape, as if pursued by the howling hounds of hell. He
climbed hills, he plunged down into narrow gorges. One after
another he came upon two streams: across he went, soaked to the
waist. Any bush that barred his path infuriated him, for his one
thought was to forge straight ahead, onwards, ever further, to get
away from himself, to get away from that other thing, the crazed
beast that he could feel within him. But he was bearing it away
with him, it could run just as fast as he. For seven months he had
thought it banished once and for all, and he had begun to take an
interest in normal life once more; but now he would have to start
all over again, he would have to struggle and make sure it didn't
leap out at the first woman he happened to bump into in a crowd.
However, the deep silence and the vast solitude were beginning
to calm him a little, and his mind was turning to thoughts of a life
as silent and deserted as this desolate region, a life in which he
would walk on and on without ever meeting another soul. He
must have been curving round unwittingly because he came out
on the far side, right next to the railway line, having moved in a
broad semi-circle through the undulating scrubland above the
tunnel. He shrank back, nervous and angry with the fear that he
might chance once more upon the living. Then, intending to cut
across behind a small hillock, he lost his way and found himself
in front of the fence beside the railway line, just at the entrance
to the tunnel and opposite the field where he had lain sobbing

not long before. And there, defeated, he had paused, standing stock still, when the thunderous roar of a train emerged from the depths of the earth, muted at first but growing with every second, barring his way. It was the Le Havre express, which left Paris at 6.30 and was passing here now at 9.25, a train which, every other day, he himself would drive.

First Jacques saw the dark mouth of the tunnel light up, like a gaping furnace filled with blazing firewood. Then, accompanied by its own cacophonous din, the engine burst forth, dazzling the darkness with its great big round eye, as the front headlamp bore into the black countryside and illuminated the oncoming rails with a double line of flame. But the apparition vanished like lightning: all at once the coaches followed, one after another, the small square windows in the doors passing in fitful flashes of light, revealing each compartment filled with passengers in such vertiginously rapid succession that the eye was left to doubt the reality of these images so fleetingly glimpsed. And in that split second Jacques very distinctly saw, in the flaming light of a coupé window, a man pinning another man down on the seat and planting a knife in his throat, while a dark shape, perhaps a third person, perhaps some tumbling luggage, was bearing down with all its weight on the flailing legs of the victim. Already the train was gone, disappearing into the distance in the direction of La Croix-de-Maufras, and all that could be seen in the darkness were its three rear lights, the red triangle.

Rooted to the spot, the young man continued to gaze after the train, as its thunder receded into the vast, dead silence of the countryside. Had his eyes deceived him? And he began to have doubts, no longer dared be quite certain of the reality of this vision which had come and gone in a flash. Not one single feature of the two actors in the drama remained clear in his memory. The brown shape must have been a travelling-rug which had fallen across the victim's body. And yet at first he was sure he had seen the thin, pale profile of a face beneath thick, tumbling hair. But everything had gone blurred now, and evaporated, as in a dream. One moment, the profile came back to him; the next, it disappeared completely. No doubt he had imagined it all. And the whole thing horrified him, seemed so extraordinary, that he

finally conceded to himself that it must have been an hallucination, brought on by the dreadful mental crisis which he had just
undergone.

For almost an hour Jacques continued to walk, his head heavy
with perplexed reflections. He was exhausted, the tension had all
gone from him now, and a great icy coldness inside him had put
an end to his fever. Without any conscious intent, he finally
returned to La Croix-de-Maufras. Then, when he found himself
in front of the crossing-keeper's house, he told himself he
wouldn't go in, that he would sleep in the small shed built on to
one of the gable-ends. But a ray of light was coming from under
the door, and automatically he pushed it open. An unexpected
sight made him pause on the threshold.

In the far corner of the room Misard had moved the butter-
jar; and, crouching on all fours, a lighted lantern beside him, he
was sounding the wall with gentle taps of his fist, searching. The
noise of the door made him straighten up. But otherwise he
seemed not in the least perturbed, merely saying casually:

'Some matches fell down the back.'

And, replacing the butter-jar, added:

'I came to get my lantern because just now, as I was coming
in, I saw someone lying on the line . . . I think he's dead.'

At first Jacques had been struck by the thought that he had
caught Misard hunting for Aunt Phasie's hoard, a fact which
transformed into sudden certainty the doubts he had been having about his aunt's allegations. But he was then so deeply
shaken by the news of a body being discovered that it quite drove
from his mind all thoughts of the other drama, the one taking
place here in this remote little house. The scene in the carriage,
that briefest of visions of one man slitting another's throat, had
just come back to him in the same flash of realization.

'A man on the track, where?' he asked, turning pale.

Misard was about to relate how he was bringing back two eels
he had caught with his ground-lines and how he had been thinking only of getting back home as fast as possible to hide them.
But why bother to let the fellow in on all that? He simply
gestured vaguely and replied:

'Over there, about five hundred metres or so . . . Need to have
a good look, so as to make sure.'

At that moment Jacques heard a dull thud above his head. His nerves were so frayed that he jumped.

'It's nothing,' Misard went on, 'just Flore moving about.'

And indeed the young man recognized the sound of two bare feet on the tiled floor. She must have been waiting for him, and was coming to listen at the half-open door.

'I'll come with you,' he went on. 'You're sure he's dead?'

'Well, it seemed like he was. We'll be able to see better with the lantern.'

'So what do you make of it, then? An accident presumably?'

'Could be. Some chap or other who's got himself run over, or maybe a passenger that's jumped from a carriage.'

Jacques was shaking.

'Come on, let's go, quick.'

Never before had he been gripped by such an urgent passion to see something, to know. Once outside, while his companion, without the slightest trace of emotion, was following the railway line, swinging the lantern to and fro, its bright circle of light gently following the rails, he ran on ahead, irritated by this slowness. It was like some physical desire, like the inner fire that quickens lovers' steps at the appointed hour of a tryst. He was afraid of what was waiting there, and he flew towards it, straining every muscle in his body. When he got there, and all but fell over a dark hump stretched out beside the down line, he stood transfixed, as a shudder ran all the way up his body from the soles of his feet to the top of his spine. And his frustration at not being able to see anything clearly soon turned to curses at the other man lagging behind, some thirty paces back.

'For Christ's sake, get a move on. If he was still alive, we could help him.'

Misard sauntered up, phlegmatic as ever. But then, when he had held the lantern over the body:

'Blimey, he's a goner all right.'

The man, having presumably fallen from a carriage, had landed on his stomach, face down, some fifty centimetres at most away from the rails. All that could be seen of his head was a thick shock of white hair. His legs were splayed. His right arm lay as if pulled from its socket, while the left was crooked under his chest. He was very well dressed, in an ample blue greatcoat,

elegant ankle-boots, and a smart shirt. The body bore no signs of
having been run over, but a considerable amount of blood from
the throat was staining the shirt-collar.

'Some gentleman as has got what was coming to him,' Misard
continued calmly, after a few moments' silent examination.

Then, turning to Jacques, who was standing there motionless,
his mouth wide open:

'Mustn't touch, it's against the law . . . You wait here and
keep an eye on him while I go and tell the station-master at
Barentin.'

He raised his lantern and consulted a kilometre post.

'Good. Exactly at Post 153.'

And, putting his lantern down next to the body, he shuffled
away.

Left on his own, Jacques remained where he was and continued to gaze at the still, slumped heap, which appeared no
more than a blurred mass in the dim lamplight cast along the
ground. And the inner agitation that had quickened his steps, the
horrible fascination that kept him standing there, culminated in
one piercing insight that burst from the depths of his being: that
man, the one he'd seen with the knife in his fist, he had dared!
that man had travelled the distance of his desire, that man had
killed! Oh! to stop being a coward, to have satisfaction at last, to
plunge the knife in! And what about him, who'd spent the last
ten years desperately wanting to do just that! There was, in
the midst of his fevered interest, a measure of self-contempt,
of admiration for the other man, and above all the need to see
the thing for himself, an unquenchable thirst to drink in the
spectacle of the tatter of humanity, the broken puppet, the
limp rag, to which a living creature is reduced by the mere stab
of a knife. What he only dreamt about that other man had done,
and there it was. If he were to kill, that's what would be lying
on the ground. His pulse raced madly, and his violent itch to
kill grew fiercer, like a sexual urge, at the sight of this sorry
corpse. He took a step forward, drew closer, like a nervous child
coming to terms with its fears. Yes! He would dare, he too would
dare!

But a thunderous roar behind him made him jump to one side.
A train was approaching, and he had not even heard it from

within the depths of his meditation. He had nearly been crushed to pulp: only the hot breath and fearsome puffing of the engine had alerted him. The train passed, amidst a whirlwind of noise, and smoke, and flame. The crowds were still coming, travellers continuing to stream towards Le Havre for the next day's celebrations. A child pressed its nose to the window, looking out at the dark countryside; men's faces stood out in profile, while a young woman pulled down a window and threw out a piece of paper covered in butter and sugar. Already the train was heading off merrily into the distance, heedless of the corpse which its wheels had so narrowly missed. And the body just lay there, face down, dimly lit by the lantern, in the melancholy quiet of the night.

Then Jacques was seized with a desire to see the wound itself, while he was still alone. The only thing that stopped him was the idea that if he touched the head they might notice. He had calculated that Misard could scarcely return with the station-master in less than three-quarters of an hour. And the minutes ticked by as he thought about Misard, that puny creature, so slow, so unruffled, who was also daring, daring to kill as calmly as can be, with drugs, dose by dose. So was it quite easy to kill, then? Everybody did it. He moved closer. The thought of seeing the wound spurred him on so sharply that his flesh burned. To see how it was done and what had come out, to see the red hole! If he replaced the head carefully, no one would ever know. But a different, unacknowledged, fear lay at the heart of his hesitation, the actual fear of blood. It had always been thus with him: terror loomed even as desire was aroused. With only another quarter of an hour to go on his own, he was nevertheless about to steel himself when a slight sound close by made him jump.

It was Flore, standing there staring, like him. She was always curious about accidents: the merest mention of an animal being run over, or a man cut in two, was sure to send her dashing off to have a look. She had just got dressed again, wanting to see the dead man. And she was not, after an initial glance, the sort to hesitate. Crouching down and raising the lantern in one hand, she took hold of the head in the other and pulled it back.

'Careful, it's against the law,' murmured Jacques.

But she merely shrugged. And there was the head, in the yellow lamplight, the head of an old man, with a large nose, and the blue eyes that went with the fair hair of earlier days, eyes that were wide open. Below the chin the horrible, gaping wound was visible, a deep gash cut into the neck, ragged as though the knife had turned and gouged. There was blood all down the right side of the chest. On the left, in the buttonhole of the overcoat, the rosette of a Commander of the Legion of Honour looked like a stray clot of blood.

Flore exclaimed softly in surprise.

'Good Lord, it's the old man!'

Bending over beside Flore, his hair mingling with hers, Jacques lent forward to get a better look, and gasped for breath as his eyes feasted on the spectacle before him. Unconsciously he repeated:

'The old man . . . the old man . . .'

'Yes, old Grandmorin . . . the President.'

She examined the pale face for a moment longer, with its twisted mouth and wide, terrified eyes. Then she let go of the head, which was beginning to grow cold with rigor mortis, and it fell back on to the ground, closing up the wound.

'No more messing with the girls!' she repeated more softly. 'And there'll be one of them at the bottom of this, I'll bet you . . . Oh, my poor Louisette. The pig! It's good riddance, I say.'

And there followed a long silence. Flore, who had set the lantern down again, waited, casting long looks at Jacques from time to time; while he, separated from her by the corpse, had still not moved, as if lost to the world, completely absorbed in what he had seen. It must have been nearly eleven o'clock. Awkwardness after what had happened earlier that evening prevented her from speaking first. But then a voice could be heard, it was her father returning with the station-master; and, not wanting to be found there, she made up her mind to speak.

'Aren't you coming back for the night?'

He shuddered, and seemed to be engaged in brief inner debate. Then, with an effort, in a desperate attempt to draw back from the brink:

'No, no!'

She made no gesture, but the sag of her powerful shoulders told of the depth of her disappointment. As though wanting to be forgiven for her earlier resistance, she now became very meek, and asked again:

'So you're not coming back home? I shan't see you again?'

'No, no!'

The voices were coming nearer, and without trying to take his hand, since he seemed to be keeping the corpse between them on purpose, without even saying goodbye the way they always had since childhood, she vanished into the darkness, breathing in harsh gasps as though choking back tears.

Suddenly the station-master was standing there, with Misard and two station-workers. He, too, identified the victim: it was indeed President Grandmorin, whom he knew from seeing him alight at his station every time he went to his sister's, Madame Bonnehon's, at Doinville. The body could remain where it was, though he did have it covered with a coat which one of the men had brought. An employee of the railway company had taken the train from Barentin at eleven o'clock to go and inform the Public Prosecutor at Rouen. But the latter wouldn't arrive till five or six in the morning, since he would have to fetch the examining magistrate with him, as well as the coroner's clerk and a doctor. So the station-master arranged for the body to be guarded: they would take it in turns throughout the night, that way there would always be someone on watch, with the lantern.

And Jacques, before finally deciding to go and find a station shed to sleep in at Barentin, since he was not due to leave for Le Havre until 7.26, remained behind for a long while, simply standing there, a prey to his obsession. Then the thought of the examining magistrate they were expecting began to worry him, as though he felt himself somehow to have been an accomplice. Should he mention what he had seen, that moment as the express went by? He decided at first that he would say something, since, after all, he himself had nothing to fear. It was clear, moreover, where his duty lay. But then he wondered what was the good of that: he wouldn't be giving them any firm evidence, he wouldn't be able to say anything at all for definite about the killer. It would be daft to get mixed up in it all, a waste of his time, having to get all worked up about it for nobody's benefit. No, no, he would say nothing! And so finally he departed, twice turning to look back at the dark hump of the corpse where it lay surrounded by the yellow circle of light coming from the lantern. Keener, colder air was coming down from the mists above, falling upon the desolate wilderness and its barren hillsides. More trains had passed, and another was approaching, a very long one, on its way to Paris. They came and went, each of them inexorable in its mechanical power, racing ahead towards some distant destination, towards the future, oblivious that mere inches away there lay the half-severed head of this man whom another man had slaughtered.

CHAPTER III

ON the following day, a Sunday, every church clock in Le Havre had just struck five when Roubaud came down into the station concourse to begin his day's work. It was still pitch dark, but the wind, blowing in from the sea, had freshened and was rolling back the mist, piling it along the hilltops from Sainte-Adresse to the fort at Tourneville; while, to the west, out to sea, could be seen a patch of clear sky, shining with the last stars of the night. Beneath the station roof gas-lamps were still burning, paled by the cold, damp air of the early hours; and the first train to Montivilliers stood there, being assembled by a gang of railway-men under the direction of the assistant station-master in charge of the night shift. The doors to the station waiting-rooms were not yet open, and the platforms stretched deserted as the station blearily awakened to the day.

Earlier, as he was leaving for work from his flat above the waiting-rooms, Roubaud had found the ticket-clerk's wife, Madame Lebleu, standing stock still in the middle of the main corridor, off which were the railwaymen's quarters. For weeks now this lady had been getting up in the middle of the night to spy on Mademoiselle Guichon, the woman from the ticket-office, whom she suspected of carrying on with the station-master, Monsieur Dabadie. Not that she had ever discovered the slightest piece of evidence, not a shred, not the merest whisper. And that morning, again, she had soon returned to her flat with nothing to report but her surprise at having seen in the Roubauds' flat, during the three seconds it took the husband to open and shut their door, the wife herself, the beautiful Séverine, standing in the dining-room all dressed, hair combed and shoes on, her who usually lay in bed till nine o'clock. Accordingly Madame Lebleu had woken her husband to apprise him of this extraordinary fact. The previous evening they had waited for the arrival of the Paris express, at 11.05,* before going to bed, consumed with curiosity to find out what had happened about that business with the Sub-Prefect. But they had been unable to read anything into the Roubauds' expression, for they had returned looking exactly as they did every day; and they had strained their ears till midnight, but to no avail: not a sound from their neighbours, who must have gone straight to bed and fallen fast asleep. Clearly their trip had not gone well, otherwise Séverine would not have been up and about at such an hour. The ticket-clerk having asked how she looked, his wife had endeavoured to describe her: very stiff, very pale, those wide blue eyes of hers shining so brightly beneath her black hair; and moving not a muscle, as if she were sleepwalking. Well, they'd soon find out what was what, as the day went by.

Down below, Roubaud located his colleague Moulin, who had done the night shift. He took over while Moulin chatted and walked with him for a while, bringing him up to date with the various little things that had happened during the night: intruders had been caught, about to break into the left-luggage office; three station-workers had been reprimanded for indiscipline; a coupling-hook had just broken while they were making up the Montivilliers train. Roubaud listened in silence, his face calm; he was merely a little pale, doubtless a trifle tired still, as the dark rings under his eyes also seemed to suggest. However, though his colleague had stopped talking, he appeared to continue listening, as though he had expected to hear of other events. But that in fact was all, and he bowed his head, gazing momentarily at the ground.

Walking along the platform, the two men reached the end of the roofed area, at the place on the right where there was a shed for rolling-stock: this contained the carriages that had arrived the night before and which were then used to make up the next day's trains. He had already looked up again, his eyes now fixed on a first-class carriage with a coupé bearing the number 293, which happened to be caught in the flickering light of a gas-lamp, when the other man exclaimed:

'Oh, I was forgetting . . .'

Roubaud's pale face flushed, and he started involuntarily.

'I was forgetting,' Moulin repeated. 'This carriage must stay here, don't have it connected to the 6.40 express this morning.'

There was a short silence, before Roubaud asked quite naturally:

'Oh, and why's that?'

'Because a coupé's been booked for this evening's express. It's not certain there'll be one arriving in the course of today, so we may as well keep this one.'

Still staring at it, he replied:

'Probably best.'

But another thought was preoccupying him, and suddenly he burst out:

'It's disgusting! Look how the buggers clean it! You'd think this carriage hadn't been touched for a week.'

'Oh,' Moulin continued, 'when trains come in after eleven, there's not much danger of the men getting their rags out . . . It's pretty good if they're even prepared to carry out their tour of inspection. The other night they left a passenger asleep across the seats, he only woke up the following morning.'

Thereupon, stifling a yawn, he announced that he was off to bed. But then, as he was walking away, he was seized with sudden curiosity:

'Incidentally, that business of yours with the Sub-Prefect, is that all sorted out now?'

'Oh yes, fine, the trip went well. I'm satisfied.'

'Good, then, so much the better . . . And don't forget, the 293's not to go out.'

Left alone on the platform, Roubaud walked slowly back towards the Montivilliers train. The waiting-rooms were opened, and passengers appeared—a few men off shooting with their dogs, two or three shopkeepers and their families taking advantage of their Sunday off, no more than a handful in total. But once that train left, which was the first of the day, he had no time to lose, he had immediately to have the men make up the 5.45 stopping train for Rouen and Paris. At that early hour there were few staff on duty, and the assistant station-master's life was made more complicated by all manner of responsibilities. When he had supervised the marshalling, with each carriage being fetched from the shed and positioned on the trolley which the men then pushed into the main station area by hand, he had to hurry off to the booking-hall and keep an eye on the sale of tickets and the registering of the luggage. A row broke out between some soldiers and a station-worker, requiring his intervention. For half an hour, surrounded by chilly draughts and shivering passengers,

his eyes still heavy with sleep, and bad-tempered from all this
rushing about in the dark, he was several different people at once,
with no time for his own thoughts. Then, when the departure of
the stopping train had cleared the station, he hurried off to the
pointsman's box to make sure everything was in order there, for
another train was arriving, the through train from Paris, which
was late. He came back to watch the train emptying and waited
till the stream of passengers had handed in their tickets and piled
into the hotel cabs, which in those days used to come and wait
inside the station itself, with just a picket-fence between them
and the tracks. And only then was he finally able to draw breath,
as silence fell once more on the deserted station.

The clock was striking six. Roubaud strolled out of the concourse and, once outside, with space before him, he looked up
and breathed more easily to see the dawn breaking at last. The
wind off the sea had now swept all the mist away, and the clear
morning sky promised a fine day. He looked northwards to the
Ingouville ridge where, as far as the trees by the cemetery, it
made a streak of violet across the lightening sky; then, turning
south and west, he observed one last flock of wispy white clouds
floating in formation above the sea; while the entire eastern side,
where the vast indentation of the Seine estuary lay, was beginning to burst into flame with the imminent rising of the sun. He
had automatically taken off his silver braided cap, as if to cool his
brow in the pure, sharp air. This familiar vista, this huge, flat
expanse of the station yard—goods reception on the left, then
the engine-shed, on the right the despatch depot—it was a whole
world of its own, and it seemed to soothe him, to restore him to
the peace and calm of his daily routine that never, ever changed.
Above the wall that ran along the Rue Charles-Laffitte, factory
chimneys poured out smoke, and huge stockpiles of coal were
visible in the depots that run the length of the Vauban dock. And
already a distant stirring could be heard from the direction of the
other docks. The whistling of the goods trains and the wind-
borne sounds and smells of the sea as it returned to life put him
in mind of the coming day's celebrations, of the ship they were
going to launch and the crush there would be to see it.

As Roubaud walked back into the station, he found the
men beginning to make up the 6.40 express. Thinking they were

loading the 293 on to the trolley, the tranquillity he had absorbed
with the freshness of the morning vanished in a sudden burst of
anger.

'Not that carriage, for Christ's sake! Leave it where it is, can't
you! It's not going out till this evening.'

The foreman explained that they were simply moving the
carriage in order to get at another one behind it. But Roubaud
didn't hear, rendered temporarily deaf by his own disproportionate rage.

'You bunch of incompetent bastards, I told you not to touch
it.'

When he eventually grasped the situation, he remained furious, going on about how badly designed the station was, and how
there wasn't room to turn even a single carriage round. And
indeed the station, one of the first on the line to be built, was
inadequate, and quite unworthy of Le Havre, with its old
wooden engine-shed, and the station roof of timber and zinc
with its narrow windows, and the bare, sorry-looking buildings
all covered in cracks.*

'It's a disgrace, I don't know why the Company hasn't demolished the lot.'

The men looked at him, surprised to hear him speak so freely,
this man who always behaved so properly. He noticed, and
stopped abruptly, standing there stiffly, in silence, continuing to
supervise the operation. A wrinkle of discontent furrowed his
narrow brow, while his round ruddy face, bristling with red
beard, tensed with his effort at self-control.

From then on Roubaud maintained his composure entirely.
He busied himself with the express and inspected every smallest
detail. Some couplings looked as if they had been badly secured,
and he demanded that they be tightened there and then in front
of him. A mother and two daughters, acquaintances of his wife,
wanted him to get them seats in the compartment for ladies only.
Then, before blowing his whistle for the train to depart, he made
one final check that everything was in order; and he stared after
it for a long while as it left, with the keen scrutiny of one who
knows that a single moment's inattention can cost lives. At that
very instant, indeed, he had to cross the track to see in a train
from Rouen which was just entering the station. In fact, there

was a man on board who worked for the mail and with whom he
was in the habit of swapping news each day. In the course of
an extremely busy morning this was his one moment's respite,
almost a quarter of an hour, in which he had time to draw breath,
there being no particular duty at this stage which required his
immediate attention. And that morning, as always, he rolled
himself a cigarette and chatted away with animation. It had
grown light now, and the gas-lamps beneath the station roof had
just been extinguished. The roof itself contained so few windows
that the place was still plunged in grey gloom; but beyond, the
vast expanse of sky on to which it opened was already ablaze with
a conflagration of sunbeams, while gradually the whole horizon
was turning pink, with every foreground detail sharply deline-
ated in the pure air of a fine winter's morning.

At eight o'clock Monsieur Dabadie, the station-master, would
come down, and his assistant would report to him. He was a
good-looking man, very dark-skinned, well-dressed, with the air
of a successful businessman fully involved in his own affairs.
Indeed he seldom took much interest in the passenger station,
preferring to devote himself primarily to the activities of the
docks with their huge shipments of cargo and the regular contact
with big business both in Le Havre and in the rest of the world.
That day he was late; and twice already Roubaud had put his
head round the door of his office, only to find him out. On the
table the mail had not even been opened. Among all the letters
the assistant station-master's eyes had just lighted on a telegram.
Then, as if rooted to the spot, he had remained by the door,
involuntarily turning from time to time to glance briefly towards
the table.

Eventually, at ten past eight, Monsieur Dabadie appeared.
Roubaud, who had taken a seat, remained silent, to give him time
to open the telegram. But the station-master was in no hurry,
preferring to exchange a friendly word with his subordinate, of
whom he thought highly:

'And Paris? Everything went all right, I expect?'

'Yes, sir, thank you.'

He had eventually opened the telegram, but he wasn't reading
it, he was still smiling at Roubaud, whose voice had died away as

he made a violent effort to control a nervous tic which was convulsing his chin.

'We are very glad to keep you on here.'

'And I'm very glad to stay on here, sir.'

Then, as Monsieur Dabadie eventually began to read the telegram, Roubaud, his face sweating slightly, watched him. But the reaction he had been expecting was not forthcoming; the station-master calmly finished the telegram and threw it on to the desk: no doubt some routine piece of business. He promptly continued to open his mail while, as happened every day, his assistant gave him an oral report on the events of the night and the early morning. Only, this particular morning, Roubaud was hesitant and had to search his memory before recalling what his colleague had told him about the intruders caught by the left-luggage office. They exchanged a few more words, and the station-master gestured to him to leave as his two deputies, the one in charge of dock traffic, the other of slow goods trains, came in to report also. They brought with them a further telegram, which a station employee had just handed them on the platform.

'You may go', said Monsieur Dabadie, seeing Roubaud still waiting by the door.

But he continued to wait, his round eyes staring, and departed only after he had seen the little piece of paper dropped on to the desk with the same gesture of unconcern. For a moment he wandered about the concourse, perplexed, in a daze. The clock said 8.35, he had no more departures before the slow train at 9.50. Normally he used this hour's lull to make a tour of inspection. He continued to walk about for a while longer, oblivious of where his feet were taking him. Then, on looking up and finding himself in front of the 293, he rapidly turned on his heels and disappeared towards the engine depot, even though there was nothing there that required his attention. The sun was now coming up over the horizon, and a golden rain of dust hung in the pale air. He found no further pleasure in the fine morning, but hastened on, with a preoccupied air, trying to subdue the obsessive tension of his waiting.

A sudden voice brought him up short.

'Monsieur Roubaud, good morning! . . . Did you see my wife?'

It was Pecqueux, the fireman, a tall, thin fellow of forty-three with large bones and a face roasted by all the heat and smoke. The grey eyes set beneath a low forehead and the full mouth with its jutting jaw were continually alive with jovial laughter.

'What are you doing here?' said Roubaud, stopping in astonishment. 'Oh, of course, the accident with the engine, I was forgetting . . . And you're not off again till this evening? Mm, a whole day off, not bad, eh?'

'Not bad at all,' the other agreed, still drunk from some merriment the night before.

Born in a village near Rouen, he had joined the Company as an apprentice fitter when he was very young. Then, reaching the age of thirty and bored with the workshop, he had decided to become a fireman with a view to qualifying later as an engine-driver; and that was when he had married Victoire, who came from the same village. But the years went by, and he was still a fireman; he'd never be a driver now, not without a licence, or a record for good conduct, not as the drunkard and womanizer he was. He'd have been sacked scores of times already if it hadn't been for the protection of President Grandmorin, and if people hadn't got used to his vices, which he compensated for by his good humour and his long years of experience as a railwayman. He was only a liability when he got drunk, for then he became a real brute and capable of anything.

'So, my wife, did you see her?' he asked again, his mouth parting wide in that broad laugh of his.

'Certainly we saw her,' the assistant station-master replied. 'We even had lunch in your room . . . Ah, that's a fine woman you've got there, Pecqueux. And it's just not right, the way you're unfaithful to her.'

He chuckled even more loudly.

'What an idea! But she's the one who wants me to have a good time!'

And it was true. Victoire, who was two years older, had become enormous and scarcely mobile, and she would slip five-franc pieces into his pockets so that he would take his pleasure elsewhere. She had never been particularly upset by his infidelities, by this natural urge of his to be always chasing skirt; and now he had his life sorted out, with two women, one at each end of the line, his woman in Paris for the nights he slept there, and another in Le Havre for the hours spent waiting between trains. Very economical in her ways and spending little on herself, Victoire, who knew everything and treated him as might a mother, was fond of saying that she did not want to see him disgrace himself in the eyes of the other woman. Indeed every time he left, she would make sure that he had clean linen, for she would have felt it keenly had the other woman been able to accuse her of not looking after their man properly.

'No matter,' said Roubaud. 'It's hardly very kind. My wife loves her wet-nurse dearly, and she's planning to give you a ticking-off.'

But he fell silent when he saw, coming out of a nearby train-shed, a tall, spare-looking woman, Philomène Sauvagnat, the depot manager's sister, who had been Pecqueux's extra 'wife' in Le Havre for the past year. The pair of them must have been talking in the shed when Pecqueux had come out to call to the assistant station-master. She still looked young, despite her thirty-two years: lanky, angular, flat-chested, with flesh that burned with continual desire, she had the long face and blazing eyes of a scrawny, whinnying mare. They said that she drank. Every man in the station had passed through the little house where she lived with her brother next to the engine depot, and which she never bothered to clean. The brother, from the Auvergne, a stubborn man and a great stickler for discipline, who was highly regarded by his superiors, had had no end of trouble over her, to the point where he had been threatened with the sack; and if now she was tolerated because of him, he himself only insisted on keeping her out of a sense of kinship; which did not, however, prevent him from giving her a good thrashing if he found her with a man, so severely indeed that he would leave her for dead on the floor. It had been quite some encounter, her and Pecqueux: she had found satisfaction at last in the arms of this great big fun-loving devil, while he, glad of the change from a wife too fat and delighted to have one too thin, was for ever merrily announcing that he had finally met his heart's desire. And only Séverine, thinking she owed it to Victoire, had stopped speaking to Philomène, whom in any case she had already been avoiding as much as she could, out of instinctive disdain, and whom she had now completely ceased to acknowledge.

'Oh, right then,' said Philomène rudely. 'See you later, my love. I'll be off, seeing as how Monsieur Roubaud wants to give you a talking-to, on the part of his wife.'

He, jovial as ever, was still laughing.

'No, stay, he's only joking.'

'No, no. Must go and take over two of my hen's eggs that I promised to Madame Lebleu.'

She had thrown this name in on purpose, aware of the unspoken rivalry between the ticket-clerk's wife and the assistant station-master's, and affecting to be on excellent terms with the first in order to infuriate the second. But she did stay, all of a sudden interested when she heard the fireman ask about the business with the Sub-Prefect.

'All sorted out, isn't it, Monsieur Roubaud? You're satisfied?'

'Yes, quite satisfied.'

Pecqueux gave a knowing wink.

'Oh, you needn't have worried, you know, 'cos when you've got yourself a bigwig up your sleeve . . . Eh? Know what I mean? My wife, now, she's very grateful to him too.'

The assistant station-master interrupted the reference to President Grandmorin by repeating brusquely:

'So, you're not leaving till this evening, then?'

'That's right. La Lison'll be repaired by then, they're just fixing the connecting-rod . . . And I'm waiting for my driver; he's been off taking the air. You know him, don't you, Jacques Lantier? He's from your part of the world.'

For a moment Roubaud did not reply, his mind vacant, miles away. Then, suddenly with a start:

'What? Jacques Lantier, the driver . . . Certainly I know him. Well, I mean, to say hello to. We met here actually, because he's younger than me, so I never met him back in Plassans . . . He did a small favour for my wife last autumn, ran an errand for her, to her cousins' at Dieppe . . . A capable sort, so they say.'

He was saying whatever occurred to him, gabbling. Suddenly he walked away.

'Cheerio, Pecqueux . . . Better take a look at how things are going over this side.'

Only then did Philomène depart, loping away like a mare; while Pecqueux, standing there, hands in pockets, and laughing easily in the carefree idleness of this cheerful morning, watched in surprise as the assistant station-master contented himself with a single turn round the shed and was already hurrying back. Take a look? That was soon over and done. What had he really been after?

It was almost nine when Roubaud returned into the main concourse. He walked to the far end near the parcels office, looked about without apparently finding what he was after, and then back he came, his stride as impatient as ever. With a glance he checked on each department's office in turn. At this hour the station was peaceful, deserted; and he paced about it all alone, looking more and more irked by the quiet, tormented like a man who is threatened with catastrophe and in the end desperately wants that catastrophe to happen. He had reached the limits of his self-control, he simply could not remain still. His eyes never left the clock now. Nine, five past nine. Normally he only went back upstairs at ten, after the 9.50 had departed, to eat. Suddenly he did go back up, remembering that Séverine would be up there waiting too.

In the corridor, at that precise moment, Madame Lebleu was opening the door to Philomène, who had dropped by, without a hat, clutching two eggs. There they stood, and Roubaud had to make his way to his flat beneath their keen gaze. He had his own key, and proceeded as swiftly as he could. Nevertheless, in the rapid opening and shutting of the door, they saw Séverine seated on one of the dining-room chairs, her hands in her lap, her face pale, just sitting there. Whereupon, having dragged Philomène inside and shut the door after them, Madame Lebleu recounted that she had already seen her sitting like that earlier: probably that business with the Sub-Prefect had turned out badly. But no, Philomène explained that she had rushed over because she had news; and she repeated what she had just heard from the mouth of the assistant station-master himself. Whereupon the two women became lost in speculation. This was how it was when-ever they met, endless gossip.

'They've had a good talking-to, my dear, I'd bet my last penny on it . . . That's it, they're for the high jump.'

'Oh, just think, love, if only they *would* get rid of 'em for us.'

The increasingly poisonous rivalry between the Lebleus and the Roubauds had started simply enough over lodgings. The whole first floor, above the waiting-rooms, was given over to housing the station-workers; and the central corridor, like a real hotel corridor, all painted yellow and lit from above, ran the length of the floor, its brown doors lined up to left and right. Except that the flats on the right had windows that looked out over the station entrance with its old elm-trees and the fine view to the Ingouville ridge beyond; while those on the left had low, arched windows that gave directly out on to the station roof, which blocked the view with its steeply pitched slope of lead flashing and dirty glass. Life in the former was as cheerful as could be, what with the constant bustle of the entrance, the greenery of the trees, and the broad sweep of the countryside; while in the latter, where one could hardly see a thing and the sky was shut out as though by prison walls, a person could have died of boredom. At the front lived the station-master, the assistant station-master Moulin, and the Lebleus; at the back, not counting the three rooms reserved for inspectors just passing through, were the Roubauds, together with the office-clerk Mademoiselle Guichon. Now it was a notorious fact that the two assistant station-masters had always lived next door to one another. That the Lebleus were there at all was thanks to the kindness of Roubaud's predecessor as assistant station-master who, being a widower and without children, had wanted to do Madame Lebleu a good turn by letting her have his flat. But shouldn't this flat have then been given to the Roubauds? Was it right to relegate them to the back when they had the right to live at the front? For as long as the two households had lived together amicably, Séverine had deferred to her neighbour Madame Lebleu, who was twenty years older, in poor health to boot, and so enormous that she was constantly out of breath. War between the two women had really only been declared the day Philomène had caused a rift between them by inventing nasty rumours.

'You know,' Philomène now continued, 'I wouldn't put it past them to have used their journey to Paris to go and ask for you to be moved out . . . Someone told me they'd written the Managing Director a long letter putting forward their case.'

Madame Lebleu was choking with rage.

'The miserable wretches! . . . And I'm absolutely sure they're trying to get that office-clerk on their side; 'cos for the past fortnight she's hardly even said hello to me . . . And there's another fine thing, what's more! I've got my eye on her all right . . .'

Lowering her voice, she expressed the certainty that Mademoiselle Guichon must be leaving her flat each night to go and see the station-master. Their doors were opposite each other. This was Monsieur Dabadie, a widower and the father of a teenage daughter still at boarding-school: he was the one responsible for this woman, a blonde of thirty, coming to the place originally, and by then she was already past it, all silent and thin, as slippery as a snake. She must have been a teacher or something. And quite impossible to catch, the way she could slither about the place, without a sound, through the merest crack. In herself she was scarcely worth bothering about. But if she was sleeping with the station-master, then her role was crucial, and the clever thing was to get a hold over her, by knowing her secret.

'Oh, I'll see to the bottom of this in the end,' Madame Lebleu went on. 'I'm not going to let them get the better of me . . . Here we live and here we stay. The good people are on our side, aren't they, my dear?'

The whole station did indeed take a passionate interest in this battle of the lodgings. The corridor itself was particularly involved. Almost the only person to take no interest was Moulin, the other assistant station-master, quite satisfied as he was to be living at the front, married to a timid, skimpy little woman whom no one ever saw and who bore him a child every twenty months.

'Well,' Philomène concluded, 'if they're for the high jump, this isn't what's going to make them leap . . . You mind out, they've got friends in high places.'

She was still holding her two eggs, and now handed them over: two eggs freshly laid that morning, which she had just taken from under the hens. The old lady was lost in gratitude:

'How kind you are! You do spoil me, you do . . . Come and have a chat more often. You know my husband's always at his ticket-office; and I get so bored, stuck here all the time on account of my legs and that! What would become of me, I wonder, if those wretches did take my view away from me?'

Then, as she showed her to the door, she placed a finger to her lips.

'Sh! Listen!'

The pair of them stood there in the corridor for a full five minutes, stock still, holding their breath. Heads cocked, they strained their ears in the direction of the Roubauds' dining-room. But not a sound could be heard, only the silence of the dead. And so, anxious not to be caught, they finally parted, nodding goodbye to each other without a further word. The one tiptoed away while the other closed her door so gently that the latch slid noiselessly back into place.

At nine twenty Roubaud was back down in the concourse again. He was supervising the men making up the 9.50 slow train; and, despite all efforts at self-control, he was gesticulating more than ever, pacing about, turning his head ceaselessly this way and that, his eyes sweeping the platform from end to end. Nothing was happening, and his hands trembled at the fact.

Then, suddenly, as once more he scanned the station with a backward glance, he heard a voice next to him, a telegraph-operator asking breathlessly:

'Monsieur Roubaud, you haven't seen the station-master, have you, or the superintendent? . . . I've got some telegrams for them, and I've been running about the place for ten minutes now . . .'

Roubaud had turned round in such a sudden stiffening of his whole being that not a muscle moved in his face. His eyes locked on to the two telegrams that the operator was holding. This time surely—and the man's anxiety left no room for doubt—disaster had struck at last.

'Monsieur Dabadie was there a minute ago,' he said calmly.

Never in his life had he felt so cold, nor known his mind so sharp, as he stood there, erect, taut, ready to defend himself. Now he was sure of himself.

'Look,' he continued, 'there's Monsieur Dabadie now.'

And there the station-master was, on his way back from the slow goods yard. On perusing the telegram he exclaimed:

'There's been a murder down the line . . . The telegram's from the inspector in Rouen.'

'What?' enquired Roubaud, 'One of our men murdered?'

'No, no, a passenger, in a coupé . . . The body was thrown off, just near the exit from the Malaunay tunnel, at post 153 . . . And the victim's one of our board directors, President Grandmorin.'

It was the assistant station-master's turn to exclaim:

'The President! Oh, my poor wife, she's going to be terribly upset!'

The outburst sounded so natural and so concerned that Monsieur Dabadie paused for a moment.

'Oh, but that's right, of course, you knew him. A fine man, wasn't he?'

Then, recalling the other telegram, the one addressed to the superintendent:

'This must be from the examining magistrate, some formality or other presumably . . . And it's only twenty-five past nine, and naturally enough Monsieur Cauche isn't here yet . . . Someone should go to the Café du Commerce, on the Cours Napoléon. They're bound to find him there.'

Five minutes later, and Monsieur Cauche was on his way, fetched by one of the station-workers. A former officer who looked on his present employment as a form of retirement, he never appeared at the station before ten o'clock, whereupon he strolled round for a while and then headed back to the café. This drama, occurring between two games of picquet, had surprised him at first, for the business which passed through his hands was rarely serious. But the telegram did indeed come from the examining magistrate at Rouen; and if it had arrived twelve hours after the body was discovered, that was because the magistrate had first telegraphed to Paris, to the station-master, to find out the details of the victim's departure; only then, informed of the number of the train and of the particular carriage, had he sent an order to the superintendent to go and inspect the coupé which was in carriage 293, if indeed the carriage was still at Le Havre. All at once the bad temper which Monsieur Cauche had displayed at being disturbed, doubtless for no good reason, vanished to be replaced by a demeanour of extreme self-importance, proportionate to this exceptionally grave turn of events.

'But,' he exclaimed, suddenly anxious at the prospect of the enquiry being taken out of his hands, 'that carriage shouldn't still be here, it ought to have gone out again this morning.'

It was Roubaud who set his mind at rest, with his unflappable air.

'No, no, excuse me, sir . . . A coupé had been booked for this evening, so the carriage is still here, in the shed.'

And off he walked, with the superintendent and the stationmaster following behind. However, news must have got out, because the men making up the train surreptitiously downed tools and followed also; while at the doors of the various offices station staff began to appear and eventually drew near, one by one. Soon a crowd had gathered.

As they were reaching the carriage, Monsieur Dabadie observed aloud:

'But there was an inspection last night. If there'd been any traces, they'd have been noted in the report.'

'Well, we'll soon see,' said Monsieur Cauche.

He opened the door and climbed into the coupé. On the instant he exclaimed, forgetting himself and swearing:

'Oh, my God! You'd think it was a pig they'd been bleeding in here!'

A small gasp of horror ran through the assembled crowd, necks were craned; and Monsieur Dabadie was one of the first to want to see, hoisting himself up on to the compartment step, while behind him Roubaud, not to seem different, also strained to see.

Inside the coupé nothing was out of place. The windows were still shut, everything seemed to be where it should. Only, a dreadful stench issued from the door of the compartment; and there, in the middle of one of the seat-cushions, a pool of blood had coagulated, a pool so deep and broad that a stream had welled from it as from a spring, spreading out over the carpet. Clots stuck to the material. And that was all, nothing but this evil-smelling blood.

Monsieur Dabadie flew into a rage.

'Where are they, where are the men who did the inspection yesterday evening? Have them brought to me.'

They were in fact present, and came forward, mumbling excuses: it was pitch dark, didn't people realize? but they always ran their hands over everything carefully to make sure. They swore that the night before they hadn't found a thing.

Meanwhile Monsieur Cauche, who had remained in the carriage, stood there with his pencil, taking notes for his report. He called to Roubaud, in whose company he often liked to take a stroll along the platform, smoking a cigarette, when things were quiet.

'Monsieur Roubaud, could you come here? You can help me.'

And, when the assistant station-master had stepped across the blood on the carpet to avoid getting it on his shoes:

'Have a look under the other seat-cushion and see if anything's slipped down behind.'

Roubaud lifted the cushion and felt carefully with his hands, wearing an expression of simple curiosity.

'Nothing here.'

But a stain on the back of the upholstered seat caught his attention, and he pointed it out to the superintendent. Wasn't that a bloody fingerprint? No, they agreed eventually, it was just a splash of blood. The crowd had drawn closer to get a better view of the investigation, scenting crime, and pressing up behind the station-master who had squeamishly remained on the carriage step.

The station-master had a sudden thought.

'Just a minute, Monsieur Roubaud, weren't you on that train? . . . You were, weren't you, you came back on the express, yesterday evening . . . Perhaps *you* might be able to tell us something!'

'But, of course, that's quite true!' exclaimed the superintendent. 'Did you notice anything?'

For three or four seconds, Roubaud said nothing. He was crouching down at that moment, examining the carpet. But he stood up almost at once, and replied in his usual, slightly gruff voice:

'Certainly, certainly, I'll tell you what I can . . . My wife was with me. If what I have to say is to go in the report, then I'd rather she came down and we checked if I've remembered things right.'

This seemed perfectly reasonable to Monsieur Cauche, and Pecqueux, who had just appeared, offered to go and fetch Madame Roubaud. Off he strode, and they bided their time. Philomène, who had come running to the scene with the fireman, watched him leave, irritated that he had volunteered. But catching sight of Madame Lebleu who was hurrying along as fast as her poor swollen legs would carry her, she rushed to her assistance; and the two women threw their hands in the air, gasping and exclaiming in their excitement at the discovery of such an abominable crime. Although absolutely nothing was known as yet, various versions of events were already circulating around them, to the accompaniment of horrified expressions and gestures of dismay. Her voice raised above the general murmur, Philomène herself was maintaining on her word of honour, without anyone having told her any such thing, that Madame Roubaud had seen the murderer. Silence fell when Pecqueux reappeared, accompanied by the woman in question.

'Just look at her!' murmured Madame Lebleu. 'Quite the princess, and her an assistant's wife! She was just like that this morning, before dawn even, all combed and corseted as if she was off visiting.'

Séverine came up, walking with short, even strides. There was a whole long stretch of platform to cover, beneath the gaze of the onlookers observing her arrival; and she did not falter, simply pressing a handkerchief to her eyes from the enormous grief that had overwhelmed her on learning the name of the victim. Dressed in a black wool dress of great elegance, she seemed to be in mourning for her protector. Her thick dark hair gleamed in the sunlight, for in her haste she had not even bothered to cover her head, despite the cold. Her eyes, so gentle and blue, full of pain and bathed in tears, made her a touching sight.

'And cry she might,' muttered Philomène. 'They're for it all right, now that someone's gone and killed their all-powerful benefactor.'

When at last Séverine stood there amongst them, in front of the open door of the coupé, Monsieur Cauche and Roubaud stepped down on to the platform; and immediately the latter began to say what he knew.

'Now then, my dear, yesterday morning, as soon as we got to Paris, we went to see Monsieur Grandmorin . . . It must have been about a quarter past eleven, wasn't it?'

He was staring at her, and she repeated in a docile voice:

'Yes, a quarter past eleven.'

But her eyes had fallen on the cushion, black with blood, and she choked: sobs rose from deep in her throat. Moved and concerned, the station-master quickly intervened:

'Madame, if you feel unable to bear the sight . . . We quite understand how painful this must be for you.'

'Oh, just a few brief words,' the superintendent broke in. 'Then we'll see Madame is taken home again.'

Roubaud hastened to continue.

'Well, after we'd talked about this and that, it was then Monsieur Grandmorin told us that he had to go away the next day, to Doinville, to his sister's . . . I can still see him sitting there at his desk. I was here, my wife sat over there . . . Didn't he, dear, he told us he'd be leaving the next day.'

'Yes, the next day.'

Monsieur Cauche, who was still busy making rapid notes with his pencil, glanced up.

'What do you mean, the next day? But he left that evening!'

'But wait,' replied the assistant station-master. 'When he knew that we were going back that evening, he thought for a moment of taking the express with us, if my wife would like to go on with him to Doinville and spend a few days there with his sister, as she'd done before. But my wife had a lot to attend to here and so she said no . . . Didn't you, dear, you said no?'

'Yes, I said no.'

'Well, that was that. He was very nice about it . . . He'd already dealt with the matter I'd come about, so he walked us to the door of his office . . . Didn't he, dear?'

'To the door, yes.'

'That evening we left . . . Before settling into our compartment I went and had a chat with Monsieur Vandorpe, the station-master. And I didn't see a thing. I was very annoyed because I thought we would have the compartment to ourselves, and there was this lady I hadn't noticed before, sitting in the corner; and to make matters worse, two other people, a couple, got in at the very last minute . . . As far as Rouen, nothing either, I didn't see anything out of the ordinary . . . And so, at Rouen when we got out to stretch our legs, you can imagine our surprise when, only three or four coaches away from ours, there was Monsieur Grandmorin standing at the door of his coupé! "So, Monsieur le Président, you did leave after all? Well, well, we had no idea we were on the same train as yourself!" And he explained how he had received a telegram . . . The whistle went and we hurried back to our compartment, where, incidentally, we found everyone gone, our fellow-passengers had all got out at Rouen, which was not exactly an unpleasant surprise . . . And there we are, that's it really, isn't it, dear?'

'Yes, that's it really.'

This account, simple as it was, had made a deep impression on the audience. They stood there gaping, waiting for answers. The superintendent had stopped writing, and spoke for them all in their surprise when he asked:

'And you're quite sure that there was no one in the coupé with Monsieur Grandmorin?'

'Oh, yes, quite sure.'

A shiver ran round the crowd. This mystery which had now presented itself was casting a chill of fear, as though each of them could feel a cold breath down the back of his neck. If the passenger was alone, who then could have killed him and thrown him from the train, three leagues further on, before the next stop?

In the midst of the silence Philomène's disagreeable voice was heard:

'It's a bit odd all the same.'

And, sensing her stare, Roubaud looked her in the eye and nodded, as if to say that he, too, found it all a bit odd. Beside her he noticed Pecqueux and Madame Lebleu, who were nodding also. Everyone's eyes were upon him, they were waiting for something else, scrutinizing him for some forgotten detail which would shed light on the affair. There was no hint of accusation in their burning, curious gaze; and yet he thought he could see the first glimmerings of vague suspicion, the sort of doubt that the merest little fact can sometimes change into certainty.

'Extraordinary,' murmured Monsieur Cauche.

'Quite extraordinary,' repeated Monsieur Dabadie.

Then Roubaud made up his mind:

'What I do know is that the express went from Rouen to Barentin as normal, without stopping, at its proper speed, and without anything unusual happening that I could see . . . I say that only because being alone as we were, I'd pulled the window down to smoke a cigarette; and I was looking out off and on, and I could hear all the sounds of the train perfectly well . . . What's more, at Barentin I saw Monsieur Bessière on the platform, the station-master, the man who took over from me. So I called him over, and we had a word or two while he was up on the footboard shaking hands . . . Isn't that right, dear? You can ask him if you like, Monsieur Bessière, he'll tell you.'

Séverine, still standing there motionless and pale, her slim face etched with grief, confirmed once more what her husband had said.

'Yes, he'll tell you.'

Thereafter all accusation became impossible if the Roubauds, who had got back into their compartment at Rouen, had been greeted in it at Barentin by a friend. The shadow of a suspicion which the assistant station-master thought he had seen pass across their faces had vanished; and the general amazement increased. The whole affair was becoming more and more mysterious.

'Look,' said the superintendent, 'are you absolutely sure that nobody at Rouen could have got into the coupé after you left Monsieur Grandmorin?'

Evidently Roubaud had not foreseen this question since, for the first time, he began to flounder, no doubt because he had not prepared an answer in advance. He looked at his wife, hesitating:

'Oh no, I don't think so . . . They were shutting the doors, the whistle was going, we only just had time ourselves to get back to our carriage . . . And anyway, the coupé was reserved, no one was allowed to get in, I don't think . . .'

But his wife's blue eyes were widening, becoming so large that he was afraid to be more categoric.

'Mind you, I don't know . . . Well, perhaps someone could have got in . . . There was such a crush . . .'

And as he spoke, his voice became firm once more, and this whole new story took shape, a thing of certainty.

'You see, because of the celebrations at Le Havre, there was an enormous crowd . . . We had to fend off passengers from second class and even third class who were trying to get in to our compartment . . . And, of course, the station's very badly lit, you could see nothing at all, people were pushing and shouting, and shoving to get on the train before it went . . . Heavens, yes, it's quite possible that somebody didn't know which carriage to get into, or maybe even took advantage of the crush and simply forced his way into the coupé at the very last moment.'

Then, breaking off:

'What do you think, dear? That must be what happened.'

Séverine, looking quite broken, her handkerchief pressed to her swollen eyes, repeated:

'That's what happened, I'm certain.'

From that point, the way forward was clear: and, without a word, the superintendent and the station-master exchanged a knowing look of agreement. There was a prolonged stir in the crowd, who could sense that the investigation was at an end but were still tormented by the desire for explanations: all at once, theories began to circulate, and everyone had his own version of events. For some time now the normal working routine of the station had been suspended, the whole workforce was there, obsessed by this drama; and it came as a surprise to see the 9.38 making its way into the station. Some people hurried away, the doors opened, and the passengers streamed out. But almost all the onlookers had remained behind, clustering round the superintendent, who, with the scruples of a methodical man, was inspecting the bloodstained coupé one last time.

At this moment Pecqueux, standing gesticulating between Madame Lebleu and Philomène, spotted his driver, Jacques Lantier, who had just alighted from the train and was watching the crowd from a distance. He beckoned to him wildly. Jacques did not move. Eventually he made up his mind, and walked slowly towards them.

'What's up?' he asked his fireman.

He knew perfectly well, and only half-listened to the news of the murder and the various theories people had about it. What he found surprising and strangely disturbing was to land up like this in the middle of the investigation, to see once more the coupé he had glimpsed hurtling at full speed through the night. He craned forward, gazing at the pool of congealed blood on the cushion; and he could see it all again, the murder taking place, and especially the body back there, lying beside the track, its throat cut. Then, turning away, he caught sight of the Roubauds, while Pecqueux continued to tell him the whole story, about how they were mixed up in it, and about their departure from Paris in the same train as the victim, and their final conversation at Rouen. The husband he knew, just to say hello to sometimes, since he'd begun driving the express; while he had glimpsed the wife occasionally, and shunned her, as he did the others, out of pathological fear. But now, at this moment, standing there pale and tearful, with a sweet, gentle, frightened look in her blue eyes under that crushing pile of black hair, she caught his attention. As he kept his gaze on her, his thoughts drifted, and he wondered vaguely what the Roubauds and he were doing there, how events had conspired to bring them together like this beside this carriage, beside the scene of the crime, when they had returned from Paris the previous evening, and he himself was just that moment back from Barentin.

'Yes, I know, I know,' he said loudly, interrupting the fireman. 'I was there, at the very spot, last night, just beyond the tunnel, and I actually think I saw something, just as the train was passing.'

There was great excitement, everyone crowded round. And he himself was the first to quiver with astonishment, completely staggered by what he had just said. Why had he spoken, having faithfully promised himself that he would say nothing? So many good reasons told him to be silent! And the words had unwittingly issued from his lips as he was gazing at this woman. She had quickly lowered her handkerchief the better to fix him with her tear-filled eyes, which now grew wider still.

But the superintendent had pushed his way closer.

'What? What did you see?'

And Jacques, beneath Séverine's unblinking stare, told them what he had seen: the coupé all lit up, passing in the night, at full speed, and the fleeting profiles of two men, the one on his back, the other knife in hand. Standing beside his wife, Roubaud listened, staring at him with his large bright eyes.

'So', asked the superintendent, 'would you recognize the killer?'

'Oh no, I don't think so.'

'Was he wearing an overcoat or a workman's smock?'

'I couldn't say. I mean, after all, the train must have been doing eighty kilometres an hour!'

Involuntarily Séverine caught Roubaud's eye, and he managed to speak:

'Well, indeed, you'd need pretty good eyesight.'

'No matter,' Monsieur Cauche concluded. 'This is an important statement. The examining magistrate will help you to sort out your story . . . Monsieur Lantier and Monsieur Roubaud, will you give me your full names, so that you can be called as witnesses.'

It was over: the onlookers gradually melted away, and station life returned to normal. Roubaud in particular had to rush off to deal with the 9.50 slow train, which the passengers were already boarding. He had given Jacques a firm handshake, firmer than usual; and, left alone with Séverine, behind Madame Lebleu, Pecqueux, and Philomène, who were walking away deep in whispered conversation, Jacques had felt obliged to accompany the young woman back into the station concourse as far as the staff staircase, finding nothing to say to her, yet prevented from leaving her side as if some bond had just been tied between them. It was an even more beautiful day now: the bright sun was climbing in triumph above the morning mists, amid the great, limpid blueness of the sky; while the wind from the sea, gathering in strength with the rising tide, brought a salty freshness on the air. And, as he left her finally, once more he encountered her wide eyes, whose sweet, imploring, terrified gaze had so profoundly touched him.

But there was a short blast on the whistle. It was Roubaud giving the signal for the train to depart. The engine answered with a prolonged whistling, and the 9.50 jolted forward, gathering speed, before disappearing into the distance beneath the golden dust of the sun.

CHAPTER IV

THAT day in the second week of March, Monsieur Denizet, the examining magistrate,* had once again summoned a number of important witnesses in the Grandmorin affair to attend him in his chambers in the Palais de Justice at Rouen.

For three weeks this affair had been causing an enormous stir. It had convulsed Rouen, and now Paris was in a high state of excitement, with the opposition newspapers adopting it as an engine of war in their virulent campaign against the Empire. Preoccupation with the coming general election, which was dominating political life, served further to fan the flames of battle. The Chamber of Deputies had seen some particularly tempestuous sessions: once, when the powers of two deputies attached to the person of the Emperor had been bitterly contested, and again when there had been fierce criticism of the administration of public finances under the Prefect of the Seine Region, with calls for the creation of a municipal council.* And the Grandmorin affair had come just at the right time to keep things on the boil, with the most extraordinary stories circulating about it, and newspapers full of new theories every morning, each one damaging to the government. On the one hand, it was intimated that the victim, who had been a frequent visitor to the Tuileries, a former magistrate, a commander in the Legion of Honour, and worth several millions, had been given to all manner of debauch; while on the other, since the enquiry had still not come up with a solution, people were beginning to accuse the police and the prosecution service of complacency, and to make jokes about this mythical killer who remained at large. That there was much substance in these attacks only made them the harder to bear.

Thus Monsieur Denizet felt all the more keenly the heavy responsibility resting on his shoulders. He, too, was in a high state of excitement about the affair, not least because he was ambitious and had been desperately waiting for a case of this importance to come his way so that he might display to advantage the great qualities of perspicacity and energy which he considered himself to possess. The son of a big cattle-breeder in Normandy, he had studied law at Caen and been called only somewhat late in life to the magistrate's bench, where the fact of his peasant origins, exacerbated by that of his father's bankruptcy, had rendered advancement difficult. Deputy public prosecutor at Bernay, Dieppe, and Le Havre, it had taken him ten years to become public prosecutor at Pont-Audemer. He had then been transferred to Rouen as deputy prosecutor, and he had now, at the age of over fifty, been an examining magistrate for the past year and a half. Lacking independent means, and consumed by needs which could not be met from his meagre salary, he lived in that total dependence upon the poorly paid office of magistrate to which the mediocre are resigned and in which the intelligent eat their hearts out, as they await an opportunity to sell themselves. He, for his part, had a sharp, unfettered intelligence, indeed he was honest, and in love with his job, intoxicated with the omnipotence which made of him, as he sat there in his judge's chambers, absolute master over other people's freedom. His self-interest alone curbed his passion; he had such an overriding desire to obtain some decoration and be transferred to Paris that, having allowed himself on his first day as an examining magistrate to be carried away by his love of the truth, he now proceeded always with extreme caution, at every stage discerning pitfalls in which his future prospects might be swallowed up.

Monsieur Denizet, it must be said, was already predisposed; for, at the outset of his investigation, a friend had advised him to go to Paris, to the Ministry of Justice. There he had had a long conversation with the Secretary General, Monsieur Camy-Lamotte,* a figure of some importance in charge of appointments, with the power to promote, and who was in regular touch with the Tuileries. He was a fine man, who, like himself, had started out as a deputy prosecutor but who, thanks to his connections and his wife, had been made a Deputy and Grand Officer in the Legion of Honour. The case had naturally landed on his desk, since the public prosecutor in Rouen, concerned about this shady drama in which the victim was a former magistrate, had taken the precaution of referring it to the Minister, who in turn had delegated the matter to his Secretary General. And at this

point there had been a curious crossing of paths: for Monsieur
Camy-Lamotte, it transpired, had been a fellow-pupil of President Grandmorin's, albeit a few years younger, and they had
remained such close friends that he knew everything there was to
know about the President, including his vices. Hence he had
spoken about his friend's tragic death with genuine sorrow, and
had said nothing at all to Monsieur Denizet other than how
desperately anxious he was to find the guilty party. But he was
obliged to say that the Tuileries were most unhappy about the
disproportionate fuss, and he had taken the liberty of advising
him to be of the utmost discretion in the matter. In sum, the
examining magistrate had understood that he would do well not
to rush things, not to risk anything without prior approval.
Indeed he had returned to Rouen convinced that the Secretary
General, in his keen desire to investigate the matter himself, had
sent out his own men. They wished to discover the truth, the
better then, if necessary, to suppress it.

However, the days went by, and Monsieur Denizet, despite
his efforts to be patient, was becoming irritated by the jokes in
the press. Then the detective in him came to the fore, and off he
went, nose to the wind, like a good gundog. He was carried away
by the need to find the right trail, by the thought of glory for
being the first to scent it, even though he was ready to abandon
it if that was the order. And so, while he waited in vain for a letter
to come from the Ministry, some piece of advice, a simple sign
even, he had begun once more actively to investigate the affair.
Two or three arrests had already been made, but in each case the
charges had had to be dropped. All of a sudden, however, the
publishing of President Grandmorin's will raised a suspicion in
his mind, one which had already crossed it at the start: namely,
that the Roubauds might be guilty. The will, full of curious
bequests, contained one whereby Séverine inherited the house at
the place named La Croix-de-Maufras. From that moment the
motive for the murder—which he had so far sought in vain—was
clear: the Roubauds, knowing of the legacy, could have murdered their benefactor in order to enter into immediate possession. This possibility haunted him all the more because
Monsieur Camy-Lamotte had spoken about Madame Roubaud
in an odd way, as if he had known her in the old days, at the

President's house, when she was a girl. Only, how improbable, how materially and psychologically impossible it all was! Since starting to conduct his investigations along these lines, he had kept coming up against facts which ran completely counter to his idea of a properly conducted judicial enquiry. Nothing became any clearer; the central illumination, the prime cause shedding light on everything, was missing.

There was, of course, another possible line of enquiry, which Monsieur Denizet had not lost sight of, the line offered by Roubaud himself, about the man who might have taken advantage of the scramble of departure and boarded the coupé. This was the notorious 'lost murderer', the legendary figure who had been the occasion of so much mirth in all the opposition newspapers. The main thrust of the enquiry had at first been to obtain a description of this man—at Rouen, where he had boarded the train, and at Barentin, where he must have got off. But nothing precise had come of it, with certain witnesses even denying that it was possible to force one's way into a reserved coupé like that, while others had provided the most contradictory pieces of information. And the trail seemed to be leading nowhere when the magistrate, on questioning Misard the crossing-keeper, accidentally stumbled on the dramatic story of Cabuche and Louisette, the young girl who had allegedly been raped by the President and gone to her friend's house to die. It was like a thunderbolt, and the whole classic charge formulated itself automatically in his mind. It was all there: the quarryman's murderous threats against the victim, his bad record, a shaky alibi that was impossible to corroborate. The previous day, in a moment of inspired initiative, he had secretly had Cabuche taken from his little house in the middle of the woods, a remote sort of lair, where they had found a pair of trousers stained with blood. And, while still resisting the conviction which was gradually overtaking him, and promising himself not to abandon his theory about the Roubauds, he was nevertheless exultant that he alone had had a nose sufficiently keen to sniff out the real murderer. It was with the purpose of making absolutely certain that he had summoned to his chambers that day several of the witnesses who had already been questioned on the day following the crime.

The examining magistrate's office was situated on the Rue Jeanne d'Arc side of the old, dilapidated building which adjoined the former palace of the Dukes of Normandy, now the Palais de Justice, and adjoined it much to its architectural detriment. The large, gloomy room, on the ground floor, received so little daylight that in winter it was necessary to light a lamp from three o'clock onwards. Done up in old, faded green wallpaper, it contained but two armchairs, four chairs, the magistrate's desk, and a small table for the clerk; while on the mantelpiece above the empty fireplace stood a black marble clock flanked by two bronze goblets. Behind the desk a door led to another room, in which the magistrate periodically concealed persons he wished to have immediately available; whereas the main door opened directly on to the wide corridor furnished with benches where the witnesses waited their turn.

Although summoned for two o'clock, the Roubauds had been there since half-past one. They had come straight from Le Havre, scarcely stopping for lunch in a little restaurant in the Grande-Rue. Dressed both in black, he in a frock-coat, she in a silk dress like a lady, they maintained the grave, somewhat exhausted, grief-stricken air of a couple that has lost a relative. She was seated on a bench, quite still, not uttering a word, while he, having chosen to remain standing, his hands behind his back, was walking slowly up and down in front of her. But each time he went by, their eyes met, and their secret fears passed like shadows across their blank faces. Although they had been delighted at the time, the bequest of La Croix-de-Maufras had added to their worries; for the President's family, and especially his daughter, outraged at such strange bequests (so numerous that they amounted to half the total estate), talked of contesting the will; and Madame de Lachesnaye, urged on by her husband, had been behaving with particular harshness towards her former friend Séverine, heaping the most grave suspicions upon her. At the same time, the thought that there existed conclusive evidence against them, which had not occurred to Roubaud at first, now filled him with constant dread: that letter which he had made his wife write to get Grandmorin to leave, a letter they were going to find if Grandmorin hadn't destroyed it, with its easily identifiable handwriting. Fortunately, time had gone by and nothing had surfaced; the letter must have been torn up. But all the same, each summons to the magistrate's chambers brought the couple out in a cold sweat, for all their proper demeanour as heirs and witnesses.

It struck two. Jacques now appeared in his turn, having come from Paris. At once Roubaud went up to him, his hand outstretched in a particularly expansive manner.

'Ah, you too then, so they've been bothering you as well . . . It is a nuisance, isn't it, this sad business dragging on like this!'

Catching sight of Séverine just sitting there motionless, Jacques had suddenly stopped. For three weeks now, every other day, when he went to Le Havre, the assistant station-master had been exceedingly cordial towards him. Once even he had had to accept an invitation to lunch with them. And in the young woman's presence he had felt himself start trembling again, in an increasingly disturbing way. Was he, then, going to want her too? His heart pounded and his hands itched at the mere sight of her white neck above the curve of her bodice. As a result he had firmly resolved to avoid her from now on.

'So,' said Roubaud, 'and what are they saying about all this in Paris? Nothing new, I suppose? They haven't found out a thing, you see, never will . . . Come and say hallo to my wife.'

He insisted, and Jacques had to go over and greet an embarrassed Séverine, who was smiling her timid child's smile. He made an effort to talk about innocuous subjects, while all the time the husband and wife observed him, as if they were trying to read beyond his thoughts and discern those vague intimations into which he himself hesitated to delve. Why was he so distant? Why did he seem to want to avoid them? Was he beginning to remember things, is that why they had all been called back, to be brought face to face? This was the one witness they feared, and they would like to have subjugated him, bound him to them with the ties of a fellowship so close that he would no longer have the courage to say a word against them.

It was the assistant station-master who, in his desperate anxiety, returned to the subject.

'So you don't know why they've called you? Eh? Perhaps something's turned up.'

Jacques shrugged.

'There was a rumour going round, just a while back, at the station, when I arrived. Something about an arrest.'

The Roubauds were dumbfounded, very agitated and perplexed. What, an arrest? Nobody had said a thing to them about it! An arrest that *had* taken place, or was about to? They asked question after question, but that was all he knew.

At that moment, in the corridor, the sound of footsteps caught Séverine's attention.

'Here come Berthe and her husband,' she murmured.

It was indeed the Lachesnayes. They walked very stiffly past the Roubauds, the young woman not so much as glancing at her former friend. And immediately an usher showed them into the magistrate's office.

'Oh, I see. Well, we had better summon up our patience,' said Roubaud. 'We've a good two hours in front of us . . . Come on, come and sit down.'

He himself had just sat down on Séverine's left, and he gestured to Jacques to sit down on the other side, next to her. Lantier remained standing a moment longer. Then, when she looked at him with her sweet, timid air, he slid down on to the bench. She seemed very fragile sitting there between them, he could sense her soft, submissive gentleness; and the slight warmth emanating from this woman, during their long wait, slowly induced in him a state of torpor which spread throughout his whole body.

In Monsieur Denizet's office the interrogation was about to begin. Already the enquiry had spawned an enormous file of documentation, bundle upon bundle of papers, all in blue folders. They had endeavoured to trace the victim's movements from the moment he left Paris. Monsieur Vandorpe, the station-master, had made a statement about the departure of the 6.30 express, recalling how carriage 293 had been added at the last minute, then his brief conversation with Roubaud, who had got into his compartment shortly before President Grandmorin arrived, and finally how he had seen the latter into his coupé, where he had certainly travelled alone. Then the chief guard, Henri Dauvergne, had been questioned about events during the ten-minute stop at Rouen, but he had been unable to tell them anything for certain. He had seen the Roubauds talking, in front of the coupé, and he was fairly sure that they had returned to their own compartment, the door of which would have been shut by an inspector; but he couldn't be absolutely definite, what with the jostling of the crowd and the semi-darkness in the station. As to saying whether a man, the notorious 'lost murderer', could have jumped into the coupé as the train was leaving, he did not think it very likely, although it was possible; for, as far as he knew, such a thing had already happened twice before. Questioned on the same points, other members of the staff at Rouen, far from shedding any light, had really only complicated matters further with their contradictory replies. However, one fact was proven, that Roubaud, in the carriage, had shaken hands with the station-master on the footboard at Barentin: the station-master, Monsieur Bessière, had formally corroborated the fact, and added that his colleague was alone with his wife, who had been half-lying across the seat and apparently sleeping peacefully. Other than this, they had gone so far as to trace the passengers who had left Paris in the same compartment as the Roubauds. The large lady and gentleman who had arrived late, at the very last minute, respectable people from Petit-Couronne, stated that they had immediately dropped off to sleep and so were unable to provide any information; and as for the woman in black, sitting silently in her corner, she had melted away like a shadow, it had proved completely impossible to trace her. And lastly there had been the other witnesses, the motley selection who had helped establish the identity of the passengers who had got off at Barentin that evening, since that was where the man himself must have got off: they had counted the tickets, and they had managed to identify all the passengers, except for one, namely a tall, strapping fellow with a blue scarf round his head, and who some said had worn an overcoat, others a workman's smock. On the subject of this man alone, who had disappeared, vanished into thin air, the file contained three hundred and ten separate items, and of such a conflicting nature that every single statement was contradicted by another.

The file was made the more complex still by the legal documents: the affidavit drawn up by the coroner's clerk whom the public prosecutor and the examining magistrate had taken to the scene of the crime, with its detailed description of the place beside the line where the victim had been found lying, the position of the body, the state of his clothes, and the objects found in his pockets, which had allowed him to be identified; the doctor's report, for he too had been taken there, a deposition containing, in scientific terminology, a long description of the throat wound, that single wound, a horrible gash made with a sharp-edged instrument, presumably a knife; and then yet other reports, other documents about transporting the body to Rouen hospital, and how long it had remained there before its remarkably rapid decomposition had obliged the authorities to return it to the family. But from all this additional documentation only two or three salient points emerged. First, his watch was missing from his pockets, as was a small wallet which should have contained ten thousand-franc notes, a sum which President Grandmorin owed his sister Madame Bonnehon and which she had been expecting. So it looked as though robbery might have been the motive, except that, conversely, a ring bearing a large diamond had still been on his finger. From which flowed a whole series of hypotheses. Unfortunately they did not have the numbers of the banknotes; but the watch was well known, a very solid watch with stem-winder, with the President's two intertwined initials engraved on the case and the maker's number, 2516, marked on the inside. Lastly, the weapon, the knife used by the murderer, had been the object of a particularly thorough search, along the whole length of the track, in the surrounding bushes, anywhere it could have been thrown; but the search had proved fruitless, the murderer must have hidden it somewhere with the banknotes and the watch. The only thing they had found, about a hundred metres from Barentin station, was the victim's travelling-rug, discarded as if it were an incriminating piece of evidence; and this was now one of the prosecution's exhibits.

When the Lachesnayes entered, Monsieur Denizet was standing in front of his desk rereading a transcript of one of the first interviews, which his clerk had just found for him in the file. He was a short, rather thickset man, clean-shaven, with prematurely greying hair. His heavy jowls, square chin, and broad nose were wan and expressionless, an effect reinforced by heavy eyelids that drooped over large, limpid eyes. But all the sagacity and skill which he believed himself to possess were concentrated in his mouth, one of those actor's mouths that parades its emotions with infinite mobility of expression, and which in his case became extremely thin-lipped in moments of particular subtlety. And subtlety was his undoing, more often than not; he could be too perceptive, would try to be too clever when in fact the truth was simple and straightforward, modelling himself on an ideal notion of his profession, and believing himself to be some kind of moral anatomist, endowed with second sight, and extremely sharp-witted. For all that, however, he was no fool.

At once he became courtesy itself towards Madame de Lachesnaye, for he was also the worldly magistrate, the man who moved in the society of Rouen and its environs.

'Madame, do please be seated.'

And he personally brought up a chair for the young lady, a blonde, scrawny woman with an ugly, disagreeable air, and dressed in mourning. But he adopted a straightforwardly polite, even slightly offhand, manner towards Monsieur de Lachesnaye, who was fair-haired also and sickly-looking; for, in his eyes, this little man—an appeal judge already at the age of thirty-six, and decorated, thanks to his father-in-law's influence and the favours which his father, also a magistrate, was owed from his days on the inter-district committees—this little man epitomized the magistracy of patronage, of the rich, of mediocrities who took up their posts sure in the knowledge of swift promotion by virtue of their connections and their wealth, while he, a man without means, without protectors, found himself constantly having to grovel as the humble applicant before the ever-grinding wheel of professional advancement. Hence he was not at all averse to making this man feel, here in his chambers, the measure of his omnipotence, of the absolute power he wielded over each person's freedom, to the extent that with a single word he could turn a witness into the accused and, if the fancy so took him, proceed at once to his arrest.

'Madame,' he continued, 'you will forgive me for having to torment you again over this painful business. I know that you are just as anxious as I am to have the matter cleared up and see the guilty party pay for his crime.'

He signalled to his clerk, a tall, sallow youth with a bony face, and the interview began.

But from the first questions addressed to his wife, Monsieur de Lachesnaye—who had taken a seat upon realizing that he was not going to be invited to do so—insisted on answering in her stead. Soon he began venting all his bitterness about his father-in-law's will. Did he make himself quite clear? Bequests so numerous, so substantial that they amounted to nearly half the estate, an estate of three million seven hundred thousand francs! And mostly to people they didn't know, to women of every class! There was even one to a little woman who sold violets in a doorway in the Rue du Rocher. It simply would not do, and he was waiting for the criminal proceedings to be at an end before he endeavoured to determine if there might not be a way of overturning this immoral will.

While he was thus lamenting, through clenched teeth, and showing himself up for the fool he was, a stubborn and obsessive provincial sunk in avarice, Monsieur Denizet observed him with his large, clear, half-hooded eyes, and an expression of envious disdain played over his thin lips at the spectacle of this ineffectual man whom two million could not satisfy, and whom one day no doubt he would see elevated to the highest rank, thanks to all that money.

'I believe, Monsieur, that you would be making a mistake,' he said finally. 'The will could only be contested if the total sum of the bequests came to more than half the estate, and that is not the case.'

Then, turning to his clerk:

'Goodness, Laurent, you're not writing all this down, I trust.'

With a faint smile, the latter reassured him with the air of one who knew what was what.

'But I say, look here,' Monsieur de Lachesnaye continued more tartly, 'I sincerely hope people don't think I'm going to let the Roubauds have La Croix-de-Maufras. A gift of that kind to the daughter of a servant! And why, for what possible reason? In any case, if it's proved that they've been involved in a crime . . .'

Monsieur Denizet returned to the matter in hand.

'Really, so you think they might be?'

'Well, I ask you! If they knew about the will, it's evident that they had an interest in seeing our poor father dead . . . And don't forget, what's more, that they were the last to speak to him alive . . . I don't know, it all seems pretty fishy to me.'

Impatient at being sidetracked from his new theory, the magistrate turned to Berthe:

'And you, Madame, do you believe your former friend to be capable of such a crime?'

Before replying, she looked across at her husband. In the space of a few months of marriage the ill humour and coldness of each had communicated itself to the other and been thereby increased. They were bad for each other, it was he who had set her at odds with Séverine, to the point where now, in order to recover the house, she would willingly have had her arrested on the spot.

'Heavens, sir,' she said finally, 'the person to whom you refer had some very bad habits as a child.'

'What do you mean? Are you accusing her of behaving badly, at Doinville?'

'Oh no, sir, my father would not have continued to have her in the house!'

In this outburst could be heard the outraged prudishness of a respectable bourgeoise who would never have anything with which to reproach herself and for whom it was a point of honour to be one of the most unquestionably virtuous women in Rouen, somebody who was acknowledged and well received wherever she went.

'It's just', she continued, 'that when people fall into frivolous, loose ways . . . Well, sir, many things I could never have believed possible now seem certain fact to me.'

Once more Monsieur Denizet felt frustrated. He was no longer in the least interested in this line of enquiry, and whoever insisted on it became his adversary and seemed to him to be attacking the sureness of his judgement.

'But look here, we must think clearly about this,' he cried. 'People like the Roubauds don't go and kill someone like your father just to enter into their inheritance the sooner; or at the very least there would be signs of their haste, I would find other evidence of their determination to possess things, to enjoy the benefit of things. No, such a motive is insufficient, there would have to be something else, and there isn't, you yourselves haven't suggested any other motive . . . And then, think of the facts, don't you see what makes it materially impossible? No one saw the Roubauds get into the coupé, one station-worker even thinks he saw them return to their own compartment. And since they were certainly in it at Barentin, one would have to allow the possibility of a person's going from their carriage to the President's and back, with three other carriages in between, and all during the few minutes which that part of the journey takes, and with the train travelling at top speed. Is it likely? I have questioned drivers, I have questioned guards. They all told me that only someone thoroughly used to doing it would have the nerve and the strength necessary . . . The woman would not have been party to it in any case, the husband would have risked it without her; and why, to kill a benefactor who had just got them out of a difficult situation? No, no, absolutely not! The theory just doesn't stand up, we'll have to try something else . . . For instance, someone who boarded the train at Rouen and then got off again at the first station after that, someone who had recently threatened to kill the victim . . .'

In his excitement he was beginning to touch on his new theory, and he was on the point of giving too much away when the door opened slightly and the usher put his head round. But before the usher could say a word, a gloved hand pushed the door wide open; and a blonde lady entered the room, dressed in extremely elegant mourning, a woman still beautiful though now in her fifties, with the strong, opulent beauty of an ageing goddess.

'It is I, my dear magistrate. I am late, I do hope you will forgive me? The roads were quite impossible, the three leagues from Doinville to Rouen seemed like at least six today.'

Gallantly Monsieur Denizet had risen from his chair.

'Have you been keeping well, Madame, since last Sunday?'

'Yes, very well . . . and you, my dear sir, have you recovered from that fright my coachman gave you? The lad told me he nearly had you in the ditch when he was taking you home, and scarcely two kilometres into your journey.'

'Oh, a slight jolt, nothing more, I had almost forgotten about it . . . Please, do have a seat, Madame, and, as I was just saying to Madame de Lachesnaye, I do hope you will forgive me for adding to your grief with this dreadful business.'

'Heavens, if needs must . . . Good day, Berthe! Good day, Lachesnaye!'

It was Madame Bonnehon, the sister of the victim. She had embraced her niece and shaken hands with the husband. Widowed since the age of thirty, having been married to a factory-owner who had brought her a large fortune, and already very wealthy in her own right, the Doinville estate having been her portion of the inheritance which she had shared with her brother, she had led a pleasant life, full, so it was said, of moments of romance, but so respectable and apparently blameless that she had remained the arbiter of Rouen society. Opportunity and inclination had led her to bestow her love among the magistracy, and for twenty-five years now she had been receiving the legal profession at her château, a whole succession of people from the Palais de Justice fetched from Rouen in her own carriages and delivered home again in one long, never-ending party. Even now the fires still burned, since she was thought to harbour a certain maternal affection for a young deputy prosecutor, Monsieur Chaumette, the son of a judge in the Court of Appeal: she was doing what she could to secure the son's promotion, while showering the father with invitations and kindnesses. And she had also retained a good friend from former times, likewise a judge, a bachelor called Monsieur Desbazeilles, who was the literary ornament of the Rouen law courts and whose finely turned sonnets were widely quoted. For years he had had his own room at Doinville. Nowadays, even though he was over sixty, he still came regularly to dinner, as an old friend, his rheumatism now permitting him naught but fond memories. Thus she maintained her regal sway by her gracious goodness, despite the threat of advancing years, and no one thought to challenge it; she had only noted a possible pretender for the first time last winter, at Madame Leboucq's, the wife of another judge, a tall, dark-haired woman of thirty-four, really very handsome, and the magistracy were beginning to go there a great deal. In the midst of her habitual gaiety, this struck a note of melancholy.

'In that case if you will allow me, Madame,' Monsieur Denizet continued, 'I shall ask you a few questions.'

The interview with the Lachesnayes was over, but he did not dismiss them: his chambers, normally so cold and cheerless, were turning into a society drawing-room. The clerk, phlegmatic as ever, prepared once more to write.

'One witness has mentioned a telegram your brother received, summoning him immediately to Doinville . . . We have found no trace of this telegram. Might you have written to him, Madame?'

Madame Bonnehon, smiling, very much at ease, began to answer in the tone of voice befitting a friendly chat.

'I didn't write to my brother, I was expecting him, I knew he'd be coming some day or other, even though no particular date had been arranged. He usually did simply turn up, just like that, and almost always by the night train. As he was in the habit of staying in a small house tucked away in the grounds, next to a deserted lane, we never even used to hear him arrive. He would hire a cab at Barentin, and he wouldn't appear till the following day, often very late on, rather like someone who's been a neighbour for years and just happens to drop in . . . If I was expecting him this time, it was because he was to bring me ten thousand francs which he owed me. He would certainly have had the ten thousand francs on him. That's why I've always thought that somebody killed him to rob him, as simple as that.'

The magistrate allowed a short pause; then, looking her in the face:

'What do you think of Madame Roubaud and her husband?'

She protested sharply.

'Ah no, my dear Monsieur Denizet, you're not going to make the same mistake again about those fine people . . . Séverine was a good little girl, very gentle, very docile even, and pretty with it, which is no bad thing. I think, since you want me to repeat it, that she and her husband are incapable of doing anything bad.'

He was nodding, glancing in triumph towards Madame Lachesnaye. Thus provoked, she permitted herself to intervene.

'I must say, Aunt, you take rather a simple view.'

At that Madame Bonnehon spoke her mind, with her customary frankness.

'Enough, Berthe, we will never agree with each other on this . . . She was cheerful, and liked to laugh, and quite right too . . . I know perfectly well what you and your husband think.

But if the truth be told, it's your own self-interest that's muddling you in the head if you're so surprised at your father leaving La Croix-de-Maufras like that to dear Séverine . . . He had brought her up, had given her a dowry, it was perfectly natural for him to include her in his will. He did look on her somewhat as his own daughter, after all, didn't he?! . . . Ah, my dear, money counts for so little when it comes to being happy!'

She herself, as it happened, having always been very wealthy, had never failed to appear thoroughly unmercenary. Indeed it was one of her refinements as the woman beautiful and adored to affect to see love and beauty as the sole reasons for living.

'It was Roubaud who mentioned the telegram,' Monsieur de Lachesnaye observed drily. 'If there was no telegram, the President cannot have told him he received one. Why has Roubaud lied?'

'But', cried Monsieur Denizet in growing excitement, 'the President may very well have invented this telegram himself, to explain his sudden departure to the Roubauds. According to their own testimony, he was not due to leave until the next day; and as he found himself on the same train as they, he needed to have some reason or other if he was not to tell them his real reason, which in any case we none of us know . . . The telegram is of no importance, it doesn't lead anywhere.'

There was a further silence. When the magistrate resumed, he was very calm, very circumspect:

'And now, Madame, I come to a particularly delicate matter, and I must beg you to excuse the nature of my questions. No one respects the memory of your brother more than I . . . There were rumours, were there not? It was said that he had mistresses.'

Madame Bonnehon had begun to smile again, in her infinite tolerance.

'Oh, my dear sir, at his age! . . . My brother was widowed early on, and I never felt I had any right to find fault with what he considered acceptable. So he lived his life after his own fashion without the slightest interference from me. What I do know is that he kept up his position in society, and that right to the end he moved in the very best circles.'

Berthe, deeply embarrassed to hear her father's mistresses mentioned in front of her, had lowered her eyes; while her husband, no less discomforted than she, had gone to stand by the window, his back towards them.

'Forgive me if I insist,' said Monsieur Denizet. 'Was there not some business or other, to do with a personal maid, who worked for you?'

'Oh, yes, Louisette . . . But, my dear sir, she was a wicked little thing, carrying on with a hardened criminal at the age of fourteen. People tried to use her death against my brother. It's outrageous, I can tell you all about that.'

Doubtless she was in good faith. Although she had no illusions about the President's morals and had not been surprised by his tragic death, she felt the need to defend the family's high standing. Moreover, as for this unfortunate business with Louisette, if she believed him more than capable of having wanted the girl, she was equally convinced of the latter's precocious taste for debauch.

'Picture for yourself a young girl, oh, so tiny, so delicate, pink and fair like a little angel, and sweet too, so sweet and gentle, as if butter wouldn't melt in her mouth, she could have had heaven itself without saying so much as a word of confession . . . Well, she wasn't yet fourteen and there she was carrying on with a sort of brute, a quarryman by the name of Cabuche, who had just spent five years in prison, for killing a man in a tavern. This fellow lived like a savage, on the edge of the Bécourt forest: his father had died of misery and left him a hovel there made out of mud and tree trunks. He was determined to carry on working part of the abandoned quarries which, I gather, once supplied half the stone used to build Rouen. And off to his lair the young thing would go, to see her werewolf: the whole district was so frightened of him that he lived absolutely alone, as though the plague were on him. They were often seen together, roaming the woods, hand in hand, she so dainty, he a huge beast. Well, in short, all quite unbelievably wicked . . . Of course, I only learnt all this later. I had taken Louisette on almost out of charity, by way of a "good work". Her family, the Misards, whom I knew to be poor, carefully omitted to tell me how they had thrashed the child, not that they ever managed to stop her running off to

Cabuche the moment a door was left open . . . And that's when the accident happened. My brother never had any servants of his own when he was at Doinville. Louisette and another woman used to do the cleaning in the house where he stayed on his own. One morning after she had gone there alone, she disappeared. I simply thought that she'd been planning her escape for a long time and that her lover had waited for her and then made off with her . . . But the dreadful thing was that five days later a rumour went round that Louisette was dead, and there was talk of her having been assaulted, by my brother, in such monstrous circumstances that the child ran off in her panic to Cabuche and, so it was said, died of brain fever. But what did actually happen? There were so many versions of events going round that it's difficult to say. For my part I think that Louisette—who really did die of a fever, a doctor confirmed the fact—that she caught it while out on some foolish escapade or other, some night spent out in the open, wandering about the marshes . . . Don't you think so, my dear sir? You can't possibly see my brother tormenting this young girl, can you? It's disgusting, quite impossible.'

During this account Monsieur Denizet had listened attentively, neither approving nor disapproving. And Madame Bonnehon had some difficulty in knowing how to finish. Then, making up her mind:

'Heavens, I'm not saying that my brother might not have wanted to have his fun with her. He liked young people, he was a very light-hearted sort beneath that stern exterior. Well, let's say he kissed her.'

At this there was a moment's shocked outrage from the Lachesnayes.

'Oh, *come*, Aunt!'

She merely shrugged: why lie before the law?

'So he kissed her, tickled her perhaps. There's no crime in that . . . And if I'm prepared to allow even this much, it's only because it can't have been the quarryman who made up such a tale. It must have been Louisette who lied, the little baggage, perhaps exaggerating things so that her lover would look after her, with the result that he—as I said, no better than a brute—ended up honestly believing that "they" had gone and killed his mistress for him . . . He really was wild with rage, he went round all the taverns repeatedly saying that if he got his hands on the President, he would bleed him to death like a pig . . .'

The magistrate, silent until then, interrupted her sharply:

'He said that? There are witnesses who will testify to the fact?'

'Oh, my dear sir, you will find as many as you please . . . Well, well, a very sorry business it has been, we have had a lot to put up with. Fortunately my brother's position placed him quite above suspicion.'

Madame Bonnehon had just realized what new line of enquiry Monsieur Denizet was pursuing; and it rather worried her, she preferred not to get further involved by asking him any questions herself. He had risen to his feet, saying that he did not wish a moment longer to abuse a grieving family's readiness to co-operate. At his behest the clerk read out the transcripts of the interviews, which the witnesses were then required to sign. The transcripts were of impeccable propriety, so expertly weeded of redundant and compromising words that Madame Bonnehon, pen poised, cast a glance of benevolent surprise in the direction of this Laurent fellow, so pale and skinny, whom she had not previously observed.

Then, as the magistrate was accompanying her to the door with her nephew and niece, she took both his hands in hers.

'Until we meet again soon, then? You are always welcome at Doinville, you know . . . And thank you, you are one of the last of my faithful.'

Her smile had clouded with melancholy, while her niece, who had preceded her out of the room, had departed coldly, with the merest tilt of the head by way of salutation.

Alone, Monsieur Denizet drew breath for a moment. He now stood there thinking. In his view, things were becoming clear, there had certainly been the use of force on Grandmorin's part, his reputation was well known. That made the investigation a delicate matter, and he promised himself to be even more cautious in future, until he received the expected instructions from the Ministry. But he was no less exultant. At last he had the criminal in his grasp.

Resuming his place, in front of the desk, he rang for the clerk.

'Show the man Jacques Lantier in.'

Out in the corridor the Roubauds still sat waiting on the bench, expressionless, as though patience had sent them to sleep, their blank faces ruffled only by an occasional nervous twitch. The clerk's voice calling for Jacques seemed to rouse them, and they gave a slight shudder. Their wide eyes followed him as he disappeared in to see the magistrate. Then they fell once more to waiting, pale still, and silent.

For the past three weeks this whole business had been haunting Jacques, making him uneasy, as if somehow it could all go against him. That made no sense, for he had nothing with which to reproach himself, not even the failure to speak up; and yet he could not help entering the magistrate's room without that little shiver of the guilty man who is afraid to find his crime discovered; and he parried the questions, watched his tongue, for fear of saying too much. He, too, could have killed: could people not see that in his eyes? He hated nothing more than being summoned as a witness like this, he felt a kind of anger, whereas all he wanted, as he kept saying, was for people to stop bothering him, especially about things that were no concern of his.

On this particular occasion, in fact, Monsieur Denizet was solely concerned with the description of the murderer. Jacques, being the only witness to have seen him, was alone able to give precise information about him. But he stuck to his first statement, he repeated that his glimpse of the murder had lasted scarcely a second, an image so rapid that it remained in his memory as though without shape, an abstraction. Just one man cutting another man's throat, nothing more. For half an hour the magistrate pursued him, slowly, obstinately, asking him the same question in every conceivable different way: was he tall? was he short? did he have a beard? was his hair long or short? what sort of clothes was he wearing? to what class did the man appear to belong? And Jacques, unsettled, kept giving non-committal answers.

'Look here,' Monsieur Denizet enquired abruptly, staring him straight in the face, 'would you recognize him if you saw him again?'

Jacques's eyelids quivered slightly, and he was filled with anxiety at this gaze boring into his skull. His conscious mind posed itself the question out loud.

'Recognize him? . . . Yes . . . maybe.'

But already his curious fear of some unconscious complicity made him revert to his systematic evasiveness.

'Except no, I don't think so, I could never be definite. Just think! At eighty kilometres an hour!'

Gesturing in defeat, the magistrate was going to show him into the adjoining room, to have him available, when he had second thoughts.

'Wait, sit down.'

And ringing once more for the clerk:

'Show Monsieur and Madame Roubaud in.'

Seeing Jacques as they entered, their eyes clouded with uncertainty and disquiet. Had he said something? Was he being kept to confront them? All their self-assurance vanished, just to feel his presence there; and their voices were somewhat muted as they replied to the initial questions. But the magistrate had simply gone over their first interview again, all they had to do was to repeat the same phrases, almost word for word, while he listened to them, head down, without so much as looking at them.

Then, suddenly, he turned towards Séverine.

'Madame, you told the superintendent—I have his report here—that in your opinion a man got into the coupé at Rouen, just as the train was leaving.'

She was dumbfounded. Why was he bringing that up? Was this a trap? Was he going to compare her statements and watch her contradict herself? So she looked enquiringly at her husband, who carefully intervened.

'Sir, I don't think my wife was as definite as that.'

'No, I'm sorry . . . While you were suggesting it as a possibility, Madame said: "That's what happened, I'm certain" . . . Well, Madame, I want to know if you had particular reasons for saying that.'

She was now thoroughly nonplussed, convinced that if she didn't look out, he was going to lead her, answer by answer, to start confessing things. And yet she had to say something.

'So you didn't see the man, there's nothing you can tell us about him?'

'No, sir, no, nothing.'

Monsieur Denizet appeared to abandon this aspect of his enquiry. But he returned to it at once with Roubaud.

'And you, how is it you didn't see the man, if there really was one, because according to your own statement you were still talking to the victim when the whistle went for the train's departure?'

This insistence succeeded in terrifying the assistant station-master, who was anxiously wondering now whether to abandon the story about this man, or to stick to it. If they had evidence against him, this theory of there being an unknown murderer could hardly be sustained and could even make things worse for him. Biding his time till he could see his way clear, he answered with confused explanations, at length.

'It really is unfortunate', Monsieur Denizet went on, 'that your memory of events should be so hazy, because you would be in a position to help us dispel certain suspicions that have attached to various individuals.'

That seemed so direct to Roubaud that he felt the irresistible need to clear himself at once. He saw himself exposed, and his mind was made up in an instant.

'It's all a question of your conscience, isn't it? A fellow hesitates, you see, it's perfectly natural. If I was to tell you that I really do think I saw this man . . .'

The magistrate gestured in triumph, believing himself to owe this onset of plain speaking to his own skill. He had learnt from experience, he was used to saying, how strangely difficult certain witnesses find it to confess what they know; and he flattered himself that he could get such people to make a clean breast of things in spite of themselves.

'Come on, out with it . . . What's he like? Tall, short, about your height?'

'Oh no, no, much taller . . . At least that's how it seemed. Just a feeling, you know. I'm almost sure I brushed past him as I was running back to my carriage.'

'Just a moment,' said Monsieur Denizet.

And, turning towards Jacques, he asked him:

'The man you glimpsed with the knife in his hand, was he taller than Monsieur Roubaud?'

Jacques, beginning to grow impatient for fear he might not be able to drive the five o'clock train, raised his eyes and examined Roubaud; and it was as if he had never looked at him before, he was startled to see that the man was short, stoutly built, with a distinctive profile, which he had seen somewhere before, in a dream perhaps.

'No,' he murmured, 'not taller, about the same height.'

But the assistant station-master protested vigorously.

'Oh, much taller, a head taller at least.'

Jacques remained staring at him, wide-eyed; and beneath his gaze, in which he discerned a growing astonishment, Roubaud writhed as though trying to escape his own resemblance to himself; while his wife, her blood running cold, also followed the silent workings of memory now visible on the young man's face. Clearly he had been surprised at first to note certain similarities between Roubaud and the murderer; then he had had the sudden certainty that Roubaud was that murderer, as had been rumoured; and now he seemed completely at the mercy of the emotions caused by this discovery, his face agape, without it being possible to tell, without his even knowing himself, what he was going to do about it. If he said anything, the couple were doomed. Roubaud's eyes had met his, and they both looked at each other, into each other's souls. There was silence.

'So you disagree,' Monsieur Denizet continued. 'If he looked shorter to you, that's probably because he was bending over, when he was struggling with the victim.'

He too was looking at the two men. He had not thought of bringing the witnesses together to this end; but some professional instinct told him that here, now, at this moment, the truth was in the air. It even shook his confidence in the theory about Cabuche. Were the Lachesnayes right after all? Might it be, thoroughly implausible though it seemed, that the guilty parties were this honest railwayman and his sweet, young, gentle wife?

'Did the man wear a full beard, like you?' he asked Roubaud.

The latter found the strength to reply in a steady voice:

'A full beard, no, no. No beard at all, I think.'

Jacques realized that he would be asked the same question. What would he say? Because he himself could have sworn that the man had indeed worn a full beard. Well, these people were no concern of his, why not tell the truth? But as he looked away from the husband, his gaze encountered that of the wife; and in this gaze he discerned such an ardent plea, such a total surrender of her whole person, that he was completely overwhelmed. The old trembling took hold of him again: did he, then, love her? was this the woman that he might love, and love properly, without that monstrous desire to destroy? And at that moment, in strange counter-reaction to his turmoil, it seemed to him that his memory was becoming hazy, that he could no longer recognize the murderer in Roubaud. His vision of the scene blurred once more, and doubt set in, such that now he would mortally have repented of saying anything at all.

Monsieur Denizet put the question:

'Did the man have a full beard, like Monsieur Roubaud?'

And he answered in good faith:

'Sir, to tell you the truth, I can't say. Again, as I told you, it was all so fast. I just don't know, I just can't say for sure.'

But Monsieur Denizet persisted, because he wanted to have done with suspecting the assistant station-master. He pressed Roubaud, he pressed the driver, finally obtaining a full description from the former, how the man was tall, well-built, without a beard, dressed in a workman's smock, in short the complete opposite of himself in every particular: while from the latter he now drew no more than evasive monosyllables which lent weight to the other man's assertions. And the magistrate reverted to his initial conviction: he was on the right track, the picture that the witness was drawing of the murderer was turning out so accurate that every new detail added to his certainty. It was this couple, themselves unjustly suspected, who by their overwhelming evidence would bring the guilty man to execution.

'In here,' he said to the Roubauds and Jacques, as he ushered them into the adjoining room after they had signed their statements. 'And wait till I call you.'

Immediately he gave the order for the prisoner to be brought; and he was so pleased with the way things were going that in his good humour he went so far as to inform his clerk:

'Laurent, we've got him.'

But the door had opened, and two gendarmes had appeared, escorting a tall man in his late twenties. At a sign from the magistrate they withdrew, and Cabuche remained alone in the middle of the room, gaping wildly, bristling like some cornered beast. He was a strapping fellow, with a powerful neck and huge hands, fair-haired, with particularly white skin and very sparse beard, the merest trace of golden down, curled and silken. The massive face and low forehead bore witness to a violent being of limited intelligence, utterly given over to the sensations of the moment; but something like an instinctive need to be submissive and loving could be seen in his broad mouth and in the squarish nose which resembled that of some faithful hound. Brutally seized from his lair at break of dawn, dragged from the forest, and infuriated by accusations he did not understand, he had already assumed, with his torn smock and terrified demeanour, the shifty air of the accused man, that look of a cunning bandit which prison confers upon even the most upright of men. Night was falling, the room was dark, and he was fading into the shadows, when the usher brought in a large lamp, with a globe of clear glass, which lit up his face in its strong light. And there he stood, bareheaded, perfectly still.

Immediately Monsieur Denizet had fixed him with his large, clear eyes beneath their drooping lids. He said nothing. This was the moment of mute engagement, the preliminary trial of strength before the savage combat began, with its weapons of ruse and trap and moral torture. This was the guilty man, everything done to him was legitimate, his only remaining right was the right to confess his crime.

The interrogation began, very slowly.

'Do you know of what crime you stand accused?'

Cabuche, his voice thick with impotent fury, growled:

'No one's told me, but I can guess. There's been enough talk about it!'

'Did you know Monsieur Grandmorin?'

'Oh yes, I knew him all right, only too well!'

'A girl, Louisette, your mistress, entered service as a lady's maid to Madame Bonnehon.'

A surge of rage welled up in the quarryman. In his anger he saw red.

'God damn it, they're bloody liars, anyone who says that! Louisette was not my mistress!'

The magistrate had watched with curiosity as he lost his temper. Then, going off at a tangent:

'You are a very violent man. You were sentenced to five years in prison for killing a man, during a quarrel.'

Cabuche bowed his head. It was a source of shame to him, that sentence. He muttered:

'He hit me first . . . I only did four years, I was let off the other.'

'So,' Monsieur Denizet continued, 'you claim that Louisette was not your mistress?'

Again, he clenched his fists. Then, in a low, choked voice:

'Look here, she was just a young girl, not even fourteen, when I came home . . . Everyone was avoiding me then, they'd have stoned me if they could. But she would come up to me, in the forest where I always met her, she would talk to me, she was kind, oh, she was kind . . . So we became friends, just like that. When we went for a walk, we would hold each other by the hand. Oh, those were good times, good times! . . . Well, of course, she was growing up, and I did have thoughts about her that way. I can't say I didn't. I was, well, crazy, I loved her so much. She loved me a lot too, and it would have happened eventually, what you say, but then they took her away from me, and placed her in service at Doinville, at that lady's . . . Then, one evening, when I got back from the quarry, I found her outside my door, half out of her mind, in such a state she was, burning with fever. She hadn't dared go home to her parents, she had come to die in my house . . . Oh, God almighty, that pig! I should have gone and slit his throat there and then!'

The magistrate pursed his narrow lips in surprise at the sincere tone of the man. Clearly he would have to play a tight game here, he was up against stronger opposition than he had expected.

'Yes, I know all about that dreadful tale you and the girl made up. I would just have you know that everything about Monsieur Grandmorin, everything he ever did, placed him above your accusations.'

Distraught, eyes bulging, hands trembling, the quarryman spluttered:

'What do you mean, made up what? . . . It's the others are lying, and we're the ones who get accused of making things up!'

'But of course you did, stop playing the innocent . . . I've already questioned Misard, the man who's married to your mistress's mother. I shall confront the pair of you if I have to. You'll soon see what *he* thinks of your story . . . And mind how you answer me. We have witnesses, we know everything, so you'd do better to tell the truth.'

This was his usual tactic of intimidation, which he used even when he knew nothing and had no witnesses.

'So: do you publicly deny that you went round telling everyone you would cut Monsieur Grandmorin's throat?'

'Oh that, certainly I did! And I said it with all my heart, I can tell you, I was bloody itching to get my hands on him!'

Monsieur Denizet was brought up short with surprise, having expected a strategy of repeated denials. What! The accused was admitting he'd made threats. What was he up to? Afraid of rushing things, he collected himself for a moment, then stared hard at Cabuche as he sprang his question:

'What were you doing on the night of the 14th to the 15th February?'

'I went to bed when it got dark, about six o'clock . . . I wasn't feeling too good, and my cousin Louis even helped me out by taking a load of stones to Doinville.'

'Yes, your cousin was seen, with the cart, crossing the line at the level-crossing. But when questioned your cousin could only say one thing: that you left him round about noon and that he didn't see you again . . . Prove to me that you went to bed at six o'clock.'

'Come on, that's daft, I can't prove it. I live in a house cut off from everybody, at the edge of the forest . . . I was there, I'm telling you I was there, and that's all there is to it.'

Monsieur Denizet decided then to administer the *coup de grâce* of an incontrovertible statement of the facts. Every muscle in his face was locked fast by the tension of his will, while his mouth played the scene.

'Then I shall tell you what you were doing on the night of the fourteenth . . . At three o'clock you boarded the Rouen train at Barentin, for some reason which the enquiry has yet to determine. You were to return by the train from Paris which stops at Rouen at three minutes past nine; and you were standing among the crowd on the platform when you saw Monsieur Grandmorin, in his coupé. You note that I am fully prepared to concede that there was no question of ambushing him, that the idea of the crime only occurred to you at that moment . . . You got in during the general scrimmage to board, and waited until you were in the Malaunay tunnel; but you mistimed things, because the train was coming out of the tunnel just as you were doing the deed . . . And you threw the body off the train, and got off at Barentin, having also disposed of the travelling-rug . . . That is what you did.'

He had been studying Cabuche's pink face carefully for the merest flicker of a reaction, and was irritated when the latter, who had been very attentive at first, finally burst out laughing with a jovial guffaw.

'What's all that about? . . . If I'd done it, I'd say so.'

Then, quite calmly:

'I didn't do it, but I should have. God damn it, yes, I really wish I had.'

And Monsieur Denizet could get nothing else out of him. Vainly he went back over his questions, again and again returning to the same points but making different tactical approaches. No! still no! he was not the man. Cabuche just shrugged his shoulders, found the whole thing daft. When they had arrested him they had searched his hovel, but found neither the weapon, nor the ten banknotes, nor the watch; but they had confiscated a pair of trousers with a few bloodstains on it, an overwhelming piece of evidence. Once more, he had begun to laugh: a good one, that was, a rabbit he'd caught in a snare had bled all down his legs! And it was the magistrate, obsessed with his one theory about the crime, who was now getting out of his depth, the professional trying to be too subtle, complicating things, going past the plain and simple truth. This ignorant man, incapable of meeting him with cunning, but of invincible strength when he

said no and again no, was gradually driving him into a fury;
because he could not see him as anything but guilty, and each
new denial outraged him further, like some stubborn commit-
ment to savagery and mendacity. He would soon catch him out,
though, see if he didn't.

'So you deny it?'

'Of course I do, since it wasn't me that did it . . . If it had 'a
been, cor, I'd be that proud of it, I'd say so.'

Brusquely Monsieur Denizet rose from his desk and went
himself to open the door to the adjoining room. And then, when
he had called Jacques back in:

'Do you recognize this man?'

'Yes, I know him,' the driver answered in surprise, 'I've seen
him before, at the Misards'.'

'No, no . . . I mean, do you recognize him as the man in the
carriage, the murderer?'

All at once Jacques became wary again. In fact he
didn't recognize him. The other man had seemed shorter,
darker. He was about to say so when it occurred to him that
this would be committing himself too much. And he remained
evasive.

'I don't know, I can't say . . . I assure you, sir, I just can't say.'

Without further ado Monsieur Denizet summoned the
Roubauds in their turn. And he asked them the same question:

'Do you recognize this man?'

Cabuche was still smiling. Showing no signs of surprise, he
gave a little nod to Séverine, whom he had known as a young girl
when she lived at La Croix-de-Maufras. But she and her husband were startled to find him there. Now they understood: this
was the person they'd arrested, the one Jacques had mentioned,
the accused who'd been the reason for their all being questioned
again. And Roubaud was dumbfounded, aghast at this fellow's
resemblance to the description of the imaginary murderer, the
one he'd invented, the opposite of himself. It was such a complete coincidence, he was so thrown by it, that he hesitated to
reply.

'I said, do you recognize this man?'

'My God, sir, as I told you, it was just a feeling I had, somebody brushing against me in the crowd . . . Well, certainly this

man is tall like the other one, and fair-haired, and he doesn't have a beard . . .'

'Do you or do you not recognize him?'

The assistant station-master gasped for breath, trembling with the silent struggle going on inside him. The instinct for self-preservation prevailed.

'I can't say for certain. But it's close all right, very close.'

This time Cabuche began to swear. That was it, he'd been bothered enough over this stupid business. Since he hadn't done it, he wanted to go. And, with the blood rushing to his head, his fists began to fly, and he became so terrifying that the gendarmes were summoned to take him away. But at the sight of this violence, of this forward lunge of the threatened beast, Monsieur Denizet was triumphant. Now he was convinced, and he made no effort to hide the fact.

'Did you notice his eyes? I can always tell from their eyes . . . Oh, his number's up, he's all ours!'

The Roubauds stared at each other, not moving a muscle. What? Was that it, then? All over, saved, since the law now had the guilty man? They were still somewhat shaken, their conscience uneasy at the role they had been forced to play by the way things had turned out. But joy soon overtook them, sweeping away all scruple, and they were just standing there smiling at Jacques, relieved, desperate simply to get out into the fresh air, and waiting for the magistrate to let the three of them go, when the usher brought him in a letter.

Briskly Monsieur Denizet had seated himself at his desk again, to concentrate, oblivious of the three witnesses. It was the letter from the Ministry, the advice he should have had the patience to wait for before proceeding further with the enquiry. And what he read must have detracted from his triumph because his expression grew gradually colder as he resumed his habitual air of gloomy impassivity. At one point he looked up and glanced sideways at the Roubauds, as though a particular sentence had served to remind him of their existence. They, their short-lived joy at an end, and plunged once more into unease, felt as though they had been recaptured. Why on earth had he looked at them like that? Had someone in Paris found those three lines of handwriting, the stupid note that haunted and terrified

them? Séverine knew Monsieur Camy-Lamotte well, from having seen him many times at the President's house, and she knew
that he had been given the task of going through the dead man's
papers. One bitter regret was tormenting Roubaud, that he
hadn't thought of sending his wife to Paris: she could have called
on one or two useful people, at the very least she could have
secured the protection of the Secretary General in case the Company lost patience on account of all the nasty rumours and
decided to dismiss him. And neither of them could take their
eyes off the magistrate, feeling their anxiety increase with every
minute as they watched his face darken in evident consternation
at the contents of this letter, which had completely upset his
good day's work.

At length Monsieur Denizet put the letter down and sat for a
moment, deep in thought, his eyes fixed on the Roubauds and on
Jacques. Then, resigning himself, and as if talking out loud to
himself:

'Well, we'll see, we'll look at all this again . . . You may go.'

But as the three of them were leaving, he could not resist the
desire to know, to clear up the vital point which was ruining his
new theory, even though he had been advised to proceed no
further without prior agreement.

'No, you, wait a moment, I have one more question to put to
you.'

In the corridor the Roubauds paused. The doors were
open, and they were unable to leave: something was preventing
them, their anxiety about what was going on in the magistrate's
chambers, the physical impossibility of departing until they
had learnt from Jacques what new question he had been
asked. They turned round, and began to pace up and down,
their legs aching with exhaustion. Once more they found
themselves side by side on the bench upon which they had
already waited hour after hour; and there they sat, slumped in
heavy silence.

When the driver re-emerged, Roubaud rose stiffly to his feet.

'We were waiting for you, we can go back to the station
together . . . Well?'

But Jacques turned his head away, embarrassed, as if he
wanted to avoid Séverine's gaze which was fixed upon him.

'He doesn't know any more, he's floundering,' he said finally. 'Now he's asked me if there weren't two people involved? And because I told him in Le Havre about seeing a dark shape pressing on the old man's legs, he asked me about that . . . He himself seems to think it was only the rug. Then he sent for the rug, and I had to say what I thought . . . Heavens, yes, I don't know, maybe it was the rug.'

The Roubauds shuddered. They were on their track, one word from this fellow could sink them. He knew all right, and he'd end up talking. The three of them were leaving the Palais de Justice in silence, the woman walking between the two men, when the assistant station-master added, in the street:

'By the way, mate, my wife has to go to Paris for the day, on a business matter. It'd be very kind if you could look after her, if she needs anyone.'

CHAPTER V

A T quarter-past eleven, exactly on time, the signal-box at
the Pont de l'Europe gave its two regulation blasts on the hooter
to announce the arrival of the Le Havre express, which was
emerging from the Batignolles tunnel. Presently the turntables
shook, and the train entered the station with a short whistle, its
brakes grinding, smoke trailing, water streaming, soaked by a
driving rain which had not let up since Rouen.

The station-workers had not yet turned the handles on
the carriage doors when one of these opened and Séverine
jumped smartly down on to the platform, before the train had
come to a halt. Her carriage was at the end of the train, and she
had to hurry to reach the engine, through the sudden flood of
passengers issuing from their compartments amidst a flurry of
children and parcels. Jacques was there, standing on the footplate, waiting to return to the depot, while Pecqueux, cloth in
hand, was wiping the brasswork.

'Is that agreed, then?' she said, standing on tiptoe. 'I'll be in
the Rue Cardinet at three, and you'll be kind and introduce me
to your superior so that I can thank him.'

Such was the pretext dreamed up by Roubaud, to thank the
manager of the Batignolles depot for some favour or other. This
way she could be entrusted to the friendly offices of the driver,
and she would be able to strengthen the bonds between them, to
work on him.

But Jacques, black with soot, drenched and exhausted from
his struggle with the wind and the rain, simply looked at her with
hard eyes and said nothing. He had not been able to refuse her
husband as they were leaving Le Havre; and he was disturbed at
the prospect of finding himself alone with her, for now he could
feel how much he desired her.

'All right?' she insisted, smiling with that sweet, tender look of
hers, despite the surprise and slight repugnance which she felt at
finding him so dirty, indeed scarcely recognizable. 'All right? I'm
counting on you.'

As she tried to raise herself further, placing her gloved hand on an iron handle, Pecqueux warned her obligingly:

'Careful, you'll get yourself dirty.'

Then Jacques had to reply, and gruffly did so:

'Yes, Rue Cardinet . . . Providing this damned rain doesn't wash me away. What filthy weather!'

Her heart went out to him in his pitiful condition, and she added, as if he had suffered for her alone:

'Goodness, look at the state of you, and while I was all tucked up in the warm . . . I thought about you, you know. It made me really cross, seeing all this rain . . . I was so glad to think it was you bringing me this morning, and taking me home this evening, on the express.'

But this note of kindness and intimacy, of such tender concern, seemed only to upset him the more. He appeared relieved when a voice cried out: 'Back up.'

Promptly his hand went up to pull the whistle, while the fireman gestured to the young woman to stand aside.

'See you at three!'

'Yes, at three.'

And as the engine set off once more, Séverine left the platform, the last to depart. Once outside in the Rue d'Amsterdam and about to open her umbrella, she was pleased to see that it was no longer raining. She walked down to the Place du Havre, thought for a moment, and finally decided that she would do better to have lunch at once. It was twenty-five past eleven, and she entered a cheap restaurant at the corner of the Rue Saint-Lazare, where she ordered fried eggs and a chop. Then, eating very slowly, she fell once more to thinking the thoughts which had been haunting her for weeks, her face pale and troubled, the biddable smile of seduction quite vanished.

It had been on the previous evening, two days after their interrogation at Rouen, that Roubaud had come to the conclusion it was dangerous to wait any longer and had decided to send her to see Monsieur Camy-Lamotte, not at the Ministry but at his home in the Rue du Rocher, where he lived in a large townhouse which happened to be right next door to Grandmorin's. She knew she would find him in at one o'clock, and she was in no hurry; she was preparing what she was going to say to him, trying to anticipate how he would reply so that nothing should fluster her. The previous evening, a new source of anxiety had just served to speed her on her way: they had learnt through station gossip that Madame Lebleu and Philomène were going round saying that the Company was about to dismiss Roubaud for bringing its name into disrepute; and the worst of it was that Monsieur Dabadie, when asked directly, had not said no, which lent considerable weight to the rumour. In these circumstances it became a matter of urgency that she should hurry to Paris to plead their cause and especially to request protection from this powerful figure, just as they had from Grandmorin. But behind this request, which at the very least would serve to explain her visit, lay a more pressing motive, the keen and irresistible need to know, that need which makes the criminal give himself up rather than remain in the dark. The uncertainty was killing them, and they felt particularly exposed ever since Jacques had told them of police suspicions about a second person being involved in the murder. They speculated endlessly: what if the letter were found, what if the true facts were established? They expected at any moment to be searched, arrested; and their torment had now reached the point where the slightest incident in their immediate vicinity seemed to assume an air of such terrible menace that they ended up wishing that disaster would strike rather than have to live with this endless series of alarms. Certainty, and an end to suffering!

Séverine finished her chop, still so absorbed in her thoughts that she came to with a start, astonished to find herself in this place. Everything was beginning to taste bitter, she could not swallow properly, and she did not even feel like a coffee. But though she had tried to eat slowly, it was still barely a quarter past twelve when she left the restaurant. Another three-quarters of an hour to kill! She who adored Paris, who so loved walking its pavements, wherever she fancied, on the rare occasions when she came, now felt lost, fearful, impatient to be done with it and then to hide herself away. The pavements were already drying, and a warm wind was sweeping away the last of the clouds. She walked down the Rue Tronchet, and found herself in the flower-market by the Madeleine, one of those March markets blooming with primulas and azaleas in the pale light of fading winter. For half an hour she walked about in this hastening spring, once more filled with vague musings, and thinking of Jacques as of an enemy whom she had to disarm. It was almost as if her visit to the Rue du Rocher were over, as if that side of things were taken care of, and that all that remained was to ensure this fellow's silence; which was a complicated matter, she could not see her way clear at all, with her head full of outlandish schemes. But such thoughts caused her no feeling of strain, no sense of fear, just a gentle, soothing calm. Then suddenly she saw the time, on a kiosk clock: ten past one. Her errand was not yet done, and she was overtaken once more by an anguished awareness of reality as she hurried back in the direction of the Rue du Rocher.

Monsieur Camy-Lamotte's house stood at the corner of this street and the Rue de Naples; and Séverine had to walk past the Grandmorin residence, which stood silent and empty, its shutters closed. She looked up and quickened her step. The memory of her last visit had returned; the great house loomed before her, terrifying. And just as she turned, some yards further on, to look back, like a person pursued by a vociferous crowd, she caught sight, on the opposite pavement, of Monsieur Denizet, the examining magistrate at Rouen, who was also walking up the street. It came as a shock. Had he noticed her glancing up at the house? But he kept on at a steady pace, and she allowed him to overtake her and then, in great consternation, followed him. It came as a further shock when she saw him stop at the corner of the Rue de Naples and ring the bell at Monsieur Camy-Lamotte's house.

She was panic-stricken. She would never dare go in there now. She turned back and cut down the Rue d'Édimbourg as far as the Pont de l'Europe at the end. Only then did she feel safe. At a loss now, not knowing what to do or where to go, she stood by one of the railings, looking down through the metal girders at the vast railway yard and the ceaseless comings and goings of the trains. Her startled eyes followed their movements, as she thought to herself that the magistrate must surely have come about the enquiry, and that the two men were in there talking about her, that her fate was, at that very moment, being decided. And then, overcome by despair, she felt the strong urge, rather than return to the Rue de Rocher, to throw herself under a train forthwith. There was one just emerging from under the roof of the mainline station, and she watched it approach and pass beneath her, puffing a warm swirl of white steam up into her face. Then the foolish pointlessness of her journey and the dreadful state of anxiety in which she would have to return home, were she to lack the resolve to go and find out for certain, struck her with such force that she gave herself five minutes in which to recover her courage. Locomotives were whistling, and she followed the progress of one of them, a small engine which was moving a local train on to a siding; and then, happening to glance up to the left, she recognized, way above the parcels yard, right at the top of the building in the Impasse d'Amsterdam, the window of Mère Victoire's flat, the window where she saw herself again leaning out next to her husband, before that dreadful scene which had been the cause of their misfortune. This served to remind her of the danger of their situation with such a sharp stab of anguish that suddenly she felt ready for anything, anything to have done with it. She was deafened by the noise of hooters and the long, thunderous rumble of trains, while thick clouds of smoke blotted out the horizon, rolling away over the clear, broad sky of Paris. And off she set once more in the direction of the Rue du Rocher, proceeding there as though engaged upon an act of self-destruction, and quickening her pace for sudden fear that there might be no one in.

When Séverine had pulled the bell, she froze once more with terror. But already a footman was bidding her be seated in an anteroom, having first asked for her name. And through the doors which were slightly ajar, she distinctly heard two voices in animated conversation. Silence had fallen again, deep and unbroken. All she could hear now was a dull thumping in her temples, and she told herself that the magistrate was still in conference, that she would no doubt be kept waiting for a long time; and this waiting was becoming unbearable. Then suddenly, to her surprise, the footman was calling her and ushering her in. Quite certainly the magistrate had not left. She could feel his presence, concealed behind a door.

It was a large study, with black furniture, a thick carpet, and heavy door-curtains, an austere room so hermetically sealed that not a single noise could be heard from outside. Yet there were flowers, some pale roses in a basket of bronze. And this pointed to a certain graciousness, a taste for the good life, behind all the severity. The master of the house was standing there, very properly buttoned into a frock-coat of equal austerity, his thin face broadened slightly by greying sideburns, but with the elegance of a former lady's man, his figure still slim, and hinting at a genial distinction beneath the studied formality of his official mien. In the half-light of the room, he looked particularly tall.

On entering, Séverine was overwhelmed by the stuffiness, the airless, curtained warmth of the room; all she saw was Monsieur Camy-Lamotte, who stood observing her approach. He did not indicate that she might sit down, and made a point of not being the first to speak, waiting for her to explain the reason for her visit. This prolonged the silence; and then, in an abrupt reversal of feeling, she suddenly recovered her self-possession in the face of danger, and became very calm, very circumspect.

'Monsieur,' she said, 'please forgive my boldness in reminding you of my presence and in coming to impose on your good will in this way. You are aware of the irreparable loss which I have suffered, and in my present abandoned state I dared to think of you as one who might defend us, who might continue to protect us a little, as your friend did, my much lamented protector.'

Monsieur Camy-Lamotte then had no alternative but to bid her be seated, for this was perfectly said, without any exaggeration of humility or grief, with all the inborn art of feminine hypocrisy. But he continued to say nothing, and himself had now sat down, still waiting. She continued, perceiving that she would have to be more precise.

'Permit me to refresh your memory by recalling that I had the honour of meeting you at Doinville. Ah, those were happy days for me! Now, the bad times have come, and I have only you, Monsieur. I beseech you in the name of the deceased. You who loved him, finish his good work, be to me as he was.'

He was listening to her, watching her, and all his suspicions were set at nought, so natural did she appear, so charming in her regrets and her supplication. It had seemed to him that the note which he had found among Grandmorin's papers, those few unsigned lines, could only have come from her, for he knew how

obliging she had been towards the President; and a moment ago
the announcement of her visit had been enough to convince
him. He had just interrupted his conversation with the
magistrate for the sole purpose of confirming his conviction. But
could one believe her guilty, seeing her like this, so calm and
gentle?

He wanted to be quite clear in his mind, and so, still maintaining his severe manner:

'Please elaborate, Madame . . . I remember perfectly. I ask for
nothing better than to be of service to you, if I can.'

And so, quite plainly, Séverine related how her husband had
been threatened with dismissal. People were jealous of him,
because he was good at his job and because of the protection he
had hitherto enjoyed in high places. Now that they thought him
defenceless, they hoped to triumph, and were redoubling their
efforts to do so. Not that she was going to mention any names;
she could still mind her words, despite the imminence of the
danger. If she had decided to come to Paris like this, it was only
because she was totally convinced of the need to act as quickly as
possible. Tomorrow might be too late: she was asking for help
here and now. And all this with such an abundance of good
reasons and logical facts that it seemed indeed impossible
that she could have come all this way with any other purpose in
mind.

Monsieur Camy-Lamotte was studying her intently, down to
the tiny, imperceptible twitching of her lips; and then he fired
his first shot:

'But why on earth would the Company dismiss your husband?
It has no serious charge to lay against him.'

She kept her eyes on him too, trying to catch the slightest
crease in his expression, wondering if he had found the letter;
and, despite the innocuousness of the question, she had the
sudden conviction that the letter was here, in this room, lying in
a drawer: he knew, for he was setting a trap for her, wanting to
know if she would dare speak about the real reasons for the
dismissal. Besides, he had spoken too emphatically, and she had
felt herself being scrutinized to the depths of her soul by the
man's pale, weary eyes.

Bravely she marched towards the guns.

'Good heavens, Monsieur, it is perfectly monstrous, but we were suspected of having killed our benefactor, because of his wretched will. We had no trouble proving our innocence, only something always sticks when people make abominable accusations like that, and no doubt the Company is afraid of any scandal.'

Once more he was surprised, disarmed, by this frankness, and especially by the sincere tone in which it was said. Moreover, having at first thought her rather ordinary-looking, he was beginning to find her extremely attractive, with that willing, submissive look in her blue eyes, beneath the black tumult of her hair. And he was thinking of his friend Grandmorin, seized with jealous admiration: how the devil had that fellow, ten years his senior, managed to have such creatures until his dying day, when he himself had already had to renounce such playthings if he was not to forfeit the remainder of his vital energy? She was really most charming, quite exquisite, and he permitted himself the smile of a now disinterested amateur, adding it to his cool manner and grand air of a functionary who finds himself with such a tiresome business on his hands.

But Séverine, out of feminine bravado, sensing her power, made the mistake of adding:

'People like us don't kill for money. There would have to have been another motive, and there wasn't.'

He observed her, saw the corners of her mouth quiver. It was her. From that moment his conviction was total. And she herself understood at once that she had given herself away, from the way he had stopped smiling, his chin now tensely pinched. She felt herself inwardly collapse, as if her whole being were draining from her. Nevertheless she remained upright in her chair, and heard his voice continue conversing in the same even tone, saying all the things that required to be said. The conversation proceeded, but from that point on neither of them had anything to learn; and in words of no consequence each was talking about what neither of them would say explicitly. He had the letter, it was she who had written it. That much was evident, even from their silences.

'Madame,' he said finally, 'I'm not refusing to intervene with the Company, if your case really does merit attention. As it happens, I'm expecting the managing director this evening, on another matter . . . Only, I shall need some details. I tell you what, why don't you write down your husband's name, his age, his previous positions, in fact anything that might give me a clearer picture of your situation.'

And he placed a little side-table in front of her, averting his eyes so as not to unnerve her unduly. She had shuddered: he wanted a sample of her handwriting, in order to compare it with the letter. For a moment she tried desperately to think of an excuse, determined not to write anything. Then she reflected: where was the use, since he already knew? They'd always be able to get their hands on some of her handwriting. Apparently un-concerned, and in the most casual manner imaginable, she wrote down what he had requested; while he, standing behind her, recognized the writing perfectly, which was a little less sloping and less shaky than that on the note. And in the end he thought her rather brave, this slip of a thing: again he smiled, now that she could not see him, with the smile of a man whom female charms alone could still reach in the midst of his worldly-wise indifference to all things. Ultimately nothing was worth the effort of being just. All that concerned him was the public face of the regime he served.

'There we are, Madame. You give me that, and I shall make enquiries, I shall do what I can for the best.'

'I am most grateful to you, Monsieur . . . So you will make sure that my husband is kept on? I may consider the matter settled?'

'Oh, come, no, I am not committing myself to anything . . . I must see first, I must think things over.'

He was, in fact, in two minds: he did not know how he was going to proceed as regards this couple. And she had but one remaining cause for anxiety, now that she felt herself to be at his mercy: this hesitation of his, the alternative of being saved or ruined by him, without being able to divine the reasons which would decide him.

'Oh, Monsieur, think what torture it is for us. You can't let me leave without setting my mind at rest.'

'Oh, my goodness, indeed I can, Madame. There is nothing for it. You will just have to wait and see.'

He edged her towards the door. She was about to leave, in despair, in disarray, and was almost ready to admit everything out loud, so immediately did she feel the need to force him to say plainly what he intended to do with them. In order to remain a moment longer, and hoping to find a way round him, she exclaimed:

'I was forgetting, I wanted to ask your advice, about this wretched will . . . Do you think we ought to refuse the legacy?'

'The law is on your side,' he answered guardedly. 'It's all a matter of interpretation and the circumstances.'

Standing in the doorway, she made one last attempt.

'Monsieur, I beg you, please don't let me leave like this, tell me if I may hope.'

In a gesture of self-abandonment she had taken hold of his hand. He withdrew it. But she was looking at him with her beautiful eyes, gazing in such ardent supplication that he was moved.

'Well, then, come back at five o'clock. Perhaps I shall have some news for you then.'

She departed, and left his house more worried than when she had arrived. The situation had become clearer now, and her fate hung in the balance, under threat of an arrest which could come perhaps at any moment. How was she to get through till five o'clock? The thought of Jacques, whom she had quite forgotten about, occurred to her all at once: someone else who could destroy her, if she were arrested! Although it was scarcely half-past two, she hurried back up the Rue du Rocher, in the direction of the Rue Cardinet.

Monsieur Camy-Lamotte, left to himself, had stopped in front of his desk. As a regular visitor to the Tuileries, where his post as Secretary General at the Ministry of Justice caused him to be summoned almost daily, and as a person with just as much power as the Minister himself, and who was even employed in preference to him on more intimate matters, he knew how much this Grandmorin affair was causing irritation and disquiet in high places. The opposition newspapers were continuing to conduct a noisy campaign, with some accusing the police of being so busy with political surveillance that they no longer had the time to arrest any murderers, while others were investigating the

President's way of life, intimating that he moved in court circles, which was a milieu of the vilest debauch; and this campaign was beginning to have disastrous effects as election day approached. Accordingly the Secretary General had been notified of a categoric wish to have done with the affair as quickly as possible, no matter what it took. The Minister having delegated this delicate business to him, he found himself solely responsible for the decision to be taken, albeit on the Minister's authority; and this required some thought, for he did not doubt that he would be made the scapegoat for everyone else if he proved clumsy in his handling of the case.

Still deep in thought, Monsieur Camy-Lamotte walked over and opened the door to the adjoining room, in which Monsieur Denizet was waiting. And he, who had been listening, exclaimed as he came back in:

'I told you we were wrong to suspect those two . . . It's quite obvious all that woman cares about is saving her husband from possible dismissal. Not one word she said could lead one to suspect her.'

The Secretary General did not reply at once. Preoccupied, his gaze fixed on the examining magistrate, and struck by his heavy face and thin lips, he was reflecting on this magistracy to which, as unseen chief of personnel, he had the power to appoint, and he was surprised at how worthy it remained despite the modest stipends, and how intelligent, too, despite the torpor of professional routine. But, well, this fellow here, no matter how subtle he thought himself, with his heavy eyelids and half-hidden gaze, he could be passionately stubborn when he thought he was on to the truth.

'So', Monsieur Camy-Lamotte resumed, 'you persist in the belief that this Cabuche person is the guilty party?'

Monsieur Denizet started in surprise.

'Oh, certainly! . . . Everything points to him. I've already set out the evidence for you, and it all adds up—if I may say so—to a classic case. Not one piece is missing . . . I checked carefully whether he had an accomplice, if a woman was with him in the coupé, as you suggested. That seemed to fit with the testimony of a driver, a man who glimpsed the murder taking place; but thanks to some skilful questioning on my part, the man did not persist in his original statement, and he even identified the travelling-rug as being the dark shape he had mentioned . . . Oh, yes, no doubt about it, Cabuche is the guilty party all right, and all the more so because if we don't have him we have no one.'

Up until this moment the Secretary General had been biding his time before informing him of the written evidence at present in his possession; and now that he himself knew for certain, he was in less of a hurry to establish the truth. Why destroy the false trail upon which the enquiry was proceeding if the right one would lead to greater problems? He would have to weigh things up first.

'Heavens!' he went on with his world-weary smile, 'I'm perfectly prepared to accept that you're on the right track . . . I just wanted to see you about one or two rather serious aspects of the matter, that's all. This is an unusual case, and now it has become thoroughly political—as you yourself are aware, are you not? So we shall perhaps find ourselves obliged to act as men of government . . . Look here, between ourselves, from the enquiries you've made, that girl, Cabuche's mistress, she was raped, wasn't she?'

The magistrate pursed his lips in the manner of a subtle man, and his eyes half-disappeared behind his eyelids.

'Well, I think she was in a bad way when the President had finished with her, I'm afraid, and the whole thing's bound to come out at the trial . . . What's more, if the defending counsel turns out to be a supporter of the opposition, one can expect a whole catalogue of embarrassing stories to be trotted out. For there's no shortage of those in our part of the world.'

This Denizet was not so stupid when he departed from routine and stopped believing himself to be seated upon the absolute throne of his own perspicacity and omnipotence. He had understood why he had been summoned not to the Ministry of Justice but to the private residence of the Secretary General.

'In short,' the magistrate concluded, seeing that the latter appeared to have no qualms, 'we shall have a messy business on our hands.'

Monsieur Camy-Lamotte simply nodded. He was in the process of calculating the consequences of the other trial, that of the Roubauds. It was absolutely certain that if the husband appeared in court, he would tell everything—about his wife who had also been abused as a young girl, and about the subsequent adultery, and about the jealous rage which must have driven him to murder: not to mention the fact they would no longer be dealing with a serving-girl and a man with a criminal record, and that this railwayman, married to this pretty woman, was going to impugn a whole section of the bourgeoisie and the railway industry. And then, did one ever quite know where one was with a man like the President? Perhaps they would turn up unforeseen horrors? No, decidedly, the case against the Roubauds, against the people who were really guilty, was an even messier business. That was absolutely plain, and he dismissed the possibility, once and for all. If he had to choose one, he would be inclined to prefer that they pursue the case against the innocent Cabuche.

'I bow to your view of the matter,' he told Monsieur Denizet finally. 'There is indeed strong circumstantial evidence against the quarryman, if he had reason to seek legitimate revenge . . . But what a sorry tale, my goodness, and what muck will have to be raked! . . . I know that justice is supposed to remain indifferent to the consequences, and that, being above particular interests . . .'

He gestured an ending to his unfinished sentence, as the magistrate, whose turn it was to be silent, glumly awaited the orders which he could sense were coming. Now that there was acceptance of his version of the truth, of this product of his own intelligence, he was quite ready to sacrifice the idea of justice to the demands of government. But the Secretary General, despite his usual adroitness in this sort of transaction, began to rush things, to speak too quickly, in the manner of one who is used to being obeyed.

'Well, in a word, they want the case thrown out . . . See that the file's closed on it, will you?'

'I beg your pardon, Monsieur,' declared Monsieur Denizet, 'it is no longer up to me to decide such a thing, it is a matter for my conscience.'

At once Monsieur Camy-Lamotte smiled, his old, polite self again, and with that knowing, courteous air which suggested that he cared not a fig for anything.

'Of course it is. And it is to your conscience that I am speaking. I leave you to take the decision which it shall determine upon, sure as I am that you will weigh the pros and cons fairly, with an eye to the best interests of sound principle and public morality ... You yourself know, and better than I do, that it is sometimes a more heroic course to accept a lesser evil rather than to incur a greater one ... In short, an appeal is being made to you in your capacity as a solid citizen, to you as a man of integrity. No one is talking about infringing your independence, and that's why I repeat that you are absolute master in this affair, just as the law requires indeed that you should be.'

Jealous of this unlimited power, especially now that he was on the point of abusing it, the magistrate welcomed each of these statements with a nod of satisfaction.

'What is more,' the other man continued in a yet smoother tone, which was beginning to sound ironic in its exaggeration, 'we know whom we are dealing with. We have been following your efforts for some considerable time now, and I am able to tell you that we would appoint you here in Paris at once if a vacancy were to present itself.'

Monsieur Denizet started. What? If he did as he was asked, they weren't immediately going to fulfil his great ambition, his dream of a place on the Paris bench? But already Monsieur Camy-Lamotte was adding, having understood:

'The position has been identified, it is merely a question of time ... But, well, since I have already been indiscreet, I am happy to tell you that your name has been put forward for the Legion of Honour, on the 15th of August next.'

For a moment the magistrate reflected. He would have preferred the promotion, for by his calculations that would have meant an increase in his salary of about one hundred and sixty francs a month; and in the genteel poverty in which he lived, that meant a more comfortable existence, new clothes for himself, Mélanie his maid better fed and less querulous. But the cross of the Legion of Honour, that was something worth having. Also, he had received a promise. And this man who would never before have thought of selling himself, brought up as he had been to the tradition of an honest and unsung magistracy, now found himself instantly yielding to a mere prospect, to this vague undertaking by his superiors that they would look favourably on him. The judiciary function had simply become a job like any other, and he was dragging the ball and chain of professional advancement along with him, a famished solicitant ever ready to bend the knee to the commands of the powers that be.

'I am very touched,' he murmured, 'please tell the Minister so.'

He had risen to his feet, sensing that anything either of them might now add would only cause embarrassment.

'So,' he concluded, his eyes expressionless, his face impassive, 'I shall bring my enquiry to a conclusion having due regard to your misgivings. Naturally, if we do not have absolutely conclusive proof against this Cabuche fellow, it will be wiser not to risk the pointless scandal a trial might bring . . . We shall release him and continue to keep him under surveillance.'

Standing in the doorway, the Secretary General remained thoroughly amiable to the last.

'Monsieur Denizet, we are counting absolutely on your great discretion and on your high standards of integrity!'

When he found himself alone once more, Monsieur Camy-Lamotte decided out of a curiosity that was now of course pointless to compare the page of Séverine's handwriting with the unsigned note which he had discovered in President Grandmorin's papers. The similarity was total. He folded the letter and carefully locked it away, for, even if he hadn't breathed a word of its existence to the magistrate, he considered that such a piece of ammunition was well worth keeping. And as he dwelt in his mind's eye on the profile of that little woman, so frail and yet so strong in her taut resistance, he gave his usual shrug of indulgent mockery. Ah, those creatures, when they want something!

Séverine, at twenty minutes to three, had reached the Rue Cardinet too early for the appointment she had made with Jacques. This was where he lived, at the top of a tall building, in a narrow room to which he seldom went except at night to sleep; and even then he was absent twice a week, the two nights he spent at Le Havre between the evening express and the morning express. That day, however, soaked to the skin and completely exhausted, he had gone to his room and thrown himself on to the bed. With the result that Séverine might have waited for him in vain, if he had not been woken by a domestic quarrel next door, a man beating his screaming wife. He had washed and dressed in a thoroughly bad humour, after seeing her waiting below on the pavement when he looked out of his attic window.

'There you are, at last!' she cried, when she saw him coming out of the main entrance. 'I thought I must have made a mistake . . . You did say the corner of the Rue Saussure . . .'

And without waiting for a reply, she looked up at the building: 'So this is where you live, then?'

Without saying so, he had arranged for them to meet like this outside his own door because the depot to which he was to accompany her was just opposite. But her question embarrassed him, he could imagine her imposing on their acquaintanceship and asking to see his room. It was so sparsely furnished and so untidy he was ashamed of it.

'Oh, I don't live there, I'm just a bird of passage,' he replied. 'We'd better hurry, I'm worried the manager may already have left.'

And indeed, when they called at the little house where he lived, behind the depot, inside the station perimeter, they found that he was out; and they went from shed to shed only to be told each time that they should come back at about a quarter past four, if they wanted to be sure of finding him, in the repair workshops.

'Very well, we'll be back,' Séverine announced.

Then, when she was once more outside, alone in Jacques's company:

'If you're free, do you mind if I stay and wait for him with you?'

He could hardly refuse, and anyway, despite the uneasiness she caused him deep down, she has beginning to exert a growing charm over him, so strongly that the intentionally sullen manners which he had promised himself to assume disappeared beneath her gentle gaze. This woman, with her long, tender, timorous face, she was just the kind to love you like a faithful dog, the sort of dog one hasn't even the heart to beat.

'Of course, I shan't leave you,' he replied less brusquely. 'Only, we've got more than an hour to kill . . . Would you like to go to a café?'

She smiled at him, happy at sensing him become cordial at last. Hastily she declined.

'Oh no, no, I don't want to be shut up indoors . . . I'd rather walk with you, round the streets, wherever you like.'

And prettily she took hold of his arm. Now that he was no longer all black from the train journey, she found that he cut a rather distinguished figure, dressed as he was in the manner of a well-to-do railwayman, a picture of respectability, yet with the added savour of a proud independence derived from his daily routine of exposure to danger and all weathers. Never before had she been quite so struck by how handsome he was, with his round face and regular features, and his very dark moustache on a white skin; and it was only those darting eyes, those eyes speckled with gold that he was continually averting from her, which kept her on her guard. If he avoided looking her in the face, was it because he didn't want to commit himself, wanted to remain free, to act as he pleased, even act against her? From that moment, uncertain as she still was and trembling each time she remembered that study in the Rue du Rocher where her fate was being decided, she had but one goal, to feel this man upon whose arm she walked become hers, totally hers, and, when she looked up, to make his eyes rest on hers, in a deep gaze. Then he would belong to her. She did not love him, the thought never even occurred to her. Simply, she was trying to make him her own, so as no longer to have to fear him.

For a few minutes they walked along in silence, amidst the constant bustle of pedestrians who throng this populous quarter. Sometimes they were obliged to step off the pavement; and then they would walk in the road, among the carriages. Soon they found themselves in front of the Square des Batignolles, which was almost deserted at this time of the year. Yet the sky, washed clean by the morning's deluge, was a very soft blue; and, under the warm March sun, the lilac-trees were budding.

'Shall we go in?' asked Séverine. 'All these people are making me dizzy.'

Jacques was about to go in anyway, unconsciously needing to have her more to himself, far from the crowd.

'As good a place as any,' he said. 'Yes, let's go in.'

Slowly they continued their stroll beside the grass, between the leafless trees. One or two women were taking toddlers for a walk, while other people hurried past using the gardens as a short cut. They stepped over the stream, and climbed the path among the rocks; then, returning aimlessly, they passed among clumps of pine, their evergreen foliage gleaming darkly in the sunlight. And, coming upon a bench, in this solitary corner, hidden from view, they sat down, this time without even asking each other, as if led there by some mutual understanding.

'It's turned out nice today all the same,' she said after a silence.

'Yes,' he replied, 'the sun's come out again.'

But they weren't thinking of that. He, who shunned women, had just been reflecting on the events which had brought him into contact with this one. Here she was, touching him, threatening to invade his whole existence, and he could not get over his astonishment. Since the last interrogation, at Rouen, he was no longer in any doubt, this woman was an accomplice to the murder at La Croix-de-Maufras. Why? What circumstances had led up to it? What passion or motive had made her do it? He had asked himself these questions, but without being able to provide clear answers. Yet he had finally managed to come up with a story: the husband, mercenary and violent, in a hurry to come into possession of the legacy; perhaps the fear that the will might be altered to their disadvantage; perhaps the intention to bind his wife to him, by a bond of blood. And he contented himself with this version of events, the more obscure parts of which intrigued him and were of particular interest, though he made no attempt to shed further light upon them. The idea that his duty would be to tell the forces of law and order everything he knew had been haunting him too. Indeed it was this very idea which had been preoccupying him ever since he had found himself sitting here on the bench, close to her, so close that he could feel the warmth of her hip against his own.

'In March', he continued, 'it's extraordinary being able to sit out like this, as if it were summer.'

'Oh,' she said, 'you soon feel it when the sun gets higher.'

And she, for her part, was reflecting that this man really would have to be stupid not to have guessed that she and her husband were the guilty parties. They had virtually thrown themselves at him, and here she was herself, at this very moment, still making up to him. And in the silence punctuated by their inconsequential remarks she followed his train of thought. Their eyes had met, and she had just read in them that he was beginning to wonder if she wasn't the person he had seen, leaning with all her weight on the victim's legs, the dark shape. What could she do, what could she say, that would bind him with an indestructible tie?

'In Le Havre this morning', she added, 'it was very cold'.

'And to think,' he said, 'after all the rain we've been having.'

And at that moment Séverine had a sudden inspiration. She did not consider rationally nor engage in any inner debate: it just came to her, like an instinctive impulse, from the dark depths of her mind and heart; for, if she had thought about it, she would have said nothing. But she could sense that it was exactly right, and that by talking to him she would conquer him.

Gently she took his hand and looked at him. The clumps of green trees hid them from the gaze of the people walking past along the nearby streets, and they could hear only the distant rumble of traffic, muffled amidst the sunlit solitude of the gardens; while at the corner of one of the paths a child was playing on its own, tipping sand into a little bucket with his spade. And, without smoothing the change of subject, she murmured from the depths of her soul:

'You think I'm guilty, don't you?'

He started slightly, and his eyes came to rest on hers.

'Yes,' he replied, in the same low voice that was tense with emotion

Then, still having hold of his hand, she squeezed it more tightly; and she paused, sensing their separate agitation blend into one.

'You're wrong, I'm not guilty.'

And she said this not to persuade him, but simply to warn him that she had to remain innocent in the eyes of other people. It was the declaration of a woman who says no and wants it to be no, always, come what may.

'I am not guilty . . . you're not to make me unhappy any more by thinking I am.'

And to her great delight she saw him allow his eyes to rest on hers, in a deep gaze. What she had just done, doubtless, was to give herself; for she was yielding to him, and if later he should ever come to claim her, she would not be able to refuse him. But the bond had been tied between them, indissolubly: she defied him to talk now, he was hers as she was his. Her declaration had united them.

'You won't make me unhappy any more, will you? You'll believe me?'

'Yes, I believe you,' he smiled.

Why force her to talk, painfully, about this dreadful business? Later she would tell him everything, if she felt the need. Her way of seeking peace of mind by confessing to him, without saying so in as many words, touched him greatly, as a mark of infinite tenderness. She was so trusting, so fragile, with her sweet, periwinkle eyes! She seemed to him so much the woman, so ready to devote herself to a man and to submit to him in order to be happy! And above all, what really delighted him as they sat there hand in hand, neither of them taking their eyes off the other, was not to have that disturbing feeling in him, that terrifying trembling that took hold of him in the presence of a woman when he thought of possessing her. With other women he had not been able to touch their flesh without experiencing the desire to devour it, as though ravenous with an abominable hunger to butcher them. But this one, could he then love her, and not kill her?

'You know I am your friend, and you have nothing to fear from me,' he murmured in her ear. 'I don't want to know your business, it shall be as you see fit . . . Do you understand me? I am yours to command.'

He had come up so close to her face that he could feel her warm breath in his moustache. Even that morning he would not have dared such a thing, still wildly afraid of having an attack. What had happened to him that all he could feel now was a slight tremor, and the contented lassitude of the convalescent? The thought, the certainty now, that she had killed, made her seem different, more considerable, a creature apart. Perhaps she hadn't simply helped but actually dealt the blow. He was convinced of the fact, without any evidence whatsoever. And from that moment she seemed sacred to him, beyond his power to reason, deep from within the unconscious realm of the terrified desire which she aroused in him.

They were both chatting away merrily now, like a courting couple at the beginning of their love.

'You should give me your other hand so I can warm that too.'

'Oh no, not here. People will see us.'

'Who will see us? We're all alone. And anyway, where's the harm? That's not how babies are made.'

'I should hope not indeed.'

She was laughing freely, overjoyed at her salvation. She didn't love this man, she thought she was quite certain about that; and though she had promised herself to him, she was already imagining ways of not paying up. He looked like a nice sort, he wouldn't torment her, everything would be fine.

'Is that agreed, then? We're friends, but no one is to know, not even my husband . . . Now, let me have my hand back, and stop looking at me like that, you'll wear your eyes out.'

But he kept her delicate fingers in his. Barely whispering, he blurted out:

'You realize I love you.'

Rapidly she had withdrawn her hand, with a slight tug. And standing in front of the bench, where he remained seated:

'Well really, I've never heard such nonsense. Careful, some-one's coming.'

A nursemaid was in fact approaching, the baby asleep in her arms. Then a girl went past in a great hurry. The sun was setting, drowning on the horizon in clouds of violet, and its rays were departing from the grass, dying in golden dust upon the green tips of the firs. It seemed as though there had been a sudden cessation in the constant rumble of traffic. Five o'clock could be heard striking on a nearby clock.

'Oh, good heavens!' cried Séverine, 'five o'clock and I've got an appointment in the Rue du Rocher!'

Joy ebbed from her, and, remembering that she was not yet saved, she was plunged back into anguished apprehension at the unknown which there awaited her. She turned completely pale, her lips trembling.

'But the depot manager you had to see?' said Jacques, who had risen from the bench to offer her his arm.

'Too bad, I'll see him another time . . . Look, my friend, I can manage without you, let me just go quickly and do my errand. And thank you again, thank you with all my heart.'

She was pressing his hands, making haste to leave.

'See you later, on the train.'

'Yes, see you later.'

Already she was hurrying away, disappearing between the clumps of trees; while he, slowly, made his way towards the Rue Cardinet.

Monsieur Camy-Lamotte had just been having a long meeting at his house with the managing director of the Compagnie de l'Ouest. Summoned on the pretext of a quite different matter, the managing director had finally admitted how much annoyance the Grandmorin affair was causing the Company. First, there were the complaints in the newspapers about the lack of security for first-class passengers. Next, the whole workforce seemed to be involved in the incident, and several employees were under suspicion, not least this Roubaud fellow, the most incriminated of all, who could be arrested at any moment. Lastly, the rumours about unsavoury behaviour on the part of the President, a member of the board, seemed to be reflecting on the board as a whole. And in this way the effects of the presumed crime of some little assistant station-manager, a strange, mean, dirty business, were gradually making themselves felt, up through a complex machinery of wheels within wheels, sending shock waves throughout the vast mechanism of railway management, and disabling even its most senior administrators. The tremor could be felt still higher, right up to the Minister, and threatened even the State in the current unsettled political climate—this critical moment for the great body politic whose decline was hastened each time it caught the slightest fever. Accordingly, when Monsieur Camy-Lamotte had learnt from his interlocutor that the Company had decided that morning to dismiss Roubaud, he had vigorously opposed such a measure. No! No! Nothing could be clumsier, the furore in the press would be twice as great if they chose to portray the assistant station-manager as a political victim. All hell would break loose, from top to bottom, and God knows what manner of disagreeable revelations there might be about this person and the next! The scandal had dragged on too long, it was vital to silence speculation as soon as possible. And, duly persuaded, the managing director had undertaken to keep Roubaud on, and not even to move him from Le Havre. People would soon see that they were all beyond reproach. That was an end of the matter, the case would be closed.

When Séverine, all out of breath, her pulse racing, found herself once more in the austere study in the Rue du Rocher, standing before Monsieur Camy-Lamotte, the latter observed her for a moment in silence, intrigued by the extraordinary efforts she was making to appear calm. Yes, he had decidedly taken a liking to her, to this dainty criminal with the periwinkle eyes.

'Well, Madame . . .'

And he paused to savour her anxiety some moments longer. But there was such an intense look on her face, he could feel her reaching out to him with all her being in such a desperate need to know the answer, that he took pity.

'Well, Madame, I have seen the managing director and arranged for your husband not to be dismissed. The matter is settled.'

Then she gave way, overwhelmed by the excess of joy that suddenly flooded over her. Her eyes were filled with tears, and she remained silent, smiling.

He said it again, stressing the phrase, to convey its full significance:

'The matter is settled . . . You may return to Le Havre and set your mind at rest.'

She understood perfectly: he meant that they would not be arrested, that they were being spared. It wasn't just that there would be no dismissal, it was the fact that the whole horrible drama would be forgotten, buried. Prompted by an instinctive desire to caress, like some sweet domestic pet rubbing itself against its benefactor by way of thanking him, she bent over his hands, kissed them, and pressed them to her cheeks. And this time he had not withdrawn them, extremely moved himself at the tender charm of this display of gratitude.

'Only', he went on, trying to reassume his stern demeanour, 'mind and make sure you behave yourselves.'

'Yes, Monsieur!'

But he wanted to keep them at his mercy, the man and woman both. He alluded to the letter.

'Remember that the file is here, and that at the slightest misdemeanour everything can be reopened . . . Above all, advise your husband to cease involving himself in politics. On that particular subject we will be merciless. I know that he has already compromised himself, I've been told about that unfortunate quarrel with the Sub-Prefect. I mean, he's said to be a republican, and that is detestable . . . Do you understand? Either he behaves himself, or we shall silence him. It is as simple as that.'

She had risen to her feet, in a hurry now to be out of the house in order to give full rein to the joy which was bursting within her.

'Monsieur, we shall do as you say, we shall be as you wish us to be . . . No matter when, no matter where, your word is our command: I am yours.'

He had begun to smile again, with that weary smile touched with the disdain of a man who has drunk for a long time of the vanity of all things.

'Oh, I shan't take advantage, Madame, I don't any more.'

And he himself opened the door of the study for her. On her way out she turned round twice, her face radiant with continuing gratitude.

Séverine walked along the Rue du Rocher like a woman possessed. She realized that she was going up the street, for no reason at all; and she came down it again, crossing the road to no particular purpose, at the risk of being run over. It all came from a need to be on the move, to gesture, to cry out. Already she understood why they were being let off, and she found herself saying:

'My goodness but they're scared! There's not much danger of any of them stirring all this up again, I've been totally stupid to torture myself like this. It's obvious . . . Oh, what luck, I'm saved, and this time saved for good! . . . And I don't care, I'm going to have to frighten that husband of mine into behaving himself . . . Saved, saved, what luck!'

As she was coming out of the Rue Saint-Lazare, she saw from a jeweller's clock that it was twenty minutes to six.

'I know, I'll treat myself to a slap-up dinner. I've still got time.'

Opposite the station she chose the most expensive restaurant, and once seated on her own at a little table with a spotless white table-cloth beside the front window, from which she delightedly observed all the comings and goings in the street, she ordered a choice meal of oysters, fillet of sole, a wing of roast chicken . . . The least she deserved was to make up for her awful lunch. She devoured everything, finding the wheaten bread particularly delicious, and ordered another little treat for herself, some beignets soufflés. Then, having drunk her coffee, she hurried out, for she only had a few minutes left in which to catch the express.

On leaving her, Jacques had returned home to change into his work clothes and proceeded immediately to the depot, where he usually arrived only half an hour before his engine was due to leave. He had ended up relying on the good offices of Pecqueux to carry out the inspection, even though, more often than not, the fireman was drunk. But on this occasion, filled with tender thoughts as he was, he began to have instinctive misgivings and determined to check for himself that all working parts were in good order—especially as that morning, on their way from Le Havre, he thought he had noticed the engine needing more power for less work.

In the vast enclosed shed, black with soot and lit by tall, grimy windows, there among the other engines standing idle, Jacques's locomotive was already positioned at the head of a track, ready to leave first. A depot fireman had just stoked the fire, and red cinders were dropping into the ashpit. It was one of those two-coupled express engines, a giant of refined elegance, with its great, lightweight wheels connected by limbs of steel, its breast huge, its haunches sleek and powerful, manifesting all the logical order and certainty that constitute the sovereign beauty of these metal creatures, precision allied to power. Like the other engines belonging to the Compagnie de l'Ouest, it bore as well as its own number the name of a station, that of Lison, a station in the Cotentin. But Jacques had affectionately turned this into a woman's name, La Lison, a name he would utter in fond tones.

And it was true that he had really loved this engine of his ever since he had started driving her four years ago. He had had others, the docile and the awkward, the courageous and the lazy; he knew that each one had its own character and that many of them were not up to much, rather like those of the flesh-and-blood variety; with the result that, if he loved this one, it was because she really did have the rare qualities of a good woman. Thanks to her good steam flow, she was gentle, obedient, easy to start, regular and unflagging in her action. Of course people said that, if she started so easily, that was due to the excellent steel tyres on the wheels and above all to the perfect adjustment of the slide-valves; just as, if she steamed so much on so little fuel, people put that down to the quality of the copper in the tubes and the happy disposition of the boiler. But he knew that there was more to it, for other engines that were identically designed and built with identical care did not manifest any of her qualities. The mystery of manufacture had given her a soul, that something that the chance blows of a hammer can bring to metal, that an assembly worker's hand can lend to the individual parts: the engine's personality, its life.

He loved her therefore, La Lison, in the manner of the grateful male, this Lison who stopped and started promptly like a vigorous and amenable mare; he loved her because she earned him extra money on top of his fixed salary, thanks to the bonuses for fuel economy. She steamed so well that she did in fact save large amounts of coal. And he had only one thing with which to reproach her, she needed too much greasing: the cylinders especially devoured unreasonable quantities of grease, a constant hunger it was, absolute gluttony. Vainly he had tried to get her to moderate her appetite. But she became breathless at once, that was just the way she was. He had resigned himself to tolerating this voracious passion, rather as one shuts one's eyes to a particular vice in persons who are otherwise full of sterling qualities; and he was content to joke with his fireman that like many a beautiful woman she was always slapping on the grease.

While the fire roared and La Lison gradually built up a head of steam, Jacques walked round her, inspecting every part of her, trying to discover why she had consumed more lubricant than usual that morning. He could find nothing, she was gleaming and spotless, with that cheerful spotlessness which bespeaks the tender loving care of a driver. He was forever cleaning and polishing; on arrival especially, he would rub her vigorously, the way one rubs down steaming animals after a race, taking advantage of the fact that she was hot to remove various stains and runs. He never rushed her either, but kept her to an even pace, making sure not to fall behind schedule, because that meant having to make unwelcome bursts of speed later on. Moreover the two of them had lived so well together that not once in four years had he had to lodge a complaint about her, in the depot's register where the drivers record their requests for repairs, particularly the bad drivers, who, being either lazy or drunk, were always quarrelling with their engines. But today it troubled him, it really did, this wanton appetite for grease; and there was something else too, something deep down which he couldn't put his finger on, that he had never felt before, an uneasiness, a mistrust of her, as if he doubted her and sought assurance that there would be no untoward behaviour once they were underway.

However, Pecqueux was not there, and Jacques let fly when he finally did appear, the worse for wear after lunch with a friend. Normally the two men got on very well together, throughout the long hours of companionship which took them from one end of the line to the other, rattling along side by side, without a word, brought together by a common need and common dangers. Although he was more than ten years younger, the driver behaved in a fatherly way towards his fireman and covered up for his lapses, letting him sleep for an hour when he was too drunk; and the other man returned this tolerance with the good-natured devotion of a faithful dog. Besides, his drunkenness apart, he was an excellent worker and experienced at his job. It must be said that he too loved La Lison, which in itself was all that it required for the two men to get on. Together the pair of them and the engine constituted a regular *ménage à trois*, and never so much as a quarrel. Hence Pecqueux, dumbstruck at being so ill received, looked at Jacques in yet greater surprise when he heard him grumbling and voicing his doubts about her.

'What are you talking about? But she's going like a bird!'

'No, no, I'm not happy.'

And despite the fact that each part was in good order, he continued to shake his head. He tried the hand-levers, checked that the steam-valve was working properly. He climbed on to the footplate, and filled the lubricant cups of each cylinder himself; while the fireman wiped the dome, on which there were still slight traces of rust. The rod on the sand-box was working well, everything should have set his mind at rest. The trouble was that La Lison no longer had sole possession of his heart. Another affection was growing there, for that slim, fragile creature he could still see sitting next to him, on the park bench, with her beguiling vulnerability, and her need to be loved and protected. Never before, even when some circumstance beyond his control had made him late and he was hurling his engine forward at eighty kilometres an hour, never had he thought of the risk to passengers. And here he was, the very thought of taking this woman back to Le Havre, this woman he had almost hated this morning and whom it had annoyed him to bring, now filling him with anxiety, with fear at the prospect of an accident, in which he could imagine her being injured through some fault of his own, and dying in his arms. From this moment on he counted love among his responsibilities: and La Lison, under suspicion, had better behave herself if she wanted to preserve her reputation as a good runner.

Six o'clock struck. Jacques and Pecqueux climbed up on to the little metal bridge connecting the tender to the engine; and after the fireman had opened the steam-cock at a sign from his chief, a swirling cloud of white vapour filled the blackness of the shed. Then, responding to the regulator as it was gradually turned by the driver, La Lison set off, making her way out of the depot and whistling for a clear road. Almost at once she was permitted to enter the Batignolles tunnel. But at the Pont de l'Europe it was necessary to wait; and it was not a moment before the scheduled time when the pointsman sent her down to the six-thirty express, to which two station-workers firmly coupled her.

Only five minutes remained before they were due to depart, and Jacques was leaning out, surprised not to see Séverine among the press of travellers. He was quite certain that she would not board the train without coming to have a word with him. At last she appeared, late, almost running. And sure enough, she came the length of the train, stopping only when she reached the engine, her face glowing, exultant with joy.

Her little feet hoisted her up and she lifted her face, laughing. 'Don't worry, here I am.'

He too began to laugh, happy that she had arrived.

'Good, good, that's all right then.'

But she raised herself still further on tiptoe, and continued in a whisper:

'My friend, I am a happy woman, a very happy woman . . . I've had a great stroke of luck . . . Everything I wanted.'

He understood perfectly, and it gave him huge pleasure.

Then, as she was dashing off again, she turned and added jokingly:

'So you make sure now, and don't go smashing me to pieces!'

'As if I would! You needn't worry about that.'

But the doors were slamming shut. Séverine just had time to board; and Jacques, at a signal from his chief guard, pulled on the whistle and opened the regulator. Off they set. It was the same departure as that of the ill-fated train in February, at the same time, to the accompaniment of the same station bustle, the same sounds, the same smoke. Only it was still daylight, a clear evening of utter peacefulness. Séverine stood with her head out of the window, watching.

And up on La Lison, on the right of the cab, Jacques, warmly dressed in woollen overall and trousers, with his cloth-sided goggles tied at the back beneath his cap, kept his eyes firmly on the track, repeatedly leaning out beyond the glass screen in order to see better. Rudely jolted by the shuddering of the locomotive, which he did not even notice, he had his right hand on the gear-wheel, like a pilot at his helm, and was continually turning it imperceptibly this way and that, slackening or increasing the speed; while with his left hand he kept pulling on the whistle, for the way out of Paris is difficult and full of hazards. He pulled the whistle at each level-crossing, each station, each tunnel, at each long curve in the track. A red signal showing up in the distance, amidst the fading light, he gave a long request for the road, and passed like a roll of thunder. He scarcely took the time to dart an occasional glance at the pressure-gauge, turning the little wheel of the injector whenever the pressure reached ten kilograms. And it was always to the track ahead that his eyes returned, utterly attentive to the tiniest details, so rapt that he saw nothing else, that he did not even feel the wind blowing around him like a hurricane. The pressure-gauge dropped, and he lifted the ratchet to open the firebox door; and Pecqueux, accustomed to this movement, understood, broke up some coal with a hammer, and then spread it with his shovel in an even layer over the whole width of the grate. A searing heat burned their legs; then, with the door shut, the icy cold wind blew once more.

Night was falling, and Jacques became twice as careful. He had rarely known La Lison more obedient: he possessed her, bestriding her as he pleased, with the absolute authority of a master; and yet he did not slacken his iron grip, treating her like some tamed beast of which one must continue to be wary. And there behind him, on the speeding train, he could see a delicate face, yielding itself up to him, trusting and smiling. It made him tremble slightly, and he clasped the gear-wheel more firmly still, his eyes piercing the gathering darkness, fixedly, in search of red lights. After the junctions at Asnières and Colombes, he had breathed somewhat more easily. As far as Mantes everything was fine, there was a level stretch where the train had an easy run. After Mantes he had to urge La Lison on a little so that she would take a fairly steep climb, of about half a league. Then, without slowing, he launched her down the gentle incline of the Rolleboise tunnel, all two and a half kilometres of it, which she covered in scarcely three minutes. There was just one more tunnel, the one at Roulle, near Gaillon, before Sotteville with its dreaded station, which was rendered especially perilous by the complexity of its lines, the continual shunting, and the constant clutter of traffic. Every ounce of strength he possessed was concentrated in his watchful eyes and in the hand with which he drove; and La Lison, whistling, her smoke trailing, raced through Sotteville at full steam, and did not stop before Rouen, from where she set off again, a little more sedate now, and proceeding more slowly as she took the climb towards Malaunay.

The moon had risen, particularly bright, its white brilliance allowing Jacques to make out the smallest bush, even the stones on the roads, as they hurtled past. Glancing to the right on leaving the Malaunay tunnel, momentarily disconcerted by the shadow cast across the track by a tall tree, he recognized the remote spot, a clump of brushwood, where he had witnessed the murder. The countryside slid past, a rugged wilderness of endless hillocks and dark, wooded hollows, pitted and desolate. Then, at La Croix-de-Maufras, beneath the motionless moon, came the sudden glimpse of the house standing at an angle, abandoned and derelict, its shutters eternally closed, a place of grim melancholy. And once again, without knowing why, but this time more than ever, Jacques felt his chest tighten, as if he were passing before his own doom.

But at once his eye caught another image. Beside the Misards' house, leaning on the crossing gate, was Flore. He saw her every trip now, standing at the same spot, waiting, looking out for him. She did not move, she simply turned her head, to follow him a moment longer amidst the flash that was already bearing him away. Her tall figure stood out, a dark shape against the white light, and her golden hair gleamed like fire in the pale gold of the moon.

Jacques, having spurred La Lison on to take the climb at Motteville, gave her a short breather along the Bolbec plateau before finally sending her hurtling down the steepest slope on the line, from Saint-Romain to Harfleur, a distance of three leagues which the engines devour at the gallop like crazed beasts with the scent of the stables in their nostrils. And he was totally exhausted when, amidst the noise and smoke of their arrival at Le Havre station, Séverine, before returning up to her flat, came rushing towards him to say, in her warm and cheerful way:

'Thank you. See you tomorrow.'

CHAPTER VI

A MONTH went by, and a great calm had once more descended upon the flat which the Roubauds occupied on the first floor of the station, above the waiting-rooms. For them, for their neighbours along the corridor, and for this whole little world of railway workers, subjected as they were to a clockwork existence by the steady revolutions of the timetable, life had resumed its monotonous course. And it was as though nothing violent or out of the ordinary had ever occurred.

The scandalous Grandmorin affair, which there had been so much talk about, was now quietly being forgotten, and the file was about to be closed in view of the apparent inability of the authorities to find the guilty man. After a further fortnight's detention, Denizet, the examining magistrate, had ordered the case against Cabuche to be dropped on the grounds of insufficient evidence; and a police myth was beginning to form, the implausible tale of an elusive, anonymous murderer, an adventurer in crime, capable of being in more than one place at the same time, who was held responsible for every murder but who disappeared into thin air the moment an officer of the law appeared. Only occasionally now did the odd joke about this imaginary killer resurface in the pages of the opposition press, which was in a ferment at the approach of the general election. The high-handedness of Prefects or the attempts of those in power to put pressure on various individuals furnished it daily with alternative subjects for its indignant articles; so much so that, with the newspapers no longer bothering about the affair, it had ceased to be the object of the public's avid curiosity. Nobody even talked about it any more.

What had finally restored calm to the Roubaud household was the happy resolution of their other problem, the one potentially posed by Grandmorin's will. On the advice of Madame Bonnehon, the Lachesnayes had finally consented not to contest the will for fear of reviving the scandal, being in any case highly uncertain as to how the case might turn out. And having now entered into possession of their legacy, the Roubauds had for the past week found themselves the proud owners of the house and garden at La Croix-de-Maufras, estimated to be worth some forty thousand francs. They had immediately decided to sell the house, this place of depravity and bloody deeds which haunted them like a nightmare and where they would never have dared to sleep for fear of the ghosts of the past—and to sell the whole thing just as it was, furniture included, without repairing it or even removing the dust. But as it would have sold at public auction for a price too far below its real value, there being few buyers ready to bury themselves away in such a remote setting, they had decided to wait for someone to take a fancy to the place, and so had been content to hang an enormous sign on the front of it, which could be easily read from the trains that were constantly passing. This appeal in large letters, a wilderness for sale, added to the sorry spectacle of closed shutters and a garden overrun by brambles. Roubaud had absolutely refused to go there, even in passing, to do some things that needed to be done. So Séverine had gone herself one afternoon; and she had left the keys with the Misards, asking them to show people round should any prospective purchasers turn up. Such persons could have moved in within a matter of hours, for the house was fully furnished down to the bedlinen in the cupboards.

And so, having no further cause for concern, the Roubauds were content to let each day go by in sleepy expectation of the next. The house would be sold in the end, they would invest the money from it, and everything would be fine. In fact they simply forgot about it, and lived as though they would never move out of the three rooms which they currently occupied: the dining-room, which gave directly on to the corridor, the moderately spacious bedroom on the right, and the tiny, airless kitchen on the left. Even the station roof outside their windows, that slope of zinc which blocked out the view like a prison wall, instead of exasperating them as it used to, now seemed to soothe them and to add to the sense of never-ending peacefulness, of reassuring tranquillity, in which they slumbered. At least you could not be seen by the neighbours, prying eyes were not always peering in to see what you were up to; and now, with the arrival of spring, their only complaint was the stifling heat and the dazzling reflections bouncing off the zinc during these first days of warm sunshine. Reaction had set in following the dreadful shock which had caused them to live for nearly two months in a continual tremble, and they revelled dumbly in their growing torpor. All they asked was to remain where they were, simply content to be, without fear, without pain. Never had Roubaud shown himself to be a more punctual or conscientious worker. When working on the day shift, he would go down to the station at 5 a.m. and not return home for his meal until 10 o'clock; then he went back down at 11 and continued until five in the afternoon, which in all made eleven hours at work. During the night shift, when he was on duty from five in the afternoon until five in the morning, he did not even have the short break for a meal at home, since he had supper in his office. He bore this hard servitude with a kind of satisfaction, seeming to delight in it, concerning himself with the minutest details, wanting to see and do everything himself, as if he had found oblivion in this exhaustion and had discovered that it restored balance and normality to his life. For her part, Séverine was almost always on her own, being a 'widow' one week and seeing Roubaud only at lunch and dinner the other; and she appeared to have been overtaken by a passion for housework. Normally she would sit doing embroidery, leaving the housework, which she hated, to an old woman, Mère Simon, who came in from nine until noon. But ever since she had found herself once more left to her own devices at home and confident of remaining there, her head had been filled with thoughts of cleaning and tidying. Now she only sat down if she had had a good sort-out. Besides which, both of them slept soundly. Neither during their rare private conversations, nor at meal-times, nor on the occasions when they shared a bed, did they ever once mention the affair again; and they must have thought that it was all over, dead and buried.

For Séverine especially, life thus became once more thoroughly undemanding. Her periods of indolence returned, and she resumed her practice of leaving the housework to Mère Simon in the manner of a young lady suited only to the most delicate needlework. She had started on an interminable piece of work, a whole bedspread to embroider, which threatened to take her a lifetime. She would rise quite late, happy to remain alone in bed listening to the comforting sound of the trains, their arrivals

and departures marking the advance of the hours with the precision of a clock. During the early days of their marriage she had
been unsettled by the violent noises coming from the station, the
whistle-blasts, the thud of the turntables, the rumblings that
sounded like thunder, and the sudden vibrations, like earth-
quakes, that made both her and the furniture shake. Then, little
by little, she grew used to it, and the clamorous, vibrant station
became part of her life; and now it gave her pleasure, her tranquil
repose was founded upon all this bustle and din. Before lunch
she would wander about from room to room, chatting with the
cleaning-lady, her own hands idle. Then she would spend long
afternoons seated by the dining-room window, with her needlework more often than not lying on her lap, quite happy to do
nothing. The weeks when her husband came home in the early
hours and went to bed, she could hear him snoring until evening;
in fact for her these had become the good weeks, like the ones she
used to have before she was married, when she had the whole bed
to herself, and then spent her time as she pleased, with a whole
free day stretching ahead of her. She hardly ever went out, and
all she could see of Le Havre was the smoke from the nearby
factories, great black swirls of it staining the sky above the zinc
ridge-flashing that blocked her view just a few yards from where
she sat. The town was there, behind that eternal wall; she could
always sense its presence, but her frustration at not being able to
see it had eventually given way to quiet acceptance. Five or six
flower-pots planted with wallflowers and verbena made a little
garden for her to tend in the gutter of the station roof, blooms to
brighten her solitary life. Sometimes she spoke of herself as
though she were a recluse, living in the middle of a wood. Only
Roubaud, when he had a spare minute, would venture out of the
window: then he would walk to the end of the gutter and climb
the zinc slope to perch on top of the ridge, above the Cours
Napoléon; and there he would finally light his pipe, out in the
open air, overlooking the town spread out at his feet, and the
docks with their tall forest of masts, and the sea, a vast expanse
of pale green stretching to infinity.

It seemed as though the same somnolence had overtaken the
other railwaymen's households, those of the Roubauds' neighbours. Their corridor, which usually whistled with the terrible

winds of gossip, was also gradually going to sleep. When Philomène visited Madame Lebleu, one could scarcely even hear the murmur of their voices. Both of them being surprised to see how things were turning out, they now spoke of the assistant station-master only in scornful commiseration: well, of course, his wife had been up to all sorts in Paris, to make sure he kept his job; whatever you said, he was a marked man, and people would always have their suspicions about him. And as the ticket-clerk's wife was now convinced that her neighbours no longer had the power to reclaim her flat, she simply treated them with great disdain, walking past them very stiffly without acknowledging them. So much so that she had even begun to irritate Philomène, who called less often now: she found her too proud, it was no fun any more. For something to do, nevertheless, Madame Lebleu continued to keep watch on the carryings-on between Mademoiselle Guichon and Monsieur Dabadie, the station-master, but still without ever catching them in the act. Out in the corridor the silent shuffling of her felt-soled slippers was all that remained. Things having thus gradually quietened down, a month elapsed, of total peace, like the long sleep that follows a great catastrophe.

But at the Roubauds' one thing still remained both as a painful reminder and as a source of further anxiety: a particular spot on the dining-room floor upon which their eyes could never chance to fall without their feeling once more troubled by unease. This was, to the left of the window, the oak block which they had removed and then replaced in order to hide the watch and the ten thousand francs taken from Grandmorin's body, together with a purse containing about three hundred francs in gold coins. Roubaud had removed the watch and money from the man's pockets only to make it look like robbery. He was no thief, and he would have starved to death right next to it, he was given to saying, rather than spend a single centime or attempt to sell the watch. The money of that old man, who'd degraded his wife and got his just deserts, money stained with blood and filth, no! no! that money was too dirty for any honest man to touch. He quite forgot about the house at La Croix-de-Maufras, this gift he was ready to accept: it was only the fact of going through the victim's pockets, of those banknotes stolen during the abominable act of murder, which revolted him and gave him a bad conscience, causing him to recoil in disgust and apprehension. However, he had not yet been able to bring himself to burn them or to go and throw the watch and purse into the sea some evening. While simple prudence counselled him to it, a deeper instinct protested within him against such destruction. Unconsciously he respected these things, he could never have brought himself to destroy such a sum. Initially, on the first night, he had buried it all under his pillow, believing nowhere else to be sufficiently secure. During the days which followed, he had racked his brains trying to think of a possible hiding-place, and chosen a different one every morning, at the slightest noise, for fear of being searched by the police. Never had he exercised his imagination so greatly. Then one day, having run out of clever ideas and tired of being afraid, he simply couldn't be bothered to remove the money and watch from where he had hidden them the previous evening, at the edge of the parquet floor; and now nothing in the world could have induced him to go near it, it was like some charnel-house, a gaping hole of horror and death where ghosts lay in wait for him. He even avoided walking on that particular block of flooring; for it gave him an unpleasant sensation, as if he could feel a slight jolt in his legs. Séverine, when she sat by the window in the afternoons, would move her chair back so as not to be directly above this corpse they kept under their floor. They did not talk to each other about it and tried to convince themselves that they would get used to it, but eventually they grew more and more irritated at finding it always there and to feel its nagging presence beneath their feet at every hour of the day. And this uneasiness was even more singular given that they were not in the least disconcerted by the knife, that fine new knife the wife had bought and the husband had driven into a lover's throat. They had simply given it a wash, and it now lay at the bottom of a drawer. Mère Simon used it occasionally to cut bread.

At the same time Roubaud had recently introduced a new source of disturbance into their tranquil existence—and one which was gradually increasing—by obliging Jacques to visit them on a regular basis. The driver's duty roster brought him to Le Havre three times a week: on Mondays from 10.35 a.m. till

6.20 p.m., and on Thursdays and Saturdays, from 11.05 p.m. till 6.40 a.m. And on the first Monday after Séverine's trip, the assistant station-master had insisted.

'Look here, mate, you've just got to come and have a meal with us . . . Goodness me, you've been ever so kind to my wife. You must at least let me say thank you.'

Twice in one month Jacques had accepted to lunch with them like this. It was as though Roubaud was embarrassed at the long silences which now occurred when he ate alone with his wife and found it a relief to have a guest with them. He would immediately remember all his old stories, and start chatting and joking.

'Come again as often as you can! You can see you're not in the way.'

One Thursday evening, all cleaned up and about to go to bed, Jacques had met Roubaud strolling round the depot; and despite the late hour, the latter, not wanting to return home on his own, had made the young man walk back to the station with him and then dragged him off to his flat. Séverine was still up, reading. They had had a drink together and even played cards until past midnight.

And now these Monday lunches were becoming a regular event, as were the little parties on Thursday and Saturday evenings. If his colleague missed a day, Roubaud would himself go looking for him and reproach him for neglecting them. He was becoming increasingly morose, and he was really only ever cheerful now when he was with his new friend. This fellow who'd given him such a dreadful fright at first, and who by rights should now have been the object of his hatred as the one witness, the one living reminder, of the dreadful things he wanted to forget, had on the contrary become indispensable to him, perhaps precisely because the man knew and had not talked. It was something they had in common, like a very strong bond, a kind of complicity. Often Roubaud would look knowingly at the other man and shake his hand in a sudden burst of emotion which went well beyond the mere expression of camaraderie.

But above all Jacques offered them a distraction in their domestic life. Séverine, too, would greet him gaily, uttering a little cry the moment he walked in, as a woman stirred by the prospect of pleasure. She would drop everything, her embroidery or her book, and in talk and laughter make her escape from the grey slumber in which she spent her days.

'Oh, it is good of you to come! I thought of you when I heard the express.'

It was always a special occasion when he lunched with them. She already knew his tastes and would go out herself to fetch fresh eggs for him: and it was all done in a kindly way, in the manner of a good housewife receiving the friend of the house, and without his being able as yet to discern anything other than a desire to please and the need for some amusement.

'And you must come again next Monday, you know! We'll be having cream!'

Nevertheless, a month later, by which time he was now an established visitor, the rift between the Roubauds had widened. She, for her part, found it increasingly agreeable to have the bed to herself and contrived to be there as seldom as possible at the same time as her husband; and he, who had been so passionate, so brutal even, in the early days of their marriage, made no effort to stop her. He had loved her without delicacy, and she had resigned herself to it with the submissiveness of a compliant wife, thinking that that was how things were, but otherwise finding no pleasure in it. Yet ever since the crime, and without her knowing quite why, it had filled her with considerable repugnance. It played on her nerves, frightened her. One evening, the candle still burning, she shrieked: there on top of her, in that red, convulsed face, she thought she had seen the face of the murderer; and thenceforward she trembled every time with the horrible sensation that the murder was being committed there and then, as though he had shoved her on to her back at knife-point. It was ridiculous, but her heart pounded in terror. In fact he forced himself on her less and less now, sensing her too resistant for his own pleasure. It was as though the weariness and indifference that normally comes with age had been brought on in them by this dreadful crime and the spilling of blood. On nights when they could not avoid being together, they each slept on the edge of the bed. And Jacques was quite clearly contributing to this process of separation in that his presence was gradually making them less exclusively taken up with each other. He was releasing them from one another.

Roubaud, meanwhile, experienced no remorse. Until the file on the case was closed, he had merely been worried about what might happen; and now his greatest anxiety was that he might lose his job. As things stood, he had no regrets. Perhaps, though, if he had had to start all over again, he would not have involved his wife; for women are quick to panic, and now he was losing his wife because he had placed too great a burden upon her shoulders. He would have remained her master if he had not descended with her into the terrified and quarrelsome companionship of crime. But that was how things were, he would just have to get used to it; especially as he had to make a real mental effort to put himself back in the frame of mind which had led him, in the wake of her confession, to consider the murder necessary to his own survival. It had seemed to him then that, had he not killed this man, he could not have gone on living. Now that jealousy had ceased to burn within him, that he no longer felt its intolerable, searing flame, a numbness had overtaken him, as though the blood in his heart had turned thick with all the blood that had been spilled, and the necessity of the murder was no longer so evident. It even occurred to him to wonder whether it had all actually been worth killing someone for. Not that this constituted repentance, more a form of disillusion at best, the idea that one often does all manner of unspeakable things in order to be happy but without in fact being any the happier. Once so talkative, he would fall into long silences, periods of turbid reflection from which he emerged in yet more sombre mood. Every day now, in order to avoid remaining alone with his wife after meals, he would climb up on to the station roof to perch on the gable; and there, in the wind coming off the sea, lulled by indeterminate daydreams, he would smoke his pipe and gaze across the town, watching the steamers vanish over the horizon bound for distant waters.

One evening, Roubaud felt a pang of the fierce jealousy of old. He had been to seek out Jacques at the depot and was bringing him back home for a drink when he met Henri Dauvergne, the chief guard, coming down the stairs. The latter looked

embarrassed and explained that he had just been to see
Madame Roubaud on an errand from his sisters. The truth was
that for some time now he had been pursuing Séverine in the
hope of a conquest.

Opening the door, Roubaud shouted roughly at his wife:

'What the hell was he doing here again? You know I can't
stand him!'

'But it was only about an embroidery pattern, dear.'

'I'll give him embroidery all right. Do you think I'm daft
enough not to know what he came looking for? . . . Just you
watch yourself!'

He was advancing towards her, his fists clenched, and she was
backing away, white as a sheet, astonished at the force of this
outburst after the quiet indifference they had felt towards each
other of late. But already he was beginning to calm down, and he
turned to his companion:

'It's true, you know, these fellows turn up on your doorstep
and think the wife's going to throw herself at 'em while the
husband shuts his eyes and thinks what an honour! It makes my
blood boil, it does . . . You know what I'd do if it happened to
me? I'd strangle my wife, there and then. I would. And that little
upstart had better not be back, or I'll give him what for . . . It
makes you sick, doesn't it?'

Jacques, extremely embarrassed by this scene, was at a loss as
to how he should react. Was this exaggerated display of anger for
his benefit? Was the man trying to warn him? He was reassured
to hear him cheerfully continue:

'Anyway, you silly thing, I know you'd send him packing
yourself . . . Come on, get us some glasses and come and have a
drink with us.'

He was patting Jacques on the shoulder, and Séverine, who
had also recovered her composure, smiled at the two men. Then
they drank together, and spent a pleasant hour.

Thus did Roubaud bring his wife and colleague together, as
though they were all good friends, and without any apparent
thought for the possible consequences. In fact this matter of
Roubaud's jealousy prompted an even greater sense of intimacy
between Jacques and Séverine, a secret affection deepened by
confidences shared; for, when he saw her again two days later,

Jacques sympathized with her over the coarse way she had been treated, and she, moist-eyed, revealed, by the very manner in which her grievances poured involuntarily from her, how little happiness she had found in her marriage. From that moment they had something of their own they could discuss, a friendly complicity in which the merest signal soon sufficed. At each visit he would look enquiringly at her to discover if she had had any new cause for sadness. She would respond in kind, with a simple flicker of her eyelids. Then their hands reached out for each other, when the husband's back was turned, and grew bolder, communicating in long squeezes, telling each other, with the tips of their warm fingers, of the growing interest they now took in the minutest detail of each other's existence. Rarely did they have the good fortune to be together, even for a minute, without Roubaud being present. He was constantly there, between them, in this dreary dining-room; and they made no effort to elude him, it did not even occur to them to arrange a meeting elsewhere, in some remote corner of the station. Thus far theirs was a genuine affection, an attraction born of keen sympathy, and he was scarcely an impediment to it, since a simple glance or clasp of the hand still sufficed for them to understand each other.

The first time Jacques whispered in Séverine's ear that he would be waiting for her the following Thursday, at midnight behind the depot, she recoiled and snatched her hand away. It was her week of freedom, the week when Roubaud was on night shift. But it had unsettled her greatly to think of leaving the flat and going off to meet this man all that way through the darkness of the station. She experienced a confusion she had never known before, the fear of the inexperienced virgin who can feel her heart beat faster; and she did not yield at once, for almost a fortnight he had to keep asking her until she finally consented, despite the fact that she herself ardently longed to make this nocturnal journey. It was the beginning of June, and the evenings were becoming oppressively warm, barely cooled by the sea breeze. Three times already he had waited for her, hoping always that she would come and meet him despite her refusal. That evening she had said no once again; but there was no moon this particular night, the sky was overcast, and not a single star gleamed above the sultry haze. And as he stood there, in the shadows, he saw her come at last, treading silently, dressed in black. It was so dark that she could have brushed past without seeing him if he had not caught her in his arms and kissed her. She gave a slight, tremulous cry. Then, laughing, she allowed her lips to linger on his. But that was all, not once would she accept to sit with him in any of the various sheds that were all around. They walked, and they talked in low voices, pressing close together. There was a huge open space here, taken up by the depot and its buildings, the whole area between the Rue Verte and the Rue François-Mazeline, each of which cuts across the tracks at a level-crossing: it was like some immense wasteland, full of sidings and water tanks and hydrants, of buildings of every sort, the two great engine-sheds, the Sauvagnats' little house surrounded by its pocket-handkerchief of a vegetable patch, the huts that housed the repair workshops, the quarters where the drivers and firemen slept; and nothing could have been easier than to hide away in all this, to vanish from sight as in the middle of a wood, among its deserted alleys and unfathomable paths. For an hour they enjoyed this delicious privacy, unburdening their hearts of all the affectionate reflections which had been accumulating for so long, waiting to be said; for she would hear only of affection, she had told him at once that she would never be his, that it simply would not do to sully this pure friendship of which she was so proud, that they needed to be able to respect each other. Then he accompanied her to the Rue Verte, and their mouths met once more, in a long kiss. And home she went.

At that very hour, in the assistant station-masters' office, Roubaud was beginning to doze off in the old leather armchair from which he would rise, with aching limbs, some twenty times a night. Until nine o'clock he had to see the evening trains in and out. The fish train in particular kept him busy, with all the shunting and coupling and the despatch dockets that had to be carefully checked. Then, when the Paris express had arrived and been uncoupled, he would sit alone at a corner of the office table and have his supper, a piece of cold meat between two slices of bread, which he had brought down with him. The last train, a slow from Rouen, came in at half-past midnight. And then a profound silence would descend on the deserted platforms; only a handful of gas-lamps were left burning, and the whole station fell into a slumber, in the flickering semi-darkness. Of the station staff there remained only two foremen and four or five workmen, under the orders of the assistant station-master. And even they were snoring away like troopers, stretched out on the floor of the sleeping-quarters; while Roubaud, obliged to wake them at the slightest alert, could only doze, ear cocked. In case tiredness should get the better of him towards dawn, he would set his alarm-clock for five, the time at which he had to be up and ready to see in the first train from Paris. But sometimes, especially recently, he had not been able to sleep, and insomnia had kept him fidgeting uncomfortably in his chair. Then he would go out and do his rounds, walking as far as the pointsman's hut where he would linger briefly to have a word. The huge black sky and the supreme peace of the night would eventually calm his fever. Since being involved in a fight with intruders he had been armed with a revolver, which he carried loaded in his pocket. And around he would go, often until dawn, stopping the moment he thought he saw the darkness stir, and walking on again in vague regret that he had not had to shoot, finally relieved when the sky lightened and drew the great pale phantom of the station out of the shadows. Now that it was getting light by three, he would go back and slump in his armchair, where he fell fast asleep, until the alarm-clock roused him, startled, to his feet.

Every fortnight, on the Thursday and the Saturday, Séverine would go to meet Jacques; and one night, as she was telling him about the revolver with which her husband was armed, they became anxious. Roubaud, it was true, never went as far as the depot. None the less this lent a semblance of danger to their walks, which further added to their charm. In particular they had found a perfect spot: it was behind the Sauvagnats' house, a sort of alleyway between two enormous piles of coal, which made it seem like the one solitary street in a strange city of great square palaces built of black marble. They were completely out of sight there, and at the end of the alleyway was a little tool-shed in which a heap of empty sacks would have made the softest of beds. But when a sudden shower one Saturday had forced them to take shelter there, she had insisted on remaining standing, yielding only her lips to him, in never-ending kisses. In these she abandoned her modesty and gave her breath to be drunk, greedily, as a favour to a friend. And when, roused to passion, he tried to take her, she would resist, each time tearfully giving the same reasons. Why did he want to make her unhappy like this? It was such a tender thing, it seemed to her, to love each other without all the dirtiness of sex! Soiled at sixteen by the depravity of that old man whose bloody spectre haunted her, and later abused by the brutal appetites of her husband, she had retained a childlike innocence, a virginal purity, all the charming bashfulness of a passion that knows not itself. What delighted her about Jacques was his gentleness, his obedient willingness to cease running his hands over her as soon as she took them gently in her own, feeble though hers were. For the first time she was in love, and she did not give herself because, precisely, it would have spoiled her love to belong to him at once as she had to the other two men. Her unconscious desire was to prolong such a delicious sensation for ever, to become the young girl again, before she had been defiled, to have a sweetheart the way one does at fifteen, kissing on the mouth behind doors. And, his moments of feverish passion apart, he made no demands on her, content to go along with this voluptuous deferral of felicity. Like her he felt as though he were returning to his childhood, as though love were just beginning, love which until then had been nothing but a source of horror. If he was amenable and withdrew his hands as soon as she removed them, it was because deep down in his feelings of love there remained an unspoken fear, a great uncertainty, which made him worry that he might be confusing desire with his old urge to murder. This woman who herself had killed was like his flesh's dream come true. That he was cured seemed to him every day more certain, since he had held her for hours, her arms around his neck, his mouth on hers, drinking in her soul, without feeling that crazed desire to be her master by cutting her throat. But he still didn't dare; and it was so good to wait like this, to leave it to their love to bring them together, when the right moment came and their willed resistance faded in each other's arms. And so their happy meetings followed one upon the other, and they never for a moment tired of seeing each other again and walking together in the darkness, between the great piles of coal that rendered the surrounding darkness yet blacker still.

One night in July, Jacques, in order to reach Le Havre on time at 11.05, had to urge La Lison on, as if the stifling heat had made her lazy. Over to his left a storm had been following him ever since Rouen, moving up the valley of the Seine with great, blinding flashes of lightning; and from time to time he looked round anxiously, for Séverine was to come and meet him that evening. He was afraid that if the storm broke too soon, it might prevent her from coming out. So, having succeeded in reaching the station before the rain, he grew impatient with the endless crowd of passengers still issuing from the carriages.

Roubaud was there, standing on the platform, tied up with the duties of the night shift.

'Goodness!' he laughed, 'you seem to be in a bit of a hurry to get to bed . . . Sleep well.'

'Thanks.'

And Jacques, having backed the train out, pulled on the whistle and made for the depot. The folding doors of the huge entrance were open, and La Lison disappeared into the covered engine-shed, a kind of gallery about seventy metres long containing two tracks, with room for six locomotives. It was very dark in there, and four gas-lamps scarcely made any impression on the blackness, seeming rather to increase it by casting great, moving shadows; only the occasional broad flash of lightning made the skylights and the tall windows on either side seem to burst into flame. And then, as when a building is on fire, one could make out the cracked walls, and the roof-beams blackened with soot, the whole shabby dilapidation of a ramshackle building no longer adequate to its purpose. Two engines were already standing there, slumbering and cold.

Immediately Pecqueux began to put out the engine's fire. He raked it violently, and the cinders fell through the grate into the ashpit.

'I'm too hungry to do this, I'm off for something to eat,' he said. 'Coming?'

Jacques did not reply. Despite being in a hurry, he did not want to leave La Lison before the firebox had been emptied and the boiler drained. It was a point of principle, the practice of a good driver, and one from which he never departed. When he had the time, he wouldn't even leave without inspecting the

engine and carefully rubbing it down as though he were groom-
ing a favourite animal.

The water gushed down into the pit, and only then did he say:
'Come on, quick.'

A tremendous clap of thunder interrupted him. This time the
tall windows had stood out so clearly against the flaming sky that
one could have counted the broken panes, of which there were
many. On the left, beside the line of vices used for repairs, a
sheet of boiler-plate which had been left upright rang out with
the echoing chime of a church bell. The whole of the roof-
timbering had cracked.

'Bugger me!' the fireman said simply.

The driver gestured despairingly. That did it, especially as
rain was now deluging down on to the shed. The glass in the roof
looked as though it might cave in under the rattling force of the
downpour. There must have been broken panes up there, too,
because it was raining on La Lison, great drops of it, bucketing
down. A furious gale was blasting in through the doors, which
were still open, and it was as if the entire shell of the old building
was about to be blown away.

Pecqueux was putting the final touches to the engine.

'There! We'll be able to see better tomorrow . . . No need to
tart her up any more just now . . .'

And then, his thoughts reverting:

'Time to eat . . . It's too wet for us to turn in yet.'

The canteen, in fact, was just around the corner, right next to
the depot itself; whereas the Company had had to rent a house,
in the Rue François-Mazeline, where there were beds for the
drivers and firemen staying in Le Havre overnight. In the time it
would have taken them to get there in such torrential rain, they
would have been soaked to the skin.

Jacques had to resign himself to following Pecqueux, who had
picked up his chief's small food-basket as though to save him the
bother of carrying it. He knew it still contained two slices of cold
veal, along with some bread and a bottle that had hardly been
touched; and this, quite simply, was what was making him
hungry. It was raining even harder now, and another clap of
thunder had just shaken the engine-shed. By the time the two
men went out through the small door on the left which led to the

canteen, La Lison was already growing cold. She settled into sleep, abandoned there in the darkness broken by violent flashes of lightning, beneath the heavy splashes of rain that soaked her haunches. Next to her, water was running from a feeder-tap which had not been properly turned off, making a large pool that flowed between her wheels, along the pit.

But, before going into the canteen, Jacques wanted to clean himself up. Hot water was always available in an adjacent room, where there were tubs to wash in. He took a bar of soap out of his basket and removed the grime from his hands and face, black from the journey; and having taken the precaution, as all drivers were advised, to bring a set of clean clothes, he was able to change completely—as he always did in fact, as though he were getting dressed up to go out, every time he arrived in Le Havre on a night they were due to meet. Pecqueux was already waiting for him in the canteen, having scarcely washed more than the tips of his nose and fingers.

This canteen consisted simply of a small, bare, yellow-painted room, with only one stove to heat the food on and just one table, fixed to the floor, with a zinc top in place of a table-cloth. Two benches completed the furnishing. The men had to bring their own food and ate off paper with the point of a knife. The room was lit by a large window.

'Bloody rain!' Jacques shouted, going over to stand by the window.

Pecqueux had sat down on a bench, in front of the table.

'Aren't you eating then?'

'No, mate, finish the bread and meat if you want . . . I'm not hungry.'

Without waiting to be asked twice, Pecqueux devoured the veal and finished off the bottle. He often had windfalls like this, since his chief had a small appetite; and he loved him the more, in his dog-like devotion, for all the crumbs he picked up after him like this. His mouth full, he continued after a pause:

'So what if it's raining? We made it in time, didn't we? Mind you, if it keeps up, I'm leaving you to it. It's off next door for me.'

He began to laugh, for he made no secret of it; he had had to tell Jacques about himself and Philomène Sauvagnat so that

Jacques wouldn't be surprised to find him sleeping out all those nights he went to her. Since her room at her brother's was on the ground floor, next to the kitchen, he had only to tap on the shutter for her to open the window, and in he stepped, simple as that. They'd all had their leg over that window, so it was said, every man jack in the station. But now she made do with the fireman, having no need, it seemed, of another.

'God damn and blast it,' Jacques swore beneath his breath, seeing the torrents come on even stronger after a lull.

Pecqueux, the last mouthful of meat poised on the tip of his knife, again laughed good-naturedly.

'So you had something on then this evening, did you? Well, between the pair of us they can hardly accuse us of wearing out the mattresses over there in the Rue François-Mazeline, can they?'

Jacques came away from the window abruptly.

'What d'you mean?'

'Well, I mean, you've been just like me since the spring, never back till two or three in the morning.'

He must know something. Perhaps he had seen them meet. In each dormitory the beds were arranged in pairs, the fireman's next to the driver's, because they tried to make the two men live as intimately as possible, given that they had to co-operate so closely at work. Hence it was not surprising that Pecqueux had noticed Jacques's irregular pattern of behaviour, since up until then he had lived very much to a routine.

'I get headaches,' Jacques replied, saying the first thing that occurred to him. 'It helps me if I have a walk round at night.'

But already the fireman was having none of it.

'Oh, you're a free man, you know . . . I was only joking . . . And what's more, if you're ever in any bother some day, don't you hesitate to come to me. Because I'm your man, you know, anything you want.'

Without further elaboration, he ventured to shake him by the hand, nearly crushing it as he pledged himself body and soul. Then he crumpled up the greasy paper in which the meat had been wrapped and threw it away, and put the empty bottle back in the basket, carrying out these menial chores in the manner of a methodical servant accustomed to broom and mop. And as the rain was still refusing to let up, even though the thunder had stopped, he said:

'Well, I'll be off then. I'll leave you to it.'

'Oh well,' said Jacques, 'since it's not going to stop, I'll go and have a lie-down on the camp-bed.'

Next to the depot was a room with loose-covered mattresses where the men came and rested, still in their clothes, when they only had three or four hours to wait in Le Havre. Sure enough, as soon as he had seen the fireman vanish into the pouring rain in the direction of the Sauvagnats' house, he decided to make a run for it himself as far as these sleeping-quarters. He did not lie down, however, preferring instead to stand by the wide-open door, so overpowering was the heat and stuffiness of the room. By the far wall a driver was stretched out on his back, snoring with his mouth open.

A few more minutes went by, and Jacques still could not bring himself to give up hope. In his exasperation at this stupid downpour he increasingly felt a mad desire to go to their meeting-place anyway and at least have the joy of being there himself, even if he no longer expected Séverine to come. His whole body urged him to it, and finally he departed beneath the rain and arrived at their favourite spot, making his way down the black alleyway between the piles of coal. And since the huge drops of rain lashing his face made it impossible to see, he continued on as far as the tool-shed where they had sought shelter once before. It seemed to him that there he would feel less alone.

No sooner had Jacques entered the profound darkness of this retreat when two slender arms enveloped him and warm lips were laid on his. Séverine was there.

'My God, so you came?'

'Yes, I saw the storm coming and hurried over before the rain came . . . How long you've been!'

Her voice faded to a sigh, he had never known her embrace him with such abandon. She slid to the floor, and found herself sitting on the empty sacks, the soft bed which took up a whole corner of the shed. And he, dropping down beside her still locked in their embrace, could feel his legs lying across hers. They could not see each other, and their breath wrapped them in a giddy blur, blotting out all consciousness of their surroundings.

But, in the ardent appeal of their kiss, the voice of intimacy had risen also to their lips, like a mingling of their life-blood:

'You were waiting for me . . .'

'Oh, I was waiting for you, waiting and waiting.'

And at once, from the very first minute, almost without words, it was she who pulled him towards her, forcing him to take her. She had not intended it. When he had arrived, she had already given up hope of seeing him; and just now she had simply been carried away by the unexpected joy of holding him in her arms, by a sudden, irresistible urge to be his, without thought or deliberation. It was so because it was meant to be so. The rain beat down still harder on the roof of the shed, and the last train from Paris passed by on its way into the station, rumbling and whistling, making the ground shake.

When eventually Jacques raised himself, he listened with surprise to the rattle of the rain. Where was he, then? And the moment his hand touched the shaft of a hammer lying on the ground, which he had already felt there when he first sat down, joy flooded through him. So he'd done it? He'd made love to Séverine and he hadn't grabbed the hammer and smashed her skull in. She was his without a fight, without that instinctive desire to sling her dead body over his shoulder like a prey snatched away from others. No longer did he feel that thirsting need to avenge some ancient, dimly remembered wrong, the sense of grievance accumulated from male to male ever since that first betrayal in the depths of some cave. No, the possession of this woman wove a powerful spell, she had cured him, because he saw her as different, as violent in her weakness, covered in a man's blood as by a breastplate of horror. She dominated him, for he was the one who had not dared. And it was with tender gratitude, the desire to melt into her, that he took her once more in his arms.

Séverine, too, was abandoning herself totally, overjoyed to be delivered from a struggle whose purpose she no longer understood. Why had she resisted for so long? She had promised herself to him, she ought to have given herself, since there could only be pleasure and sweetness in it. Now she saw clearly that she had always wanted to, even when it had seemed so good to wait. All that kept her heart and body alive was this need for one absolute, continuing love, and it had been a dreadful, cruel thing the way events had conspired to involve her in these terrifying abominations. Life until now had abused her with its blood and filth, and so violently that her beautiful blue eyes, though they retained their look of innocence, now stared in terror beneath the dark, dramatic helmet of her black hair. She had remained a virgin in spite of everything, and she had just given herself for the first time, to this man she adored, with the desire to lose herself in him, to be his servant. She belonged to him now, he could do with her as he pleased.

'Oh, my darling, take me, keep me, I want only what you want.'

'No, no, my dearest, you shall command, I am here only to love you and obey.'

Hours passed. The rain had long since stopped, and a great silence hung over the station, broken only by the sound of some indistinct, far-off voice coming up from the sea. They were still lying in each other's arms when a gunshot brought them trembling to their feet. It was almost daybreak, and a faint patch of light was paling the sky over the Seine estuary. Why the shot? Suddenly conscious of their heedlessness, their madness in lingering like this, they had visions of the husband pursuing them with a revolver.

'Don't go out! Wait, I'll go and see.'

Feeling his way carefully, Jacques had got as far as the door. And there in the shadows, for it was still quite dark, he heard men running towards them and recognized Roubaud's voice urging the foremen on and shouting to them that there were three intruders, that he had clearly seen them stealing coal. During the last few weeks especially, not a night had gone by without his having hallucinations like this about imaginary brigands. This time, seized by a sudden panic, he had fired at random into the darkness.

'Quick, come on, we can't stay here,' murmured Jacques. 'They'll come and search the shed . . . You make a run for it!'

They had seized each other once more in a breathless, tight embrace, lips pressed upon lips. Then Séverine flitted softly away, running along the side of the depot, concealed by the huge wall; while he quietly hid among the piles of coal. And just in time, in fact, for Roubaud did indeed want to search the shed. He swore the intruders must be in there. The foremen's lanterns danced along the ground. There was an argument. Eventually they all headed back towards the station, annoyed at this wild-goose chase.

Sensing that the coast was clear, Jacques was just deciding to go and get some sleep at last in the Rue François-Mazeline when, to his surprise, he nearly bumped into Pecqueux, who was doing up his clothes and cursing beneath his breath.

'What's up, mate?'

'Ah, Christ, don't ask! The bloody fools woke Sauvagnat, didn't they? He heard me with his sister and came down in his nightshirt to see. I jumped out the window as fast as I could . . . Wait! Just listen to that.'

They could hear the screams and sobbing of a woman being beaten, and the loud voice of a man shouting abuse and telling her off.

'Hear that? Off he goes, giving her what for yet again. She might be thirty-two, but he whips her as though she was a girl whenever he catches her . . . Ah well, can't be helped, it's none of my business. He is her brother after all!'

'But', said Jacques, 'I thought he didn't mind about you, that he only got worked up when he found her with someone else.'

'Oh, you can never be sure. Sometimes he turns a blind eye, and then other times, you see, it's out with the fists . . . It doesn't stop him loving his sister, he'd rather give it all up than be parted from her. It's just that he wants her to behave herself . . . God almighty! She's getting her fair share this time.'

The screams were dying down, to be replaced by loud groaning, and the two men moved away. Ten minutes later they were fast asleep, side by side, in the little yellow-painted dormitory, with its simple furnishing of four chairs and a table, and a single metal basin.

Thereafter, every night they met, Jacques and Séverine knew great happiness. They did not always have the protection of a storm like this. Starlit skies and blazing moons were trouble-some; but on these occasions they hurried into bands of shadow, seeking out dark corners where it felt so good to hold each other close. And during August and September there were some wonderful nights of this kind, nights so mild that the sunrise would have caught them still languishing in each other's arms had not the noises of the station stirring into life and the distant puffing of locomotives already parted them. Even the first chilly nights of October were not unwelcome. She would come more warmly dressed, wrapped in a large coat, under which he too half-vanished. Then they would barricade themselves in the tool-shed, which they had found a means of shutting from the inside with an iron bar. For them this was home, and the November gales with their sudden gusts of wind could tear the slates off the roofs, they did not so much as feel a draught. However, ever since that first evening, Jacques had had one desire, to possess her in her own home, in that cramped flat, where she seemed different, more desirable, with that calm, smiling air of a respectable housewife; and she had always refused, less because of the corridor spies than out of a last remaining scruple of virtue, wishing to keep the marriage bed separate. But one Monday, in broad daylight, when he was there for lunch and her husband was late getting back having been detained by the station-master, he jokingly carried her to the bed in a mad fit of incaution, which left them both helpless with laughter; with the result that they quite forgot where they were. After that she offered no further resistance, and he would go up and meet her there, after midnight, every Thursday and Saturday. They were taking a dreadful risk: because of the neighbours they hardly dared to move, but this only added to their love and brought them new pleasures. Often the fancy would take them to dash out into the night, a desire to flee like escaped animals into the dark solitude of the freezing night. In December once, during a bitter frost, they made love out there.

Jacques and Séverine had already been living like this for four months, and with growing passion. They were both genuinely inexperienced and at that infant stage in their emotional lives when innocence is startled by first love and delights in the merest caress. Between them the contest in submissiveness continued, as each vied with the other in the sacrifice of self. Jacques, for his part, no longer had any doubt, he had found a cure to his awful hereditary disorder; for since he had first made love to her, the thought of murder had never once troubled him. Was it that physical possession satisfied this thirst for death? Did possessing and killing amount to the same thing deep within the dark recesses of the human beast? He did not reason consciously, he was too ignorant for that, nor did he endeavour to prise open the gates of horror. Sometimes, as they lay together, he would suddenly remember what she had done, the murder to which she had confessed by the merest glance on the bench in the Square des Batignolles; and yet he had no desire to know the details. She, on the other hand, seemed more and more tormented by the need to tell him everything. When she held him, he could feel her all bursting, gasping, with her secret, as if she only wanted to fuse into one with him like this so that she could unburden herself of that which was suffocating her. A great tremor would spring from her loins, lifting her breasts in passion and rising to her lips in a mingling stream of sighs. Hadn't that voice been about to say something before it faltered in the spasmic moment? But quickly, with a kiss, he would close her mouth, setting a seal upon her confession, suddenly anxious. Why let this unknown thing come between them? Could one be sure that it would make no difference to their happiness? He sensed a danger, and his shuddering would return at the idea of their going over these bloody deeds again. And no doubt she guessed as much, for, as she lay against him, she would become fondly yielding once more, a creature of love, meant only to love and to be loved. Then a frenzied lust for possession would take hold, and leave them sometimes completely senseless in each other's arms.

Roubaud had grown even stouter since the summer, and just as his wife was recovering the gaiety and freshness of a woman of twenty, so he was ageing and seemed increasingly morose. In the space of four months he had, as she told him herself, changed a great deal. He still shook Jacques cordially by the hand and invited him back, and he was really only happy when he had him sitting at his table. Except that this distraction was no longer sufficient, and he often went out the moment he had downed his last mouthful, sometimes leaving his friend there with his wife, on the pretext that he found the heat oppressive and that he needed some fresh air. The truth was that he was now frequent-

ing a small café on the Cours Napoléon, where he would meet
Monsieur Cauche, the superintendent. He never drank much,
just the occasional small glass of rum; but he had developed a
taste for card-playing which was becoming an obsession. He only
came alive again, could only truly forget, when he had cards in
his hand and was immersed in endless games of piquet. Monsieur Cauche, who was also fanatically keen, had decided that
they would play for money, and they had now reached the level
of a hundred sous a game; and from that point on, Roubaud,
astonished at the change in himself, had burned with a rabid
thirst for gain, with that raging fever for winning money that
ravages a man to the point where he will risk his position, his
whole life even, on a single throw of the dice. So far his work had
not suffered; he got away as soon as he was free and returned
home only at two or three in the morning, on the nights when he
was not on duty. His wife did not complain, merely reproaching
him for being in an even worse mood when he finally did come
home: for he had extraordinarily bad luck, and this meant that he
was getting into debt.

One evening, the first quarrel broke out between Séverine and
Roubaud. While she did not yet hate him, things had got to the
point where she found him difficult to bear, for she could feel
him weighing on her life, she who could have been so happy and
carefree had he not been there to burden her with his presence!
Moreover, she felt no remorse at being unfaithful to him: wasn't
it his fault, hadn't he virtually forced her into it? They were
slowly drifting apart, and by way of alleviating this unwholesome
disorder in their lives, they were each seeking solace and amusement in their own particular way. Since he had his gambling, she
could perfectly well have a lover. But what did make her especially angry, something she could not just quietly accept, were
the straitened circumstances resulting from his continual losses.
Ever since the housekeeping had been disappearing in five-franc
pieces at the café on the Cours Napoléon, she had sometimes
been at her wits' end to know how she was going to pay her
laundrywoman. She herself wanted for all sorts of little comforts
and personal requisites. And this particular evening it was precisely over a pair of ankle-boots she needed that they had begun
to quarrel. About to go out and unable to find the kitchen-knife

to cut himself a slice of bread, Roubaud had used the big knife, the murder weapon, which had been lying in a drawer of the dresser. She stared at him as he refused the fifteen francs for the boots—he didn't have the money, didn't know how he could lay his hands on it; and she kept asking him, stubbornly, forcing him to repeat his refusal in increasing exasperation. But then, suddenly, she pointed to the spot on the floor where their ghosts lurked, and told him that there was money there all right, and that she wanted some of it. He turned very pale and let go of the knife, which fell back into the drawer. For a moment she thought that he was going to hit her, for he had drawn near, spluttering that the money could rot where it was, that he would cut his own hand off rather than touch it; and, with fists clenched, he threatened to brain her if she took it into her head to lift the wooden block while he was out and take so much as a centime. Never, never! It was dead and buried! But in any case she too had blanched, her resolve failing her at the thought of having to feel around under there. Let them be ruined, they would die of starvation right there beside it. And indeed they never mentioned it again, even when money was tightest. Every time they trod on that particular spot, the burning sensation had got worse, and was now so unbearable that they ended up walking round it.

Then there were other disputes, about La Croix-de-Maufras. Why were they having no success in selling the house? And each accused the other of not doing what was necessary to hasten its sale. He still violently refused to have anything to do with it; while she, on the rare occasions when she wrote to Misard, received only evasive replies: no buyer had appeared, the fruit hadn't ripened, the vegetables weren't growing for lack of water. Little by little, the great calm which had descended on the household after the crisis was thus disrupted, banished, it seemed, by a terrible new onslaught of fever. All the seeds of contention, the hidden money, the advent of the lover, had now germinated and become a source of friction between the couple, driving them apart. And in this growing turmoil life was set to become hell.

Moreover, as if in inevitable consequence, things were taking a similar turn for the worse all around the Roubauds. A new wind of gossip and argument was blowing in the corridor. After a violent altercation Philomène was no longer talking to Madame Lebleu, following the latter's slanderous accusation that she had sold her a chicken that had died of disease. But the real reason for the break in their relations was a reconciliation between Philomène and Séverine. Because Pecqueux had seen her on Jacques's arm one night, Séverine had overcome her previous scruples and decided to make herself agreeable to the fireman's mistress; and Philomène, much flattered by this connection with a lady who was unquestionably the most beautiful and most distinguished around the station, had turned on the ticket-clerk's wife, that old bag, as she put it, who was always stirring up trouble. She accused her of all manner of things, and now went round saying that the flat on the street side belonged to the Roubauds, that it was disgraceful not to let them have it back. Things, therefore, were beginning to go very badly for Madame Lebleu, especially as her relentless spying on Mademoiselle Guichon in the hope of catching her with the station-master also threatened to land her in serious trouble: she still didn't catch them, but she had made the mistake of getting caught herself, listening at doors; so that Monsieur Dabadie, extremely cross at being spied on like this, had told Moulin, his assistant, that if Roubaud claimed the flat again, he was ready to countersign the letter. And when Moulin, not usually a chatterbox, had repeated this, there had almost been door-to-door combat up and down the corridor, so high were feelings now running once more.

In the midst of these growing pressures, Séverine had just the one good day, the Friday. Since October she had had the quiet temerity to invent a pretext, a painful knee (the first thing that had occurred to her) which required her to see a specialist; and every Friday morning she would leave on the 6.40 a.m. express, driven by Jacques, and spend the day with him in Paris before returning on the 6.30 express in the evening. At first she had felt obliged to give her husband news of her knee: it was getting better, it was worse again; then, seeing that he wasn't even listening any more, she had simply stopped telling him about it. And sometimes she would look at him, wondering if he knew. How did this ferociously jealous man, this person who had killed, who had seen red in a fit of imbecilic rage, manage to tolerate her having a lover? She could not believe it, and merely thought that he was losing his wits.

One bitterly cold night in early December, Séverine waited up particularly late for her husband. The following day, a Friday, she was to catch the express before dawn; and on these evenings she usually had a long wash and set out her clothes, so as to be dressed and ready in a moment when she got up. At length she went to bed, and finally fell asleep about one o'clock. Roubaud had not yet come home. Twice already he had not reappeared before dawn, being now completely taken up with his growing obsession and unable to drag himself away from the café, where a small room at the back was gradually turning into a veritable gamblers' den: they had taken to playing écarté in there, for large sums. Happy in any case to have the bed to herself, and lulled to sleep by the prospect of her pleasant day to come, Séverine slept soundly in the soft warmth of the bedclothes.

But just before three she was woken by a peculiar noise. At first she could not make out what it was, and thinking she had been dreaming, she went back to sleep. There were muffled sounds of something being prised open, of wood splintering, as if someone was trying to force a door open. A sudden crack and a more violent ripping sound made her sit bolt upright. She was seized with terror: no doubt about it, someone outside in the corridor was forcing the lock on the door. For a whole minute she did not dare move, straining to listen, her ears humming. Then she found the courage to get out of bed to go and look; she walked noiselessly across the room in her bare feet and gently opened her bedroom door ajar, so petrified with cold that she looked quite white and even slimmer than usual beneath her nightgown. The spectacle she beheld in the dining-room rooted her to the spot in horrified amazement.

Sprawled on the floor and leaning on his elbows, Roubaud had just prised up the wooden floor-block with the help of a chisel. A candle placed nearby gave him light, casting his enormous shadow on to the ceiling. And at that moment his face was bent over the hole, a black slit in the flooring, and he was staring with bulging eyes. His cheeks were purple with blood, he wore his murderer's expression. Violently he plunged his hand in, but he was shaking so much that he found nothing and had to bring the candle closer. Down at the bottom of the hole the purse, the banknotes, and the watch became visible.

Séverine let out an involuntary cry, and Roubaud spun round, terrified. For a moment he did not recognize her and might even have thought he'd seen a ghost, as she stood there, all in white, with a look of horror on her face.

'What on earth are you doing?' she asked.

Then, realizing who it was, rather than reply he simply gave a low grunt. He stared at her, embarrassed by her presence and wanting to send her back to bed. But he could think of nothing sensible to say, all she deserved was a good smack, standing there shivering like that half-naked.

'So,' she continued, 'you won't let me have the boots, and yet you take money for yourself because you've lost again.'

In an instant this sent him into a rage. Was she going to ruin his life all over again and stop him having his fun? Her? This woman he no longer desired? When making love to her was now no better than an unpleasant disturbance? Since he could find his amusement elsewhere, he had absolutely no need of her. He felt around again and took just the purse containing the three hundred gold francs. And when he had put the floor-block back with his heel, he came over to her and, through clenched teeth, spat out:

'You're a bloody nuisance, you are, and I'm going to do exactly as I like. I don't ask questions, do I? Like about what you're going to be up to in Paris, for instance?'

Then, with a furious shrug of his shoulders, he departed once more for the café, leaving the candle on the floor.

Séverine picked it up and went back to bed, frozen to the bone. She left the candle to burn, unable now to go back to sleep, and waited with growing impatience, eyes wide open, for it to be time to take the train. There could no longer be any doubt, a gradual process of disintegration had taken place, as though the crime had been eating away at this man, causing him to decompose, and rotting every bond that had once united them. Roubaud knew.

CHAPTER VII

ON that particular Friday morning, the passengers who were to take the 6.40 express from Le Havre exclaimed in surprise upon waking: snow had been falling since midnight, and in such thick, steady flakes that it lay thirty centimetres deep in the streets.

Already, in the main concourse, La Lison stood puffing steam and smoke, coupled to a train of seven coaches, three second-class and four first. When Jacques and Pecqueux had arrived at the depot about half-past five to inspect the engine, they had groaned anxiously at the snow stubbornly spilling from the black sky. And now they stood at their post waiting for the whistle to blow, their eyes staring into the distance beyond the gaping entrance to the station, and watching the silent, ceaseless fall of flakes striping the darkness with ripples of ghostly white.

The driver muttered:

'I'm damned if I'll be able to see a signal!'

'That's if we can even get through', said the fireman.

Roubaud was there on the platform with his lantern, having returned punctually to begin his shift. From time to time his heavy eyelids closed with exhaustion, but he remained watchful. Jacques having asked him if he knew what state the line was in, he had just been across to shake his hand, replying that he hadn't yet had any reports; and when Séverine came down, wrapped in a thick coat, he escorted her himself to a first-class compartment and settled her in. No doubt he had caught the look of anxious affection that passed between the two lovers; but he didn't even bother to warn his wife that it was unwise to set off in such weather and that she would be better advised to postpone her journey.

Passengers arrived, all muffled up and laden with suitcases, a whole hustle and bustle in the bitter, early morning cold. Even the snow on their shoes remained frozen, and the doors slammed immediately shut as each person barricaded himself in. The platform lay deserted, barely lit by the eerie glimmer of a few gas-lamps; while the engine's headlamp, hanging from the base of its chimney, blazed alone, like a giant eye, spreading its sheet of flame far into the darkness.

But Roubaud raised his lantern, giving the signal. The chief guard blew his whistle, and Jacques replied, having opened the regulator and turned the tiny gear-wheel. They were off. For a further minute the assistant station-master gazed placidly after the train as it disappeared into the blizzard.

'And you watch out,' Jacques told Pecqueux. 'I don't want any nonsense today!'

He had noticed quite distinctly that his companion, too, seemed to be dropping with exhaustion—the result, no doubt, of his excesses on the previous night.

'Oh, no danger of that, no danger,' stammered the fireman.

The moment they emerged from under the station roof, the two men had entered the snow. The wind was blowing from the east, and the engine met it head on, lashed by its gusts. In the shelter of the cab they did not suffer unduly at first, dressed as they were in heavy woollen clothes and wearing goggles to protect their eyes. But in the darkness the brilliant beam from the headlamp seemed to be swallowed up by the thick, wan drapes of falling snow. Instead of being lit at a distance of two or three hundred metres, the track appeared through a kind of milky fog, from which objects loomed into view only at the very last moment, as if from the depths of a dream. And just as he had feared, the driver's main source of anxiety was confirmed by his experience of the light on the first section point: he would certainly not be able to see red warning signals at the regulation distance. From then on he proceeded with extreme caution, but without being able to reduce speed because the wind resistance was enormous and delay of whatever kind would in any case be just as dangerous.

As far as Harfleur station, La Lison kept up a good steady pace. As yet the amount of fallen snow gave Jacques no cause to worry; there were at most only sixty centimetres, and the snow-plough could easily push back a metre. He was exclusively concerned to maintain his speed, knowing full well that the true quality of a driver, after temperance and love for his engine, consisted in driving at an even speed, without jerkiness, and at the highest possible pressure. Indeed his one failing was this stubborn determination never to stop, disobeying the signals and thinking he would always have sufficient time to bring La Lison to a halt; so that sometimes he went too far and ran over deton-ators* (or 'trod on the corns', as they called it), which had twice brought him a week's suspension. But at this moment, in the midst of the great danger which he sensed, the thought that Séverine was with him and that a life so precious was in his charge, made him ten times as determined as he willed his way onwards towards Paris along this double line of metal, beset by obstacles which were his to overcome.

So, standing on the metal footplate which connected the en-gine to the tender, and constantly shaken by its jolting, Jacques leaned out to the right, in spite of the snow, to get a better view. He could see nothing through the cab window, which was blurred with water; and he remained like this, his face turned to the tearing wind, his skin flayed by a thousand needles and so pinched with cold that he felt as though he were being cut by razors. From time to time he would draw back in to recover his breath, removing his goggles and wiping them; and then he would return to his observation post in the teeth of the blast, his eyes staring ahead, waiting for the red signals, and so absorbed in his effort that twice he had the hallucinating vision of sudden, blood-red sparks staining the pale curtain that trembled in front of him.

But all at once, in the darkness, something told him that his fireman was no longer there. The only light was from a tiny lamp by the water-gauge, to save the driver's eyes being dazzled. But on the enamel dial of the pressure-gauge, which seemed to retain a gleam of its own, he had just seen the quivering blue needle sink rapidly: it was the fire burning low. The fireman had slumped across the tool-chest, overcome by sleep.

'Bloody drunkard!' Jacques screamed, shaking him furiously.

Pecqueux got up and apologized with an unintelligible grunt. He could scarcely stand, but by force of habit he returned at once to his fire, hammer in hand, breaking up the coal and shovelling it on to the grate in a good, even layer, after which he swept up. And for as long as the firebox door had remained open, a beam of flaming light had shone back along the train, like the blazing tail of a comet, setting the snow on fire as it fell showering through it in large golden drops.

Beyond Harfleur began the great three-league climb up to Saint-Romain, the steepest on the whole line. So the driver returned to his driving, concentrating hard and waiting for the sudden tug as they began to ascend this incline, which was testing enough even in fine weather. His hand on the gear-wheel, he watched the telegraph poles flash past, trying to calculate his speed. It was dropping fast, La Lison was labouring, and he could feel the increasing resistance of the snow against the plough. With his foot he opened the firebox door again; and the fireman, still half-asleep, understood and stoked the fire afresh, in order to build up the pressure. By now the door itself was turning red, casting a purplish glow over their legs. But they couldn't feel its blazing heat in the icy blast around them. At a sign from his chief, the fireman had also raised the lever on the ashpan, which increased the draught. The needle on the pressure-gauge had rapidly gone back up to ten atmospheres; La Lison was producing all the power of which she was capable. For a moment even, seeing the water-level drop, the driver had to adjust the little injector-wheel, even though that reduced the pressure. But it soon recovered, and the engine was snorting and spitting like an animal being driven too hard, rearing and jolting so much one could almost hear its limbs cracking. And Jacques bullied her along as if she were an old woman whose strength was failing, someone he no longer loved as once he had.

'She'll never make it, the lazy bitch,' he said through gritted teeth, he who normally never spoke throughout the journey.

Pecqueux looked at him in sleepy astonishment. Why had he turned against La Lison now? Wasn't she still the fine, obedient engine she'd always been, moving off so smoothly that it was a pleasure to set her going, and such a good steamer that she saved a tenth of her coal between Paris and Le Havre? When an engine had slide-valves like hers, perfectly adjusted and cutting off the steam with miraculous precision, you could forgive her any number of failings, the way you can a nagging housewife if she's thrifty and efficient. No doubt she did use too much grease. So what? You just got on and greased her, and there was an end of it!

And indeed at that precise moment Jacques was repeating in exasperation:

'She'll never make it unless we grease her.'

And he did what he had seldom ever done, he grabbed the grease-gun to lubricate her while she was running. Stepping over the rail, he climbed on to the footplate and walked the length of the boiler. But it was an extremely perilous operation: his feet were slipping on the narrow strip of iron, which was wet from the snow; he could see nothing, and the terrible wind threatened to sweep him away like chaff. And La Lison, with this man clinging to her side, pursued her breathless path into the night, opening up a deep furrow for herself through the vast blanket of white. She seemed to be trying to shake him off, as she bore him away into the distance. Having reached the front bumper-beam, he crouched down by the lubricating cup on the right-hand cylinder, which he had the greatest difficulty in filling as he clung with one hand to the handrail. Then he had to go all the way round, crawling like an insect, to grease the left-hand cylinder. And when he returned, exhausted, his face was completely white, for he had sensed the proximity of death.

'Filthy beast,' he muttered.

Struck by this unaccustomed roughness towards their Lison, Pecqueux could not help venturing yet again his usual joke:

'Should have let me do it. I know all about lubricating the ladies!'

Having woken up a little, Pecqueux had now also returned to his post and was keeping an eye on the left-hand side of the track. Normally he had good eyesight, better than his chief's. But in this blizzard everything had disappeared, and they who knew every inch of the route could scarcely recognize the places they passed through: the track had sunk beneath the snow, and the hedges, and even the houses themselves, seemed to have been swallowed up, leaving just one flat, endless plain, a jumble of indeterminate white shapes in which La Lison appeared to be galloping about wherever she liked, like some crazed beast. And never had the two men felt so keenly the brotherly bond which

united them, here upon this speeding engine as it hurtled forwards in the face of every conceivable peril, and upon which they
felt more alone, more abandoned by the world, than if they had
been locked away in a room together, and with this additional,
crushing responsibility for the human lives they were pulling
along behind them.

So Jacques, who had previously begun to find Pecqueux's
joke irritating, had eventually smiled back, controlling the
anger which was welling inside him. This was certainly not
the moment for a quarrel. The snow was falling even harder,
a thickening curtain between them and the horizon. They were
continuing to climb when the fireman in turn thought he saw a
red light glittering in the distance. Briefly he informed his
chief. But already he couldn't see it any more; his eyes had
been dreaming, as he put it. And Jacques, who had seen nothing,
was left feeling even more anxious, disturbed at this hallucination glimpsed by another, and losing confidence in himself.
What *he* imagined he could see beyond the pallid swirl of snowflakes were huge black shapes, great masses, like giant pieces of
the night seemingly on the move and coming towards the engine.
Were they landslips, mountains of earth blocking the line, all set
to smash the train to pieces? Then, seized with fear, he gave a
long, desperate pull on the whistle; and this lamentation echoed
mournfully through the storm. Then he was completely astonished to find that he had whistled as he should, for the train was
tearing through Saint-Romain station, which he had thought
was still two kilometres away.

Having by now successfully managed the dreaded incline, La
Lison began to run more smoothly, and Jacques could draw
breath for a moment. From Saint-Romain to Bolbec the track
climbs imperceptibly, and everything would no doubt be fine as
far as the other side of the plateau. Nevertheless, when he made
his three-minute stop at Beuzeville, he called to the station-
master whom he saw standing on the platform, wanting to tell
him of his misgivings about the snow which was lying more
thickly by the minute: he would never make it to Rouen, the best
thing would be to double-head by adding a second locomotive
while they were here at a depot which had a ready supply of relief
engines. But the station-master replied that he had no orders to

this effect and felt he ought not to take it upon himself to authorize it. All he offered was to give them five or six wooden shovels with which to clear the track if the need arose. So Pecqueux took the shovels and stacked them in a corner of the tender.

Up on the plateau, La Lison did in fact make good speed, and without undue difficulty. But she was flagging nevertheless. The driver had constantly to keep opening the firebox door as a sign to the fireman to put more coal on; and each time he did, there rose above the sombre-looking train—itself black against all this white and covered in a shroud—the blazing comet's tail, boring into the night. It was a quarter to eight, and day was breaking; but the paling of the sky was scarcely perceptible through the huge tumbling swirl of white which filled the space from one horizon to the other. This eerie light, in which nothing was yet visible, worried the two men still more, as they peered into the distance with eyes that watered in spite of their goggles. Without letting go of the gear-wheel, the driver also kept his hand on the whistle-rod, whistling almost continuously, for safety's sake, a sad whistle of distress amidst the snowy wasteland.

They went through Bolbec, then Yvetot, without a hitch. But at Motteville Jacques once again called over to the assistant station-master, who was unable to give him any precise information about the state of the line. No other train had yet been through, and the telegraph simply said that the slow train from Paris had been stopped at Rouen as a precaution. So La Lison set off again, making her laboured, weary way down the three leagues of gentle gradient to Barentin. It was getting light now, a very pale light, more of a livid gleam that seemed to issue from the snow itself. This was falling more thickly, like a cataract of jumbled, frosty dawn, engulfing the earth in the debris of the sky. As it grew lighter, the wind increased in strength and the snowflakes were blown along like bullets, and the fireman had continually to take his shovel and clear it off the coal piled at the back of the tender between the sides of the water-tank. The countryside was now visible to right and left, but so unrecognizable that both men felt as though they were speeding through a dream-world: the vast, flat fields, the lush pastures surrounded by hedgerows, the orchards planted with apple-trees, all now but one single white sea, barely rippled by a few tiny waves, a pale, quivering immensity in which everything had succumbed beneath the whiteness. Standing there with his face lacerated by the biting wind and his hand on the wheel, the driver was beginning to suffer horribly from the cold.

Eventually, during the stop at Barentin, the station-master Monsieur Bessière himself approached the engine to warn Jacques that considerable quantities of snow were reported in the vicinity of La Croix-de-Maufras.

'I think you can still get through,' he added. 'But it'll be touch and go.'

At that Jacques let fly.

'Bloody hell! I told them so at Beuzeville! What skin off their nose was it to put another engine on? . . . Well, that's bloody marvellous.'

The chief guard had just got down from his van, and he too was angry. He was frozen stiff from keeping a look-out and said how he couldn't tell a signal from a telegraph-pole. Proper blind man's buff, it was, in all this white!

'Well, now you know,' continued Monsieur Bessière.

Meanwhile the passengers were already beginning to wonder at this protracted stop in a completely silent station buried in snow, where not a porter shouted and not a door was slammed. A few windows were lowered, and heads appeared: a very stout lady and two charming blonde girls, her daughters probably, all three of them undoubtedly English; and, further along, a young, very pretty dark-haired woman who was being told to come back in by an elderly gentleman; while two men, the one old, the other young, were leaning half out of their windows and conversing from one carriage to another. But as Jacques glanced behind him, he saw only Séverine, who was leaning out also and looking anxiously in his direction. Oh, the dear creature, how worried she must be, and how his heart ached at the thought of her there, so near and yet so far, in the midst of this danger! He would have given every drop of blood in his body to be in Paris now, and to have delivered her there safe and sound.

'Come on, off you go,' concluded the station-master. 'No point putting the wind up everyone.'

He had given the signal himself. Back in his van the chief guard blew his whistle, and once more La Lison moved off, having responded with one prolonged, doleful hoot.

At once Jacques sensed a change in the state of the line. This was no longer the plain, with its thick carpet of snow endlessly unrolling and the engine gliding along like a steamer in advance of its wake. They were entering the rugged part of the countryside, the vast groundswell of hills and valleys that stretched as far as Malaunay in endless humps and bumps; and here the snow had piled up in irregular drifts, leaving the track clear in places while other sections were blocked by great mounds. The wind swept the embankments bare but filled the cuttings. So there was a continual succession of obstacles to be overcome, lengths of clear track intermittently barred by veritable ramparts. It was broad daylight now, and beneath its covering of snow the wild countryside, with its narrow gorges and precipitous slopes, had assumed the desolate air of some ice-bound ocean, frozen still in the surrounding tempest.

Never before had Jacques experienced such penetrating cold. Pricked by the myriad needles of the snow, his face felt as though it were bleeding; and he had lost all feeling in his hands, which were stiff and achingly numb, so numb indeed, as he shuddered to realize, that his fingers could no longer feel the little gear-wheel. When he lifted his elbow to pull the whistle, his arm hung from his shoulder with the dead weight of a corpse. He could not have said whether his legs were supporting him, amidst the endless jarring and jolting that tore at his entrails. Immense fatigue had overtaken him in this cold, as its icy grip spread to his skull, and he was afraid of simply ceasing to be, of not knowing any more whether he was driving or not, for already he was merely turning the gear-wheel in mindless, automatic response as he gazed in vacant bewilderment at the falling pressure-gauge. All the well-known stories about hallucination went through his head. Wasn't that a fallen tree up ahead, lying across the track? Hadn't he spotted a red flag waving above that bush? Weren't those detonators going off all the time amidst the clatter of the wheels? He could not have said; he kept on telling himself that he should stop, and yet he could not muster the firm will to do so. He had undergone this acute torture for several minutes when suddenly the sight of Pecqueux slumped fast asleep across the tool-chest again, completely knocked out by the overwhelming cold from which he himself had just been suffering, sent Jacques into such a fit of rage that it almost made him warm.

'Oh, you fucking bastard!'

And he, who was normally so forgiving of the man's drunken ways, kicked him awake and slapped him till he was on his feet. In his groggy state Pecqueux simply muttered complainingly and grabbed his shovel.

'All right, all right, I'm up.'

Once the firebox was stoked, the pressure rose again; and not before time, for La Lison had just entered a cutting where she would have to plough through snow more than a metre thick. She was now making progress only under the utmost strain, and her whole frame shook with it. For a moment she faltered, as though she might grind to a halt like a ship running onto a sandbank. What weighed her down was the heavy layer of snow which had gradually accumulated on the roofs of the carriages. On they rolled, black against white along a furrow of white, with their white pall stretched out above them; while La Lison herself was merely trimmed in ermine, that clothed her dark flanks where the snowflakes melted into watery trickles. Once again, despite the weight, she freed herself, and through she went. And up on the broad curve of an embankment, the train could still be seen running easily, like a ribbon of dark shadow lost in a wonderland of dazzling whiteness.

But soon there were further cuttings, and Jacques and Pecqueux, who had felt La Lison catch on something, steeled themselves against the cold, standing at this post they could not desert even in the face of death. Once again the engine was losing speed. She had run between two banks, and the final halt came slowly, without a jolt. It was as though she had run into glue and it was sticking to every one of her wheels, holding her tighter and tighter till her breath was gone. She stopped moving. That was that: the snow held her powerless in its grip.

'That does it,' Jacques growled. 'Damn and blast it!'

For a few seconds further he remained at his post, his hand on the wheel, opening all the valves to see if the obstacle would give. Then, hearing La Lison puffing and spluttering in vain, he closed the regulator and swore louder than ever in his fury.

The chief guard had lent out of the door of his van, and seeing Pecqueux, shouted in turn:

'That's it, we're stuck!'

The guard jumped smartly down into the snow, which came up to his knees. He joined them, and the three men debated what to do.

'All we can do is try and dig our way out,' the driver said at last. 'Fortunately we've got the shovels. Call the second guard, and between the four of us I'm sure we'll be able to get the wheels clear.'

They waved to the guard at the rear of the train, who had also got down from his van. He had great difficulty reaching them, occasionally sinking right into the snow. But by now the passengers had become alarmed at stopping like this in the middle of nowhere, in such a wintry wilderness, and at the sharp sound of these voices discussing what to do, and this guard hopping the length of the train in great, clumsy leaps. Windows were lowered. People were shouting, and asking questions, in vague but growing confusion:

'Where are we? . . . Why have we stopped like this? . . . What's going on? . . . My God, has there been an accident?'

The guard felt the need to reassure everyone. And indeed, as he went along, the English lady, whose broad, ruddy features were framed by the two charming faces of her daughters, enquired in a strong accent:

'Monsieur, there is no danger, I hope?'

'No, no, Madame,' he replied. 'A bit of snow, that's all. We'll be off again shortly.'

And the window was raised again to the sound of the girls' youthful chirping and that bright lilt of English vowels on their pink lips. They were both laughing, hugely entertained.

But further along the elderly gentleman was now hailing the guard, while his young wife ventured to poke her dark, pretty head out behind him.

'Why didn't they anticipate this? It's intolerable . . . I'm on my way back from London, and I have important business in

Paris this morning. I warn you, I shall hold the Company responsible for any delay.'

'Monsieur,' the guard could only repeat, 'we shall be off again in a couple of minutes.'

It was bitterly cold, and the snow was coming in; the heads vanished, and windows were shut. But inside the closed carriages there was continuing agitation, a sense of anxiety that could be discerned in the dull murmur of voices. Only two windows remained lowered; and leaning out, three compartments away from each other, two passengers were holding a conversation, an American of about forty and a young man from Le Havre, both of them very interested in the operation to clear the track.

'In America, Monsieur, everyone gets down from the train and shovels.'

'Oh, this is nothing. I've been snowed in twice before, last year. My job takes me to Paris once a week.'

'And mine about every three weeks, Monsieur.'

'What? From New York?'

'Yes, Monsieur, from New York.'

Jacques was directing the operation. Having caught sight of Séverine at a window in the front carriage, where she always travelled in order to be nearer him, he had beseeched her with a look; and realizing what he meant, she had withdrawn into the compartment out of the icy wind searing her face. His thoughts now on her, he worked with great heart. But he was beginning to realize that their getting stuck in the snow had nothing to do with the wheels; these could cut through the thickest of layers. It was the ashpan between them which was getting in the way, rolling the snow up and compressing it into enormous hard lumps. And he had an idea.

'We'll have to unscrew the ashpan.'

At first the chief guard objected. The driver was under his orders, and he did not want to authorize him to start tinkering with the engine. Then he let himself be persuaded.

'Well, all right, but on your head be it.'

Only it was a devil of a job. Stretched out under the engine, with the snow melting beneath their backs, Jacques and Pecqueux had to work for nearly half an hour. Fortunately they'd had some spare screwdrivers in the tool-chest. Eventually, at the risk

of being burned or crushed twenty times or more, they managed
to remove the ashpan. But they weren't finished yet, they still
had to get it out from underneath. It was enormously heavy
and kept getting caught between the wheels and the cylinders.
However, between the four of them, they managed to pull it out
and drag it clear of the track as far as the bank.

'Now, let's finish clearing the snow,' said the guard.

The train had been broken down for nearly half an hour, and
the anxiety of the passengers had increased. With each minute
that passed, a window would be lowered, and a voice would ask
why they hadn't left yet. There was panic: some people were
shouting, while others were crying, amidst mounting hysteria.

'No, no, it's clear enough,' declared Jacques. 'Climb aboard,
and leave the rest to me.'

Once more he was at his post, together with Pecqueux, and
when the two guards had returned to their vans, he turned the
tap on the steam-cock himself. There was a muffled sound, and
a scalding jet of steam melted the last lumps of snow sticking to
the rails. Then, his hand on the wheel, he put the engine into
reverse. Slowly he backed it out some three hundred metres to
give himself room. And then, having stoked the fire, beyond
even the permitted pressure, he came again at the wall that was
blocking their way and hurled the full weight of La Lison into it,
as well as that of the train behind. She let out a terrible 'uhn!',
like a woodman driving home his axe, and her mighty frame of
cast-iron and metal seemed to crack with the force of it. But still
she could not pass, and she had come to a halt, belching smoke,
shuddering all over from the impact. Then, twice more, he had
to repeat the operation, backing out and then charging at the
snow in an attempt to shift it; and each time La Lison braced her
haunches and breasted the snow, huffing and puffing like a giant
in a fury. Finally she seemed to draw a deep breath, tensed her
metal sinews in one supreme effort, and through she went; and
the train lumbered heavily along after her between the two walls
of sundered snow. She was free.

'Ah, she's a fine beast all the same!' growled Pecqueux.

Unable to see, Jacques removed his goggles and wiped them.
His heart was beating wildly, and he could no longer feel the
cold. But suddenly he remembered that there was a deep cutting

about three hundred metres from La Croix-de-Maufras. It lay in the direction of the wind, so there would be a considerable quantity of snow in it by now; and at once he had the certain knowledge that this was the reef elect upon which he would founder. He leant out. In the distance, after one last bend, the cutting appeared, stretching straight ahead, like a long ditch, filled with snow. It was now broad daylight, and the whiteness was boundless, dazzling, as the snowflakes continued to fall.

Meanwhile La Lison was moving along at an average speed, having encountered no further obstacles. As a precaution they had left the front and rear lamps burning; and the white head-lamp, at the base of the chimney, gleamed in the daylight like the living eye of a cyclops. On she ran, getting closer and closer to the cutting, her eye bulging wide. Then it seemed as though she began to breathe more quickly, in short gasps, like a spooked horse. Deep shudders ran through her, and she began to bridle, maintaining her progress only at the insistent hand of the driver. He had opened the firebox door as a sign to the fireman to stoke the fire. And now, instead of a comet's tail setting the night on fire, there was a plume of thick, black smoke soiling the vast pale shimmer of the sky.

On La Lison went. Eventually there was nothing for it but to enter the cutting. To right and left the banks lay buried in snow, and up ahead it was impossible to make out the line of the track. It was like the bed of a mountain torrent filled to the brim with undisturbed snow. In she ran, and continued on for about fifty metres, puffing madly, gradually slowing. As she pushed the snow back, it frothed up into a barrier in front of her, like resistant floodwater, threatening to engulf her. For a moment she seemed overwhelmed, beaten. Then, with one last heave of her haunches, she broke free and advanced a further thirty metres. This was the end, the final death throes: lumps of snow fell back down, covering the wheels and tumbling into every moving part, binding them one by one in chains of ice. And La Lison came definitively to a halt, expiring in the intense cold. Her breath gave out; she was motionless, dead.

'Well, this time we're done for,' said Jacques. 'Just as I thought.'

Immediately he tried to reverse, to repeat his previous manœuvre. But on this occasion La Lison would not budge. She refused to go either forwards or backwards; she was wedged tight on all sides, held fast to the ground, inert, unresponsive. Behind her the rest of the train, too, seemed dead, buried up to its doors in the thick drifts. And the snow kept coming, thicker and thicker, in prolonged flurries. It was like a quicksand into which engine and carriages, already half submerged, were about to disappear amidst the tremulous silence of this white solitude. Nothing moved, and the snow continued to weave its shroud.

'Same again?' asked the guard, leaning out of his van.

'Buggered,' shouted Pecqueux simply.

Now the situation was indeed becoming critical. The guard at the rear went and laid detonators to protect the train from behind, while the driver pulled desperately on the whistle, in urgent bursts, the gasping, mournful whistles of distress. But the snow muffled the sound, and the whistles faded, probably not even reaching Barentin. What should they do? There were only four of them, they would never clear drifts like this. It would have needed a whole gang. It was absolutely essential that they should send for help. And the worst of it was that panic was breaking out once more among the passengers.

A door opened, and the pretty dark-haired lady jumped down, in a great state, thinking there had been an accident. Her husband, the elderly businessman, followed her, shouting:

'I shall write to the Minister. It's an absolute disgrace!'

The sound of women crying and men shouting furiously could be heard coming from the carriages, as people slammed down the windows. Only the two little English girls found it all rather fun, grinning away happily. As the chief guard endeavoured to reassure everyone, the younger girl asked him in French with a slight English lisp:

'So we stop here, M'shieur?'

Several men had got down, despite the thick drifts which were waist high. Thus the American found himself next to the young man from Le Havre, both of them having decided to head for the engine to see what was going on. They shook their heads.

'It'll take them four or five hours to dig her out of all this.'

'At least. And even then they'll need twenty workmen to do it.'

Jacques had just persuaded the chief guard to send the second guard to Barentin to fetch help. Neither he nor Pecqueux could leave their engine.

The railwayman moved off and soon disappeared from sight at the end of the cutting. He had four kilometres to cover, and it might be more than two hours before he was back. Desperately anxious, Jacques left his post for a moment and ran to the front carriage, where he saw Séverine who had lowered her window.

'Don't worry,' he told her quickly. 'There's nothing to be afraid of.'

She replied in kind, avoiding any intimate form of expression in case they were overheard:

'I'm not afraid. It's just that I was really concerned about you.'

And it was said so sweetly that both drew comfort and smiled. Then, turning to go back, Jacques was surprised to see Flore and then Misard coming along the top of the bank, followed by two other men whom he did not at first recognize. They at least had heard the distress signal, and Misard, who was off duty, had come rushing to the scene with the two friends to whom he had happened at that moment to be offering a glass of white wine: the quarryman Cabuche, who was unable to work because of the snow, and the pointsman Ozil, who had come through the tunnel from Malaunay, still courting Flore despite her unwelcoming response. And she had come along out of curiosity, being the big girl who liked to wander and who was as brave and strong as any young man. For her, and for her father also, having a train stop like this on their very doorstep was no small event, indeed was something quite exceptional. How many trains they had seen over the five years they had lived here, each one rushing past in a sudden squall of speed at every hour of the day and night, come rain or shine. They all seemed to be blown on the same wind, not one of them had ever so much as slowed down, and they would watch them tear away into the distance, disappearing from view before they could discover a thing about them. The whole world went by like that, the madding crowd of humanity transported past them at full steam, and all they ever knew of it was the occasional face glimpsed in a flash, some

which they were never to see again, others which periodically
became familiar when they saw them again and again at the same
times, but who to them remained forever nameless. And here, in
the snow, a train had turned up at their door: the natural order of
things had been turned upside down, and they stared at this
unknown world tipped out on to the track by an accident, be-
holding it with the goggling eyes of savages who have come
running to a shore where Europeans might be shipwrecked.
They stood rooted to the spot in amazement at the sight of these
open doors revealing women wrapped in furs, and these men
standing beside the track in their thick overcoats, all this comfort
and luxury stranded upon a frozen sea.

But Flore had recognized Séverine. Keeping an eye out as she
did for each of Jacques's trains, she had for some weeks now
noticed the presence of this woman on the Friday morning
express, especially as she used to put her head out of the window
as they approached the level-crossing in order to have a look at
her property at La Croix-de-Maufras. Flore's eyes darkened as
she watched her in intimate conversation with the driver.

'Ah, Madame Roubaud!' cried Misard, who had also just
recognized her, and who immediately assumed his obsequious
air. 'What an unfortunate business! . . . But you can't stay here,
you must come in to our house.'

Jacques shook hands with the crossing-keeper and urged her
to accept.

'He's quite right . . . It may take us hours, certainly long
enough for you to freeze to death.'

Séverine declined; she was perfectly well wrapped up, she
said. In any case, she was not at all sure about walking three
hundred metres in the snow. Whereupon Flore, coming closer
and observing her with big, staring eyes, said finally:

'Come, Madame, I'll carry you.'

And before Séverine had accepted, Flore had seized her in her
strong, manly arms and was lifting her up like a small child. She
then set her down on the other side of the track, where the snow
had already been well trodden and her feet would not sink in.
Some of the passengers had begun to laugh in amazement. What
a lass! A dozen of her, and it wouldn't take them two hours to
clear the track!

Meanwhile Misard's offer of his crossing-keeper's house, with its promise of shelter and warmth, perhaps even some bread and wine, communicated itself from carriage to carriage. The panic had subsided when people realized that they were in no immediate danger; still, their situation remained wretched none the less: the foot-warmers were going cold, it was nine o'clock, and they would soon be hungry and thirsty if there were the slightest delay in help arriving. And this could drag on for hours; who knows if they might not have to spend the night there? Two bodies of opinion had formed: those who despaired and refused to leave the carriages, ensconcing themselves as though in preparation for death, all wrapped up in their rugs and stretching out angrily across the seats; and those who preferred to risk the dash across the snow at the prospect of better conditions, and desirous especially of escaping the nightmare of this stranded train which had expired with the cold. A whole group gathered, the elderly businessman and his young wife, the English lady with her two daughters, the young man from Le Havre, the American, and a dozen others, all ready to set out.

Jacques had quietly persuaded Séverine to go, whispering a promise to bring her news if he could get away. And as Flore was still looking at them with her dark eyes, he spoke to her gently like an old friend:

'All right, is that agreed? You'll show these ladies and gentlemen the way? . . . I'll keep Misard here with me, and the other two. We'll make a start and do what we can while we're waiting.'

In fact Cabuche, Ozil, and Misard had immediately grabbed shovels and gone to join Pecqueux and the chief guard, who were already setting about the snow. This small team of men was attempting to free the engine, digging under the wheels and casting shovelfuls of snow up on to the bank. No one said another word, and all that could be heard was the silence of dogged determination amidst the muffled gloom of the white countryside. And as the little group of passengers moved off into the distance, they turned to take one last look at the train where it stood, abandoned, now no more than a thin black line crushed beneath a thick layer of snow. People had shut the doors and raised the windows. Still the snow continued to fall, slowly but surely burying the train with a quiet obstinacy.

Flore had wanted to pick Séverine up again. But the latter had refused, determined to walk like the others. The three hundred metres proved very hard going, especially in the cutting where the snow came up to their waists; and twice they had to launch a rescue for the large English lady, who was half-submerged. Her daughters were still laughing, absolutely delighted. The young wife of the elderly gentleman lost her footing and was obliged to accept the helping hand of the young man from Le Havre, while her husband fulminated to the American about the state of France. Once they were out of the cutting, progress became easier; but now they were following an embankment, and the small band walked in single file, buffeted by the wind and taking care to avoid the edges that lay ill-defined and treacherous beneath the snow. At last they arrived, and Flore installed the passengers in the kitchen, though she was unable to give them each a chair for there were at least twenty people crowding into the room, which fortunately was reasonably large. All she could think of was to go and fetch some planks and set up two benches with the chairs she did have. She then threw some wood into the stove and gestured as if to say that nothing more should be demanded of her. She had not uttered a word, and just stood there gazing at all these people with her large, greenish eyes and the wild, valiant air of a tall, blonde savage. She recognized only two of the faces, having often noticed them on the trains these past few months—those of the American and the young man from Le Havre; and she examined them as one might inspect a buzzing insect which has finally settled after an invisible flight. They seemed singular to her, she had not pictured them quite like this, not that she knew anything about them beyond their facial features. As for the others, they struck her as belonging to a different race, inhabitants of an unknown planet who had dropped from the sky and brought with them, here into her very own kitchen, clothes, customs, ideas, that she would never have dreamed of encountering there. The English lady was confiding to the young wife of the businessman that she was on her way to India to join her eldest son, a senior civil servant; and the young wife was joking about her bad luck in happening to choose this particular occasion to accompany her husband to London, where he went twice a year. Everyone was lamenting the prospect of being stranded in this godforsaken place; they would need to eat, they would need a bed for the night, what *were* they going to do, for heaven's sake?! And Flore, who had been listening to them impassively, caught Séverine's eye where she sat on a chair by the fire, and gestured to her to accompany her to the adjacent room.

'Maman,' she announced on entering, 'it's Madame Roubaud . . . Won't you have a word with her?'

Phasie was lying in bed, her face yellow, her legs swollen, so ill that she had not got up for the past fortnight; and here in this sad little room, where a cast-iron stove maintained a stifling heat, she would spend the hours stubbornly mulling over the fixation which obsessed her, with nothing to distract her but the shake and rattle of the trains as they tore past at full speed.

'Ah, Madame Roubaud,' she murmured, 'how nice, how nice!'

Flore told her about the accident, and about all these people she had brought back and who were there now. But none of this was of any concern to her mother.

'How nice, how nice!' she repeated in the same weary voice.

Nevertheless she remembered, and raised her head a little to say:

'If Madame wants to go and see her house, you know where the keys are, hanging up by the cupboard.'

But Séverine declined. She had begun to shiver at the thought of going back to La Croix-de-Maufras, in the snow, in this pale, ghostly light. No, no, there was nothing she needed to see, she would prefer to stay here and wait where it was warm.

'Do sit down, Madame,' Flore went on. 'It's even cosier in here than it is next door. And besides, we'll never have enough bread for all these people. But if you're hungry, there'll always be some for you.'

She had pulled a chair up and was continuing her show of considerate hospitality, visibly making an effort to overcome her usual roughness of manner. But she refused to take her eyes off Séverine, as if she wanted to read her mind, to have a clear answer to a question she had been asking herself for some time;

and beneath all the attentiveness lay this need to get near her, to observe her closely, to touch her, in order to find out.

Séverine thanked her and settled herself near the stove, indeed preferring to be alone with the sick woman in this room where she hoped Jacques might find a way of joining her. Two hours passed, and after some conversation about matters of local interest, she was beginning to yield to the heat and fall asleep, when Flore, who was continually wanted in the kitchen, opened the door again and said in her harsh voice:

'This way, seein' as she's in here.'

It was Jacques, who had managed to get away to bring the good news. The man they had sent to Barentin had brought a whole gang back with him, some thirty soldiers whom the railway authorities had despatched to emergency areas in case of accidents; and they were all at work with picks and shovels. Only it would be a long business, and they might not get away again before nightfall.

'Anyway, you don't seem to be doing too badly,' he added, 'so just be patient. Eh, Aunt Phasie? You won't let Madame Roubaud starve, will you now?'

On seeing her big boy, as she called him, Phasie had painfully sat up in bed, alive again and happy as she watched him and listened to him talking. When he had approached her bed:

'Not likely, not likely!' she declared. 'Ah, my big boy, here you are. So you're the one that's got himself stuck in the snow! . . . And that dumb thing who never tells me anything!'

She turned towards her daughter and berated her:

'You might at least be polite. Just you go back in there and see to those ladies and gentlemen, so they don't go telling people in high places that we're all a lot of savages.'

Flore had planted herself between Jacques and Séverine. For a moment she appeared to hesitate, wondering if she might not insist on remaining there, despite her mother. But there would be nothing for her to see, her mother's presence would ensure that the pair did not give themselves away. So silently she left the room, with a last lingering stare.

'But what's all this, Aunt Phasie?' Jacques went on, with a worried expression. 'Are you in bed permanently now? Does that mean it's serious?'

She pulled him towards her, forced him even to sit on the edge of the mattress, and without bothering about Séverine, who had discreetly moved away, she poured it all out in hushed whispers:

'Oh yes, it's serious all right! It's a miracle you've found me still alive . . . I didn't want to write to you about it because, well, things like this, you don't . . . I was nearly a goner. But I'm feeling much better already now, and I really think I may pull through this time, again.'

He was examining her, horrified at the progress which the illness had made, and finding no trace left in her of the beautiful, healthy creature he had once known.

'So, my poor Aunt Phasie, still the same old cramps and dizzy spells, eh?'

But she was squeezing his hand, nearly crushing it, and she continued in an even lower whisper:

'Would you believe it, I caught him at it . . . You remember how I was at my wits' end, not knowing what on earth he could have been putting the drug *in*! I wasn't drinking, I wasn't eating anything he'd touched, and yet even so, every night my insides were on fire . . . Well, he was shoving it in the salt! I saw him at it, one evening . . . And me who used to put salt on everything, lots of it, to clean me out!'

Ever since the physical possession of Séverine appeared to have cured him, Jacques had sometimes thought about this tale of slow, deliberate poisoning as one does about a nightmare, with scepticism. He in turn tenderly squeezed the sick woman's hands, to soothe her:

'But do you honestly think all of that's really possible?. . . I mean, you've got to be quite sure before you go saying things like that . . . And anyway, it's gone on too long! No, look, it's more likely some illness, something the doctors don't understand.'

'An illness,' she sneered in reply. 'Oh yes, an illness he's gone and poured down me, more like . . . As for doctors, you're right. There've been two of them here, didn't understand at all, didn't even agree! I don't want any of them bird-brains setting foot in here again . . . But in my salt, do you hear, he was shoving it in my salt. I swear to you, I actually saw him! It's to get his hands on my thousand francs, the thousand Papa left me. He tells himself that as soon as he's finished me off, he'll soon find them.

Well, he can try. But they're somewhere where no one will ever
find them, never ever! . . . It won't matter if I do give up the
ghost, no one will ever, ever, have that thousand francs of mine.'

'But, Aunt Phasie, if it were me, I'd send for the police if I was
so sure.'

She made a gesture of disgust.

'Oh no, not the police . . . This is our business. It's between
him and me. I know he wants to do me in, and I don't want him
to, simple as that. So all I can do is defend myself, isn't it, and try
not to be as stupid as I have been, over the salt . . . Eh? Who
would believe it? That a runt like that, that a scrap of a man you
could stick in your pocket, might end up getting the better of a
big woman like myself, if I was to let him! Him and those rat's
teeth of his!'

She had begun to shake slightly, and fought for her breath
before saying finally:

'Anyway, it won't be this time. I'm on the mend, and I'll be up
and about in a fortnight . . . And next time he'll have to be pretty
cunning if he's going to catch me again. Oh yes, I can't wait to
see. If he does find some way of giving me that drug of his again,
well, all right, so he wins. Too bad, it'll be the end of me . . . But
nobody's to interfere!'

Jacques thought it was the illness that was filling her head with
these dark imaginings; and in order to take her mind off things,
he was trying to make light of it when she began to tremble
beneath the bedclothes.

'Here he is,' she whispered. 'I always know when he's
coming.'

And indeed, some seconds later, in walked Misard. She
had turned deathly pale, seized by the involuntary terror of the
colossus at the sight of the insect gnawing away at it. For in
her stubborn determination to defend herself singlehandedly,
he now filled her with a growing dread which she would not
admit. However, having taken in the scene with a swift glance
from the doorway, Misard then appeared not even to have
noticed them, her and the driver together there, next to each
other, and he proceeded instead, with his dull eyes and thin lips
and his meek, puny air, to fall over himself in profuse attention
to Séverine.

'I had thought that perhaps Madame might be wanting to take advantage of this opportunity and look over her property. So I absented myself for a moment . . . If Madame would like me to accompany her.'

And when Séverine again declined, he continued in his whining voice:

'Perhaps Madame was surprised about the fruit . . . They all had maggots, and it simply wasn't worth packing them up . . . And then, on top of that, there was a gale which caused a great deal of damage . . . Ah, it's very sad that Madame cannot find a buyer! One gentleman did come to look at it, but he wanted repairs done . . . Well, I am at your service, Madame, and Madame may rely on me to act for her here as if I were Madame herself.'

Then he insisted on offering her some bread and pears, pears from her own garden, ones which were not full of maggots. She accepted.

On his way through the kitchen, Misard had informed the passengers that the clearing of the track was proceeding, but that it would take a further four or five hours. It had gone noon, and there was further groaning, for people were beginning to feel extremely hungry. Flore was just saying that she would not have enough bread to go round. She had wine all right, she had come back up from the cellar with ten litre bottles and lined them up along the table. Only there weren't enough glasses, and they had to share, the English lady with her two daughters, the elderly gentleman with his young wife. The latter, meanwhile, had discovered a zealous and resourceful servant in the young man from Le Havre, who was attending to her every need. He disappeared and returned with some apples and a loaf of bread which he had found at the back of the woodshed. Flore became angry, saying it was bread for her sick mother. But he was already cutting it up and distributing it among the ladies, beginning with the young lady, who smiled at him, flattered. Her husband was still in a fury, no longer even concerning himself with her and busy extolling to the American the merits of commercial practice in New York. Never had the young English girls crunched on an apple so gladly. Their mother, who was very weary, dozed. On the floor, in front of the stove, sat two ladies, exhausted from waiting. Some men who had gone outside for a smoke, to kill another quarter of an hour, came back in, frozen and shivering. Gradually their disquiet grew, as their hunger went barely satisfied and as their fatigue was made worse by frustration and lack of comfort. It was turning into an encampment of shipwreck victims, manifesting all the desolation of a band of civilized people washed up on a desert island.

As and when Misard left the door open during his comings and goings, Aunt Phasie would watch them from her sickbed. So these were the people that she, too, had seen flashing past like thunderbolts for nearly a year, ever since she'd been reduced to dragging herself between bed and chair. She was only rarely able to get as far as the platform outside now, and she spent her days and nights stuck here alone, her eyes fixed on the window, with no other company but these trains that went rushing by so fast. She had always complained about this godforsaken part of the country where no one ever called; and here was a whole throng descending on them out of the blue. To think that in there, among all those people who were in such a hurry to get on with their own affairs, not one of them had any inkling of what was happening, of the filth he'd been shoving in her salt! It rankled with her, it did, that clever trick of his, and she asked herself how in God's name it was possible to be such a sly old rogue and for nobody to spot a thing. After all, so many people went past their house, thousands upon thousands; but all in such a rush, and not one of them would have imagined that here, in this tiny little house, one person was quietly and simply murdering another. Aunt Phasie looked at them each in turn, all these people who had dropped from the skies, and reflected that with everyone so busy, it was no wonder they could step in the muck and not notice a thing.

'Are you going back?' Misard asked Jacques.

'Yes, yes,' the latter replied, 'I'm just coming.'

Misard left, closing the door behind him. Phasie held on to the young man and began to whisper in his ear once more:

'If I do give up the ghost, just you wait and see the look on his face when he can't find my little nest-egg . . . Oh, that's the bit I like whenever I think about it. I shall depart this world a happy woman all the same.'

'So you mean, Aunt Phasie, that no one's to get it? You won't leave it to your daughter?'

'To Flore?! So he can take it from her?! I should think not indeed! . . . And not even to you either, my big boy, because you're too daft as well: he'd still get his hands on some of it . . . No, to nobody, I leave it to the earth where I shall go to join it!'

She was tiring herself, and Jacques made her lie down again, soothing her with a kiss and a promise to come and see her again soon. Then, as she seemed to be dozing off, he went behind Séverine, who was still sitting beside the stove: he raised a finger, smiling, as a sign to be careful; and with a pretty, silent move-ment, she tilted her head back, offering her lips, and he bent over and pressed his mouth to hers, in a long, discreet kiss. They closed their eyes, drinking in each other's breath. But when they opened them again in a daze, Flore had come in and was standing there in front of them, watching.

'Would Madame like any more bread?' she asked in a hoarse voice.

Séverine, embarrassed and thoroughly put out, stammered a brief reply:

'N-no, no thank you.'

For a moment Jacques glared at Flore with blazing eyes. He hesitated, and his lips quivered as if he were about to say some-thing; but then, with a broad, angry gesture which was intended as a threat, he decided to leave. Behind him the door slammed shut.

Flore had remained standing there, like the tall figure of a warrior virgin, beneath her heavy helmet of blond hair. So her anxiety at seeing this lady on Jacques's train every Friday had not been ill-founded. She now had the clear answer she'd been seeking ever since she'd had the pair of them here together, an absolute answer. Never would the man she loved ever love her; it was this slender woman, this slip of a thing, that he had chosen. And her regret at having refused herself that night, when he had so brutally tried to take her, still ached within her, pain-ing her so much that she could have sobbed; for, by her simple calculations, it would now be her he was kissing if she'd given herself before this other woman. Where could she find him alone at this very moment, to throw her arms round him and cry: 'Take me, I've been so stupid, I didn't realize!' But in her powerlessness she could feel her fury mounting against this fragile creature sitting there stammering in embarrassment. With one squeeze of her firm, pugilist's arms, she could choke the breath out of her, like a little bird. Why then did she not dare? But she swore to avenge herself all the same, for she knew a thing or two about this new rival of hers which could have landed her in prison, about this woman they'd allowed to go free like all the other whores who sold themselves to rich and powerful old men. And so, tortured by jealousy and bursting with anger, she began to clear away what was left of the bread and pears, with the extravagant movements of the wild, beautiful girl she was.

'Since Madame doesn't want any more, I'll give it to the others.'

Three o'clock came, then four. Time dragged by, each long minute of it, under the crushing weight of a growing weariness and irritation. Here was night falling once more, casting a livid gleam across the vastness of the white countryside; and every ten minutes men would go out and gaze into the distance to see how the work was coming along, only to come back in saying that the engine still did not seem to have been cleared. Even the two little English girls had begun to cry with nervous exhaustion. In a corner the pretty dark-haired woman had gone to sleep on the shoulder of the young man from Le Havre, completely un-noticed by the elderly husband amid the general unrestraint in which all convention had been swept away. The room was getting colder, and people were shivering without even thinking they might put more wood on the stove; so that eventually the American departed, believing that he would be better off stretched out on a seat in one of the carriages. This was now how they all thought, what they all regretted: they should have stayed where they were, and then at least they would not have been consumed with anxiety at not knowing what was going on. They had to dissuade the English lady, who was also talking of returning to her compartment to lie down. After a candle had been placed on a corner of the table to give everyone in the pitch-black kitchen some light, an enormous feeling of dismay set in, and they sank into dark despair.

Meanwhile, outside, the work of unblocking the line was nearly complete; and while the team of soldiers who had freed the engine were clearing the track in front of it, the driver and the fireman had returned to their post.

Seeing the snow finally begin to let up, Jacques was beginning to feel more confident. Ozil the pointsman had assured him that beyond the tunnel, towards Malaunay, considerably less snow had fallen. Again he asked him:

'When you walked through the tunnel, were you able to get in and out without any difficulty?'

'But I've told you! You'll get through, I promise!'

Cabuche, who had toiled with the enthusiasm of a friendly giant, was already withdrawing into the background in his timid, uncouth way, which his recent brush with the law had served only to exacerbate; and Jacques had to call across to him.

'Hey, mate, pass us our shovels over, those ones there lying against the bank. We may need them.'

And when the quarryman had done him this last service, Jacques shook him firmly by the hand to show that he still respected him despite everything, having seen him at work.

'You're a good man, you are.'

This mark of friendship moved Cabuche in an extraordinary way.

'Thanks,' he said simply, choking back his tears.

Misard, who had patched things up with Cabuche after previously denouncing him to the examining magistrate, nodded and pursed his lips in a thin smile. He had stopped shovelling a long time ago, standing there with his hands in his pockets and surveying the train with a jaundiced eye as though he were waiting to see if he would find any lost property under the wheels.

The chief guard had at last decided with Jacques that they might try to set off, when Pecqueux, having got down on to the track again, called the driver over:

'You'd better have a look. One of the cylinders has taken a knock.'

Jacques went over and bent down to see for himself. He had already noticed this damage in the course of his earlier, careful inspection of La Lison. During the clearing operation they had discovered that the combination of wind and snow had caused some oak sleepers, which had been left lying along the embankment by men working on the line, to slip down and block the track; and the train must even have stopped partly because of this, since the engine had evidently bumped into the sleepers. They could see the scratch along the cylinder-casing, and the piston-rod inside seemed to have been slightly bent. But this was the only apparent damage, a fact which had originally reassured the driver. But perhaps there were serious problems inside, for nothing is more delicate than the complicated mechanism of the slide-valves: here beats an engine's heart, its living soul. Jacques climbed aboard again, blew the whistle, and opened the regulator on La Lison to see how her moving parts responded. It took her a long time to jolt into action, like someone after a bruising fall who has lost all feeling in his limbs. Finally, with a strained chuff, she moved off, managing several revolutions of her wheels but still dazed and lumbering. It would be all right, she would be able to move, she would complete the journey. Only he shook his head, for he knew her inside out and had just felt how strange she was to the touch, how altered and aged, as though somewhere inside her she had been dealt a mortal blow. She must have got it in the snow, some blow to the heart, or a fatal chill, like those sturdy young women who die of pneumonia having come home from a dance some night in the cold and the rain.

Once more Jacques pulled on the whistle, after Pecqueux had opened the steam-cocks. The two guards were at their post. Misard, Ozil, and Cabuche climbed on to the footboard of the front van. And gently the train emerged from the cutting, between the soldiers armed with their shovels who had lined up to right and left along the top of the embankment. Then it stopped at the crossing-keeper's house to take on the passengers.

Flore was standing outside. Ozil and Cabuche went over to join her, while Misard was now all eagerness, bidding farewell to the ladies and gentlemen coming out of his house, and steadily pocketing silver coins. Free at last! But they had waited too long, and everyone was shivering with cold, hunger, and exhaustion. Off went the English lady with her two daughters, both half-asleep; and the young man from Le Havre boarded the same compartment as the pretty dark-haired woman, she now very weary, and he having offered her husband his assistance. And in the middle of all this trampled snow it was like a routed army boarding the train, pushing and shoving, letting themselves go completely and with not a thought left for their personal appearance. Briefly, behind the glass panes of the bedroom window, Aunt Phasie appeared: curiosity had torn her from her bed, and she had dragged herself across the room, to look. Her great, hollow, invalid eyes watched this crowd of strangers, these passers-by from a world on the move, people she would never see again, blown in by the storm and swept away once more in its path.

But Séverine was the last to leave. She turned her head and smiled at Jacques, who was leaning out and watching till she reached her carriage. And Flore, who was waiting for them, paled once again to see this tranquil exchange of affection pass between them. Abruptly she moved closer to Ozil, whom she had until then rejected, as if now, in the midst of her hatred, she felt the need of a man.

The chief guard gave the signal, La Lison responded with a plaintive whistle, and Jacques set off, this time bound non-stop for Rouen. It was six o'clock, and from a pitch-black sky night had almost fallen over the surrounding white countryside; but a pale gleam of cheerless, dismal light hovered just above the ground, illuminating the desolation of this wilderness. And there at an angle, in the eerie glow, stood the house at La Croix-de-Maufras, looking even more dilapidated, completely black against the snow, with its 'For Sale' sign nailed up high on its shuttered façade.

CHAPTER VIII

THE train did not reach Paris until 10.40 that night. There had been a twenty-minute stop at Rouen to allow the passengers time to eat; and Séverine had hastened to telegraph to her husband to let him know that she would not be returning to Le Havre until the following day, by the evening express. A whole night with Jacques! The first they would spend together alone in one room, free as they pleased and without fear of being disturbed!

As they were leaving Mantes, Pecqueux had had an idea. His wife, Mère Victoire, had been in hospital for a week with a serious ankle-sprain following a fall; and having another of the city's beds to sleep in, as he put it with a snigger, it had occurred to him to offer Madame Roubaud the use of their room: she would be much more comfortable there than in a local hotel, and she was welcome to treat the place as her home until the following evening. At once Jacques had realized the practical advantages of such an arrangement, especially as he could think of nowhere else to take the young woman. So, when later in the station she approached the engine through the crowd of passengers now finally able to detrain, he advised her to accept, holding out the key which the fireman had handed him. But she hesitated, refusing out of embarrassment at the ribald smile on Pecqueux's face, for he surely knew.

'No, no, I have a cousin. She'll have a mattress I can sleep on.'

'Come on, take it,' Pecqueux said finally in his good-natured, jocular way. 'The bed's nice and soft, you know. And a big one, too, you could get four in it!'

Jacques was looking at her so pressingly that she took the key. He had leant over and whispered very softly:

'Wait for me.'

Séverine did not have far to go, just a little way up the Rue d'Amsterdam and then down the Impasse; but the snow was so slippery that she had to take great care as she walked. By a piece of luck the front entrance was still unlocked, so she climbed the stairs without being seen by the concierge, who was absorbed in a game of dominoes with a woman from next door; and on the fourth floor she opened and closed the door so softly that none of the neighbours could possibly have suspected she was there. On the other hand, when passing the third-floor landing, she had very distinctly heard singing and laughter coming from the Dauvergnes': no doubt one of the sisters' musical evenings, to which they invited their female friends once a week. And now that Séverine had shut the door and was standing in the thick darkness of the room, she could still hear the lively merriment of these young people coming up through the floor. For a moment the darkness seemed total; and she jumped when, out of the pitch blackness, came the deep tones of the cuckoo-clock striking eleven in a voice she recognized. Then her eyes grew accustomed to the dark, and the two windows emerged as two pale squares illuminating the ceiling with the light reflected from the snow. Already she had begun to get her bearings, as she felt around for the matches on the dresser where she remembered having seen them before. But she had more trouble finding a candle. Eventually she discovered the remains of one at the bottom of a drawer; and having lit it, the room brightened, and she cast a quick, nervous glance around her as if to make quite sure that she really was alone. It all seemed very familiar, the round table where she had lunched with her husband, and the bed with its red cotton counterpane on to which he had knocked her down with his fist. Yes, this was the place; nothing in the room had changed during the ten months since she had been there.

Slowly Séverine removed her hat. But as she was about to take off her coat as well, she shivered. It was freezing in this room. Beside the stove, in a small chest, there was some coal and sticks. Immediately, without further removing her clothes, she decided to light the fire; and she was glad to, because it took her mind off the sense of uneasiness which she had felt at first. Making the place ready like this for a night of love, the thought that they would be nice and cosy here, allowed her to recover her mood of loving delight in their escapade: for so long now, and without ever believing it could actually happen, they had dreamt of such a night! Once the stove was going, she thought of all sorts of other preparations: she arranged the chairs to her liking, she fetched white sheets and completely remade the bed, which gave her considerable bother for it was indeed very large. Her one

problem was that she could find nothing in the sideboard to eat
or drink: no doubt for the three days that he had been master in
his own house, Pecqueux had emptied the place, down to the
crumbs off the floorboards. It had been the same with the light,
with just this one candle-end left; but still, once you're in bed,
you don't need to be able to see. And being now very warm, and
excited, she paused in the middle of the room and looked round
to check that nothing was missing.

Then, as she began to be surprised that Jacques had not yet
arrived, the sound of a whistle drew her over to one of the
windows. It was the 11.20 through train to Le Havre, which was
just leaving. The vast open space beneath her, with its swathe of
track stretching from the station to the Batignolles tunnel, was
one great sheet of snow, and all she could see were the railway
lines, fanning out into black branches. The engines and rolling-
stock standing in the sidings were mere heaps of white, apparently slumbering under ermine wraps. And between the
immaculate, snow-covered window-panes of the great station
roofs and the lace-trimmed girders of the Pont de l'Europe, the
houses opposite in the Rue de Rome could still be seen in the
darkness, dirty blotches of yellow amidst all this white. The Le
Havre train came into view at a sombre crawl, its front headlamp
burning a bright hole of fire into the night; and she watched it
disappear under the bridge, its three rear lamps staining the
snow a bloody red. When she turned back into the room, she
gave another brief shiver. Was she really alone? She thought she
had felt hot breath warming the back of her neck, and the rough
touch of a hand stroking her body through her clothes. Her wide
eyes travelled round the room once more. No, no one there.

What on earth was Jacques up to, being late like this? Ten
further minutes passed. She was alarmed to hear a faint scraping
noise, like fingernails scratching on wood. Then she realized and
ran to open the door. It was Jacques, carrying a bottle of Malaga
wine and a cake.

Shaking with laughter, she threw her arms wildly round his
neck.

'Oh, you wonderful man! You thought of it!'

But he bid her abruptly be quiet.

'Sh, sh!'

So she lowered her voice, thinking the concierge was following him. No, fortunately, just as he'd been about to press the
bell, the door had opened for a lady and her daughter, who were
presumably on their way down from the Dauvergnes; and he'd
been able to slip upstairs without anyone knowing. Only, back
there on the landing, he had glimpsed the newspaper woman
through a half-open door, who was just finishing washing some
clothes in a basin.

'Do you mind if we try not to make too much noise? We'd
better speak softly.'

By way of reply she held him in a passionate embrace, covering his face with silent kisses. It amused her to play at mysteries
and to speak only in low whispers.

'Yes, yes, fine. We'll be as quiet as two little mice, you'll see.'

So she laid the table with all possible care, two plates, two
glasses, two knives, pausing on the verge of helpless laughter the
moment something made a sound when she put it down too
hard.

Watching her, and also finding it funny, he continued softly:

'I thought you'd be hungry.'

'Oh I'm starving. The food was so bad at Rouen!'

'Well then, what about me going back down to get us a
chicken?'

'Oh no. And not be able to get back in again? . . . No, no, the
cake'll be plenty.'

Immediately they sat down side by side, almost on the same
chair, and the cake was shared out and consumed with the play-
fulness of lovers. She complained of being thirsty and drank two
glasses of Malaga straight off, which brought the colour well and
truly to her cheeks. The stove was getting red-hot behind them,
and they could feel its pulsing heat. But as he began to plant
noisy kisses on the back of her neck, she in her turn stopped him:

'Sh, sh.'

She gestured to him to listen; and in the silence they heard a
dull thumping coming up from the Dauvergnes' again, to the
rhythm of some music: the girls were having a knees-up. Next
door the newspaper woman was emptying the soapy water from
her basin into the sink on the landing. She closed her door again,
the dancing downstairs stopped for a moment, and the only

sound came from beneath the window outside, muffled by the snow, the faint rumbling of a departing train, which seemed to be crying as it tooted feebly on its whistle.

'An Auteuil train,' he murmured. 'The 11.40.'

Then he breathed in a soft voice:

'Bedtime, my love, don't you think?'

She did not reply, for at this moment of excited happiness she had been reclaimed by her past and was now, despite herself, reliving the hours which she had spent here with her husband. Was it not as though the lunch they had shared were now continuing with this cake, eaten here on the same table and to the accompaniment of the same sounds? She felt increasingly aroused by the objects around her, and the memories came flooding back; never had she felt such a burning need to tell her lover everything, to deliver herself up entirely. She had an almost physical longing to do so, which she could no longer distinguish from her sensual desire; and it seemed to her that she would belong to him more, that she would drink fullest of the joy of being his, if she were to whisper a confession in his ear as they lay together in the one embrace. She began to relive the events of the past: her husband was standing there, and she turned her head, thinking she had just seen his stubby, hairy hand reach over her shoulder to grab the knife.

'Don't you think, my love, time for bed?' repeated Jacques.

She quivered, feeling his lips crushing against hers as if once again he wanted to seal the confession within. So without a word she rose, slipped quickly out of her clothes, and slid into bed, not even stopping to pick her skirts off the floor. He, too, left everything as it was: and the table lay strewn with the remains of their meal, while the candle-end finally began to burn out, its flame already flickering. And when he in turn had undressed and got into bed, they entwined at once in a frenzy of possession, which left them choking for breath. In the still air of the room, with the music still continuing below, not a cry came, not a single sound, only one long, abandoned shudder, a deep spasm into oblivion.

Already Jacques could no longer recognize in Séverine the woman he had known during their first encounters, so gentle and passive, with those clear blue eyes of hers. She seemed to have grown daily more passionate, beneath that dark helmet of black hair; and he had felt her gradually awaken in his arms from the long, cold virginity out of which neither the senile practices of Grandmorin nor the conjugal brutality of Roubaud had been able to draw her. This creature of love, once merely docile, now loved and gave herself without reserve, and felt a burning gratitude for such pleasure. She had developed a violent passion, an adoration, for this man who had brought her such a revelation of her senses. And it was the great happiness she now felt in being able to hold him close at last, freely, to be able to press him to her breasts and wrap her arms around him, which had made her thus clench her teeth so that not a sigh should escape.

When they opened their eyes again, he was the first to express surprise:

'Oh, the candle's gone out.'

She gestured vaguely as if to say what did she care. Then, with a stifled giggle:

'I was a good girl, wasn't I?'

'Oh, yes, no one will have heard . . . Two proper little mice!'

When they returned to bed, she took him once more in her arms, snuggling up against him and pressing her nose to his neck. And sighing contentedly:

'Oh God, isn't this wonderful?!'

They spoke no further. The room was pitch black, and the pale squares made by the two windows were scarcely visible; on the ceiling there was just the one ray of light from the stove, a round, blood-red patch. They both lay there staring at it. The music had stopped, doors banged, and the whole building was sinking into the heavy peace of sleep. From down below the muffled thuds of the incoming Caen train as it rumbled over the turntables scarcely even reached them and seemed very far away.

But holding Jacques like this soon made Séverine begin to long for him again. And together with her desire there arose once more within her the need to confess. It had been tormenting her for so many weeks now! The round patch on the ceiling grew wider, seeming to spread like a bloodstain. She began to see things as she stared at it, and the objects round the bed seemed to be finding their voice, to be telling the whole story out loud.

She could feel the words of it rising to her lips on the mounting wave of excitement that bore up her flesh. How good that would be, to have nothing more to hide, to melt into him completely!

'You don't realize, my love . . .'

Jacques, who was also staring at the blood-red patch, knew perfectly well what she was going to say. Next to him, in that delicate body knotted to his own, he had been following the rising tide of this obscure, enormous thing which each of them thought about but neither of them mentioned. Until then he had silenced her, fearful of the trembling that would herald the return of his former malady, anxious that it might alter things between them if they were to talk of the spilling of blood. But this time he was powerless, even to lean over and seal her mouth with a kiss, so overwhelmed was he by the delicious languor of lying here in this warm bed, in the soft arms of this woman. He thought it was too late, that she would tell him everything. And so he was relieved in the midst of his nervous expectancy when she appeared to think twice and hesitate, before drawing back and saying instead:

'You don't realize, my love, but my husband suspects I'm sleeping with you.'

At the last second, without her intending it, it was the memory of the previous night in Le Havre which had sprung from her lips, not the confession.

'Oh really, do you think so?' he murmured disbelievingly. 'He seems so friendly. He shook me by the hand only this morning.'

'I tell you, he knows everything. At this very moment he must be telling himself that this is how we are, part of each other, loving each other! I can prove it.'

She paused and hugged him tighter in her embrace, as her happiness at possessing him took on the sharp edge of rancour. Then, after a moment's tremulous reflection:

'Oh, I hate him, I hate him!'

Jacques was surprised. He himself had absolutely nothing against Roubaud. Indeed he found him very obliging.

'Goodness, why on earth?' he asked. 'He doesn't bother us much.'

She made no reply, but repeated:

'I hate him . . . It's sheer torture now to have him anywhere near me. Oh, if only I could, I'd run away, I'd be with you.'

Touched by this outburst of fervent love, he in turn pulled her closer, holding her against his flesh, down the whole length of his body, all his. But once again, as she nestled against him, hardly taking her lips from his neck, she said gently:

'What you don't realize, my love . . .'

It was the confession coming back again, fatally, inevitably. And this time he had the clear sense that nothing in the world would stop it, for it rose within her frantic desire to be taken and possessed once more. There was not a sound to be heard in the building now, even the newspaper woman must have been fast asleep. Outside not a vehicle moved, as Paris lay snowbound, draped in silence; and the last train to Le Havre, which had departed at 12.20, seemed to have taken the residual stirrings of the station with it. The stove no longer roared, and the embers of the dying fire intensified the red stain on the ceiling, which stared down like an eye rounded in terror. It was so hot in the room that a heavy, suffocating fog seemed to weigh down on the bed, where the pair lay spent, mingling their limbs.

'My love, what you don't realize . . .'

Then he too spoke, insistent:

'But yes, I do know.'

'No, you suspect perhaps, but you can't actually know.'

'I know he did it for the legacy.'

She started, and gave a short, nervous laugh in spite of herself.

'Oh, yes, the legacy!'

And very softly, so softly that a nocturnal insect buzzing against the window-panes would have made more noise, she told the story of her childhood at President Grandmorin's; she wanted to lie and not confess the nature of her relations with him, but then she yielded to her need for openness, and found relief, pleasure almost, in telling it all. After that her gentle murmuring flowed on, unstoppable.

'Just imagine! It was here in this room, last February—you remember, when he had that business with the Sub-Prefect. We had just had lunch, as happy as can be, like now when we were having supper over there on the table. He knew nothing about it, of course, and I wasn't going to be the one to tell him . . . And we just happened to be talking about a ring, one I'd been given a long time ago, talking about nothing really. And then, I don't know how, but it all simply came to him . . . Oh, you just can't imagine, my love, you just can't imagine how he treated me then!'

She was shaking, and he felt her small hands clenching against his bare skin.

'He knocked me to the ground with his fist . . . And then he dragged me, by the hair . . . And then he lifted his heel over my face as if he wanted to crush it . . . Oh, I shan't forget that as long as I live, I can assure you . . . Then he hit me again, my God! But if I were to tell you all the questions he asked me, and all the things he forced me to describe to him! As you can see, I've no wish to hide anything. Here I am telling you everything when there's nothing to make me, is there? Well, I shan't dare give you even an inkling of the filthy questions I *had* to answer, because if I hadn't, he'd have smashed my head in, that's for sure . . . No doubt he did love me, and it must have been hard for him to find all that out. And, granted, it would have been more honest of me to have told him everything before we were married. Only, you see, it was all over and done with, gone and forgotten. Only a real savage could go mad with jealousy like that . . . I mean, take you, my love: are you going to stop loving me now that you know?'

Jacques had not stirred, and he lay there motionless, thinking, wrapped in these woman's arms that were tightening round his neck and waist like coiling knots of snakes. He was very surprised, having never suspected such a story. How much more complicated things were, when the legacy would have been such a satisfactory explanation. What's more, he preferred it this way; to know for sure that the couple hadn't killed for money relieved him of the feeling of contempt which he had sometimes dimly felt, even when kissing Séverine.

'Me not love you any more, why? . . . I don't care about your past. It's no business of mine . . . You're married to Roubaud, but you might just as easily have been married to someone else.'

There was a silence. They held each other tight, almost till they choked, and he could feel her round breasts, all swollen and hard, against his side.

'So you were the old man's mistress, then. It's funny all the same.'

But she stretched up his body to his mouth, mumbling through a kiss:

'You're the only man I love, I've never loved anyone but you . . . Oh, the other two, if you only knew! You see, with them I didn't even learn what it could be like, while you, my darling, make me very happy!'

She was arousing him with her caresses, offering herself, wanting him, claiming him back with her straying hands. And so as not to yield at once, though he longed as she did, he had to restrain her with both his arms.

'No, no, wait, in a minute . . . So what about the old man?'

Very quietly, in a convulsion of her whole being, she confessed:

'Yes, we killed him.'

The tremble of desire merged with trembling of another sort, as she shuddered at the memory of death. It was, as at the climax of every sensual ecstasy, like the new beginning of a final agony. For a moment a sensation of lingering vertigo quite took her breath away. Then, with her face pressed once more to her lover's neck, she continued in the same even murmur:

'He made me write to the President telling him to leave on the express, at the same time as us, and not to show himself until we got to Rouen . . . I just sat in my corner of the compartment trembling, horrified at the prospect of the terrible thing that lay ahead of us. And opposite me there was a woman in black who never said a word and who frightened the life out of me. I didn't even look at her, I just imagined that she could read our thoughts exactly and knew perfectly well what we were going to do . . . That's how the two hours went by, from Paris to Rouen. I didn't utter a word, didn't move, just shut my eyes to pretend I was asleep. I could feel him beside me, not moving either, and what terrified me was knowing the dreadful things that were going through his mind and not being able to tell exactly what he'd decided to do . . . Oh, what a journey, with all those thoughts going round in my head, and the train whistling, and the jolting and clattering of the wheels!'

Jacques's mouth was buried in the thick, scented fleece of her hair, and he kept kissing her, at regular intervals, with long, absent-minded kisses.

'But since you weren't in the same compartment, how did you manage to kill him?'

'Wait, you'll see in a moment . . . That was my husband's plan. To be honest, it was only a matter of luck that it succeeded . . . There was a ten-minute stop at Rouen. We got off, and he forced me to walk as far as the President's coupé as though we were simply stretching our legs. When we got there, he pretended to be surprised to see him standing at the door, as if he'd had no idea he was on the train. There was a lot of pushing and shoving on the platform, and a crowd of people were trying to board in second class, because of the celebrations the next day in Le Havre. When they started to shut the doors again, it was the President himself who asked us to travel with him. I mumbled something about our suitcase, but he wouldn't listen, said that absolutely no one was going to steal our suitcase, and that we could go back to our own compartment at Barentin because he was getting off there. My husband looked anxious for a moment, as if he wanted to run and fetch it. But at that moment the guard blew his whistle, so he made up his mind and pushed me into the coupé. Then he climbed in himself and shut the door, and the window. How did no one see us? That's what I can't understand. Lots of people were rushing about, the station staff were in a panic . . . well anyway, there wasn't one witness who saw things clearly. And then the train slowly left the station.'

She was silent for a few moments, reliving the scene. Her limbs were so relaxed that, without her realizing it, her left thigh had developed a tremor and was rubbing up and down against his knee.

'Oh, that first moment in the coupé when I felt us moving! I was in an absolute daze, all I could think of was our suitcase: how could we get it back, and wouldn't it give us away if we left it where it was? It all seemed stupid to me, impossible, a kind of nightmare murder imagined by a child, which it would be madness to carry out. We'd be arrested the next day and convicted. So I tried to tell myself that my husband wouldn't go through with it, that it wouldn't happen, couldn't happen. But no, I could see just by the way he was talking to the President that he was fiercely determined, nothing was going to change his mind. And yet he was very calm, he was even chatting away quite cheerfully, the way he used to; and it must just have been from the clear look in his eyes, when he glanced at me occasionally, that I could see he was still stubbornly resolved. He was going to kill him, in the next kilometre, in the next two perhaps, at the precise spot which he'd chosen, and which I knew nothing about: it was evident, as plain as day even in the calm way he looked at him, at that man who in a few minutes' time would cease to exist. I said nothing, I was trying to hide the quaking going on inside me and simply smiled if either of them looked at me. So why didn't I even think of trying to prevent it? It was only later when I thought about it that I was surprised I hadn't shouted from the window or pulled the communication cord.* At the time it was as though I were paralysed, I was absolutely powerless to act. I suppose it seemed as if my husband were within his rights. And I ought to tell you this as well, my darling, while I'm about it: in spite of myself, every ounce of me was on his side against the other man, because I'd been with both of them, hadn't I, and he was young, while the other one, ugh, the caresses of that man . . . But in the end who can say? You do things you never thought you were capable of. When I think I wouldn't even dare bleed a chicken! Oh, that feeling of being out on a dark stormy night, that horrible blackness screaming inside me!'

This fragile creature, so slender lying here in his arms, now seemed quite impenetrable to Jacques, a bottomless pit filled with the darkness of which she spoke. Try as he might to hold her more tightly, he could no longer feel quite part of her. Excitement gripped him as he listened to this tale of murder being blurted out from the depths of their embrace.

'So tell me, did you help him kill the old man?'

'I was sitting in a corner,' she continued, without answering directly. 'My husband was between me and the President, who was sitting in the other corner. They were talking about the forthcoming elections . . . From time to time I saw my husband lean forward and look out to make sure where we were, as if he were in a hurry . . . Each time I followed his eyes, I too looked to see where we'd got to. It wasn't totally dark that night, and the black shapes of the trees went rushing past at a furious rate. And always that clattering of the wheels, I've never heard anything like it, like a dreadful babble of voices raging and moaning, or the pitiful howling of dying animals! The train was travelling at top speed . . . Suddenly there were flashes of light, and the noise of the train echoed between the buildings of a station. We were at Maromme, already two and a half leagues out of Rouen. Just Malaunay to come, and then Barentin. Where was it going to happen? And when? Would it take till the very last minute? I no longer knew what time it was or how far we'd come, and I was beginning to let myself be just carried along by that deafening plunge through the darkness, like a stone falling, when all at once, as we were passing through Malaunay, I realized: it would be done in the tunnel, one kilometre ahead . . . I turned towards my husband, and our eyes met: yes, in the tunnel, in two minutes' time . . . On the train went, and we passed the branch-line to Dieppe, I saw the pointsman at his post. There are hilly slopes there, and I distinctly thought I saw men standing there raising their fists at us and shouting abuse. Then the engine gave a long whistle: it was the entry to the tunnel . . . And when the train disappeared inside, oh, what a noise it made beneath that low roof! You know, like the clanking sound of a hammer on an anvil, and at that moment of panic it sounded to me like the crash of thunder.'

She shivered, and broke off to say in a different, almost laughing voice:

'Isn't it stupid, darling? The whole thing still chills me to the bone. And yet I'm perfectly warm here with you, and so happy! . . . Anyway, you know, there's nothing at all to be afraid of now. The case has been closed, not to mention the fact that the bigwigs in the government are even less keen than we are to clear the matter up . . . Oh, I've seen how things stand all right, I've no need to worry.'

Then she added, laughing out loud:

'And as for you! A proper fright you gave us, you'll be pleased to know! . . . And by the way, I've always wondered: what precisely did you see?'

'Only what I told the magistrate, nothing else: one man cutting another man's throat . . . You both behaved so strangely

towards me that in the end I began to suspect. For a moment I
even recognized your husband . . . It was only later, though, that
I became absolutely certain.'

Gaily she interrupted him:

'Yes, in the Square, that day I said no, do you remember? The
first time we were alone together in Paris . . . Isn't it odd?! I was
telling you it wasn't us, and I knew perfectly well that you were
thinking the opposite. Eh? It was as if I'd told you the whole
thing, wasn't it? . . . Oh, my love, I've often thought back to that
time, and do you know, I think that's when I first started to love
you.'

Involuntarily they squeezed each other tight, as though they
might fuse together. And then she continued:

'The train was in the tunnel . . . It's very long, that tunnel.
You're in there for all of three minutes, but I really thought we'd
been in it for a whole hour . . . The President had stopped talking because of the deafening racket of clanking metal. And then,
at that crucial moment, my husband's nerve must have failed
him for a second because he still didn't move. All I could see
in the flickering lamplight was that his ears were turning
purple . . . Was he going to wait till we were out in open countryside again? The whole thing now seemed to me so inevitable,
so much a matter of fate, that I had only one desire: to put an end
to this awful suspense, to get it over with. Why didn't he kill him
now, since kill him he must? I'd got myself into such a state of
fear and torment that I could have grabbed the knife myself just
to have had done with it . . . He looked at me. It must have
shown on my face. And then all of a sudden, as the President
turned towards the window, he lunged forward and grabbed him
by the shoulders. In his surprise the President instinctively
broke free and reached for the communication cord, which was
just above his head. He touched it but my husband grabbed him
again and shoved him back on to the seat with such force that he
was almost bent double. His mouth was wide open in terrified
astonishment, but his confused cries were lost in the racket,
though I could distinctly hear my husband saying "Swine!
Swine! Swine!" over and over again with a sort of hiss as he got
more and more furious. Then the noise began to fade as the train
left the tunnel and the shadows of the countryside reappeared,

with the black trees rushing by . . . I had stayed in my corner, completely rigid, and pressing myself against the back of the seat to get as far away as possible. How long did the struggle last? A few seconds at most. But it seemed to me that it would never end, and that all the passengers could hear the screams, that the trees themselves were watching. My husband had his knife open but couldn't strike because he kept getting kicked away, and he found it difficult to stand up with the floor of the carriage swaying all the time. He nearly fell to his knees at one point, and meanwhile the train just continued on its way, carrying us along at top speed, with the engine whistling as we approached the level-crossing at La Croix-de-Maufras . . . That was the moment, and I have never been able to remember since exactly how it happened, when I threw myself across the President's legs as he struggled to get free. Yes, I just let myself drop like a package on top of him, crushing his legs with all my weight so that he couldn't move. I didn't see what happened, but I felt the whole thing: the impact of the knife entering his neck, the long shuddering of his body, and then death coming in three wheezing gasps, like the whirring of a clock with a broken spring. . . . Oh, those final death throes! I can still feel the trembling going through my arms and legs like an echo.'

Jacques, listening avidly, wanted to interrupt and ask her questions. But now she was in a hurry to finish:

'No, in a minute . . . As I was getting off him, we were passing La Croix-de-Maufras at full speed. I distinctly saw the front of the house, all closed up, and then the crossing-keeper's hut. Just four kilometres to Barentin, five at the outside. The body was bent over on the seat, and the blood was making a thick pool. And my husband was standing there in a daze, jolted by the movement of the train and wiping the knife with his handkerchief. A minute went by like that, and neither of us did anything to save ourselves . . . If we kept the body with us, if we stayed there ourselves, people might discover everything at Barentin . . . But by now he'd put the knife back in his pocket and seemed to be coming to. I saw him search the body, and take the watch and the money, in fact anything he found; and then he opened the door and tried to push the body out on to the track, but without getting his arms round it properly because of the

blood. "Help me, can't you! Come and give it a shove!" I didn't
even try, I had lost all feeling in my arms and legs. "For Christ's
sake, give me a hand!" The head had been pushed out first and
was hanging over the footboard, while the trunk was all rolled up
in a bundle and wouldn't go through the door. And the train just
kept on going . . . Finally, after a harder shove, the body teetered
on the edge and then disappeared amidst the clattering of the
wheels. "There, that's the end of him, the swine." Then he
picked up the rug and threw it out as well. That left the two of
us standing there, not daring to sit down on the seat where there
was the pool of blood . . . The door was still wide open, banging
to and fro, and in my exhausted, panic-stricken state I didn't
understand at first when I saw my husband climb out and also
disappear. He came back. "Come on, quickly, follow me, if you
don't want us both to get the chop!" I didn't move, and he began
to lose patience.

"For Christ's sake, come with me! Our compartment's empty,
we can go back." Empty? Our compartment? Had he actually
been to see? That woman in black, the one who didn't say
anything, the one you didn't notice, was he really sure she hadn't
remained behind in a corner? . . . "Come, now, or I'll bloody
throw you out like the last one!" He had climbed back in and was
shoving me forward, brutally, like a madman. And I found myself outside the train, on the footboard, clinging with both hands
to the brass handrail. He had climbed out after me, making sure
to shut the door. "Go on, move." But I didn't dare, I was dizzy
with the speed of the train and being lashed by the roaring wind.
My hair came loose, and I thought my numbed fingers were
going to let go of the handrail. "For God's sake, move." He kept
shoving me, so I had to move, hand over hand and hugging the
side of the carriages, with my skirts all blowing round me and
flapping against my legs so I couldn't move properly. Already,
after going round a bend, we could see the lights of Barentin
station in the distance. The engine began to whistle. "Go on, for
God's sake!" Oh, that hellish noise, that violent shaking as I went
along. It was as though a gust of wind had grabbed me in a gale
and was whirling me about like a wisp of straw before crushing
me against some wall. Behind me the countryside was racing
past, and the trees seemed to be galloping after me in a mad

stampede, twisting round on themselves and letting out a short moan every time one of them went by. At the end of the carriage I had to step across on to the footboard of the next one and grab its handrail, but courage failed me and I stopped. I'd never have the strength. "Go on, for God's sake." He was right behind me, shoving me forward, and I shut my eyes, and somehow or other I managed to keep going, by sheer force of instinct, like an animal that has dug its claws in and simply refuses to let go. And how were we not seen? We went along three carriages, and one of them, in second-class, was crammed full of people. I remember seeing the rows of heads in the lamplight. I think I'd recognize them if I ever saw them again one day: there was a fat man with red sideburns, and I remember especially two young girls leaning forward and laughing. "Go on, for God's sake, go on." I remember nothing after that: the lights of Barentin were coming closer, the engine was whistling, and the last thing I was conscious of was being dragged, carried, hauled along by my hair. My husband must have grabbed hold of me, opened the door above my shoulders, and thrown me into the compartment. When we stopped, I was lying half conscious in a corner, gasping for breath; and I didn't move an inch as I listened to him exchanging a few words with the local station-master. Then the train set off again, and he collapsed on to the seat, completely exhausted himself. And all the way to Le Havre neither of us said a word . . . Oh, I hate him, I hate him, do you hear, for all the dreadful things he's made me go through! But you, my darling, I love you, you give me so much happiness!'

For Séverine, after the mounting excitement of her long tale, this exclamation was like the final burgeoning of her pent-up need for joy amidst the horror of her memories. But Jacques, on whom this story had made a deep impression and who wanted her as much as she did him, restrained her a little longer.

'No, no, wait . . . So you were lying flat across his legs and actually felt him die?'

Within him that unknown other was stirring once more; a wave of ferocity welled up from his entrails and flooded his head with a vision of red. His fascination with murder had taken hold of him again.

'And the knife? You felt it go in?'

'Yes, with a sort of thud.'

'Ah, a thud. Not a kind of tearing? Are you sure?'

'No, no, just a sudden jolt.'

'And then he gave a shudder. Is that right?'

'Yes, three shudders, oh! from one end of his body to the other, and so protracted that I could follow them all the way down to his feet.'

'And he went all stiff when he shuddered, did he?'

'Yes, the first time very stiff, and then the next two times not quite so much.'

'And then he died. And what did it do to *you*, feeling him die like that, from a knife wound?'

'To me? Well, I don't know exactly.'

'You don't know? Why won't you tell me the truth? Tell me, tell me honestly how you felt. Did you feel sorry?'

'No, no, not sorry!'

'Did you feel pleasure?'

'Pleasure? Oh, no, not pleasure!'

'What then, my love? Please, tell me all about it . . . If you but knew . . . Tell me how it feels.'

'My God! how can one describe such a thing? . . . It's horrible, it takes hold of you and carries you away, so far, far away! I experienced more in that one minute than in the whole of my previous life.'

This time, with teeth clenched and barely muttering, Jacques had taken her; and Séverine took him also. They possessed each other, finding love in the midst of death, and with the same excruciating pleasure as animals that eviscerate one another while they mate. Only the sound of their rasping breath could be heard. On the ceiling the blood-red patch of light had disappeared; and now that the stove had gone out, the bedroom was beginning to grow chilly from the great icy cold outside. Not a voice was to be heard from the city that lay wrapped in its wadding of snow. For a moment there had been the sound of snoring coming from the newspaper woman's next door. Then everything had subsided again into the great dark abyss of the sleeping building.

Jacques, still holding Séverine in his arms, at once felt her yield irretrievably to sleep, as though suddenly struck down.

The train journey, the long wait at Misard's, and this night of passion, had exhausted her. She mumbled goodnight like a child, and already she was asleep, breathing evenly. The cuckoo-clock had just struck three.

And for almost another hour Jacques continued to hold her on his left arm, which grew gradually numb. He could not keep his eyes closed; some invisible hand seemed to insist on opening them again in the darkness. He could scarcely make out anything in the room now, where the engulfing blackness of the night had swallowed up stove, furniture, and walls alike; and he had to turn his head to locate the two pale squares of the windows, which stood motionless and ethereal, as though glimpsed in a dream. Despite his overwhelming fatigue, his brain was still extraordinarily active, and he remained quiveringly alert as he unwound his single spool of thoughts over and over again. Each time he thought that by an effort of will he was beginning to drift off to sleep, the same haunting vision returned, and the same images followed each other in procession, bringing with them the same sensations. And the scene that would unfold before him with this mechanical regularity, as his wide, unblinking eyes absorbed the darkness, was the scene of the murder, detail by detail. It kept repeating itself, always the same, compulsive, maddening. The knife would enter the neck with a dull thud, the body would shudder three times, and life would ebb away in a stream of warm blood, a red stream which he thought he could feel running over his hands. Twenty, thirty times, the knife went in and the body jerked. The whole thing was assuming monstrous proportions in his mind, stifling him, spilling out into the darkness, bursting the night asunder. Oh! to plunge a knife in like that, to satisfy that distant longing, to know what it felt like, to savour that minute in which you experience more than in the whole of your previous life!

As this feeling of suffocation increased, Jacques thought it was only Séverine's weight on his arm which was preventing him from sleeping. Gently he released himself and laid her next to him without waking her. In his initial relief he breathed more easily, thinking that sleep at last was coming. But despite his efforts the invisible fingers prised his eyelids open again, and against the blackness the murder scene once more unfolded in its gory detail; the knife went in, the body jerked. A red rain streaked the darkness, and the wound in the neck gaped hugely as though a wedge had been removed by an axe. Then he gave up the struggle and continued to lie there, a prey to this obsessing vision. He could almost hear the humming activity of his brain, a whirring in the works. It all stemmed from a long way back, from his early youth. And yet he had thought himself cured, for the urge had lain dead for months, ever since he had first possessed this woman; but now here he was feeling it more intensely than ever, having listened to her whisper this reconstruction of the murder as she lay pressed against his flesh and entwined in his limbs. He had now moved to one side to avoid her touch, scorched by the merest contact with her skin. A sensation of unbearable heat was running up his spine, as if the mattress beneath him had turned into a bed of hot coals. Pinpoints of fire pricked the back of his neck. For a moment he tried having his hands outside the bedclothes; but they turned at once to ice, and made him shiver. He took fright at these hands and drew them in again, first clasping them over his stomach, then sliding them beneath his buttocks, pressing them under, imprisoning them there as if he dreaded some abomination on their part, an act which he would not intend but which he would no less certainly commit.

Each time the cuckoo-clock struck, Jacques would count. Four, five, six o'clock. He yearned for the day to begin, hoping that the dawn would dispel this nightmare. Thus he now continually turned his head towards the windows, watching the panes. But still all that could be seen was the faint reflected light from the snow. At a quarter to five, only forty minutes late, he had heard the arrival of the direct from Le Havre, which meant that trains were getting through again. And it was not until after seven that he saw the window-panes begin to pale and slowly turn a milky white. At last the room was growing lighter, revealing a dim blur in which the furniture seemed to float. The stove reappeared, and the wardrobe, and the dresser. Still he could not close his eyes, indeed now they itched with his need to see. Immediately, even before it was sufficiently light, he had more sensed than seen, lying on the table, the knife which he had used the previous evening to cut the cake. All he could see now was this knife, a small knife with a pointed blade. As day broke, every glimmer of white light from the two windows now entered the room only to be reflected in this slender blade. And in his terror at his own hands he buried them even more firmly beneath his body, for he could feel them twitching in revolt, stronger than his will. Were they going to cease to belong to him? These hands that must have come down to him from someone else, hands that were the legacy of some ancestor from a time when man used to strangle wild beasts in the forest!

Wanting not to look at the knife, Jacques turned towards Séverine. She was sleeping very peacefully, breathing like a child in her exhaustion. Her thick black hair fell in a loose tumble to her shoulders, making a dark pillow for her head; and beneath her chin, among the curls, her breasts could be seen, as delicately white as milk, with scarcely a trace of pink. He looked at her as if he did not know her. And yet he adored her, carrying her image with him everywhere, desiring her, often achingly so, even when he was driving his engine; to such an extent that one day he had awoken as though from a dream just as he was passing through a station at full speed against the signals. But the sight of these white breasts took complete hold of him, filling him with a sudden, inexorable fascination; and with as yet conscious horror he could feel the imperious need rising within him to fetch the knife from the table and to come back and plunge it up to the hilt into this womanly flesh. He could hear the dull thud of the blade going in, he could see the body shudder three times and then stiffen in death beneath a stream of red. As he struggled to tear himself free from this haunting vision, he forfeited a further portion of his will with every second that passed, as though he were gradually sinking beneath the waves of his fixation, teetering on that extreme edge beyond which one yields, defeated, to the promptings of instinct. Everything became a blur, and his rebellious hands, having won the battle against his efforts to conceal them, unclasped themselves and escaped. And he understood so clearly that he had ceased to be their master, and that they were about to gain brutal satisfaction if he continued to gaze at Séverine, that he devoted his one last ounce of strength to throwing himself out of bed and on to the floor, where he rolled around like a drunkard. He picked himself up but nearly fell again when his feet became tangled in the skirts that were still lying there. He stumbled around, casting about wildly for his own clothes, with his one thought being to get dressed quickly, grab the knife, and go and kill some other woman in the street. This time his tormenting desire was too strong, he simply had to kill one. He could not locate his trousers, though he laid his hands on them three times without realizing he had found them. Putting on his shoes caused him infinite trouble. Although it was now broad daylight, the room seemed to be filled with a red mist, like a freezing fog at dawn in which everything merges into everything else. Shivering feverishly and finally dressed, he had seized the knife and hidden it up his sleeve, quite certain that he was going to kill one of them, the first woman he met on the pavement, when a rustling of bedclothes and a prolonged sigh brought him up short beside the table; and he stood there, the blood draining from his face.

It was Séverine waking up.

'What's up, my love? Are you going out already?'

He made no reply, not even looking at her, and hoping she would go back to sleep.

'Where are you going, my love?'

'It's nothing,' he stammered, 'just something at work. Go to sleep, I'll be back soon.'

Then, as drowsiness overtook her once more, and with her eyes already closed, she muttered a few unintelligible words.

'Oh, I feel ever so sleepy! . . . Come and give me a kiss, darling.'

But he just stood there, knowing that if he turned round with this knife in his hand, if he so much as looked at her again, all dainty and pretty in her naked, dishevelled state, then that would be an end to the willpower which held him there near her, tensely resisting. Despite himself his hand would go up and plunge the knife into her neck for him.

'Darling, come and kiss me . . .'

Her voice tailed away, and she fell back to sleep, very gently, an affectionate murmur on her lips. And he, distraught, opened the door and fled.

It was eight o'clock when Jacques found himself down on the pavement in the Rue d'Amsterdam. The snow had not yet been cleared, and one could barely hear the footsteps of the few people walking by. He had immediately spotted an elderly woman; but she was turning into the Rue de Londres, and he did not follow her. Various men jostled him, and he walked down towards the Place du Havre, clasping the knife with its pointed end hidden up his sleeve. When a young girl of about fourteen came out of a house opposite, he crossed the street but only to see her walk into a baker's next door. His impatience was such that he did not wait for her to come out but continued his search on down the street. Ever since he had left the room, knife in hand, it had not been him doing things but the other man, the one he had so frequently sensed stirring in the depths of his being, that unknown person from far back who burned with this hereditary thirst for murder. He had killed in times gone by, he wanted to kill again. And everything around Jacques now seemed to exist in a dream state, for he saw them through his fixation. It was as if his normal everyday life had been obliterated, and he walked as though in his sleep, with no memory of the past nor any thought for the future, entirely given over to his obsessive need. His body moved along, but his own self was absent from it. Two women brushed past as they overtook him, making him quicken his step; and he was just catching them up when a man stopped them. The three of them were laughing and talking. Put off by the man's presence, he began to follow another woman who happened to come past, a dark, scrawny woman who looked poverty-stricken in her thin shawl. She was walking very slowly, probably on her way to some hated form of labour that was arduous and badly paid, for she was in no hurry and her face looked desperately sad. And nor did he hurry either, now that he had got one, rather waiting for the right spot where he could strike at his ease. No doubt she had noticed this fellow following her, and her eyes turned towards him with an expression of indescribably bleak despair, astonished that anyone could be interested in someone like her. Already she had led him halfway down the Rue du Havre, and she turned round twice more, each time preventing him, as he pulled the knife from his sleeve, from planting it in her neck. Her eyes were the eyes of destitution, and so imploring! Over there, when she stepped off the pavement, that's when he would strike. But then suddenly he veered off in pursuit of another woman, who was walking in the opposite direction. And he did so quite without reason, without wanting to, but simply because she was passing at that particular moment, and because that was how it was.

Jacques followed her back towards the station. This one was walking at a brisk pace, her short steps tap-tapping along the pavement; and she was adorably pretty, twenty at most, already plump, blonde, with lovely eyes full of a gaiety that laughed at life. She did not even notice that a man was following her; and she must have been in a hurry, for she darted nimbly up the steps of the Cours du Havre into the booking hall and continued the length of it, almost running, before rushing over to the ticket-windows for the Ceinture line. And as she was asking for a first-class ticket to Auteuil, Jacques bought one too and accompanied her through the waiting-rooms, out on to the platform, and into the same compartment, where he sat down beside her. The train left at once.

'I've got time,' he thought, 'I'll kill her when we go through a tunnel.'

But opposite them an old lady, the only other passenger to board the train, had just recognized the young woman.

'Why, it's you! Where are you off to at this time of the day?'

The young woman laughed good-naturedly and gestured in comic despair.

'One can't go anywhere without being recognized these days! I hope you won't give me away . . . It's my husband's birthday tomorrow, and as soon as he left for work, I ran. I'm off to a nursery at Auteuil where he saw an orchid he's just dying to have . . . It's a surprise, you see.'

The old lady nodded with benevolent affection.

'And is baby doing well?'

'Oh, the dear little thing, she's a real joy . . . I weaned her a week ago, you know. You should just see her eating her soup! We're all of us terribly well, it really shouldn't be allowed!'

She was laughing even louder, her white teeth showing between her blood-red lips. And Jacques, who had placed himself on her right, with the knife clenched in his fist and hidden by his thigh, told himself that he was well placed to strike. All he had to do was lift his arm and make a half-turn, and he would have her just where he wanted her. But as they went through the Batignolles tunnel, the thought of her hat-strings gave him pause.

'There's a bow there', he reflected, 'that's going to get in my way. I want to be sure.'

The two women continued to chat away merrily.

'So you're happy, I see.'

'Happy? Oh, I can't tell you! It's like a dream . . . Two years ago, I was just nobody. As you remember, there wasn't much fun to be had at my aunt's, and not one centime for a dowry . . . I was a nervous wreck when he used to call, I'd come to love him so much. But he was so handsome, so rich . . . And now he's mine, he's my husband, and we have baby as well! I tell you, it's all too much!'

While studying the bow that tied her hat-strings, Jacques had just noticed that underneath, attached to a black velvet neck-band, was a large gold medallion; and he planned carefully what he would do.

'I'll grab her neck with my left hand, and then I'll get the medallion out of the way by pulling her head back, so as to have the neck bare.'

The train was continually stopping and starting. There had been two short tunnels one after another, at Courcelles, and then at Neuilly. Any moment now . . . It would only take a second.

'Did you go to the seaside this summer?' the old lady went on.

'Yes, to Brittany, for six weeks, in the middle of nowhere. It was paradise. Then we spent September in the Poitou, at my father-in-law's. He owns a lot of woodland there.'

'And weren't you going to take something in the south for the winter?'

'Yes, we shall be in Cannes from about the 15th . . . We've taken the house. With a lovely little garden, and facing the sea. We've sent someone down to get everything ready for us . . . It's not that either of us feels the cold, but oh! the sun, it does you good! . . . Then, after that, we shall be back in March. Next year we'll stay put in Paris. Then in two years' time, when baby's a big girl, we'll travel. Oh, I don't know, life seems to be just one long holiday!'

She was so overflowing with happiness that, yielding to her expansive nature, she turned towards Jacques, this stranger, and gave him a smile. As she did so, the bow of her hat-strings shifted, the medallion moved to one side, and the neck appeared, all rosy pink, with a slight dimple that was golden with shadow.

Jacques's fingers had tightened round the handle of the knife as he came to an irrevocable decision.

'There, that's where I'll strike. Yes, a moment from now, in the tunnel, before Passy.'

But at Trocadero station a railwayman got on, and since he knew Jacques, he began to talk about work, about the theft of some coal for which a driver and his fireman had just been convicted. And from then on everything was a blur, and he was never able subsequently to piece together exactly what happened. The laughter had continued, a happiness so infectious that it had communicated itself to him and calmed him. Perhaps he had gone as far as Auteuil with the two women; except that he could not remember them getting off there. He himself had ended up on the banks of the Seine, without being able to explain how. One thing he did very clearly remember was the sensation of throwing away the knife from the top of the river-bank, that knife which had remained in his fist, pointing up his sleeve. After that he didn't know, he had been in a daze, as though absent from his own being—from which also that other self had now departed, vanishing with the knife. He must have walked for hours, through streets and squares, wherever his body chose to take him. People, houses, went past, all very pale-looking. No doubt he must have gone somewhere and had a meal in the middle of a room full of people, for he could distinctly recall white plates. He also had the persistent impression of a red poster on a shop that had closed down. And then everything had sunk into a dark chasm, a nothingness beyond time and space, in which he had lain motionless, perhaps for centuries.

When he came to, Jacques was in his tiny room in the Rue Cardinet, sprawled fully dressed across his bed. Instinct had brought him back there, like an exhausted dog that drags itself back to its kennel. Indeed he could not remember either climbing the stairs or falling asleep. He was stirring from a deep sleep, shocked and startled to find himself suddenly in possession of his faculties once more, as though he had passed out. He might have been asleep for three hours or three days. And at once his memory returned: the night spent with Séverine, the confession of the murder, his rushing out like some carnivorous beast in pursuit of blood. He had taken leave of himself, and now he was back, stupefied at the things which had taken place beyond his control. Then he remembered that she would be waiting for him, and he was on his feet in a trice. Glancing at his watch, he saw that it was already four o'clock; and with his head now clear and quite calm, as though he had been copiously bled, he hurried back to the Impasse d'Amsterdam.

Séverine had slept soundly until noon. When she then woke and found to her surprise that he was not yet back, she had relit the stove. Having finally got dressed, she was dying of hunger and so decided about two o'clock to go down and eat in a nearby restaurant. When Jacques appeared, she had just returned to the flat having done some shopping.

'Oh, my love, I was so worried about you!'

She had flung herself round his neck, and was looking closely into his eyes.

'What on earth happened?'

Now exhausted, his flesh numb, he was able to reassure her calmly, without any hint of disturbance.

'Oh, nothing. A boring chore, that's all. Once they've got their claws into you, they never let you go.'

Then, lowering her voice, she began to speak in humble, winning tones.

'You'll never guess what I pictured . . . Oh, it was a horrid thought, and it was making me so unhappy! . . . But, well, I said to myself that maybe, after what I'd told you, you wouldn't want me any more . . . And so I convinced myself that you'd left for good, and that you'd never ever be coming back!'

The tears were welling up, and she burst into sobs, hugging him wildly.

'Oh, my darling, if you only knew, knew how much I need people to be kind to me! . . . Love me, love me all you can, because, you see, only your love can ever make me forget . . . Now that I've told you all the bad things that have happened to me, you won't leave me, will you?! Oh please, I beg you, don't leave me!'

Jacques was deeply touched by this display of emotion. Slowly and surely he began to soften, and he stammered:

'No, no, I do love you, don't be afraid.'

And now, overcome himself, he wept in turn at his fate in suffering from this gruesome malady which had gripped him once more and of which he would never be cured. He felt a shame, a despair, that knew no end.

'Love me, love me too! Oh yes, with all your strength, because I need you just as much!'

She quivered, wanting to know.

'You've got troubles too, you must tell me what they are.'

'No, no, not troubles, things which don't exist, fits of misery which leave me horribly unhappy, things I can't even talk about.'

They held each other close, merging the awful sadness of their plights. For theirs was a suffering unto eternity, without prospect of oblivion or forgiveness. They wept together and felt the blind forces of life weighing upon them, a life of struggle and death.

'Come on,' said Jacques, breaking away, 'it's time to think of leaving . . . By tonight you'll be back in Le Havre.'

With a gloomy, vacant expression, Séverine murmured presently:

'Oh, if only I were free, if only my husband weren't there any more . . . Oh, how quickly we could forget!'

He gestured wildly, thinking aloud:

'Yes, but we can't actually kill him.'

She stared at him, and he shuddered, astonished at having said such a thing, something he'd never even thought of before. Since he wanted to kill, why didn't he kill *him*, this man who was in their way? And as he was finally saying goodbye before hurrying off to the depot, she took him once more in her arms and covered him with kisses:

'Oh, my darling, love me with all your heart. And I shall love you, more and more . . . We shall be happy, you'll see.'

CHAPTER IX

In Le Havre, during the days which followed, Jacques and Séverine exercised the greatest care, for they had become nervous. Since Roubaud knew everything, would he not be out to spy on them, to catch them and take dramatic revenge? They recalled his jealous outbursts of old, his brutal ways as a former station-worker who liked to use his fists. And the mere sight of him now, heavy and silent, with those glazed eyes, was enough to convince them that he must be hatching some cruel, cunning plan, some trap which would place them in his power. And so, for the first month, they would meet only after taking countless precautions, and even then they remained constantly on the alert.

Roubaud, meanwhile, came home less and less. Perhaps he only disappeared like this so that he could return unexpectedly and find them in each other's arms. But this fear proved unfounded. On the contrary, his absences grew so prolonged that he was simply never there, slipping away the moment he was off duty and returning only at the precise minute his duties demanded. During his weeks on the day shift he would contrive to eat his ten o'clock meal in five minutes and then disappear until half past eleven; and in the evening, when his colleague went down to replace him at five o'clock, away he vanished again, often for the entire night. He scarcely spent even a few hours asleep. It was the same with his weeks on the night shift, when he got away at five in the morning, presumably eating and sleeping somewhere else but in any case never coming home until five in the afternoon. For a long time, despite this disorderly existence, he had continued to display the punctuality of a model employee, always arriving on time, sometimes so exhausted that he could scarcely stand up, but standing nevertheless, and conscientiously going about his duties. But recently there had been gaps. Twice already the other assistant station-master, Moulin, had had to spend an hour waiting for him; and one day, on being told after lunch that Roubaud had not yet reappeared, he had even stood in for him, like the decent fellow he was, to save him from an official reprimand. And Roubaud's entire work schedule began to show the effects of this gradual want of orderliness. By day he had ceased to be his old active self, who never despatched or accepted a train until he had inspected everything with his own eyes, and entered the minutest details in his report to the station-master, ever as hard on himself as he was on others. By night, he would fall fast asleep in the big armchair in his office. Even when he was awake, he still seemed to be dozing as he came and went on the platform, hands behind his back, issuing orders in an expressionless voice and never checking to see if they had been carried out. Nevertheless everything still proceeded as it should, through sheer force of routine, except for one minor collision which was due to negligence on his part, when a passenger train was sent down a siding by mistake. His colleagues just laughed, saying it must be the wine, women, and song.

The truth was that Roubaud now virtually lived on the first floor of the Café du Commerce, in the little private room which had gradually turned into a gambling den. It was said that women went there every night; but in reality only one woman was ever to be found there, and she was the mistress of a retired sea captain, at least forty, and herself an inveterate gambler. Her sex was of no consequence. The only passion which Roubaud sought to satisfy in this place was his grim lust for gambling, a taste which he had acquired in a casual game of piquet shortly after the murder, and which had subsequently developed into a compulsive habit as a result of the total mental absorption, the utter oblivion, which it brought him. It had so taken him over that even in this brute of a man it had banished all desire for women; and now it held him entirely in its grip, as his one source of gratification and contentment. It was not that remorse had ever tormented him with the need to forget; but amidst the upheaval caused by the breakdown of his domestic existence, and with his life in ruins, he had discovered the numbing consolation of selfish happiness, something to be savoured alone; and this obsession had now become all-consuming, leaving him in a state of total moral collapse. Alcohol could not have made time hang less heavily nor pass more rapidly, nor afforded him such a complete sense of deliverance. He had ceased even to care about life itself, and he felt as though he were living at a level of extraordinary intensity, but somewhere else, uninvolved, and unaffected by the tribulations that would previously have sent him into a rage. And he was in very good health, apart from the tiredness caused by lack of sleep; he was even putting on some weight, in the form of thick sallow fat, which was making his eyelids begin to droop over those glazed eyes. When he did come home, his movements sluggish with fatigue, he brought with him nothing but a sovereign indifference to all things.

The night Roubaud had returned to take the three hundred francs in gold from under the floor, it was because he wanted to pay Monsieur Cauche, the superintendent, following a series of losses. The latter was a seasoned gambler, and his fine poker-face made him a fearsome opponent. Of course, as he said, he only played for the fun of it, being obliged by his official position to maintain the façade of a retired army bachelor who liked to while away the hours as a café regular—which didn't stop him playing cards all evening and taking everyone's money. There had been rumours that he, too, was accused of neglecting his duties and that as a result there was some question of his being forced to resign. But things had dragged on, and as there was so little for him to do anyway, why would they insist on greater effort? And he continued to content himself with making brief appearances on the platform, where everyone would duly greet him.

Three weeks later, Roubaud again owed Monsieur Cauche nearly four hundred francs. He had explained that his wife's inheritance had made them very comfortably off; but he would add with a laugh that it was she who held the purse-strings, which excused his slowness in settling his debts. Then, one morning when he was alone and feeling particularly pressed, he lifted the wooden floor-block again and took a thousand-franc note from the hiding-place. His whole body was trembling, he had not felt nearly so anxious the night he had taken the gold coins: doubtless that had just seemed like spare change, whereas now, with this banknote, theft proper began. His flesh prickled with unease when he thought of this sacrosanct money which he had promised never to touch. He had sworn then that he would rather die of starvation, and yet here he was taking some of it, and he could not have said how his scruples had come to disappear like this, a little every day he supposed, as the rot set in after the murder. At the bottom of the hole he thought he had felt something damp, something pulpy and foul-smelling which gave him the horrors. Rapidly he replaced the flooring, vowing once more that he would rather cut off his hand than open it again. His wife had not seen him, and he breathed again with relief, drinking a large glass of water to steady himself. His heart was now pounding with delight at the thought of paying his debt and having all this money with which to gamble.

But when it came to changing the banknote, Roubaud's worries began all over again. He had once been brave, and he would have given himself up had he not been foolish enough to involve his wife in the affair; whereas now the very thought of the police brought him out in a cold sweat. While he knew perfectly well that they didn't have the numbers of the missing banknotes, and that anyway the case had been shelved and lay buried for ever in the files, he was still terrified at the prospect of going in somewhere and asking for change. For five days he carried the note round with him; and it became his habit, his constant need, to touch it, or to put it in a different place, or to make sure that he had it by him at night. He devised the most complicated schemes, but kept coming up against unforeseen problems. First, he had thought of the station: why shouldn't a colleague in charge of cash-receipts change it for him? Then that had seemed extremely risky, and he had thought of taking himself off instead to the other end of Le Havre, without his uniform cap, and buying something. Only wouldn't they be surprised to see him breaking into such a large sum just for something small? And then finally he had decided to present the note at the tobacconist's on the Cours Napoléon, where he went every day. Wasn't that simplest in the end? They knew he'd come into an inheritance, the lady behind the counter couldn't possibly be surprised. He got as far as the door, but then lost his nerve and had to walk down to the Vauban dock to pluck up courage again. After walking around for half an hour he came back, still not knowing what to do. And that evening at the Café du Commerce, in front of Monsieur Cauche, he suddenly took the note from his pocket out of sheer bravado and asked the proprietor's wife to change it for him; but she had insufficient change and was obliged to send a waiter with it to the tobacconist's. They even joked about the note, which seemed to be in mint condition even though it dated back ten years. The superintendent had inspected it and said there could be no question, it must have lain buried in some hole or other; which then started the captain's mistress off on an interminable story about a hidden fortune that had turned up beneath the marble top of a chest of drawers.

The weeks went by, and the ready availability of this money brought Roubaud's passion for gambling to fever pitch. It was not that he played for high stakes, but he was dogged by such continual and desperate ill-luck that the small daily losses accumulated into considerable sums. Towards the end of the month he found himself penniless once more, already owing several louis on the security of his word, and it drove him mad to think that he dared not touch another card. But he kept up the struggle, almost falling ill in the process. The thought of the nine banknotes lying there beneath his dining-room floor became an obsession that possessed him every minute of the day: he could see them through the wooden floor-blocks, he could feel them warming the soles of his shoes. To think that if he had wanted, he could have taken one more! But this time he really had vowed, and he would rather have put his hand in the fire than go rummaging about in there again. And then one evening, when Séverine had gone to sleep early, he pulled up the floor-block, furious at himself for giving in and so distraught with misery that his eyes filled with tears. What was the use in fighting against it like this? It would only mean suffering to no purpose, for he now realized that he would end up taking them all, one by one.

The following morning Séverine happened to notice a new scratch at the edge of the parquet flooring. She bent down and saw where the floor-block had been levered up. Evidently her husband was still helping himself to the money. She was surprised at how angry she felt, for she didn't normally care about money; apart from which she, too, believed herself resolved to die of starvation rather than touch any of these banknotes tainted with blood. But were they not hers as much as his? Why was he disposing of them in secret, and without even consulting her? During the time which elapsed before their evening meal, she was tortured with the need to know for certain, and she would have removed the floor-block herself to find out, if she hadn't felt her scalp tingle at the very thought of delving in there on her own. Mightn't the dead man himself rise up from the hole? This childish fear made the dining-room so disagreeable to her that she took her needlework into the bedroom and shut herself in.

Then, that evening, as they both sat silently eating the remains of some stew, her irritation returned as she saw him keep glancing involuntarily at the edge of the floor.

'You took some more, didn't you?' she asked sharply.

He looked up in surprise.

'More what?'

'Oh, don't come the innocent, you know perfectly well . . . But listen to me. I want you to stop, because it's no more yours than mine, and it sickens me to think you've had your hands on it.'

Usually he avoided scenes. Their marital life now amounted to little more than the unavoidable contact of two beings bound together, spending whole days without exchanging a single word, each going their separate ways, like complete strangers, indifferent and alone. So he merely shrugged his shoulders and offered no comment.

But she was particularly agitated, and intended once and for all to settle the matter of this hidden money, which had caused her such unhappiness ever since the day of the crime.

'I want an answer . . . I dare you to tell me that you haven't touched it.'

'What business is it of yours?'

'It's my business that it turns my stomach. Only today I was afraid, I just couldn't stay in this room. Every time you disturb the stuff, I get terrible dreams for nights afterwards. We never talk about it; so leave it be, and don't make me start now.'

He looked at her with his large, unblinking eyes and repeated wearily:

'What business is it of yours if I touch it, if I don't make *you* touch it. It's up to me, it's my affair.'

She was about to make an angry gesture, but controlled herself. Then, thoroughly nonplussed and with a look of pain and disgust on her face, she said:

'Really, I just don't understand you . . . I mean, you were an honest man once. You were, you'd never have taken a penny from anyone . . . And what you did, that could be forgiven, you were out of your mind, and so was I, thanks to you . . . But this money, oh, this dreadful money, which you said wasn't even going to exist as far as you were concerned, and which now you're stealing, bit by bit, for your own pleasure . . . What's happening, how can you have fallen so low?'

He was listening to her, and in a moment of lucidity he, too, found it surprising that he had been reduced to stealing. The separate stages of his slow moral collapse were fading into the past; he couldn't remake the connections which, all around him, the murder had severed, and he couldn't explain how another life, almost an entirely new mode of being, had begun, in which his domestic life was in ruins, and his wife estranged and hostile. But then at once his sense of the irreparable nature of things took hold of him again, and he gestured as though to rid himself of importunate reflections.

'When a person's bored at home', he grunted, 'he looks elsewhere for his amusements. And since you don't love me any more . . .'

'No, indeed, I don't love you any more.'

He stared at her and then smashed his fist down on to the table, his face suddenly flushing.

'So fucking well leave me alone, then! I don't stop *you* having your piece of fun, do I? I don't judge *you*, do I? . . . There are a lot of things a respectable man would do in my place, things I don't do. For a start I should throw you out, with a kick up the backside. Perhaps I'd stop stealing, then.'

She had turned very pale, for the thought had often occurred to her also that when a man, a jealous man, is so ravaged by his inner malaise that he tolerates his wife having a lover, then that means the moral gangrene is spreading, destroying each remaining scruple and dissolving conscience altogether. But she would not give in, she refused to be held responsible. And she stammered out:

'I forbid you to touch that money.'

He had finished eating. Calmly he folded his napkin, then rose and said in a bantering tone:

'If that's what you're after, we can split it.'

Already he was bending down as though to lift the floor-block. She had to rush across and plant her foot on it.

'No, no! You know I'd rather die . . . You're not to open it. No, not while I'm here, you're not!'

That evening Séverine had arranged to meet Jacques, behind the goods station. When she returned after midnight, the evening's scene came back to her, and she locked herself in her bedroom. Roubaud was on night duty, so she had no need to worry that he might come home to bed, as occasionally he still did. But even with the blankets pulled up to her chin and the lamp on low, she could not get to sleep. Why had she refused to share? She found that her honest principles didn't balk quite so strongly now at the idea of benefiting from this money. Had she not accepted the bequest of La Croix-de-Maufras? In that case she might just as well take the money, too. Then the shivering returned. No, no, never! Had it been just money, then perhaps; what she dared not touch, as though for fear it might scorch her fingers, was this money stolen from the body of a dead man, this horrible money from a murder. But she calmed down again, and reasoned with herself: she wouldn't have taken it to spend; on the contrary, she'd have hidden it somewhere else, buried it where only she could find it, where it would have lain for all eternity; and that way, at least, half would have been rescued from her husband's clutches. He wouldn't have the satisfaction of keeping the lot, he wouldn't be able to go gambling away what belonged to her. By the time the clock struck three, she was bitterly regretting having refused to share. But one idea did occur to her, vaguely, still only as a remote possibility: to get up and delve beneath the floor, so that there was none left for him. Except that she went so cold at the very idea that she could not contemplate it. Take it all, and keep it all, and he wouldn't even dare complain! And this plan of action gradually imposed itself upon her, while from the depths of her unconscious self there rose a determination which she was powerless to resist. She did not mean to and yet suddenly she jumped out of bed, for she was helpless to do otherwise. She turned up the wick on the lamp and went into the dining-room.

From that moment Séverine ceased to tremble. Her terrors
had gone, and she proceeded coolly, with the slow, precise movements of a sleepwalker. She had to fetch the poker, which served
to lift the floor-block. Once the hole was open, and being unable
to see clearly, she brought the lamp closer. But she froze in
astonishment, craning forward, motionless: the hole was empty.
Evidently, while she had been hurrying off to her rendezvous,
Roubaud had come back up, having anticipated her in the same
idea: take it all, and keep it all; and he'd pocketed every single
banknote, not one remained. She knelt down, and all she could
see at the bottom was the watch and chain, its gold glistening in
the dust between the joists. Cold fury held her there for a moment, her half-naked body completely rigid, as she repeated
aloud twenty times or more:

'Thief! Thief! Thief!'

Then angrily she seized the watch, disturbing a large black
spider that made off across the plaster. Banging the floor-block
back into place with her heel, she returned to bed and placed the
lamp on the bedside table. When she had warmed up again, she
examined the watch which she still held in her clenched fist, now
turning it over and inspecting it at length. She looked with
interest at the President's two interwoven initials engraved on
the casing. Inside she read the number 2516, the manufacturer's
code. It was an extremely dangerous valuable to keep since the
police knew its number. But in her anger at having been able to
salvage only this, she was no longer afraid. Indeed she even felt
somehow that her nightmares were over, now that there was no
longer a corpse beneath her floor. At last she would be able to
walk about unhindered in her own home, wherever she liked.
She slipped the watch under the bolster, extinguished the lamp,
and went to sleep.

The next day Jacques, being off duty, was to come up and
have lunch with her, having waited until Roubaud had gone off
to ensconce himself as usual in the Café du Commerce. They
treated themselves like this sometimes, whenever they dared. So
that day during their meal, and being still in a state of some
agitation, she told him about the money and how she had found
the hiding-place empty. Her resentment towards her husband
had not abated, and the same word kept coming back:

'Thief! Thief! Thief!'

Then she fetched the watch and insisted on giving it to Jacques, despite his evident repugnance.

'Don't you see, darling, no one's going to look for it at your place. If I keep it, he'll try and take that as well. And at that point, well, I think I'd rather let him have my right arm than . . . No, he's already had too much. I didn't want the money, any of it. It always gave me the creeps, I'd never have spent a penny of it. But did that mean *he* had any right to benefit from it? Oh, I hate him!'

She was crying, and she pleaded with him so insistently that finally he put the watch in his waistcoat pocket.

An hour went by, and Jacques was continuing to sit with Séverine, who was still only half-dressed, on his knee. She was lying back against his shoulder with one arm draped languidly round his neck when Roubaud, who had a key, entered the room. She leapt sharply to her feet, but they had been caught in the act, there was no point in denying it. The husband had stopped in his tracks, unable to proceed, while the lover remained seated, dumbfounded. Then, without even bothering with some tortuous explanation, she advanced on him and repeated furiously:

'Thief! Thief! Thief!'

For a second Roubaud hesitated. Then, with that shrug of the shoulders with which he now brushed everything aside, he went through to the bedroom and picked up an official notebook which he had forgotten to take with him. But she pursued him, shouting:

'You've been in there again, just you dare tell me you haven't . . . And you took it all, you thief! Thief! Thief!'

Without a word he crossed the dining-room. Only at the door did he turn and fix her with his gloomy stare.

'Just fucking well leave me alone, do you hear?'

And off he went, not even slamming the door. It was as if he hadn't seen, not once had he referred to this lover sitting there.

After a long silence, Séverine turned to Jacques:

'Well, would you believe it!'

Jacques, who had said nothing, finally stood up. And he gave his opinion:

'He's done for, that man.'

Both agreed. Their surprise at his tolerating one lover after murdering another was shortly followed by disgust at this spectacle of the accommodating husband. When a man gets to that stage, he's in the mire, and he might as well roll in the gutter.

From that day onwards Séverine and Jacques enjoyed total freedom, and they exploited it without a further thought for Roubaud. But now that the husband no longer troubled them, their principal anxiety was the spying of the neighbour, Madame Lebleu, who was always on the look-out. Clearly she suspected something. Try as Jacques might to creep quietly each time he came, he would see the door opposite open imperceptibly and an eye stare at him through the slit. It was becoming intolerable, and he dared not go up any more; for if he did risk it, his presence was immediately known, and an ear would come and press itself to the keyhole; so that it was impossible to kiss or even to talk freely. So it was at this point, in her exasperation at the new obstacle to her passion, that Séverine renewed her old campaign to take over the Lebleus' flat. It was a well-known fact that it had always been occupied by the assistant station-master. But what attracted her was no longer the flat's superb view, with its windows that looked out over the main entrance to the station and towards the Ingouville heights. The sole reason for her wish, but which she did not mention, was that the flat had a second entrance, a door which opened on to a service staircase. Jacques could come and go that way without Madame Lebleu even knowing he had visited. Then at last they would be free.

The battle was terrible. This question had already caused much excitement in the corridor, and it now became a live issue again, turning more poisonous by the hour. Thus threatened, Madame Lebleu defended herself with desperation, convinced it would kill her if they shut her away in that dark flat at the back, blocked off by the station roof and as dismal as a prison cell. How did they expect her to live in such a hole, accustomed as she was to her lovely, light room with its open view to the wide horizon, and where there was always some life to cheer her thanks to the constant to-ing and fro-ing of the passengers. What with her legs, she couldn't go for a walk any more, and all she would ever see again would be that zinc roof, so they might as well kill her and have done with it. Unfortunately these were merely sentimental reasons, and she was forced to admit that she had taken the flat over from the last assistant station-master, Roubaud's predecessor, who, being a bachelor, had ceded it to her out of gallantry; there must even have been a letter from her husband undertaking to give it back if a subsequent assistant station-master wanted it. Since they had not yet found this letter, she denied its existence. The more hopeless her cause became, the more violent and aggressive she grew. At one point she had tried to get Madame Moulin, the wife of the other assistant station-master, on her side by compromising her with the allegation that she, Madame Moulin, had seen men kissing Madame Roubaud on the stairs; and Moulin had become angry, for his wife, a sweet and thoroughly nondescript creature whom no one ever met, tearfully swore that she had never seen nor said anything of the sort. For a week this particular piece of gossip circulated like the winds of a gale from one end of the corridor to the other. But Madame Lebleu's great mistake, and which would lead to her defeat, was that she was always irritating Mademoiselle Guichon, the office-clerk, by her obstinate spying: it was a mania of hers, this obsession that Mademoiselle Guichon went to meet the station-master every night, and her now almost pathological need to catch her was made even more acute by the fact that she had been spying on her for two years and not once discovered a thing, not even a whisper. She was convinced they were sleeping together, and it drove her mad. So Mademoiselle Guichon, furious at not being able to come in or go out without being spied on, was now urging that she be banished to the back: that way there would be a flat between them and she would at least not have her living opposite any more and be obliged to pass her door. It was becoming evident that Monsieur Dabadie, the station-master, who had hitherto remained neutral in the dispute, was siding against the Lebleus more and more each day, and this boded ill.

Further quarrels added to the complexity of the situation. Philomène, who now brought her freshly laid eggs to Séverine, was extremely rude every time she met Madame Lebleu; and as the latter deliberately left her door open just to annoy everyone, unpleasant words were continually exchanged between the two women whenever Philomène passed. This intimacy between Séverine and Philomène had reached the point where they confided in one another, and Philomène was now taking messages from Jacques to his mistress when he dared not come up himself. She would arrive with the eggs, rearrange their meetings, say why he'd had to be careful the day before, and tell Séverine about the hour he'd spent chatting at her house. For sometimes, when he was prevented from meeting her, he would happily pass the time in the little house belonging to Sauvagnat, the depot manager. He would follow his fireman Pecqueux there, as if he needed something to take his mind off things and was afraid of spending a whole evening on his own. Even when Pecqueux went off on drinking bouts in the sailors' bars, he would still go and see Philomène, give her a message to take, and then sit down and fail to leave. And as she gradually became involved in the affair, she began to have a soft spot for him, for until then she had known only brutal lovers. The small hands and polite manners of this sad-looking fellow, who had such a gentle air about him, seemed to her to be delicacies of which she had yet to taste. With Pecqueux it was like being married, with drunken scenes and more often the harsh word than the gentle caress; whereas when she was delivering some amiable message from the driver to the assistant station-master's wife, she could savour for herself the subtle flavour of forbidden fruit. One day she took him into her confidence and complained of the fireman, who was not to be trusted, she said, for all his jovial air, and who was more than capable of doing something nasty when he was drunk. Jacques noticed that she was taking greater care of that big, burnt-out body of hers, like a scrawny mare's but desirable all the same, with those lovely, passionate eyes, and also that she was drinking less, and keeping the house rather cleaner. Her brother Sauvagnat, hearing the sound of a man's voice one evening, had walked in brandishing his fist, all ready to punish her; but then, seeing whom she was talking to, he had simply brought out a bottle of cider. Jacques, made welcome and free of his trembling, seemed to like it there. So Philomène became more and more friendly towards Séverine, railing against Madame Lebleu whom she went round calling an old hag.

One night after she had chanced on the two lovers behind her little garden, she walked with them in the dark as far as the shed where they generally hid.

'Really, you're far too kind, you know. Seeing as how the flat's actually yours. If it was me I'd go and drag her out by the hair . . . Go on, give her what for.'

But Jacques was not in favour of a showdown.

'No, no, Monsieur Dabadie's looking into it, it's better to wait for things to go through the proper channels.'

'Before the month is out', declared Séverine, 'I shall be sleeping in her bedroom, and then we'll be able to see each other whenever we like.'

Despite the darkness, Philomène had sensed her giving her lover's arm an affectionate squeeze at this prospect. And, leaving them, she returned home. But some thirty paces on, still hidden by the shadows, she stopped and turned. It affected her considerably to think of the pair of them there together. Yet she wasn't jealous, she simply felt a basic need to love and be loved like them.

With each day Jacques grew more and more despondent. Twice now, when he could have seen Séverine, he had invented excuses; and if he sometimes lingered at the Sauvagnats', that too was so that he could avoid her. He still loved her nevertheless, with a frustrated desire which had never ceased to grow. But now, in her arms, the dreadful malady would take hold of him again, such a dizziness that he would quickly let go of her, frozen with terror at ceasing to be himself, at feeling the beast ready to take him in its jaws. He had tried resorting to the exhaustion of long journeys, asking for extra work, spending twelve hours at a stretch standing in his cab, his body shattered by the vibration of the engine and his lungs seared by the wind. His workmates used to complain about how hard the engine-driver's life was, how twenty years of it, they said, could finish a man; but he wished it would finish him now, he could never feel exhausted enough, and he was only happy speeding along on La Lison, not thinking, just a pair of eyes searching for the signals. On arrival sleep would knock him out, without his even having time to wash. But, on waking, the torture of his obsession would return. He had also tried reviving his love for La Lison, once more spending hours cleaning her and insisting that Pecqueux have the steel shining like silver. The inspectors who came aboard during the journey used to congratulate him. He would shake his head, still not satisfied; for he well knew that since her halt in the snow she was no longer the healthy, valiant engine of old. Presumably, when her pistons and valves had been repaired, she had forfeited something of her soul, that mysterious equilibrium of vitality which is due to the chance of assembly. It pained him, and this decline in her powers became a source of bitter anxiety to him, to the point where he pursued his superiors with unreasonable complaints, demanding needless repairs and dreaming up impracticable refinements. These were refused, and he would become still gloomier, convinced that La Lison was very sick and that there was now no decent work to be had from her. He felt discouraged in his feelings of affection towards her: where was the good of loving if he was going to kill everything he loved? And so he would come to his mistress in a rage of exasperated love, which neither suffering nor fatigue could dull.

Séverine had fully sensed a change in him, and she too was miserable, believing him to be unhappy because of her, now that he knew. When she felt him shudder in her arms and avoid her kisses in brusque recoil, wasn't this because he'd remembered, because she now filled him with revulsion? She had never once dared bring the subject up again. She was sorry she had spoken in the first place, and surprised at how much she had been carried away by confession, in that strange bed where they had each burned with desire; she no longer even remembered her earlier need to confide, as though now she were simply content to have him there with her, a party to her secret. And she had certainly loved him, desired him, much more since he had known everything. Hers was the insatiable passion of a woman finally awakened, a creature intended solely to caress and be caressed, a lover first and last, a woman who was not a mother. She lived only through Jacques, and she was not exaggerating when she spoke of her efforts to melt into him, for she had but one dream, that he should carry her off and keep her with him in his flesh. Still very gentle, very passive, she derived her pleasure only from him, and she would like to have dozed like a cat upon his knee from morning till dusk. From her dreadful ordeal she retained only a sense of amazement at having been involved in it at all, rather as she seemed to have emerged an innocent virgin from the degradations of her childhood. All that was in the past now, she could smile, she would not even have been angry with her husband if only he had not been in the way. But her loathing for the man intensified as her passion, her need, for this other man increased. Now that he knew and had absolved her, he was the master, the man she would follow and who could dispose of her as his chattel. She had persuaded him to give her his picture, a photograph; and she would take it to bed with her and fall asleep with her mouth pressed to his image, deeply unhappy to see him unhappy, but without ever managing to discover quite what it was that ailed him.

Meanwhile they continued to meet out of doors, until such time as they would be free to see each other undisturbed in her new flat, when finally it had been won. Winter was coming to an end, February was very mild. They extended their walks, continuing for hours over the open ground around the station; for he avoided stopping, and when she clung to him and he was forced to sit down and take her, he insisted that it must be in the dark, so terrified was he of striking her if he should catch so much as a glimpse of her bare skin. As long as he didn't see her, perhaps he would be able to resist. In Paris, where she still followed him every Friday, he would carefully close the curtains, saying that the bright light spoilt his pleasure. She now made this weekly journey without even offering her husband an explanation. With the neighbours her former pretext of a knee injury still served; and she said also that she was going to visit her old nurse, Mère Victoire, in hospital, where her recovery was taking longer than expected. They both still took great pleasure in the trip; he in being especially attentive to the smooth running of his engine that day, and she in her delight at seeing him less gloomy and in her enjoyment of the journey itself, even though she was beginning to know every little hill and clump of trees along the way. From Le Havre to Motteville there was grassland, flat fields divided by hedges and planted with apple-trees; and then, as far as Rouen, the countryside became hilly and uninhabited. After

Rouen there was the Seine, winding its way along. They crossed
it at Sotteville, at Oissel, at Pont de l'Arche; then, across vast
plains, it would keep reappearing, spreading itself wide. After
Gaillon it was always there, on the left, flowing less rapidly now
between its shallow banks lined with poplar and willow. They
would run along the slope of a ridge, leaving the river behind
at Bonnières only to encounter it again suddenly at Rosny as
they came out of the Rolleboise tunnel. It was like a friendly
travelling-companion. Three more times they would cross it
before journey's end. Then came Mantes with its church tower
among the trees, Triel with the white patches of its chalk-pits,
Poissy where they cut right through the centre, the two green
walls of the forest at Saint-Germain, the sloping banks at
Colombes overflowing with lilac, and finally the suburbs and the
first glimpse of Paris, from the Pont d'Asnières, with the Arc de
Triomphe in the distance, rising above the shabby buildings that
bristled with factory chimneys. The engine disappeared into the
Batignolles tunnel, and people were soon getting out in the noisy
station; and from then until the evening they belonged to each
other, they were free. On the way back it was dark, and she
would shut her eyes and relive her happiness. But each morning
and evening as she passed La Croix-de-Maufras, she would lean
forward and take a cautious look, not letting herself be seen, sure
always to find Flore standing there by the crossing-gate, holding
the flag up in its sheath and enveloping the train in her blazing
stare.

Ever since this girl had seen them kissing on the day of the
snow, Jacques had warned Séverine to be careful of her. He now
realized with what passion she was pursuing him from the
depths of her young being, like a feral child, and he could sense
her jealousy in all its manly potency and unbridled, murderous
resentment. Moreover she must know a thing or two, for he
remembered her allusion to the President's relationship with a
young lady whom no one suspected and whom he'd married off.
If she knew that, she must certainly have guessed the truth about
the murder: so she would probably talk or write someone a letter,
to gain her revenge by denouncing them. But the days and weeks
had gone by, nothing had happened, and he only ever saw her
like this, on duty beside the railway line, standing there rigid

with her flag. He could feel her burning eyes upon him from the moment she saw the engine in the distance. She was always able to see him despite the smoke, and she would seize his whole person in her gaze and follow him as he flashed past amidst the thunderous roar of the wheels. And the train, too, was plumbed, probed, scrutinized, from the first carriage to the last. And she would find that other woman every time, that rival she now knew would be always there on Fridays. It was no good her leaning forward just ever so slightly like that, in her compulsive need to have a look: she had been seen, and their glances met like crossed swords. Already the train was tearing away, voraciously, into the distance, leaving one of them behind on the ground, and that one powerless to follow, furious at the happiness it was carrying away. She seemed to be growing in height, and Jacques found her taller with every trip, as he worried now about her inaction and wondered what plan would finally take shape in the mind of this towering, brooding girl, whose motionless presence he could not escape.

Séverine and Jacques were also worried about another railway worker, the chief guard, Henri Dauvergne. It was he, it so happened, who was in charge of this Friday train, and he had been forcing his attentions on Séverine. Having noticed her affair with the driver, he told himself that perhaps it would soon be his turn too. During their departure from Le Havre the mornings he was on duty, Roubaud would laugh about it, so evident had Henri's intentions become: reserving a whole compartment for her, seeing she was comfortably settled in, checking the temperature of the foot-warmer himself. Still quite happy to speak to Jacques, Roubaud had even pointed out to him one day with a wink what the young man was up to, as if to enquire whether he tolerated such a thing. Moreover, during their quarrels, he roundly accused his wife of sleeping with the pair of them. For a moment she had imagined that Jacques believed it and that this was the cause of his periods of gloom. Sobbing her heart out, she had protested her innocence, telling him to kill her if she had been unfaithful. Then, looking very pale, he had made light of it, kissing her and telling her he knew that she was a good woman and that he very much hoped he would never kill anyone.

For the first few evenings in March the weather was terrible, so they had temporarily to suspend their meetings; and the trips to Paris, those few hours of freedom they travelled so far to enjoy, now no longer sufficed for Séverine. She felt a growing need to have Jacques to herself, all to herself, to live with him day and night, never to be parted again. Her loathing of her husband intensified further, and the mere presence of the man filled her with unbearable, feverish agitation. Docile as she was, and every bit the compliant, affectionate woman, she became irritated as soon as he was involved in anything, and lost her temper the moment he placed the slightest obstacle in the way of her wishes. At such moments it seemed as though the blackness of her hair cast a dark shadow over the limpid blue of her eyes. She grew wild and accused him of having ruined her life, to the point where it had become impossible for them to live together. Hadn't he been responsible for everything? If nothing remained of their life together, if she did have a lover, wasn't it all his fault? The stolid tranquillity in which she saw him now live, the indifference with which he met her angry outbursts, the hunched shoulders, the spreading stomach, the dreary flabbiness with its air of contentment, it had all come to provoke her beyond measure, and while *she* was suffering! To separate, to go away and start a new life somewhere else, this was all she could think of now. Oh to begin again and, more especially, to make things as though the past had never been, to start life afresh as it was before all these abominations, to be once more as she had been at fifteen, and to love, and be loved, and live as then she had dreamed of living! For a week she nursed the idea of running away: she would elope with Jacques, they would go into hiding in Belgium and set up house together as a hardworking young couple. But she didn't even mention it to him, for she had immediately seen the problems: the irregularity of their situation, the continual anxiety they would feel, and above all the aggravation of letting her husband have her fortune, the money, La Croix-de-Maufras. Together they had drawn up wills leaving everything to the one who should survive the other; and she discovered that he had her in his power, for as a wife she was under his legal tutelage, her hands were tied. Rather than depart and abandon one single centime to him, she would have pre-

ferred to die where she was. One day he came home looking
deathly white and said that, while crossing the track in front of a
moving locomotive, he had felt its buffer brush his elbow. And
she reflected that if he had died, she would be free. She stared at
him with wide, unblinking eyes: why didn't he die indeed, since
she didn't love him any more, since now he was in everybody's
way?

From that day on Séverine's dream changed. Roubaud had
been killed in an accident, and she was leaving for America with
Jacques. But they were married, they had sold La Croix-de-
Maufras and liquidated all her assets. Behind them they left
nothing that might cause them concern in the future. If they
were leaving the country, it was in order to start a new life
together, in each other's arms. There would be nothing over
there to remind her of what she wished to forget, she would be
able to believe that her life had begun afresh. Since she had taken
a wrong turning, she would start again on her experience of
happiness. He would soon get a job; she herself would find
something to do; there would be plenty of money, children too in
all likelihood, a whole new life of work and happiness. The
moment she was alone, whether in bed in the morning or doing
her needlework during the day, she would resume her fantasy,
improving it, enlarging on it, adding further happy details, and
finally convincing herself that she was blessed with every possible joy and material possession. She who used rarely to go out
now had a passion for watching the liners depart: she would walk
down and lean on the harbour wall, and follow the ship's smoke
until it vanished into the haze of the open sea; and she became
another person, imagining herself standing on the deck with
Jacques, already far from France, bound for the paradise of her
dreams.

One evening in the middle of March, when he had risked
coming up to see her, Jacques told her that he had just brought
one of his old schoolfriends back from Paris, on his train, and
that this man was off to New York to promote a new invention,
a machine for making buttons; and as he needed a partner,
someone who knew about machines, he had actually offered to
take Jacques with him. Oh! what a brilliant opportunity it was, he
wouldn't need to put in more than about thirty thousand francs,

and there were perhaps millions to be made. He was only saying it out of interest, adding that in any case he had, of course, refused the offer. Nevertheless he still felt rather sorry he had, for it's not easy all the same, giving up the chance of a fortune like that when one comes along.

Séverine stood there listening to him with faraway eyes. Wasn't this her dream about to come true?

'Yes,' she murmured finally, 'and we would be sailing tomorrow . . .'

He looked up in surprise.

'What do you mean, we would be sailing tomorrow?'

'We would, if he were dead.'

She had not mentioned Roubaud by name, merely indicating him with a jut of her chin. But Jacques had understood, and he gestured vaguely to say that well, unfortunately, he was not dead.

'We would be sailing away,' she went on in a slow, resonant voice, 'and we'd be so happy over there! I could get the thirty thousand francs by selling the property, and I'd still have some over to set us up . . . You'd see to it that the money was well invested, and I'd make us a little home, where we'd love each other with all our might . . . Oh, how good that would be, how very, very good that would be!'

And she added in a whisper:

'Away from all our memories, nothing but new days stretching ahead of us!'

An enormous feeling of sweet gentleness swept over him, while their hands met and instinctively clasped each other's tight; neither of them said anything, both totally absorbed in this prospect of hope. Then once more it was she who spoke:

'All the same, you ought to go and see your friend again before he leaves, and ask him not to take on a partner without letting you know first.'

Again he looked surprised.

'But why?'

'Well, my goodness, you never know! The other day, with that engine, one second more and I was free . . . I mean, a person can be alive one minute, and dead the next.'

She looked at him hard and repeated:

'Oh, if only he were dead!'

'Still, you don't want me to kill him, I suppose?' he asked, forcing a smile.

Three times she said no; but her eyes said yes, those eyes of a woman in love who is committed body and soul to the inexorable cruelty of her passion. Since he'd killed someone himself, why shouldn't *he* be killed? This thought had suddenly come to her, like a logical consequence, a necessary conclusion. Kill him and leave, what could be simpler? With him dead it would all be over, she'd be able to start again from scratch. Already she could see no other possible outcome, her mind was made up, absolutely; while all the time, with a slight shake of the head, she continued to say no, not having the courage of her violent conviction.

Leaning against the sideboard, Jacques still affected to smile. He had just noticed the knife lying there.

'If you want me to kill him, you'd better give me the knife as well . . . Since I've already got the watch, I'll be able to start a little collection.'

He was laughing more loudly. She replied solemnly:

'Take the knife.'

And when he had put it in his pocket, as though to play along with the joke, he kissed her.

'Well, goodnight then . . . I'll go and see my friend immediately and tell him to wait . . . On Saturday, if it's not raining, come and meet me behind the Sauvagnats'. All right? . . . And don't worry, we're not going to kill anyone, it's only a joke.'

Nevertheless, despite the lateness of the hour, Jacques walked down to the hotel by the port where his friend was to spend the night before leaving the next day. He told him of a possible legacy and asked for a fortnight to reflect before giving him a definite answer. Then, on his way back to the station along the broad, dark avenues, he reflected in surprise on what he had just done. Had he then decided to kill Roubaud, since here he was already making arrangements for his wife and his money? No, of course not, he had not decided anything yet, it was really more of a precaution, in case he did decide. But the memory of Séverine came back to him, the burning pressure of her hand, her hard stare which said yes while her mouth said no. Quite plainly she did want him to kill the man. He was suddenly very confused: what was he going to do?

Back in the Rue François-Mazeline, next to the snoring Pecqueux, Jacques could not sleep. In spite of himself his mind was working on this idea of murdering Roubaud, arranging the successive scenes of the drama and calculating its remotest consequences. He went over it carefully, debating the arguments for and against. In sum, on reflection, all things calmly and coolly considered, every argument spoke in favour. Wasn't Roubaud the one single obstacle to their happiness? With him out of the way he could marry Séverine whom he adored, he wouldn't have to hide any more and she would be his, for ever, completely. Then there was the money, a fortune. He would be giving up his arduous job and becoming a boss himself, in America, this land he had heard his workmates talk about as a place where mechanical engineers moved gold around by the shovelful. His new life over there passed before him as though in a dream: a wife who loved him passionately, millions to be made in no time, a comfortable existence, limitless opportunities, anything he wanted. And for this dream to come true, all it took was just one single action, just one man to be eliminated, like crushing a plant or animal that gets in your way. This man was of no interest even, all fat and heavy now, mired in his stupid passion for gambling that had drained him of all his former energy. Why spare him? Not a single circumstance, not one, argued in his favour. Everything condemned him because, whichever way one looked at the matter, it was in other people's interests that he should die. To hesitate would be foolish and cowardly.

Now Jacques, who was lying on his front because of the prickling heat in his back, suddenly turned over, startled by a thought which, vague until then, had all of a sudden become so vivid that it had struck him like something sharp jabbing into his skull. He'd always wanted to kill someone ever since he was a child, and he'd been tortured to screaming-point by the horror of this obsession: why indeed should he not kill Roubaud? Perhaps, upon this chosen victim, he would be able to assuage for ever his need to murder; and in that way he would not only be helping their situation, he would also be cured. Cured! Oh God! Never again to feel himself shaking with that thirst for blood, to be able

to possess Séverine without that wild awakening of the primordial male, wanting to slit women's bellies open and carry them
away on his shoulders. Sweat poured off him, and he could see
himself, knife in hand, stabbing Roubaud's throat just as
Roubaud had stabbed the President, and then satisfied, sated, as
the wound bled over his hands. Yes, he would kill him, his mind
was made up, for this was the road to being cured, to the woman
he adored, to a fortune. If someone had to be killed and he had to
do it, this was the person he would kill, knowing what he was
doing, rationally, out of self-interest, with logic.

His decision taken, and as it had just gone three, Jacques tried
to sleep. He was on the point of dozing off when his whole body
roused itself with a deep jolt, and he shot up in bed gasping for
breath. Kill this man, my God, had he any right to? When a fly
bothered him, he crushed it with a tap of his hand. One day a cat
had got entangled in his legs and he had broken its back with a
kick—unintentionally, it was true. But this man, his fellow-man!
He had to retrace his entire train of thought to prove to himself
once more that he had the right to murder, the right of the strong
who find the weak in their way, and who devour them. This was
him now, loved by this other man's wife, and she herself wanted
to be free so that she could marry him and bring him all she
owned. He was simply removing the obstacle, that was all. If two
wolves meet in the woods, and a she-wolf is there, doesn't the
stronger get rid of the weaker with one snap of its jaws? And in
ancient times, when men lived in caves like the wolves, didn't the
woman they desired belong to the member of the pack who could
win her with the blood of his rivals? Well, since that was life's law
one should obey it, irrespective of the scruples which had been
thought up later so that human beings could co-exist. Gradually
his right to kill came to seem absolute, and he felt his resolve
return in full: the very next day he would choose the time and the
place, he would prepare for the deed. It would probably be best
to stab Roubaud at night, in the station, during one of his
rounds, so as to make it look as though he had disturbed intruders, who had then killed him. He knew of a good spot over
behind the coal-stacks, if only he could be lured there. Despite
his efforts to get to sleep, he was now arranging the scene,
debating where he would position himself, how he would strike

so as to lay him out flat; but quietly, irresistibly, as he began to plan things down to the last detail, his repugnance returned, an inner protest which again roused his whole being. No, no, he would not strike! It seemed a monstrous, unfeasible, impossible thing to do. Within him the civilized human being was fighting back, with the strength derived from education, from the slowly erected and indestructible edifice of inherited ideas. One should not kill, he had been suckled on that idea by the milk of generations: and his brain, thus refined and furnished with scruples, rejected murder with horror as soon as he began to rationalize it. To kill from need, in a flash of instinct, yes! But to kill with intent, from calculation and self-interest, no, never, that he could never do!

Day was dawning by the time Jacques managed to fall asleep, but he slept so lightly that the debate continued, at once confused and terrible, in his mind. The days which followed were the most painful of his whole life. He avoided Séverine, having sent word not to come to their Saturday meeting, afraid of her eyes. But on the Monday he had to see her again; and, as he feared, those big, blue eyes, so gentle, so intense, filled him with anguish. She did not talk about it, she did not do or say anything to urge him on. But her eyes spoke only of one thing, as they questioned him, pleaded with him. He could not mistake their impatience, their look of reproach, and he found them constantly fixed on his own eyes, expressing astonishment that he could hesitate to be happy. When he kissed her as he left, he gave her a short, firm hug, as a sign that he was now resolved. And indeed he was, and remained so as far as the foot of the stairs, when the struggle with his conscience began once more. When he saw her again two days later, he had the seedy pallor and furtive look of a coward unable to face a necessary deed. She burst out sobbing, without a word, weeping on his neck in utter misery; and he, thoroughly distraught, was filled with self-contempt. The matter would have to be settled once and for all.

'Thursday, at the usual place?' she asked softly.

'Yes, Thursday, I'll be waiting.'

That Thursday it was a very dark night, and the starless sky was heavy with sea-mists, impenetrable to the gaze and muffling all sound. As usual, Jacques had arrived first and was standing behind the Sauvagnats' house on the look-out for Séverine. But the darkness was so complete, and she came running towards him with such light footsteps, that he jumped when she brushed against him without his even seeing her. Already she was in his arms, where she noted his trembling with concern.

'Did I give you a fright?' she murmured.

'No, no, I was expecting you . . . Let's walk, no one will be able to see us.'

And, putting their arms gently round each other's waist, they walked across the open space. On this side of the depot there were very few gas-lamps; certain dark corners had none at all, while there was an abundance of them over towards the station, where they glowed like sparks.

For a long time they walked like this, without a word. She had her head on his shoulder, raising it from time to time to kiss him on the side of the chin; and he would lean over and return her kiss, on the temple, where it met her hair. The single, solemn chime marking one o'clock had just rung out from the churches in the distance. If they did not speak, it was because in their embrace they each knew what the other was thinking. For now it was all they did think about, it was impossible for them to be together without their being completely preoccupied by it. The inner debate was still going on, so what was the point in saying useless words out loud when what was needed was action? When she stretched up to stroke him, she could feel the knife bulging from his trouser pocket. Did that mean that he had finally made up his mind?

But her thoughts did begin to spill out, and her lips opened as she breathed almost inaudibly:

'He came up to the flat just now. I couldn't think why . . . Then I saw him take his revolver. He'd forgotten it . . . That must mean he's going to do his rounds.'

There was a further silence; and only when they had gone another twenty paces did he in turn say:

'Last night intruders took some lead near here . . . He's bound to come and have a look soon.'

Then she shivered slightly, and they both fell silent once more, as they began to walk more slowly. A doubt had struck her: was it really the knife which was making that lump in his pocket?

Twice she kissed him, to see if it was. Then, still unsure even after rubbing herself against his leg, she dangled her hand as she kissed him again and felt it. It was the knife all right. But he had understood, and he crushed her roughly to his chest as he stammered in her ear:

'He'll come. You'll soon be free.'

The murder was decided, and they felt as though they were no longer walking but being borne along the ground by some alien force. Their senses had suddenly become particularly acute, especially their sense of touch; it hurt just to hold hands, and the merest brush of the lips was like the scratch of a fingernail. Away in the blackness they could hear sounds which had previously escaped them, the rumbling and puffing of distant trains, dull thuds, footsteps. And they could see in the dark, they could make out the black shapes of things, as though a fog had lifted from their eyes: a bat flew past, and they could follow its sudden, darting loops. They had stopped at the corner of a coal-stack and stood motionless, their eyes and ears on the alert, every fibre of their being stretched taut. By now they were whispering.

'Did you hear that, over there, somebody calling?'

'No, it's just a carriage being shunted.'

'But over there, to our left, there's somebody walking. The gravel crunched.'

'No, no, it's just rats running through the coal-stacks, a piece of coal rolling down.'

Minutes went by. Suddenly she squeezed him harder.

'There he is.'

'Where? I can't see anything.'

'He's just turned the corner of the goods shed, he's coming straight towards us . . . Look, there's his shadow moving along that white wall!'

'Are you sure? That dark spot? . . . Is he alone then?'

'Yes, he's alone, quite alone.'

And at this decisive moment she flung her arms round him and pressed her burning mouth against his. It was a kiss of living flesh, a long, protracted kiss, as though she would have given him of her blood. How she loved him, and how she loathed that other man! Oh, if she had but dared, she would have done the deed herself a score of times already, to spare him the horror of it; but her hands failed her, she could feel she was too gentle, it needed the firm grip of a man. And this never-ending kiss was all she could give him of her courage, promising him full possession, full communion with her body. An engine whistled in the distance, sending forth a lament of doleful distress into the night; and the sound of regular banging, like the noise of a giant hammer, was coming from somewhere; while the mists blowing in from the sea filed across the sky like chaos on the march, their errant shreds seeming periodically to snuff out the glowing sparks of the gas-lamps. When she finally took her mouth away, she had nothing left of her own self, and she felt as though her entire being had passed over into his.

With a swift movement of his hands he had already opened the knife. But then he swore beneath his breath.

'Damn, it's no use, he's going back.'

It was true: having come within fifty paces of them, the moving shadow had just turned left and was walking away at the steady pace of a night-watchman who finds nothing to concern him.

So then she pushed him.

'Go on, after him.'

And off they went, he in front, she on his heels, flitting behind the man in hurried pursuit, trying not to make a sound. Once, at the corner of the repair workshops, they lost sight of him; then, as they took a short cut across a siding, they came on him again, at most twenty paces in front of them. They had to take advantage of the merest fragment of wall to hide behind, one false move would have given them away.

'We'll never get him,' he growled quietly. 'If he gets as far as the pointsman's box, he's safe.'

She was still at his shoulder, repeating:

'Go on, after him.'

There at this moment, in these vast open spaces plunged in darkness, and surrounded by the emptiness of a large, deserted railway station in the middle of the night, he felt as resolute as if he were standing in the helpful seclusion of a cut-throat's alley. And as he hurried furtively along, he grew more and more excited, debating with himself and rehearsing the arguments that would make of this murder a wise and legitimate action which had been logically considered and decided upon. Really he was exercising a right, the right to life itself, since this blood that belonged to another was indispensable to his own very survival. He simply had to plunge the knife in, and happiness would be his.

'We shan't get him, we shan't get him,' he repeated furiously, as he saw the shadow go past the pointsman's box. 'It's no use, look, he's away.'

But suddenly her anxious hand gripped his arm, holding him motionless by her side.

'Wait, he's coming back.'

And indeed he was. He had turned right and begun to walk back towards them. Perhaps he had dimly sensed the presence of the murderers stalking him from behind. Nevertheless he continued on with the calm tread of a conscientious watchman unwilling to finish until his inspection was complete.

Halted in their tracks, Jacques and Séverine stood stock still. By chance they had ended up at the corner of a coal-stack. They pressed themselves against it, seeming almost to become part of it as their spines stuck fast to its black wall, merging with it, disappearing into a pool of inky blackness. They held their breath.

And Jacques watched Roubaud coming straight towards them. Barely thirty metres separated them, and each step reduced the distance, regularly, rhythmically, like the inexorable pendulum of fate. Twenty to go, then ten: in a moment he would have him there in front of him, he would raise his arm like this, he would plant the knife in his throat, and then he would draw it from right to left, to stifle the scream. Each second seemed interminable, such a welter of thoughts came flooding through the vacant reaches of his skull that time had lost all dimension. Every argument which had decided him filed past once more in procession, and again he could see the murder absolutely clearly, its causes and its consequences. Five more steps. His resolve, taut to breaking-point, remained unshakeable. He would kill, and he knew why he would kill.

But then, two steps to go, one step . . . he disintegrated. Everything crumbled within him, all at once. No, no, he would not kill, he could not kill a defenceless man like this. Murder would never be done by reasoning; it needed the instinct that makes the jaw snap, the leap that launches you on to the prey, and the hunger or the fury which tears it to pieces. What did it matter if conscience was but a set of ideas handed down from one generation to the next, the gradually accumulated, inherited notion of what is just! He simply did not feel that he had the right to kill, and despite his efforts he was unable to persuade himself that he could give himself this right.

Roubaud quietly walked by. His elbow came within inches of these two people, there amidst the coal. One breath would have given them away, but they stood like corpses. The arm did not go up, the knife did not go in. Nothing, not even a shiver, stirred the thick darkness. Although he had already gone some distance, ten paces now, they both continued to hold their breath, still standing there motionless, their backs pressed to the black pile, terrified of this solitary, defenceless man who had just brushed past them on his calm, untroubled way.

Jacques choked back a sob of shame and angry frustration.

'I can't, I can't.'

He wanted to take Séverine in his arms again, to lean on her in his desire to be forgiven and comforted. Without a word she broke free. He had stretched out his hands only to feel her skirt slipping through his fingers; and all he could hear were her soft footsteps as she made her escape. Briefly he went after her in vain pursuit, for this sudden disappearance was the final straw. Was she, then, so angered by his weakness? Did she despise him? Prudence prevented him from going to her. But when he found himself once more alone in this vast open space, dotted with the tiny yellow tear-drops of the gas-lamps, a dreadful despair took hold of him, and he hastened to leave it, to go and bury his head in his pillow and blot from his mind the awful horror of his existence.

It was ten days later, towards the end of March, that the Roubauds finally triumphed over the Lebleus. The management had recognized the validity of their claim, which was supported by Monsieur Dabadie, especially as the celebrated letter from Lebleu, undertaking to vacate the flat if a new assistant stationmaster wanted it, had just been found by Mademoiselle Guichon while she was looking for some old accounts in the station archives. And Madame Lebleu, furious at her defeat, at once talked of moving out: since they wanted her dead, she might as well get it over without waiting to be asked. For three days this historic move was the talk of the corridor. Even little Madame Moulin, so unobtrusive that no one ever saw her go in or out, became implicated by carrying Séverine's work-table from one flat to the other. But it was Philomène in particular who stirred up trouble, arriving at the very outset to help, packing things up, shoving furniture about, bursting in on the front flat before the occupant had even left; and she was the one who finally evicted her, amidst the general chaos of the move as the two sets of furniture merged indistinguishably into one. She now displayed such zeal on behalf of Jacques and all that he cared for that Pecqueux, at once surprised and suspicious, had asked her in his nasty, sly way, and in the tone of a spiteful drunkard, if she were now sleeping with his driver; and he warned her that he would make them both pay for it, and no mistake, the moment he caught them. This had simply increased her infatuation with Jacques, and she now performed the role of servant, both to him and to his mistress, in the hope of having a small part of him to herself by involving herself in their lives. When she had shifted the final chair, the doors slammed shut. Then, noticing a stool which Madame Lebleu had forgotten, she opened the door again and threw it across the corridor. And that was that.

Then, slowly, life resumed its monotonous course. While Madame Lebleu was dying of boredom in the flat at the back, confined to her armchair by rheumatism, sitting there with large tears in her eyes now that her only view was the zinc roof of the station blocking out the sky, Séverine would be working at her interminable bedspread by one of the windows that looked out at the front. Below her she had the cheerful bustle of the station entrance, a constant stream of pedestrians and vehicles. Already the buds on the tall trees lining the pavements were turning green in the early spring; and beyond, the distant hillsides of Ingouville unfurled their wooded slopes, dotted with white houses. But she was surprised to derive so little pleasure from this realization of her dream, from being in this coveted flat at last and having space in front of her, daylight, and sunshine. And like Mère Simon, her daily help, who would grumble with fury

at the change in her routine, she even lost patience herself sometimes, and there were moments when she missed the old dump,
as she called it; at least there the dirt didn't show so much.
Roubaud, for his part, had simply left her to it. He didn't seem
to notice that he had moved kennels: indeed he would often still
go to the wrong flat, and only discover his mistake when his key
wouldn't fit the old lock. In any case, he was out more and more
now, and his decline continued. Once, though, he did seem to
come back to life, roused by his political views; not that these
were particularly definite nor ardently held, but he still felt a
grudge about that business with the Sub-Prefect which had
nearly cost him his job. Ever since the Empire had found itself in
a state of crisis, brought on by the general election, he had been
gloating and going round saying that these people wouldn't always be the masters. But in any case Monsieur Dabadie had got
wind of this from Mademoiselle Guichon, in front of whom this
revolutionary sentiment had been expressed, and a friendly
warning from him had been sufficient to calm Roubaud down.
Since the corridor was at peace and people were living in harmony now that Madame Lebleu was getting weaker, dying of
misery, why cause further trouble by discussing the government's affairs? He simply shrugged, he couldn't give a fig for
politics, nor anything else for that matter! And so, growing fatter
by the day and without a single moment's remorse, off he would
trudge, his back rounded in complacency.

Jacques and Séverine were increasingly ill at ease with each
other now that they could meet whenever they wished. There
was nothing left to prevent them from being happy: he could go
up and see her by the back staircase whenever he pleased, without fear of being spied on; and the place was theirs, he could have
spent the night there if he had dared. But it was the thought of
the unaccomplished act—which they desired and had agreed
upon but which he had still failed to carry out—that was now
causing this awkwardness and creating an insurmountable barrier between them. Full of shame at his own weakness, he found
her increasingly morose each time they met, sick of waiting in
vain. Even their lips no longer sought each other's, for they had
exhausted this stage of semi-union; it was total happiness they
wanted, departure, marriage across the seas, that other life.

One evening Jacques found Séverine in tears; and when she
saw him, she did not stop but sobbed even more, clinging to his
neck. She had wept like this before, but then he would soothe her
with his embrace; whereas this time the closer he pressed her to
his heart, the more he could sense the ravages of her growing
despair. He was profoundly upset; and eventually he took her
head between his hands, and, gazing closely into her watery eyes,
he made a solemn promise: for he understood perfectly that if
she despaired like this, it was because she was a woman, because,
in her passivity and gentleness, she dared not strike the blow
herself.

'Forgive me, wait just a little longer . . . Soon, I swear to you,
as soon as I possibly can.'

At once she pressed her mouth to his, as though to set a seal
upon this oath; and they shared one of those deep kisses in which
they merged, each with the other, in the communion of their
flesh.

CHAPTER X

AUNT PHASIE had died that Thursday evening, at nine o'clock, in a final seizure; and Misard, having waited by her bedside, had endeavoured in vain to close her eyelids. But the obstinate eyes were still open, and the head had stiffened and tilted slightly across her shoulder, as though to gaze across the room, while a slight retraction of the lips seemed to have made them curl in a jeering grin. A single candle stood burning on the corner of a table beside her. And the trains which had been passing at full speed since nine o'clock, quite oblivious to the dead woman whose body was not yet cold, made her corpse shake momentarily in the flickering light of the candle.

Misard at once got rid of Flore by sending her to Doinville to register the death. She would not be back before eleven, so he had two hours in front of him. First he proceeded calmly to cut himself a piece of bread, for his stomach felt empty; thanks to the death agony which had seemed to go on for ever, he had had no dinner. And he ate standing up, moving to and fro, tidying things. Coughing fits made him stop, and he would bend double, half-dead himself, so thin and puny, with his colourless hair, that it did not seem as though he would long enjoy his victory. No matter, he had devoured her, that strapping wench, that tall, fine-looking woman, as an insect devours an oak; and there she was, on her back, finished, reduced to nothing, while he lived on. But a thought occurred to him, and he knelt down to remove an earthenware pot from beneath the bed, which contained the remains of some bran-water prepared for an enema. Ever since she had suspected what was going on, he had been putting the rat poison not in the salt but in her enema water; and being too stupid, and having no suspicions in that quarter, she had taken it all the same, and this time for good. As soon as he had emptied the pot outside, he came back and sponged the tiled floor of the bedroom, which was covered in stains. Anyway, why had she been so stubborn? She'd tried to outsmart him, so hard luck on her! When a couple starts trying to see which one can see the other off, and without a word to anyone, then they need to keep their eyes open! He sniggered as though at a good joke, at this poison so innocently taken from below when she'd been paying such careful attention to everything that went in from above. At that moment a passing express shook the little house with such a blast that, despite being accustomed to it, he turned towards the window and trembled. Oh yes, that never-ending stream of people from the four corners of the earth, who knew nothing of what they crushed in their path and who were in such a hurry to go to the devil that they couldn't have cared less either! And in the heavy silence after the train had gone, his eyes fell upon the goggling gaze of the corpse, its motionless eyeballs seeming to follow his every movement, its lips curled in a grin.

Usually so phlegmatic, Misard was suddenly seized with a moment's anger. He could hear her all right, she was telling him to 'keep looking, keep looking!' But she couldn't have taken her thousand francs with her, that was for sure; and now that she was gone, he'd find them in the end. In any case, shouldn't she have handed them over with good grace? That would have prevented all this trouble. The eyes followed him everywhere. 'Keep looking, keep looking!' He glanced round this bedroom that he had never dared to search as long as she was alive. The cupboard first: he took the keys from under the bolster, ransacked the shelves of household linen, emptied both drawers, and even took them out to see if there was a secret hiding-place. No, nothing! Next, he thought of the bedside table. He removed its marble top and turned it upside down, to no avail. Above the mantelpiece was a flimsy gimcrack mirror held in place by two nails, which he investigated by sliding a flat ruler down the back, only to dislodge a shower of flaky black dust. 'Keep looking, keep looking!' Then, to escape the staring eyes which he could feel fixed upon him, he got down on his hands and knees, gently tapping the tiles with his knuckles and listening for any hollow sound that might reveal a cavity. Several tiles were loose, and he lifted them. Nothing, still nothing! When he had stood up again, the eyes gripped him anew, and he turned to try and outstare the fixed gaze of the corpse; while at the corners of her curled lips the terrible grin seemed to grow wider. There was no longer any question of it, she was laughing at him. 'Keep looking, keep looking!' He was beginning to get in a frenzy, and he approached her, struck by a suspicion, a sacrilegious idea, that turned his pasty face paler still. Why had he been so sure she couldn't have taken the thousand francs with her? Perhaps, in fact, she had. And he dared to pull back the bedclothes, to undress her. He examined her all over, searching in the folds of every limb: after all, she had told him to keep looking. Beneath her, behind her neck, under the small of her back, on he searched. The bed was ransacked, and he thrust his arm into the mattress right up to his shoulder. He found nothing. 'Keep looking, keep looking!' And her head, which had fallen back on to the crumpled pillow, continued to watch him through its mocking eyeballs.

Just as Misard was trying to straighten the bed again in trembling fury, Flore came in, back from Doinville.

'It's all arranged for the day after tomorrow, Saturday at eleven.'

She meant the funeral. But one glance had told her the nature of the task which had left Misard so out of breath during her absence. She gestured in scornful indifference.

'Give up. You'll never find it.'

He imagined that she, too, was defying him. And coming nearer, his teeth clenched:

'She gave you the money, didn't she? You know where it is.'

She shrugged her shoulders at the thought of her mother being able to give her thousand francs to anyone, even to her, her own daughter.

'Oh, didn't she just! . . . Gave it to the earth more like! . . . Go on, that's where it is, away you go and look for it.'

And with a wave of the arm she indicated the entire house, the garden with its well, the railway line, the whole vast expanse of countryside. Yes, out there, in some hole, where no one would ever find it. Then, as he went back to moving the furniture and tapping the walls, beside himself with anxious frustration and quite unperturbed by her presence, she stood at the window and continued softly:

'Oh, it's so mild out, such a beautiful night . . . I made good time. It's almost like daylight, the stars are so bright . . . And what a sunrise there'll be in the morning!'

For a moment Flore remained by the window, her gaze resting on the tranquil countryside which lay softening in the early warmth of April and from which she had returned in pensive mood, feeling all the more keenly the open wound of her hurt. But when she heard Misard leave the bedroom and continue his desperate search in the adjacent rooms, she in her turn drew near to the bed and sat down, her eyes now fixed upon her mother. At the corner of the table the candle continued to burn, with a steady, upright flame. A train went by, and the house shook.

It was Flore's intention to spend the night there, and she began to reflect. At first the sight of the dead woman took her mind off her obsession, off the thing which haunted her and which she had been debating with herself beneath the stars all the way to Doinville, in the peace and quiet of the darkness. A sense of surprise now numbed her pain: why had she not been more upset by the death of her mother? and why, even now, was she not crying? And yet she loved her all right, despite being the big, silent girl, the wild thing that was always running away and chasing across the fields the moment she was off duty. During the final crisis which was to kill her mother, she had come and sat here twenty times or more to beg her to have a doctor come; for she suspected what Misard was up to, and hoped that the fear of being discovered might stop him. But all she had ever got out of the sick woman was a furious 'No', as if in her struggle the honour of the battlefield demanded that she accept no assistance, certain as she was of her victory come what may, since she would be taking the money with her. And so Flore had not intervened, and found herself once more in the grip of her own malaise, disappearing from the house and tearing all over the place simply to forget. This, certainly, was what was blocking her feelings: with one great sorrow in one's heart, one has no room for another. Her mother had gone, and she looked at her lying there, destroyed, so pale, but she could not feel sad, despite her every effort. Should she call the police, denounce Misard? Why bother, since everything was about to come tumbling down. And gradually, irresistibly, although her gaze remained fixed on the dead woman, she ceased to see her and returned to her inner vision, wholly taken up again by the idea which had planted its stake in her skull, and sensing nothing beyond the deep shudder of the trains, whose passing tolled the hours.

For some moments the distant rumbling of a slow train to Paris had been drawing nearer. When the engine finally went past the window, with its headlamp blazing, it was as though a flash of lightning had set the room on fire.

'One eighteen,' she thought to herself. 'Seven hours to go. This morning, at eight sixteen, they will come past.'

For months now she had been obsessed by this weekly expectation. She knew that on Friday mornings the express driven by Jacques was also taking Séverine to Paris; and, in a torment of jealousy, she lived only for the moment when she could watch out for them, see them, tell herself how they were off there again, to make love to each other without let or hindrance. Oh! that train vanishing into the distance, that awful feeling of not being able to hang on to the last carriage so that she, too, might be borne away! All those wheels seemed to be cutting her heart in two. She had suffered so much that one evening she had hidden herself away to write a letter to the police, for that would be an end to it if she could get the woman arrested; and since she had once caught President Grandmorin and her at their filthy tricks, she had no doubt that in revealing these to the authorities, she would virtually be handing Séverine over. But once the pen was poised, she had never been able to find the words. And anyway, would the law listen to her? All those grand people were in it together. Perhaps she was the one they'd put in prison, the way they had Cabuche. No! she wanted revenge, and she would seek it alone, without help from anyone. It wasn't even vengeance she wanted, in so far as she had heard it described, the idea of doing harm as a cure for the harm done to oneself. Rather it was a need to have finished with it, to bring everything toppling down, as if a thunderstorm had swept them away. She was very proud, she was stronger and more beautiful than that other woman, and convinced of her right to be loved; and when she went off on her own, along the paths of this godforsaken region, with her thick helmet of blond hair, her head always uncovered, she would like to have had that other woman there and to have settled their differences in the middle of a forest, like two warring Amazons. Never yet had a man been able to lay a hand on her, she could beat the males; and that was her invincible strength, she would be victorious.

The week before, the idea had suddenly come to her, implanted as by the hammer blow of some unseen hand: she would kill them, and that way they would stop going by, they would stop going off like that together. She didn't reason it out logically, she was simply following the primitive instinct to destroy. When she got a thorn in her flesh, she tore it out; she'd have cut her finger off if she'd had to. She would kill them, kill them the next time they passed; and for this purpose she'd derail the train, drag a sleeper across the track, remove a section of rail, whatever, smash everything, bring it all crashing down. Him on his engine, he'd certainly not survive, his limbs would be crushed to pulp; and that woman, always in the first carriage so as to be nearer him, she wouldn't escape either. As for the others, that constant stream of people, she didn't even give them a thought. They were nobody, what did she know of them? And this thought of smashing a train, of sacrificing so many lives, became the obsession that filled every hour of her day, the one disaster sufficiently huge and sufficiently steeped in blood and human suffering for her to be able to bathe her enormous heart in it, a heart swollen with tears.

But by Friday morning her resolve had weakened, since she had been unable to decide where or how she would remove a rail. But that evening, once she was off duty, she had an idea and set off through the tunnel to explore as far as the Dieppe junction. This stretch of more than half a league underground was one of her regular walks, a vaulted avenue which was completely straight and in which she had the thrill of trains coming directly at her, with their dazzling headlamp: she only just avoided being crushed to death every time, and it was no doubt the danger of this which drew her there, in her thirst for daring. But that evening, having dodged the vigilant eye of the watchman and reached the middle of the tunnel, keeping to the left so as to ensure that any train would pass her on the right, she had foolishly turned to watch the lights of a train disappearing quite evidently in the direction of Le Havre; but then, when she had begun walking forward again, a stumble had caused her to turn round once more, so that she no longer knew in which direction the red lights had just vanished. Despite her courage, and still dazed by the noise of the wheels, she had stopped, her hands cold, her uncovered hair standing on end in terror. Now she had visions of not being able to tell, when the next train passed, whether it was an up train or a down train; she'd have to choose whether to jump to the right or the left, and run the risk of being sliced in two. With some effort she tried to remain rational, to remember, to think things through. Then suddenly panic had taken hold of her, and she had begun to rush blindly forward in headlong desperation. No! no! she didn't want to be killed, not before she'd killed those two! Her feet got caught in the rails, she kept slipping and falling, and then she would run even faster. It was tunnel madness, the walls seemed to press together as though to crush her, and the vaulted roof echoed with imagined sounds, with threatening voices and formidable rumblings. She kept glancing behind her, thinking she could feel the burning breath of an engine panting down her neck. Twice a sudden certainty that she'd chosen wrongly, that she'd be killed if she went that way, had made her change directions at a single bound. And on she raced, and raced, when far ahead a star appeared, a round, flaming eye that was growing bigger. But she had nerved herself against the irresistible temptation to turn yet again and run the other way. The eye became a brazier, the ravenous mouth of a furnace. Blinded, she had jumped to the left, at random; and the train was passing, like thunder, merely buffeting her with its stormy blast. Five minutes later she was emerging on the Malaunay side, safe and sound.

It was nine o'clock; a few minutes more, and the Paris express would be there. Immediately she had continued on her way, at a walking pace, as far as the Dieppe junction two hundred metres further on, examining the track, looking for some incidental feature that might serve her purpose. And it so happened that a ballast train was standing on the Dieppe line, which was undergoing repair, her friend Ozil having just sent it down there; and in a sudden moment of illumination she found and fixed upon a plan: she would simply prevent the pointsman from switching the points back to the Le Havre line, with the result that the express would collide with the ballast train. Ever since the day he'd lunged at her in a frenzy of desire and she'd half brained him with a stick, she had felt some friendship for this Ozil, and she liked to pay him unexpected visits through the tunnel, like some she-goat coming down off its mountain. He was a gaunt, taciturn ex-soldier, completely devoted to his duties; he had never yet been guilty of negligence, and kept his eyes open day and night. But this wild girl who had hit him and who was as strong as a young lad could make his flesh turn to jelly with the merest summons of her little finger. Although fourteen years her senior, he wanted her and he had sworn to have her, by biding his time and being nice to her, since brute force had not succeeded. So that night in the darkness, when she had approached his signal-box, calling to him from outside, he had gone to join her, forgetting everything. She turned his head, leading him off into the countryside and telling him complicated stories about how her mother was ill and how she wouldn't stay at La Croix-de-Maufras if she were to lose her. Meanwhile she was listening out for the distant rumbling of the express leaving Malaunay and now approaching at full speed. And when she sensed that it had come, she had turned round to look. But she had forgotten about the new system of interlocking: by entering the Dieppe line, the engine had automatically tripped the signal to red, and the driver had had time to stop just a few feet short of the ballast train. Ozil screamed like a man awaking to find his house collapsing on top of him, and rushed back to his post; while she stood rigid and motionless in the dark, observing the manœuvres necessitated by the accident. Two days later the pointsman was transferred, and he came to say goodbye to her, suspecting nothing, begging her to join him when she lost her mother. Oh well, the plan had failed, she'd just have to think of something else.

At the memory of this, Flore's dreamy gaze now unclouded, and once again she beheld the dead woman in the yellow light of the candle. Her mother was no more: should she leave, then, and marry Ozil, who wanted her, who might even make her happy? Her whole being rose in revolt. No, no! if she was going to be cowardly enough to let the other two live and continue to live herself, she would rather take to the roads and hire herself out as a servant than belong to a man she didn't love. An unusual sound caught her attention, and she realized that Misard had taken a pick and was excavating the earthen floor of the kitchen: he was so desperate to find the money, he could have ripped the whole house apart. And yet she didn't want to stay with him either.

What was she going to do? There was a sudden rush of wind, the walls shook, and upon the white face of the dead woman's corpse there passed the gleam of a furnace, casting a blood-red hue over the staring eyes and the ironic rictus of the lips. It was the last stopping train from Paris, with its slow, lumbering engine.

Flore had turned her head to gaze at the stars shining from the serene sky of a night in spring.

'Ten past three. Five more hours to go, and then they will pass.'

She would try again, it all hurt too much. Just seeing them, seeing them every week going off to their love together like that, it was simply more than she could bear. Now that she was certain that she would never have Jacques for her own, she preferred that he should cease to exist, that everything should cease to exist. And this lugubrious room in which she was keeping her vigil wrapped her in mourning, amidst her growing need that everything should be destroyed. Since there was no one left who loved her, the rest of them might just as well depart along with her mother. There would be more dead people, and more, and they'd all be carried off together. Her sister was dead, her mother was dead, her love was dead. What should she do? Live alone, whether she stayed or went, always alone, when those two would be a couple? No, no! rather that everything should come crashing down; that death, which was here in this smoky room, should breathe upon the line and sweep away the world!

And so, her mind made up after this long debate, she considered the best way of putting her plan into execution. And she came back to the idea of removing a section of track. That was the surest means, the most practical, and it was simple to carry out: all she had to do was to knock the wedges out with a hammer and prise the rail off the sleepers. She had the tools, no one would see her in this remote spot. The best place was surely the one beyond the cutting towards Barentin, where the curve crossed a valley on an embankment seven or eight metres high: at a spot like that, derailment was a certainty, and the crash would be appalling. But calculating the times, as she then did, gave her pause. The only traffic on the up line before the Le Havre express at 8.16 was a slow train at 7.55. That would give her twenty minutes to carry out her work, which was enough. Except

that they often sent down extra goods trains between the scheduled trains, especially at times when a considerable amount of
cargo had been landed. And what a pointless risk then! How
could she know in advance if it was the express which would
crash? For a long time she mulled the chances over in her head.
It was still dark outside: and the candle continued to burn,
drowning in tallow, with its long, charred wick that she had
ceased to trim.

Just as a goods train was approaching, from Rouen, Misard
came back into the room. His hands were covered in soil following his inspection of the woodshed; and he was panting for
breath, distraught at the futility of his searches, so feverish with
impotent rage that he began once more to hunt beneath the
furniture, up the chimney, everywhere. The endless train went
on and on, its great wheels clattering rhythmically past, each
thud jolting the dead woman on her bed. And as he stretched out
to unhook a small picture from the wall, he again caught sight of
the staring eyes following him round the room, and the lips that
parted in a grin.

He turned white, and shivered, stuttering with terrified anger:
'Oh yes, "keep looking", "keep looking"! . . . I'll find it, you
know, I'll bloody find it, if I have to look under every stone in the
house and every sod of earth for miles around!'

The black train had gone past, grinding slowly away into the
darkness, and the dead woman, motionless once more, continued
to look at her husband with such mockery, with such an air of
certain victory, that out he went once more, leaving the door
open behind him.

Disturbed in her thoughts, Flore had risen to her feet. She
shut the door after him, so that the man should not return to
trouble her mother. And she was astonished to hear herself say
out loud:

'Ten minutes beforehand, that should be enough.'

And indeed ten minutes would give her sufficient time. If, ten
minutes before the express arrived, no train had been signalled,
she could set to work. And at once, with the thing now settled
and certain, her anxiety vanished, and she became totally calm.

At about five o'clock the day began to break, a fresh new dawn,
pure and clear. Despite the sharp chill in the air she opened the

window wide, and the delicious morning entered the gloomy room, full of the miasma and smell of death. The sun was still beneath the horizon, behind a hill crowned with trees; but it rose into view, vermilion red, streaming over the hillsides and flooding the sunken paths, amidst that blithe animation that stirs the land with each new spring. She had not been mistaken the night before: it would be a fine morning, one of those days of youth and radiant health when it is a joy to be alive. Here in this deserted region, among the endless hills and narrow valleys, how good it would be to take herself off along the goat-tracks and wander where she pleased! And when she turned back into the room, she was surprised to see that the candle looked almost extinguished, no more than a pale tear against the daylight. The dead woman now appeared to be looking towards the railway line, where the trains continued to come and go, quite heedless of the pale gleam of candlelight beside the corpse.

Flore normally resumed her duties only at daybreak. And the first time she left the room was for the slow train to Paris at 6.12. Misard too, at six o'clock, had just relieved his colleague, who did the night shift. It was when he sounded his hooter that she went and took up her position beside the crossing gate, flag in hand. For a moment her eyes followed the departing train.

'Two hours to go,' she thought aloud.

Her mother had no further need of anyone, and Flore now felt insuperable disgust at the thought of going back into that bedroom. It was over, she had kissed her, and now she could see to her own existence and that of the rest of them. Normally she would clear off between trains; but this morning some particular interest seemed to be keeping her at her post next to the crossing gate, seated on a bench, a simple plank, beside the track. The sun was coming up, and a warm shower of gold sprinkled through the clear air; and she did not stir, basking in this gentle warmth amidst the vast countryside all quivering with the rising sap of April. For a moment she had directed her attention towards the wooden hut on the other side of the line, where Misard was clearly agitated and roused from his habitual somnolence: he kept on coming out and going in, nervously adjusting his instruments, continually glancing towards the house as if his mind were still there, still searching. Then she had forgotten about him, and was now quite unaware of his presence. She was completely absorbed in her waiting, her face tense and impassive, her eyes fixed on the furthest point on the track, towards Barentin. And there, before her, in the cheerful sunshine, there must have loomed some vision to hold the stubborn savagery of her gaze.

The minutes ticked by, and still Flore did not move. Finally, at 7.55, when Misard signalled the slow train from Le Havre on the up line with two blasts on the hooter, she rose to her feet, closed the gate, and took up her position beside it, flag in hand. And already, having made the ground tremble, the train was vanishing into the distance; it could be heard plunging into the tunnel, when the noise suddenly stopped. She did not return to her bench but remained standing there, once more counting the minutes. If in the next ten minutes no goods train were signalled, then she would run up there, beyond the cutting, and remove a rail. She was very calm, and felt only a tightening in the chest, as though the enormity of the act weighed upon it. But in any case, at this final moment, there was the knowledge that Jacques and Séverine were approaching and that unless she stopped them, they would again be passing by, on their way to love; and this sufficed to stiffen her resolve, rendering her blind and deaf in her determination, and ending all further internal debate. Here was the irrevocable moment, the cuff of the she-wolf's paw as it breaks the back of a passing prey. In the egotism of her vengeance she still saw only the two mutilated bodies, and gave no thought to the crowd, the stream of people, anonymous people, which had been rolling past her for year upon year. There'd be dead bodies, and blood, and maybe it would all block out the sun, this sun whose cheerful, tender warmth was now getting on her nerves.

Two more minutes, one more, and then away she would go, she was off already, when a distant rumbling along the Bécourt road stopped her. A cart coming, a quarryman's dray no doubt. They would ask to cross, she'd have to open the gate, have a chat, remain there: it would be impossible to do anything, she'd have missed her chance. And with a gesture of furious disregard, she took to her heels, abandoning her post and leaving the cart and its driver to fend for themselves. But a whip cracked in the morning air, and a voice cried out gaily:

'Hey! Flore!'

It was Cabuche. She stood rooted to the spot, halted almost before she'd begun, right beside the gate.

'What's up?' he continued. 'Still asleep? And on a lovely day like this? Quick, let me through before the express comes.'

She felt everything crumble inside her. It had all gone wrong, those two would go off and be happy, and she'd have found no way of smashing them to pieces, here, as they passed. And while she slowly opened the old, half-rotten gate, its iron hinges creaking in their rust, she searched furiously for an obstacle, something she could throw across the track, now so desperate that she herself would have lain across it if she had believed her bones sufficiently hard to derail the engine. But her eyes had just lit on the quarryman's dray, this heavy, low cart laden with two blocks of stone, which five strong horses could hardly pull. And here they were, these huge, tall, wide blocks, a gigantic mass that filled the roadway, offering themselves to her; and her eyes flashed with sudden concupiscence, a mad desire to take them and place them just there. The gate was wide open, and the five beasts stood waiting, steaming and snorting.

'What's up with you this morning?' Cabuche continued. 'You seem very odd.'

Then Flore spoke:

'My mother died last night.'

He exclaimed in friendly sympathy with her pain. Putting down his whip, he took her hands in his:

'Oh, my poor Flore. It had been expected for a long time, but it's so hard all the same! . . . Well, if she's in there I'd like to see her, because we'd have made up in the end if that other business hadn't happened.'

Quietly he walked with her to the house. But at the door he glanced back towards his horses. She reassured him briefly:

'Not much danger of them moving! Anyway, the express is miles away.'

She was lying. With her practised ear, through the tremulous warmth of the countryside, she had just heard the express leaving Barentin station. Another five minutes and it would be there, coming out of the cutting a hundred metres from the level-crossing. While the quarryman stood in the dead woman's room, lost in his thoughts of Louisette and deeply upset, she remained outside, by the window, and continued to listen in the distance to the regular puffing of the engine as it came closer and closer. Suddenly she thought of Misard: he would see her, try to stop her; and her heart missed a beat when she turned and saw that he was not at his post. She found him on the other side of the house digging beneath the rim of the well; he had not been able to resist his compulsion to search, no doubt suddenly convinced that this was where the money was. Completely engrossed by his passion, blind, deaf to everything else, he went on digging and digging. And that, for her, was the final spur: things were conspiring, urging her to it. One of the horses began to whinny, while the engine, beyond the cutting, was puffing very hard, like a person arriving in a hurry.

'I'll go and calm them,' Flore told Cabuche. 'Don't worry.'

She rushed forward, grabbed the leading horse by the bit, and pulled with all the mighty strength she used when she was fighting. The horses strained, and for a moment the heavy dray with its enormous load rocked backwards and forwards without advancing; but then, as though she had harnessed herself to them as an extra shaft-horse, it did begin to move across the track. And they were right in the middle when there was the express, a hundred metres away, coming out of the cutting. Whereupon, in order to halt the dray in case it should cross completely, she tugged sharply at the team of horses, restraining it with a superhuman effort that made her limbs crack. And this girl who was the subject of legend, of whom people related exploits demanding extraordinary strength—a runaway wagon stopped on a slope, or a cart pushed clear of an approaching train—here she was now doing this, holding these five horses in her iron grip as they reared and whinnied in their instinctive awareness of peril.

What seemed a terrifying eternity lasted barely ten seconds. The two giant blocks of stone seemed to shut out the horizon; while the engine, with its shining brass and gleaming steel, continued to glide forward, pursuing its smooth, thunderous course towards them beneath the showering gold of this fine, sunny morning. The inevitable was in place, nothing in the world could now prevent the collision. And the waiting continued.

Misard had rushed back to his post and was screaming his head off, waving his arms in the air and shaking his fists in a wild attempt to warn and stop the train. Having come out of the house when he heard the sound of the wheels and the horses whinnying, Cabuche had dashed across, screaming also, intending to make the horses go forward. But Flore, who had just jumped clear, held him back, which saved his life. He thought she had not had the strength to control the horses, that it was they who had dragged her. And he was blaming himself for it, sobbing in a desperate wail of terror, while she stood there motionless, taller than ever, her pupils blazing wide, watching. At the very moment when the breast of the engine was about to make contact with the blocks of stone, when it still had perhaps a metre to go, during that split second, she clearly saw Jacques, standing there with his hand on the gear-wheel. He had turned, and their eyes met in a gaze which seemed to her immeasurably long.

That morning in Le Havre Jacques had smiled at Séverine when she came down to the platform to catch the express, as she did every week. Why ruin one's life with nightmares? Why not take advantage of the happy days as and when they presented themselves? Perhaps everything would sort itself out in the end. And he had resolved to make the most of this day at least, planning what they would do, picturing himself having lunch with her in a restaurant. So, when she pulled a face to find that there was no first-class carriage at the head of the train and that she would therefore have to sit far away from him, at the rear, he had tried to console her with this cheerful smile. They would still arrive together, and they'd make up for this separation when they did. Indeed, after leaning out to watch her find a compartment, right at the end of the train, he had been in such good humour that he had even shared a joke with the chief guard, Henri Dauvergne, whom he knew to be in love with her. The previous week he had imagined that Dauvergne was growing bolder, and that she had been encouraging him, wanting a diversion, an escape from the dreadful life she had made for herself. Roubaud had said as much, that she would end up going to bed

with that young man, not for the pleasure of it but simply out of
the desire to make a fresh start. So Jacques had asked Henri who
it was he'd been blowing kisses to, the night before, when he'd
been hiding behind one of the elm-trees outside the station
entrance; and this had made Pecqueux roar with laughter as he
stoked the firebox on La Lison, which stood puffing away in
readiness to depart.

From Le Havre to Barentin the express had proceeded at its
regulation speed, without incident; and it was Henri, perched up
high in his look-out, who, as they were leaving the cutting,
signalled the presence of the quarryman's dray across the track.
The front guard's-van was crammed full of luggage, since the
train was packed with a whole shipload of passengers who had
disembarked from a steamer the night before. Hemmed in between the piles of trunks and suitcases which bounced about
with the shaking of the train, the chief guard stood at his desk,
sorting papers; while the little bottle of ink hanging from a nail
likewise swung to and fro with the motion of the train. After each
station where he set down luggage, he had four or five minutes'
worth of forms to fill in. Two passengers had got out at Barentin,
and he had just finished his paperwork when he climbed to his
seat in the look-out and glanced in his usual way up and down
the track. He used to remain on watch up there in the glass booth
during all the time he was free. The tender prevented him seeing
the engine-driver, but thanks to his elevated vantage-point he
could often see further and sooner than the driver. Thus the
train was still rounding the bend in the cutting when he saw
the obstacle ahead. He was so astonished that for a moment he
did not believe it, and he sat paralysed with horror. Several
seconds were lost, and the train was already speeding out of the
cutting and a great cry had gone up from the engine when he
finally decided to pull the communication cord hanging in front
of him.

At this crucial moment Jacques was standing with his hand on
the gear-wheel, gazing vacantly ahead in a moment of mental
absence. He was thinking of vague, faraway things, among which
even the picture of Séverine herself had ceased to figure. The
mad ringing of the alarm-bell roused him, as well as the sound of
Pecqueux screaming behind him. Having raised the firebox door

because he was dissatisfied with the way the fire was drawing, Pecqueux had just seen the dray as he leant out to check the train's speed. And Jacques, deathly pale, saw it all, saw what it meant, the dray across the line, the engine at full speed, the terrible collision, and all with such absolute clarity that he could even make out the grain in the two blocks of stone, while already he could feel the force of the impact entering his bones. Here was the inevitable. In a desperate last effort he had turned the gear-wheel, shut off the regulator, and applied the brakes. The engine was in reverse, and his hand had gone up automatically to pull the whistle and sound a warning, in a furious, futile attempt to remove the giant barrier ahead. But as this awful whistle of distress rent the air, La Lison refused to respond and just kept on running, barely slackening her speed. She was no longer the docile creature she once had been, before the snow had taken away her gift for generating steam, her talent for smooth depar- ture, and now she had become crotchety and cantankerous, like an elderly woman whose chest has been ruined by a chill. She was panting and snorting, bridling at the resistance of the brakes, and on she went, on and on, with the heavy obstinacy of her mass. Pecqueux, crazed with terror, jumped off. Jacques, rigid at his post, his right hand clamped on to the gear-wheel, the other still unconsciously pulling the whistle, waited. And then, steam- ing and smoking amidst an endless, high-pitched roar, La Lison crashed into the dray with the full, enormous weight of the thirteen carriages which she was pulling along behind her.

Twenty metres away, frozen with horror at the side of the track, Misard, Cabuche, both with their arms still raised, and Flore, goggle-eyed, then witnessed this terrifying thing: the train rearing up into the air, seven carriages climbing one on top of the other, and then everything falling back down with the most dreadful splintering sound into a jumbled mass of wreckage. The first three carriages were smashed to pieces, the next four noth- ing but a mountainous heap, a tangle of collapsed roofs, broken wheels, doors, chains, buffers, and broken glass. And above all they had heard the noise of the engine grinding into the blocks of stone, a dull, crunching sound that ended in a scream of agony. La Lison toppled over to her left on to the dray, as though disembowelled; while the blocks of stone had split asunder, exploding in fragments as though shattered by a quarry blast, and of the five horses, four were rolled, dragged along, killed on the instant. The tail of the train, the remaining six carriages which were all intact, had come to rest without even leaving the rails.

But cries went up, appeals for help, the words dissolving into the inarticulate howling of beasts.

'Help! Over here! . . . Oh, my God, I'm dying. Help! Help!'

They heard, saw, nothing further. Upside down, her belly gaping, La Lison was losing steam through burst tubes and wrenched-off taps, her thunderous puffing like the desperate, dying gasps of some female giant. A white breath was coming out of her, inexhaustibly, thick swirls of it rolling across the ground; while the burning coals that had fallen from the firebox, as red as though they were the very blood from her entrails, added their plumes of black smoke. The chimney had been driven into the ground by the force of the collision; at the point of impact the engine's frame had split, making the two side-members buckle; and like a monstrous mare gored by some formidable horn, La Lison lay with her wheels in the air, her connecting-rods twisted, her cylinders broken, and her valves and eccentrics all smashed, a horrible wound gaping at the sky and from which her soul continued to seep with a furious hiss of impotent despair. And just beside her was the horse which had not died, lying there with both its forelegs gone and, like the engine, losing its entrails through a rent in its belly. By the look of its head straining stiffly upwards in a spasm of extreme pain, it could be seen to give one last terrible whinny, of which no sound reached the ear above the roar of the dying engine.

Strangled cries went unheard, lost and borne away on the air.

'Save me! Kill me! . . . I can't bear it, kill me, just kill me!'

Amidst the deafening tumult and blinding smoke, the doors of the undamaged carriages had opened, and a panicked throng of passengers was rushing about outside. They were stumbling over the line, picking themselves up again, fighting their way clear with fist and foot. Then, as soon as they felt they were on solid ground, with open countryside ahead of them, they took to their heels, jumping over hedges, cutting across fields, yielding to their overriding instinct to get far away from the danger, far,

far away. Women, men, all screaming, disappeared into the
woods.

Trampled on, her hair dishevelled and her dress in tatters,
Séverine had managed to get clear; but she was not running
away, she was racing towards the roaring engine, when she came
face to face with Pecqueux.

'Jacques, Jacques, he *is* safe, isn't he?'

The fireman, who by a miracle had not so much as sprained a
limb, was also rushing to the scene, sick at heart with remorse at
the thought of his driver being underneath all this. Together
they had travelled so far, and toiled so hard, in the constant
buffeting of the great winds! And their engine, their poor engine,
the beloved mistress in their threesome, there she was lying on
her back, yielding up every breath in her body from her punctured lungs!

'I jumped off,' he stammered, 'I've no idea, none at
all . . . Quick, let's hurry!'

On the platform they ran into Flore, who was watching them
approach. She had not yet moved, still stupefied at having done
it, at the massacre she had brought about. It was all over, it had
worked; and she felt only relief at having satisfied a need, not pity
for the harm done to others, the others she didn't even see. But
when she recognized Séverine, her eyes opened enormously
wide, and a shadow of awful pain darkened her pale face. What?
This woman was still alive, and when he most certainly was
dead! As she felt the sharp agony of her murdered love, of this
knife which she had driven into her own heart, she suddenly
realized the full horror of her crime. She had done this, she had
killed him, she had killed all these people! A great cry ripped
from her throat, as she wrung her hands and began to run like
mad.

'Jacques, oh Jacques . . . He's over there, he was thrown backwards, I saw him . . . Jacques, Jacques!'

La Lison was panting less loudly now, a rasping lament that
was gradually fading, and above it one could hear the increasingly heartrending screams of the injured. But the smoke was
still thick, and the enormous pile of wreckage from which these
tortured, terrified voices came seemed to be cloaked in a black
dust which hung motionless in the sunlight. What should they

do? Where should they begin? How could they get to the poor
wretches?

'Jacques!' Flore continued to shout. 'I tell you he looked at
me, he was thrown over there, under the tender . . . Hurry, can't
you, come and help me!'

Cabuche and Misard had already helped Henri, the chief
guard, to his feet, for he too, at the very last second, had jumped.
He had sprained his ankle, and they sat him down against the
hedge from where he watched the rescue operation, dazed and
silent but apparently not in pain.

'Cabuche, come and help me. Jacques is under there, I tell
you!'

The quarryman didn't hear her, he was busy running to help
other injured people, carrying away a young woman whose legs
were hanging limply, broken at the thighs.

And it was Séverine who rushed forward in answer to Flore's
appeal.

'Jacques, Jacques! . . . Where? I'll help you!'

'Yes, that's right, you can help me!'

Their hands touched as they both pulled on a broken wheel.
But the delicate fingers of the one were powerless, while
the other, with her strong arms, was removing obstacle after
obstacle.

'Careful!' said Pecqueux, who had also come to help.

He had quickly grabbed Séverine just as she was about to step
on a person's arm, severed at the shoulder and still wearing a
blue serge sleeve. She recoiled in horror. But she didn't recognize the sleeve: it was an unfamiliar arm which had rolled there
from a body which would no doubt turn up somewhere. And she
began to tremble so much with the shock that she was as though
paralysed, standing there weeping as she watched other people at
work, incapable even of removing the pieces of broken glass on
which people were cutting their hands.

By now the rescue of the dying and the search for the dead
were fraught with anxiety and danger, because the fire from the
engine had spread to some of the timber, and they had to shovel
earth over it to prevent the blaze spreading. While someone went
off to Barentin to seek help and a telegram was sent to Rouen, the
business of clearing the wreckage began to organize itself as

vigorously as possible, and everybody lent a hand, showing great courage. Many of those who had fled had now returned, ashamed of their panic. But everyone proceeded with infinite care; each piece of wreckage to be lifted required special attention for they were afraid of finishing off the wretched victims beneath by causing further slippages. Some of the injured stuck out from the pile of wreckage, caught fast up to the chest, as though gripped in a vice, and screaming. They spent a quarter of an hour freeing one man, who, while white as a sheet, gave no sign of being in pain and kept saying that there was nothing the matter with him, that he couldn't feel a thing; and when they got him out, he had no legs, and he died immediately, without knowing or feeling this horrible mutilation, so great had been the shock of his terror. A whole family was retrieved from a second-class carriage, where the fire had caught: the father and mother had knee injuries, the grandmother a broken arm; but they couldn't feel their pain either, as they sobbed and called out for their little girl who had disappeared in the crash, a little fair-haired child barely three years old, who eventually turned up beneath a scrap of roof, safe and well, all smiles. Another little girl, this one covered in blood, her poor tiny hands crushed, had been carried over to one side, where she waited for her parents to be found under the wreckage, a forlorn, anonymous figure so overcome that she could not utter a word, with only her face convulsing in an expression of unspeakable terror if anyone went near her. They were unable to open the doors whose catches had been twisted in the collision, and they had to get down into the compartments through the broken windows. Already four corpses had been laid out in a row beside the track. Ten or so of the injured lay on the ground beside the corpses, waiting, with no doctor to attend to their injuries, without assistance of any kind. And the process of clearing the wreckage was only just beginning; some new victim turned up beneath every next piece of debris, and the pile did not appear to be getting any smaller, all heaving with this human butchery and running with its blood.

'But Jacques is under there, I tell you!' Flore kept saying, finding relief in this obstinate cry which she repeated without thinking, as though it were a lament for her own despair. 'Can't you hear him? He's calling, listen, listen!'

The tender was buried beneath the carriages, which had piled up on each other and then collapsed on top of it; and indeed, now that the engine had ceased to groan so loudly, one could hear the strong voice of a man roaring from beneath the wreckage. As they progressed, the agonized clamour of this voice grew louder and louder, its pain so great that the rescue-workers could bear it no longer and were screaming and crying themselves. And when at last, having freed his legs, they got hold of him and pulled, the screaming stopped. The man was dead.

'No,' said Flore, 'that's not him. He's lower down, underneath.'

And with her Amazon's arms she picked up wheels and cast them aside, twisted the zinc on the roofs, broke doors in, and ripped away lengths of chain. And as soon as she came upon a dead body or one of the injured, she called for them to be removed, unwilling to cease even for a second from her manic excavation.

Behind her Cabuche, Pecqueux, and Misard were working away, while Séverine, grown faint from standing around without being able to do anything, had sat down on a crumpled carriage-seat. But Misard, now calm and indifferent, having recovered his customary phlegm, was avoiding the more exhausting jobs and was helping mainly to carry away the bodies. Like Flore he examined the corpses as though hoping to recognize them from among the throng of thousands upon thousands of faces that had been filing past them at top speed for the last ten years, leaving only the indeterminate memory of a crowd as they came and went in a momentary flash. No! it was still the same old stream of unknown people on the move; and brutal, accidental death was as anonymous as the hurry-scurry of life which habitually tore past them on its way to the future; and they were unable to attach any name, any precise piece of information, to the horror-struck faces of these unfortunates who had fallen in transit, trampled and crushed like soldiers whose bodies serve to fill the holes in the path of an advancing army mounting an assault. Yet Flore thought she spotted one man she had spoken to, the day the train had been caught in the blizzard: that American whose profile had become familiar and yet whose name she did not know, just as she knew nothing else about him or his family. Misard carried him away like the rest of the dead, come from God knew whence and halted here on their way to God knew whither.

Then there was a further heartrending spectacle. In the up-turned shell of a first-class compartment a young couple had just been discovered, newly-weds probably, thrown on top of one another in such an unfortunate way that the woman was crushing the man beneath her and could not move to ease his position. He was suffocating and already in the throes of death; while she, able to open her mouth, was wildly imploring them to hurry, hor-rified, her heart breaking at the thought that she was killing him. And when they were finally released from each other, it was she, suddenly, who passed away: her side had been ripped open by a buffer. And the man, having recovered consciousness, was screaming with grief, kneeling next to her where she lay, her eyes still filled with tears.

By now there were twelve dead, and more than thirty injured. But they were managing to free the tender; and Flore, from time to time, would stop and plunge her head in among the splintered wood and twisted metal, searching desperately for any glimpse of the driver. Suddenly she gave a great cry:

'I see him, he's underneath there! . . . Look, there's his arm, and his blue woollen jacket . . . He's not moving, he's not breathing . . .'

She had stood up again, and swore like a man.

'But for Christ's sake hurry, can't you, get him out of there!'

With her bare hands she tried to pull a carriage floor away, which was jammed by other pieces of wreckage. Then she ran off, and returned with the axe which they used at home for chopping logs; and brandishing it like a woodcutter in a forest of oak, she began to hack furiously at the floor. People had moved aside, out of her way, shouting at her to be careful. But there were no other injured there apart from the driver, who was protected by a twisted mass of axles and wheels. Anyway she wasn't listening, she was completely carried away on a surge of unwavering, irresistible intent. She brought the shaft down again and again, and each blow disposed of a further obstacle. With her blond hair falling loose, and her ripped bodice

revealing her naked arms, she resembled some fearsome reaper
scything a path through all this destruction for which she herself
was responsible. One last blow, which landed on an axle, broke
the blade of the axe in two. And then, with the others helping,
she parted the wheels which had saved Jacques from certain
destruction, and she was the first to seize him and bear him away
in her arms.

'Jacques, Jacques! . . . . He's still breathing, he's alive. Oh, my
God, he's alive . . . I knew I'd seen him fall, I knew that's where
he was!'

Séverine rushed frantically after her. Between them they laid
him at the foot of the hedge, next to Henri, who sat there in a
stupor without seeming to understand where he was or what was
going on around him. Pecqueux had come up and was standing
in front of his driver, shattered to see him in such a bad way;
while the two women, now kneeling on either side of the casualty, were supporting his head and anxiously scanning his face
for the merest ripple of expression.

At last Jacques opened his eyes. With a dazed expression he
looked at each of them in turn, but without apparent recognition.
They meant nothing to him. But when his eyes fell on the dying
engine just a few metres away, they seemed startled at first, and
then began to stare, flickering with increasing emotion. La
Lison . . . he recognized her all right, and the sight of her
brought it all back to him, the two blocks of stone across the line,
the dreadful crash, the crumpling sensation he had felt both in
her and in himself, and from which he was recovering but she
was surely going to die. She couldn't be blamed for not responding: ever since catching that illness in the snow, it had been no
fault of hers if she'd been less alert than before; and besides,
limbs grow heavy with age, and the joints begin to seize. And so
he readily forgave her, overcome by enormous grief at seeing her
lying there, fatally injured, in her dying throes. Poor Lison had
but a few minutes to live. She was growing cold, the hot coals
from her fire were turning to ash, and the breath which had been
escaping with such force from her gaping sides had dwindled to
the gentle whimper of a tearful child. Once so shiny but now
filthy with earth and scum, and sprawled upside down in a black
mire of coal, hers was the tragic end of a lustrous steed run over

in the middle of a street. For a moment, through her punctured entrails, it had been possible to see her vital organs still at work, with her pistons pumping like twin hearts, and the steam circulating in her slide-valves as though it were the blood in her veins. But, like arms twitching in spasm, the connecting-rods were now merely jerking with the last, defiant pulses of residual life; and her soul was departing in the loss of that power which gave her life, that immense store of breath which she could not quite manage wholly to exhale. The disembowelled giant continued her descent into peace, sliding gradually into the gentlest of sleeps, until at length she fell silent. She was dead. And the heap of iron, steel, and brass which she left behind her, this crumpled colossus with its trunk split, its limbs scattered, and its organs bruised and exposed to the light of day, assumed the terrible sadness of an enormous human corpse, a whole world that once had lived and from which life had now been ripped, in pain.

Realizing that La Lison was no more, Jacques closed his eyes again and wished that he might die also, in any case feeling so weak that he thought the last, tiny gasp of the engine was carrying him off too. Tears slowly welled from beneath his closed eyelids and began to course down his cheeks. It was too much for Pecqueux, who was still standing there motionless, with a lump in his throat. The love of their life was dying, and now his driver wanted to go with her. So this was the end of their threesome? The end of all those journeys when they would travel hundreds of miles mounted on her back without exchanging a word but all three understanding each other so well that they did not even need to make a sign to be sure of being understood. Oh, poor Lison, so gentle in all her strength, so beautiful when she gleamed in the sunlight! And Pecqueux, without having had a drop to drink, burst into violent sobbing, and his large frame shook uncontrollably.

Séverine and Flore, too, were beginning to despair, deeply concerned that Jacques had lapsed back into unconsciousness. The latter ran into the house and returned with some camphorated spirit, which she rubbed on him, out of the simple need to do something. But the anguish of the two women was made worse by the interminable death throes of the horse, the only one of the five to have survived, the one with its front legs missing. It was lying near them, and it continued to whinny with an almost human cry that was so loud and sprang from such terrible pain that two of the injured had found it contagious and themselves begun to howl like beasts. No dying man ever rent the air with such a deep, unforgettable cry of agony; it made the blood run cold. This torment was becoming excruciating, and voices trembling with angry compassion began to lose patience and begged someone to finish off this wretched horse which was in such pain, and whose interminable death rattle seemed, now that the engine was dead, like a last, lingering lament for the disaster. So then Pecqueux, still sobbing, picked up the axe with its broken blade and, with a single blow to the skull, destroyed it. And silence fell upon the field of slaughter.

Help finally arrived after a wait of two hours. The impact of the collision had thrown all the carriages to the left, so that it was going to be possible to clear the down line in a matter of hours. A train consisting of three carriages, pulled by a pilot-engine, had just arrived from Rouen bringing the Prefect's chief assistant, the public prosecutor, and the Compagnie de l'Ouest's own engineers and doctors, a whole flock of horrified people eager to help; while the station-master at Barentin, Monsieur Bessière, was already there setting to with a team of men to clear the wreckage. An extraordinary atmosphere of tension and feverish activity prevailed in this remote place, normally so deserted and silent. Among the passengers who had escaped unharmed, the frenzy of panic had turned into a frantic compulsion to keep on the move: some were looking for horse-drawn transport, terrified at the thought of ever boarding a train again; others, seeing that not even a handcart was to be found, were already worrying about where they were going to eat and sleep; and all of them were asking for the nearest telegraph office, while several people were setting off for Barentin themselves, bearing messages. As the authorities began their enquiry with the help of company officials, the doctors were hurriedly setting about treating the injured. Several lay unconscious, surrounded by pools of blood. Others groaned weakly as clamps and needles were applied. Altogether fifteen passengers had died, and thirty-two lay seriously injured. The dead had been left lying in a row along the side of the hedge, face upwards, pending identification. The only person attending to them was a little deputy prosecutor, a pink-faced, fair-haired young man, who was zealously going through their pockets to see if any papers, visiting cards, or letters might allow him to label each one with a name and address. Meanwhile a large circle of people was forming; for although there wasn't another house for almost a league around, curious onlookers had arrived from nowhere, some thirty men, women, and children who were getting in the way and doing nothing to help. And now that the black dust and all-enveloping veil of smoke and steam had lifted, the glorious April morning shone in triumph over the scene of the carnage, and its bright, cheerful sunshine fell like a gentle shower upon the dying and the dead, on La Lison, disembowelled, and on the piles of wreckage being cleared by the team of workmen, like ants repairing the ravages done to their antheap by the casual footfall of a passer-by.

Jacques was still unconscious, and Séverine had stopped a passing doctor, begging him to help. He had just examined the young man and found no evident sign of injury; but he was worried that there might be internal bleeding, for tiny trickles of blood were appearing at his lips. Not yet able to give a firmer opinion, he advised that the injured man be moved as soon as possible and laid in a bed, taking every care not to jolt him.

Feeling the hands examining him, Jacques had opened his eyes again with a slight cry of pain; and this time he recognized Séverine and stammered desperately:

'Take me away from here, love, take me away from here!'

Flore had leaned forward, and when he turned his head, he recognized her too. A child's look of terror came into his eyes, and he recoiled towards Séverine in hatred and horror.

'Quick, love, quick! Take me away!'

And in similarly intimate tones—for she was alone with him, this girl no longer counted—she suggested:

'How about La Croix-de-Maufras, darling, would that do? . . . If you didn't mind too much, it's just across there, and there'll be no one to disturb us.'

He agreed, still trembling, his eyes on that other woman.

'Wherever you like, but now!'

Sitting there motionless, Flore had turned pale at this look of terrified loathing. And so, amidst all this carnage of unknown, innocent people, she had failed to kill either of them: the woman had escaped without a scratch; Jacques, too, perhaps might now survive; and in this way all she had managed to do was to bring them closer, to throw them together, alone with each other, in that empty house. She pictured them installed there, the lover saved and convalescing, the mistress all ministering angel, rewarded for her vigils by constant caresses, and both of them prolonging this honeymoon sequel to catastrophe, far from the eyes of the world, completely undisturbed. A great chill fell upon her, and she gazed at the bodies of the dead: she had killed for nothing.

Surveying the slaughter at that moment, she noticed Misard and Cabuche being questioned by some gentlemen, no doubt the police. And indeed the public prosecutor and the Prefect's chief assistant were trying to establish how the quarryman's cart had ended up across the track. Misard maintained that he hadn't left his post, though he could give no precise information: he really didn't know how it had happened, he claimed that his back had been turned while he was busy with his instruments. As for Cabuche, who was still very shaken, he told a long, confused story about how wrong he'd been to leave his horses unattended, how he'd wanted to see the dead woman, how the horses had moved forward of their own accord, and how the girl hadn't been able to stop them. He kept getting in a muddle, and would start all over again, but none of it in the end made any sense.

A wild urge to be free stirred Flore's frozen blood to life. She wanted to be left to her own devices, to be at liberty to reflect and decide for herself, for she had never needed anyone else to choose the right path. Why wait to be bothered with questions, to be arrested even? For apart from the crime itself there had been dereliction of duty, and she would be held responsible. Nevertheless she remained there, unable to leave as long as Jacques himself was still there.

Séverine had been so insistent with Pecqueux that he had finally gone off to find a stretcher; and he came back with another railwayman to carry the injured man away. The doctor had also persuaded the young woman to take the chief guard, Henri, in as well; he seemed merely concussed, and not sure where he was. They would come and fetch him once they had taken Jacques across.

And as Séverine leant over to loosen Jacques's collar, which was too tight, she kissed him on the eyes, quite openly, wanting to give him the courage to stand the pain of being moved.

'Don't worry, my darling, we shall be happy.'

Smiling, he kissed her back. And that, for Flore, was the moment of final severance, tearing her from him, for ever. She felt as though her blood, too, were now pouring from an unstaunchable wound. When they carried him away, she took to her heels. But as she passed in front of the little house, she caught sight of the dead woman's bedroom through the window and the patch of pale candlelight which was still burning in broad daylight, beside her mother's body. Throughout the disaster the dead woman had been left on her own, with her head half-turned to one side, her eyes staring, and her lips contorted, as though she had been watching all these people she did not know being crushed to death.

Flore ran on, straight round the corner on the road to Doinville and then plunging into the bushes on the left. She knew every inch of the terrain and defied the police to catch her if they were sent after her. So she suddenly stopped running and continued at a stroll, making for a hiding-place where she liked to go to ground on the days she was feeling miserable, a hollow above the tunnel. She looked up and saw from the position of the sun that it was midday. When she had reached her lair, she stretched out on the hard rock and lay there motionless, her hands clasped behind her neck, thinking. But then a dreadful void opened up within her, and a sensation of being already dead gradually numbed her limbs. It was not remorse at having killed all these people to no purpose, for she had to make an effort to feel any regret or horror. But, and she was sure of this now, Jacques had seen her holding the horses back; and she had just realized from the way he had recoiled that he now felt for her that terrified repulsion one feels for monsters. He would never forget. Anyway, when you fail with other people, you mustn't fail with yourself: she would kill herself by and by. She had no other hope, she had felt the absolute necessity of this more and more since she had been lying here, calming herself and turning things over. Only exhaustion, an annihilation of her whole being, prevented her from getting up, looking for a weapon, and dying. And yet, from the depths of the sleepiness which was gradually overtaking her, there rose still the love of life, the need to be happy, one last dream that she too might be happy, since she was leaving those two to the happiness of living together in freedom. Why not wait for nightfall and then go and find Ozil, who adored her and would be able to protect her? She began to think fond, confused thoughts, and she fell into a black, dreamless sleep.

When Flore awoke, night had already fallen, and it was pitch dark. She felt about her in a daze, suddenly remembering, as she felt the bare rock, where it was that she had lain down. And, like a thunderbolt, the implacable necessity of it came back to her: she had to die. It was as though her cowardly softness, the weakening at the prospect of life's possible continuance, had vanished with her exhaustion. No, no! only death was good. She couldn't go on living surrounded by all this blood, with her heart torn from her, and execrated by the only man she'd ever wanted, and who belonged to another. Now that she had the strength for it, she had to die.

Flore stood up, and came out of the rocky hollow. She did not hesitate, for it had just come to her instinctively where she should go. Once more consulting the sky, the stars this time, she knew that it was nearly nine o'clock. As she was approaching the railway line, a train went by at top speed on the down line, which seemed to please her: everything would be all right, evidently they had cleared that line, while the other was presumably still blocked since normal traffic did not yet seem to have resumed on it. From there she followed the hedge, surrounded by the deep silence of this wild, deserted region. There was no hurry, there wouldn't be another train before the Paris express, which would not come past until nine twenty-five; and she walked on slowly beside the hedge in the thick darkness, quite calmly, as though she were out for one of her usual walks along the empty paths. But just before she came to the tunnel, she climbed over the hedge and continued along the track itself, at her customary stroll, towards the oncoming express. She had to be cunning and avoid being spotted by the watchman, just the way she usually did every time she visited Ozil over at the other end. And once in the tunnel, on she walked, and walked, always forward. But this was not like the previous week, she was no longer afraid of turning round and forgetting which direction she was going in. Her head wasn't pounding with tunnel madness, that sudden moment of panic when everything—objects, time, space—becomes a blur amidst the thundering echoes and crushing sides of the vault. What did she care! She wasn't thinking rationally, she wasn't even thinking, she simply had this one fixed resolve: to walk, to walk straight ahead, for as long as no train came, and then still to walk, straight towards its headlamp, as soon as she saw it blazing through the darkness.

Flore was nevertheless surprised, for she felt as though she had been walking along like this for hours. How distant it was, this death which she desired! She despaired for a moment at the idea that it might not come to her, that she might go on and on for miles and never meet it face to face. Her feet were growing tired. Would she have to sit down, to stretch out across the rails and wait for it? But that seemed unworthy; her instincts as a warrior virgin told her that she must keep on walking right to the end, that she must die standing. And when, far away in the distance, she saw the headlamp of the express, like a tiny lone star twinkling in an inky sky, her energy returned, pushing her forward once more. The train had not yet entered the tunnel, no sound heralded its approach; there was just this light, so bright and cheerful, which was growing and growing. Drawing herself up to her full height, like a lithe statue, and swinging along on her strong legs, she now lengthened her stride, but still without running, as though she were going to meet a friend and wanted to spare her some part of the journey. But the train had just entered the tunnel, and the dreadful roar was coming closer and closer, making the ground shake with a stormy blast of air; while the star had become an enormous eye, getting bigger and bigger, as though bursting from a socket of darkness. Then, in response to some mysterious prompting, perhaps in order to be quite alone at the moment of death, she emptied her pockets, without pausing in her stubborn, heroic stride, and deposited a whole collection of articles beside the track, a handkerchief, keys, some string, two knives; she even removed the scarf round her neck, and left her bodice unbuttoned, half hanging off her shoulders. The eye was turning into a brazier, into the mouth of a furnace spewing fire, and the panting breath of the monster was coming closer, already warm and moist, amidst a rumble of thunder that became more and more deafening. And on she strode, straight towards this furnace, so that the engine should not miss her, like a bewitched moth drawn to a flame. And in the horrendous impact of collision, at the moment of embrace, she drew herself up once more as though the fighter in her had wanted, in one last effort of resistance, to seize the colossus in her arms and hurl it to the ground. Her head had collided directly with the lamp, which went out.

More than an hour elapsed before they came to collect Flore's body. The driver had perfectly well seen the tall, pale figure walking towards the engine, looking like some strange, terrifying apparition in the shaft of bright light; and when suddenly the light had gone out and the train was left thundering along in total darkness, he had shuddered to feel the passage of death. At the exit from the tunnel he had tried to alert the watchman to the accident. But it was only at Barentin that he had been able to report that someone had just got themselves sliced in two back there: it was certainly a woman; hair, mixed with the remains of a skull, was still sticking to the shattered glass of the headlamp. And when the men who had been sent out to look for the body eventually found it, they were struck at how white it was, as white as marble. It was lying on the up line, thrown there by the force of the impact, the head smashed to pulp and the limbs without a scratch, half-naked, marvellously beautiful in its purity and its power. Silently the men wrapped it. They had recognized her. She must have killed herself, in a moment of madness, to escape the terrible responsibility weighing upon her.

By midnight Flore's body was lying at rest in the little house beside her mother's. A mattress had been placed on the floor, and a new candle lit and placed between them. Phasie, her head still turned to one side and her mouth still twisted in its horrible grin, seemed now to be watching her daughter with her big, staring eyes; while in the solitude, amidst the profound silence, one could hear on every side the sound of dogged effort, the panting exertions of Misard who had resumed his search. And at the regulation intervals trains were passing to and fro on both tracks, normal service having been completely restored. Past they went, inexorably, in their mechanical omnipotence, indifferent, unaware of these dramas and these crimes. What did it matter if a few, faceless members of the crowd had fallen by the wayside, crushed by its wheels! The dead had been removed, the blood wiped away; and people were on the move once more, bound towards the future.

CHAPTER XI

THE scene was the main bedroom at La Croix-de-Maufras, the one hung with red damask and which had two tall windows that looked out on to the railway line only a few metres away. From the bed, an old four-poster on the opposite side of the room, the trains could be seen passing. And for years not one object had been removed, nor a single piece of furniture shifted from its spot.

Séverine had given instructions for the injured and unconscious Jacques to be brought up to this room, while Henri Dauvergne had been left on the ground floor, in another, smaller bedroom. For herself she reserved a room close to Jacques's, just across the landing. Within a matter of hours they were all installed with a sufficient degree of comfort, for the house had remained fully furnished, down to the linen in the cupboards. Wearing an apron over her dress, Séverine now found herself transformed into a nurse, having simply telegraphed to Roubaud to tell him not to expect her, that in all likelihood she would be remaining here for several days to care for some of the injured, whom she had taken in at their house.

And on the following day the doctor had already been able to pronounce Jacques out of danger, and indeed counted on having him on his feet within the week: an absolute miracle, just some minor internal bruising. But he advised the utmost care and that he be kept completely still. So, when the patient opened his eyes, Séverine, who had been watching over him as though he were a child, begged him to be good and to do exactly as he was told. Still very weak, he promised with a nod. He was completely lucid, and he recognized this bedroom which she had described to him on the night of her confession: the red room in which, from the age of sixteen and a half, she had yielded to the brutal advances of President Grandmorin. This was the very bed in which he now lay, and those were the windows through which, without even lifting his head, he could see the trains go past, suddenly making the whole house shake as they did so. And he could feel this house all around him now, just as he had so often seen it as he passed by aboard his engine. He could still picture it standing at an angle to the track, derelict and abandoned, with its shutters closed and, ever since it had been put up for sale, looking even more miserable and eerie thanks to the huge sign, which added to the melancholy of its garden all overgrown with brambles. He remembered the awful sadness that came over him each time he passed, and the haunting dread he felt, as though it stood there ready to bring misfortune upon his life. Today, lying in this bedroom and in such a weak state, he thought he understood why, for there could be only one explanation: plainly he was going to die here.

As soon as she saw that he was in a fit state to understand her, Séverine had hastened to reassure him by whispering in his ear as she pulled up the bedclothes:

'Don't worry, I emptied your pockets, I've got the watch.'

He stared at her, wide-eyed, trying to remember.

'The watch . . . Oh, yes, the watch.'

'They might have searched you. So I've hidden it among my own things. You've nothing to be afraid of.'

He thanked her with a squeeze of his hand. Turning his head, he caught sight of the knife lying on the table; it had also been in one of his pockets. Only there was no need to hide that: it was a knife like any other.

But already by the following day Jacques was feeling stronger, and he began to hope that he was not going to die here. He had been genuinely pleased to find Cabuche busying himself around him, trying to deaden the sound of his colossus feet on the wooden floor; for since the accident the quarryman had not left Séverine's side, as though he too were possessed by the need to devote himself to others. He forsook his own work and came every morning to help with the heavy jobs around the house, serving her like a faithful dog, his eyes always fixed on hers. As he said, she was some woman all right, despite her frail appearance. And the least he could do was to help her, seeing that she was doing so much to help other people. So the two lovers got used to having him around, and spoke intimately to each other, even kissed, without worrying about him as he crossed the room discreetly, trying to make his huge body as small as he could.

Jacques, however, was surprised at Séverine's frequent absences. The first day, on doctor's orders, she had said nothing
about Henri's being downstairs, sensing that it would bring
Jacques peace and comfort to think that they were absolutely
alone.

'We are alone, aren't we?'

'Yes, my darling, we are alone, all alone . . . Sleep now.'

Only she kept disappearing, and on the following day he had
heard footsteps and whispering downstairs. Then next day there
was the sound of stifled merriment, and bright peals of laughter,
and two eager young voices talking incessantly.

'What's going on? Who is it? . . . Are we not alone, then?'

'Well, no, my darling, there's another injured person here, in
the room just below yours. I had to take him in.'

'Oh, who then?'

'Henri, you know, the chief guard.'

'Henri . . . Oh.'

'And this morning his sisters arrived. It's them you can hear,
they laugh at anything . . . He's much better, so they'll be leaving this evening, on account of their father who can't manage
without them. And Henri will be staying another two or three
days, just to make sure he's completely well again . . . Can you
imagine? He jumped, and not a bone was broken. Except that he
seemed to have lost his mind. But he's recovered now.'

Jacques was silent, fixing her with such a long stare that she
added:

'You do see, don't you? If he weren't here, people might
talk . . . As long as I'm not alone with you, there's nothing my
husband can say, and I have a good excuse for staying on here.
You do understand?'

'Yes, yes, it's fine.'

And until evening came, Jacques listened to the laughter of
the young Dauvergne girls, which he remembered having heard
in Paris coming up from the floor below just like this, in that
bedroom where Séverine had confessed in his arms. Then there
was quiet, and all he could hear was the soft tread of Séverine as
she went from him to the other patient. The door downstairs was
shut again, and the house fell once more into a profound silence.
Twice, when he was very thirsty, he had to bang on the floor

with a chair to get her to come up. And when she reappeared, she was all smiles, all anxious to help, explaining how she was never done because she had to keep changing cold compresses on Henri's head.

By the fourth day Jacques was able to get up and sit for two hours in an armchair next to the window. If he leant forward a little he could see the narrow garden, cut off short by the railway and enclosed by a low wall overgrown with pale dog-rose. He remembered the night when he had hoisted himself up to look over that wall, and he could see once more the quite extensive grounds which lay on the other side of the house, bounded simply by a hedge, the hedge he had come through and behind which he had run into Flore sitting on the step of the little tumbledown greenhouse, busy untangling some stolen rope with the help of scissors. Oh, that dreadful night, full of the horror of his malady! And there was Flore, like a blonde Amazon with that tall, lithe figure of hers, and those blazing eyes fixed hard on his; he just couldn't get her out of his mind once the memory of her had begun to return to him with increasing clarity. From the start he had made no reference to the accident, and no one mentioned it in his company, just in case. But every detail was coming back to him, and he was beginning to piece the whole thing together; it was the only thing he thought about, and so insistently indeed that now, sitting at this window, his sole occupation was to search for traces of the disaster, to look out for the principal actors in the drama. So why didn't he see her any more, at her post by the crossing gate, flag in hand? He dared not put the question, but it added to the uneasiness he felt in this gloomy house, which seemed to be full of ghosts.

One morning, however, when Cabuche was there helping Séverine, he eventually decided to ask.

'What about Flore, is she ill?'

The quarryman, startled, misunderstood Séverine's gesture and thought she was telling him to speak.

'Poor Flore is dead!'

Jacques was looking at them and shaking, so they were obliged to tell him the whole story. Between them they related the girl's suicide, how she had got herself run over by a train, in the tunnel. They had delayed the mother's burial until the evening so that they could take the daughter with them at the same time; and they were now at rest, side by side, in the little cemetery at Doinville, where they had gone to join the first deceased, the younger daughter, that sweet, unfortunate Louisette, who had also met with a violent end, covered in blood and dirt. Three wretched creatures, of the kind who fall by the wayside and are crushed, and now departed as though swept away by the terrible gust of wind created by the passing trains!

'Dead, my God!' Jacques repeated softly. 'My poor Aunt Phasie, and Flore, and Louisette!'

At this last name, Cabuche, who was helping Séverine move the bed, instinctively looked up at her, troubled by the memory of his former affection in the midst of this new passion which had overtaken him and against which, being the affectionate creature of limited intelligence he was, he had absolutely no defence, like a good dog that bestows its loyalty from the first moment it is stroked. But Séverine, who knew about his tragic love-affair, maintained a grave expression and shot him a look of sympathy; he was deeply touched and, his hand brushing accidentally against hers as he passed her the pillows, he choked back a sob before stammering out a reply to the question which Jacques was asking him.

'Were they saying that she caused the accident, then?'

'Oh, no, no . . . Only, it *was* her fault, you see.'

In broken sentences Cabuche told what he knew. He himself had seen nothing, for he was inside the house when the horses had moved forward and so placed the dray across the track. That was his one abiding regret, and the gentlemen of the law had reprimanded him severely for it: one did not leave one's animals unattended, the dreadful calamity would not have happened if he had remained with them. So the enquiry had found in the end that simple negligence on Flore's part was to blame; and as she had punished herself in that atrocious manner, there the matter rested, they weren't even going to transfer Misard who, with that meek, deferential way of his, had got out of trouble by blaming it all on the dead girl: she'd always been a law unto herself, and he'd forever had to leave his hut to go and shut the gate for her. Moreover the Company had been unable to find other than that he had conscientiously carried out his duties that morning; and until such time as he remarried, it had authorized him to take on an old woman of the neighbourhood to look after the gate, a former serving-girl called Ducloux, who lived on ill-gotten gains amassed in earlier days.

When Cabuche left the room, Jacques with a look bid Séverine remain behind. He was very pale.

'You do know it was Flore who pulled the horses across and blocked the track with all that stone?'

Séverine blenched in turn.

'Darling, what on earth are you saying! . . . You're feverish, you must get back into bed!'

'No, no, I'm not imagining things . . . Don't you understand? I saw her, as plainly as I can see you now. She was holding the horses back, she was stopping the dray from going any further, with that strong grip of hers.'

Then Séverine sank into a chair opposite him, her legs no longer able to support her.

'My God, my God, that's terrifying . . . It's monstrous, I shall never sleep sound again.'

'It's perfectly simple, damn it,' he continued. 'She tried to kill us, the pair of us, amongst the rest . . . She'd been after me for ages, she was jealous. On top of which, she was not quite right in the head, she had some funny ideas . . . So many murdered at a stroke, all those people covered in blood! Ah, the bitch!'

His eyes widened, and a nervous twitch began to pull at his lips; he fell silent, and they continued to look at each other for a full, long minute more. Then tearing himself away from the awful things they were both picturing in their minds, he continued in a low voice:

'So she's dead, so it's been her coming back, then! Ever since I came to, I've been feeling all the time as though she were here. Only this morning I turned round, thinking she was standing at the head of the bed . . . She is dead, and we are alive. As long as now she doesn't seek vengeance!'

Séverine shuddered.

'Shut up, just shut up! You'll drive me out of my mind.'

And she left the room. Jacques heard her going down to the other patient. He remained at the window and became lost once more in his scrutiny of the railway line, and the little crossing-keeper's house with its large well, and the section-post, the tiny wooden hut in which Misard seemed to doze his way through his regular and monotonous duties. These things absorbed Jacques's attention for hours on end, as though he were seeking the answer to a problem he could not solve and upon the solution of which his salvation nevertheless depended.

As to Misard, he never tired of watching him, that puny, meek, pasty-faced creature, continually racked by a nasty little cough, who'd poisoned his wife, who'd seen off that sturdy woman like some gnawing insect, driven on by his stubborn obsession. Quite evidently he had had no other idea in his head for years, night or day, through the twelve long hours of his shift. Each time the electric bell rang signalling the arrival of a train, sound the hooter; then, once the train was past and the section blocked, press one button to alert the next section-post and press another to give the line clear to the preceding section-post: these were simple, automatic movements which had become like bodily functions in his vegetable existence. Illiterate and dull-witted, he never read anything but just sat there, his hands dangling by his side, his eyes glazed and vacant, waiting to be summoned by his instruments. Since he spent almost the whole time seated in his hut, his only distraction was to spend as long as possible over his lunch. Then he would relapse into his usual dazed stupor, with his mind totally blank, not a thought in it, tormented only by terrible drowsiness, and sometimes falling asleep with his eyes open. At night, in order not to succumb to this irresistible torpor, he had to get up and walk about, his legs unsteady as though he were drunk. And this was why his battle with his wife—that silent struggle for the hidden thousand francs, to see which of them would have the money after the other was dead—must have been the sole subject of reflection, for months on end, inside the numbed brain of this solitary man. When he sounded the hooter or changed his signals, watching like an automaton over the safety of so many lives, he would be thinking of the poison; and when he was sitting there waiting, with his arms hanging limply by his side and his eyes flickering with sleep, he would still be thinking of it. And of nothing else: he would kill her, he would search, it was he who would have that money.

Today Jacques was astonished to find him quite unchanged. So one could kill without a tremor, and life went on as before. And indeed after the first, feverish searching, Misard had become his old phlegmatic self again, full of the sly gentleness of a feeble creature who is afraid of being knocked about. In the end he had devoured his wife to no purpose, she had triumphed all the same; for he was beaten, he kept turning the house upside down and finding nothing, not a centime; and in his pallid face only the eyes, those anxious, darting looks, told of his preoccupation. He kept seeing the dead woman's staring eyes, and the hideous grin on her lips repeating: 'Keep looking! Keep looking!' He was looking all right, he was powerless to give his brain even a moment's respite now; endlessly it worked, and worked, seeking out the place where the hoard was buried, going over all the possible hiding-places, rejecting those which he had already searched, in a fever of excitement when he thought of a new one, and then burning with such impatience that he would abandon everything and hasten to it, but all in vain: an intolerable torment in the end, a form of vengeful torture, a kind of mental insomnia which kept him awake, stupefied, yet still thinking in spite of himself, as his brain ticked on with its obsession. When he blew his hooter, once for the down trains and twice for the up, he was searching; when he responded to the bells, when he pressed the buttons on his instruments, blocking and clearing the line, he was searching; ceaselessly he searched, desperately he searched, by day during his long periods of waiting and when heavy with the torpor of inactivity, and again by night, tormented with the need to sleep, as though exiled to the far end of the world in the silence of the vast, dark countryside. Meanwhile the Ducloux woman, who now looked after the gate, was, in her keenness to procure herself a husband, full of little attentions towards him and worried that he seemed never to sleep a wink these days.

One night, Jacques, who was beginning to take a few steps around the bedroom, had got out of bed and approached the window, when he saw a lantern moving to and fro at Misard's: evidently the man was searching. But the following night, as he was watching again, he was astonished to recognize the great, dark shape of Cabuche standing on the road outside the adjacent room in which Séverine slept. And, without knowing why, instead of it irritating him, this filled him with sadness and a feeling of commiseration: another poor devil, that great brute of a man, stuck there like some demented, faithful beast. Clearly Séverine, who was so slight and not at all beautiful in her separate features, must have been able to exercise some considerable charm, with her ink-black hair and pale, periwinkle eyes, if even savages, half-witted hulks, were so possessed in their flesh that they spent the night at her gate like nervous young boys! He remembered certain details, the quarryman's eagerness to help her, the slavish looks with which he offered his services. Yes, there was no doubt, Cabuche loved her, desired her. And next day he watched him closely and saw him furtively pick up a hair-grip which had fallen from her chignon while she was making the bed, and then keep it in his fist so as not to have to give it back. And Jacques thought of his own torment, of all he had suffered through his own desire, of all the fear and agitation which were returning with his health.

Two more days went by, the week was coming to an end, and, as the doctor had predicted, the injured men would soon be able to return to work. One morning, standing at the window, Jacques saw his fireman, Pecqueux, go past aboard a brand-new engine, waving his hand as though beckoning to him. But Jacques was in no hurry, he was detained here by the renewed stirrings of his passion, a sort of anxious expectancy as he awaited what was due to take place. That same day he again heard the sound of fresh, young laughter downstairs, the merriment of teenage girls filling the gloomy house with the clamour of a school at break-time. He had recognized the Dauvergne girls. He did not mention them to Séverine, who in any case kept absenting herself that day, unable to spend more than five minutes at his side. Then, that evening, the house relapsed once more into deathly silence. And as she lingered in his bedroom, looking serious and a little pale, he looked hard at her and asked:

'So he's left, has he? His sisters have taken him?'

Her reply was curt:

'Yes.'

'And so finally we're alone, absolutely alone?'

'Yes, quite alone . . . Tomorrow we shall have to part, I'm going back to Le Havre. It's all over, no more camping out in the wilds.'

He smiled awkwardly, as he continued to gaze at her. All the same he steeled himself:

'You're sorry he's gone, aren't you?'

She gave a start, and made to demur, but he stopped her:

'It's all right, I'm not trying to pick a quarrel. You can see I'm not jealous. One day you told me to kill you if you were ever unfaithful to me, and, well, do I look like a lover who's thinking of killing his mistress? . . . But it's true, you know, you were always down there. It was impossible to have you to myself even for a minute. I finally remembered what your husband used to say, how one fine day you'd end up sleeping with that chap, not so much for the pleasure of it but more for the sake of making a fresh start.'

She had ceased to protest, and slowly she repeated the words:

'A fresh start, a fresh start . . .'

Then, in a burst of irrepressible candour:

'Well, yes, it's true . . . We can tell each other everything, can't we? There are so many things that bind us together after all . . . He'd been pursuing me for months, that man. He knew I was going with you, and he thought I could just as easily go with him. And when I found myself in his company again downstairs, he mentioned it once more, and he kept telling me he was madly in love with me, and with such a look of gratitude on his face for my looking after him, and in such a sweet, loving way that, well, it's perfectly true, I did think for a moment that I loved him too, that I could make a fresh start, a start on something better, on something quiet and gentle . . . Yes indeed, something with no pleasure in it perhaps, but which would have brought me peace . . .'

She broke off, hesitating before continuing:

'Because now, for you and me, there's just no way forward, we're not going anywhere . . . Our dream of going away, the hope that we might be rich and content over there in America, all that happiness which depended on you, it's impossible now, because you weren't able . . . Oh, I'm not blaming you, indeed it's better the deed wasn't done. But I want you to understand that with you I've nothing more to look forward to. Tomorrow will be the same as today, the same problems, the same torments.'

He was letting her run on, and put his question only when he saw her fall silent.

'And so that's why you slept with him?'

She had begun to walk away, and she turned back, shrugged:

'No, I haven't slept with him, and I can tell you that quite simply, and you'll believe me, I know you will, because from now on there's no point in us lying to each other . . . No, I couldn't bring myself to, no more than you could with that other business. That surprises you, doesn't it, that a woman can't give herself to a man even though she's thought the matter through and decided it would be in her interests. In my case I didn't even weigh it up like that, I'd never had any difficulty doing what was asked of me, giving pleasure I mean, to my husband or to you, when I saw how much each of you loved me. Well, this time, I couldn't. He kissed my hands, but apart from that not even on the lips, I swear to you. He's waiting for me in Paris, for me to join him later, because I could see how unhappy he was and I didn't want to leave him with no hope at all.'

She was right, Jacques believed her; he could see perfectly well that she wasn't lying. And again he was seized with panic as the awful tumult of his desire increased within him at the thought that he was now shut up alone with her, cut off from the world, surrounded by the flames of their rekindled passion. He wanted to escape, and cried out:

'But there's still someone else, there's still Cabuche.'

In a moment she was back beside him.

'Ah, so you've noticed, you've seen that too . . . Yes, that's right, there's him as well. I sometimes wonder what gets into them all . . . He's never said a word to me. But I can see him squirming every time you and me kiss. He hears me speaking intimately to you and goes off to have a cry. And he keeps taking all my things, gloves, handkerchiefs even, all disappearing off to his cave, his treasures . . . But you can't think I'd ever give in to that wild thing. He's too enormous, I'd be terrified. Anyway, he never asks for anything . . . No, no, when big brutes like that are timid, they die of love and ask for nothing. You could leave me in his keep for a month, and he wouldn't lay a finger on me, no more than he ever laid a finger on Louisette. I can vouch for that now.'

Their eyes met at the memory of this, and there was a silence. The past rose before them: their meeting at the magistrate's in Rouen, and then their first trip to Paris, which had brought such sweet pleasure, and their love-making at Le Havre, and everything that had then followed, the good as well as the bad. She came closer, and stood so near to him that he could feel the warmth of her breath.

'No, no, even less likely with him than with Dauvergne. No chance of it with any of them, you see, because I couldn't . . . And do you want to know why? Oh yes, I can feel it now, I know I'm right: it's because you have totally taken possession of me. There's no other word for it: yes, taken possession, the way one takes something in one's two hands and carries it away and uses it every minute of the day, like some personal belonging. Before you I was no one's. Now I am yours, and yours I will remain, even if you don't want me to be, even if I don't want to be . . . I just can't explain it. We've simply been brought together. With the others it frightens me, and repulses me, whereas with you, you've made it into a delicious pleasure, true heavenly bliss . . . Oh, I love only you, I shall only ever be able to love you!'

She was reaching out her arms, about to take him to herself in an embrace, to lay her head against his shoulder, with her lips to his. But he had seized her hands and was holding her at a distance, distraught, terrified to feel the trembling of old once more travelling up his legs, and the blood pounding in his skull. It was the same ringing in the ears, the same hammer-blows, the same thronging tumult of his terrible, erstwhile attacks. For some time now he had been unable to make love to her in daylight or even by the light of a candle, for fear of going mad if he caught sight of her. And now there was a lamp beside them, shining its light fully on both of them; and if he was trembling like this and beginning to grow wild, it was no doubt because he could see the white curves of her breasts through the unbuttoned collar of her dressing-gown.

Imploring him in the heat of her passion, she continued:

'What does it matter if there's no way forward? It's just too bad! So I can't expect anything different from you, so I know that tomorrow will bring us the same problems: what do I care? All I can do is live on as before and suffer with you. We'll go back to Le Havre, and what will be will be, just as long as I can have you to myself for an hour or two like this, once in a while . . . The last three nights I haven't slept a wink, lying there in my room across the landing, tortured with the need to come to you. You'd been so ill, you seemed so depressed, that I didn't dare . . . But, please, keep me with you, this one night. You'll see how good it will be, and I'll make myself as small as possible so as not to be in your way. And, well, it *is* our last night . . . Here we are in this house, at the end of the world. Listen, not a sound, not a soul. No one can disturb us, we're alone, so absolutely alone that nobody would ever know if we were to die in each other's arms.'

In the frenzy of his desire to have her, and excited by her caresses, Jacques, having no other weapon, was already stretching out his fingers to strangle Séverine when she herself, from habit, turned and put out the lamp. Then he took her, and they lay together. It was one of their most passionate nights of love, the best of all, the only time when they had felt completely merged together, completely obliterated each in the other. Exhausted by their pleasure and numbed to the point where they could no longer feel their own bodies, they nevertheless remained awake, locked in an embrace. And just as he had in Paris during the night of her confession in Mère Victoire's room, he listened in silence while she whispered word after word into his ear. Perhaps this evening she had felt the proximity of death, just before she put out the lamp: until now she had remained blithe and unaware in the face of the constant threat of murder which hung over her as she lay in her lover's arms. But this time she had felt the tiny, cold shiver of death, and it was this unaccountable feeling of terror and her need for protection which made her cling so fast to this masculine chest. Her gentle breathing was like the very gift of her person.

'Oh, my darling, if only you'd been able to manage it, how happy we would have been over there . . . ! No, no, I'm not asking you any more to do what you cannot do; it's just that I'm so sad our dream never came true! . . . I was scared a moment ago. I don't know, I feel as though something's threatening me. I'm being silly probably, but I keep looking round all the time as though someone were there, ready to strike me down . . . And I only have you, my darling, to protect me. All my joy depends on you, you are now my one and only reason for living.'

Without replying, he held her tighter, putting into this squeeze that which he left unsaid: his feeling for her, his sincere desire to be good to her, the violent love which she had never ceased to inspire in him. And yet that evening he had wanted to kill her: for if she hadn't turned to put out the lamp, he would have strangled her, there was no doubt of it. He was never ever going to get better, the attacks came on as circumstances dictated but without his ever being able to identify or analyse their cause. After all, why this evening, when he'd found she'd been faithful to him, when she'd been so unreserved and trusting in her passion? Was it that the more she loved him, the more there rose within him, from out of the terrible shadows of male egotism, the desire to possess her, and to possess her to the point of destroying her? To have her even as the earth itself might have her: dead!

'Tell me, my love, why am I afraid like this? Do you know anything that might be threatening me?'

'No, no, don't worry, nothing's threatening you.'

'It's just that at times my whole body starts trembling. There's some constant danger or other, behind me, that I can't see but that I can sense perfectly well . . . But why *am* I afraid, then?'

'No, you mustn't, you're not to be afraid . . . I love you, I shan't let anyone harm you . . . Just feel how good it is to be here like this, each of us in the other's arms.'

There was a moment of silence, of bliss.

'Oh, my darling,' she continued in her caressing whisper, 'just think, night after night, all like this, nights without end when we'd be together as we are now, completely at one . . . We could sell this house, you know, and take the money and go and join that friend of yours in America, he's still waiting . . . Not a day goes by that I don't go to bed thinking of how our life might be over there . . . And every evening would be like this one. You would take me, I would be yours, and afterwards we would fall asleep in each other's arms . . . But you can't, I know. I don't talk about it to upset you, it just comes out, I can't help it.'

A sudden resolve seized hold of Jacques, as he came to a decision which he had already often taken: to kill Roubaud so as not to kill her. This time, like all the other times, he believed that his mind was firmly, unshakeably, made up.

'I couldn't manage it before,' he murmured in turn, 'but I shall. Didn't I promise you?'

Faintly she protested.

'No, don't promise, please don't . . . We feel dreadful afterwards, when you haven't had the courage . . . And anyway, it's a terrible thing, we mustn't. No, no, we mustn't.'

'Yes, but we must, you know perfectly well. It's because we've got to do it that I shall find the strength . . . I've been wanting to talk to you about it, and now we *are* going to talk about it because, being all on our own here, with no one to bother us, we don't really appreciate what it is we're saying.'

Already she was yielding, with a sigh, her heart pounding so violently that he could feel it beating against his own.

'Oh, my God, as long as it wasn't going to happen, I wanted it to . . . But now that it's in earnest, I shall never be able to stand it.'

They stopped talking, and a silence fell, heavy with the weight of this resolve. Around them they could feel the remoteness, the empty desolation, of this wild place. They were very hot, lying there with their damp limbs entwined, fused into one.

Then, as he idly caressed her and kissed her under the chin, it was she who continued in her soft murmur:

'He'd need to come out here . . . Yes, I could tell him to come, on some pretext or other. I don't know what. We can think of that later . . . And you could be waiting for him, couldn't you, hiding somewhere; and everything would take care of itself, because we're certain not to be disturbed here . . . Isn't that it? Isn't that what we've got to do?'

Obediently, as his lips travelled down from her chin to her breasts, he replied simply:

'Yes, yes.'

But she was thinking hard, weighing every detail; and as the plan developed in her head, she would comment and improve on it.

'Except, my darling, that we'd be stupid not to take precautions. If it meant being arrested the next day, I'd rather go on the way we are now . . . Look, I've read somewhere, I can't remember where, it must have been in a novel, that the best thing would be to make it look like suicide . . . He's been so odd for some time, so jumpy and depressed, that no one would be surprised to learn all of a sudden that he'd come out here to kill himself . . . But, well, we'd have to arrange it in such a way that the idea of suicide seemed plausible . . . Wouldn't we?'

'I suppose so.'

She continued thinking about it, a little breathlessly because he was pressing her breasts upwards to his lips so that he could kiss them all over.

'You know, something to cover our traces? . . . I know, that's an idea! What if he got it in the neck, all we'd have to do would be to carry him over between us and lay him across the line. Do you see? We could put his neck on a rail so that the first train that came along would cut his head off. And then they could search as they pleased: with everything crushed, there'd be no wound, nothing at all! . . . What do you think, would that do?'

'Yes, certainly, that would do very well.'

They were both becoming more and more aroused, and she was almost in high spirits, proud at her own inventiveness. Following a more insistent caress she trembled:

'No, stop, wait a moment . . . I'm thinking, my darling, it still won't do. If you stay here with me, suicide will look strange all the same. You'll have to leave. Do you see? Tomorrow you leave, but quite openly, in front of Cabuche, and Misard, so that your departure is firmly established. You take the train to Barentin and get off at Rouen for some reason or other; then, as soon as it's dark, you come back, and I let you in by the back door. It's only four leagues, you can be back in under three hours . . . That's it, I've got it now. That's all we need to do—if you want to, that is.'

'Yes, I want to, that's all we need to do.'

He had stopped kissing her and was now lying there thinking. And another silence ensued, in which they remained like this, motionless in each other's arms, as though completely absorbed in their future deed, which now was fixed upon, definite. Then slowly the feeling in their bodies returned, and they were crushing each other in an increasingly passionate embrace when she stopped and relaxed her grip.

'But wait! What's the pretext to make him come here? He'll only be able to catch the 8.00 train in the evening, when he finishes work, and he won't get here before ten: it's better that way . . . I know! The person Misard told me about who might buy the house, he's coming to look over it the day after tomorrow, in the morning! That's it, I'll telegraph my husband when I get up and tell him his presence is absolutely necessary. He'll be here tomorrow evening. You can leave in the afternoon and be back before he arrives. It will be dark, there's no moon, nothing to trouble us . . . It all fits perfectly.'

'Yes, perfectly.'

And this time, borne off into oblivion, they made love. When finally they fell asleep amidst the great silence, still in each other's arms, it was not yet light, but the first glimmerings of dawn were beginning to lighten the darkness in which they had lain concealed from one another as though wrapped in a black cloak. He slept until ten o'clock, deeply, in a dreamless sleep; and when he opened his eyes, he found himself alone, she was dressing in her room across the landing. A sheet of bright sunlight was coming in at the window, making flames of the red curtains round the bed and the red wallpaper, of all the red with which the room was now ablaze, while the house shook with the roar of a train which had just gone by. It must have been the train which had woken him. Dazzled, he gazed at the sunlight and the red shimmering brightness in which he lay. Then he remembered: it was settled, this coming night he would kill, when this great sun had gone down.

Things proceeded that day as Séverine and Jacques had planned. Before breakfast she asked Misard to go to Doinville with a telegram for her husband; and at about three o'clock, when Cabuche was there, Jacques openly made ready for his departure. Indeed when he left, to catch the 4.14 at Barentin, the quarryman went with him, partly for something to do but also out of an unspoken need to be near him, being content to find in the lover a little of the woman he desired. Arriving in Rouen at twenty minutes to five, Jacques went to stay at an inn near the station, which was run by a woman who came from the same part of the world as him. He talked of going to see some friends of his the next day before returning to his duties in Paris. But he said how exhausted he was, how he'd been overdoing things; and at six o'clock he retired to his room to sleep, a room which he had requested on the ground floor and which had a window that opened on to a deserted alley. Ten minutes later he was on his way back to La Croix-de-Maufras, having climbed out of the window without being seen and taken care to close the shutter in such a way that he would be able to get back in without being discovered.

It was not until a quarter past nine that Jacques found himself once more in front of the lonely house, standing in its sorry state of abandon at an angle to the railway line. It was a very dark night, and not a gleam of light could be seen coming from the façade of the house, which seemed hermetically sealed. And once again he felt that stab of pain in the heart, that sudden jolt of dreadful misery, which was like a presentiment of the calamity awaiting him there, ready to play itself out to its inevitable conclusion. As arranged with Séverine, he tossed three small pebbles against the shutter of the red bedroom; then he went behind the house where in due course a door silently opened. Closing it behind him, he followed the sound of gentle footsteps up the stairs, groping his way. But when, upstairs, he saw by the light of the large lamp standing on the corner of a table, the bed already disturbed, Séverine's clothes strewn over a chair, and Séverine herself standing bare-legged in a nightdress, with her hair piled up high in thick strands ready for bed and revealing her bare neck, he stood still in astonishment.

'What, had you gone to bed already?'

'I think it's probably better this way . . . It occurred to me, you see, that when he arrives and I go down to let him in, dressed like this, he will be even less suspicious. I'll tell him that I had a headache. Misard already thinks I'm not feeling well. That will mean I can tell him that I never left this room, when they find him tomorrow morning down there on the line.'

But Jacques was shaking and becoming angry.

'No, no, get dressed . . . You must be up. You can't stay like that.'

She had begun to smile in surprise.

'But why ever not, my love? Don't worry, I promise I don't feel cold . . . Look, feel how warm I am!'

Playfully she sidled up to him and put her bare arms round his neck, raising her round breasts towards him as her nightdress slipped off one shoulder. But as he drew back in growing irritation, she became submissive.

'Don't be cross, I'll get back into bed. Then you needn't worry about me catching cold.'

When she had got back into bed and pulled the sheets up to her chin, he seemed indeed to become a little more calm. And she continued talking quite unperturbed, explaining how she envisaged things:

'As soon as he knocks, I shall go down and let him in. At first I thought of letting him come up here, where you could be waiting for him. But then getting him down again would have complicated things further; and anyway the floor in this room is wooden whereas in the hall it's stone, which I'll be able to wash easily . . . In fact, as I was getting undressed just now, I remembered a novel where the author describes how a man who's about to kill someone takes all his clothes off first. Do you see? You can wash afterwards, and there won't be a single mark on your clothes . . . So, why don't you take off your clothes too, why don't we both take everything off?'

He looked at her in terror. But with her sweet face and bright, girlish eyes, she was simply preoccupied with carrying things through to success. All this was simply what was going through her mind. But at the thought of them both naked and splashed with blood during the murder, he was seized once more by that dreadful shuddering which shook him to his core.

'No, no . . . we'd be like savages. Why not eat his heart while we're at it? You really do hate him, don't you?'

Séverine's expression suddenly darkened. This question plunged her, from her thoughts of prudent, housewifely preparation, into the horror of the act itself. Tears welled up in her eyes.

'I've suffered too much in the last few months, I can hardly be expected to love him. I've said it a hundred times: anything, anything rather than stay even another week with that man. But you're right, it's awful that it should have come to this, we really must want desperately to be happy together . . . Anyway, as I was saying, we'll go down without the light. You can stand behind the door, and when I've opened it and he has come in, you can do what you will . . . My part is just to help you, so that you don't have to do it all on your own. I'm just trying to plan it as best I can.'

He had stopped beside the table on seeing the knife, the weapon which had already been used by the husband himself, and which she had evidently placed there for him to strike Roubaud with in his turn. Fully opened, the knife lay gleaming in the lamplight. He picked it up and examined it. She was silent, gazing at it also. Since he was now holding the knife, there was no point in her elaborating further. And she went on only when he had put it down again on the table.

'I mean, my love, it's not that I'm trying to make you do it. There's still time, leave now if you think you can't manage it.'

But with a violent gesture he insisted:

'What do you take me for, a coward? This time I'll do it, I swear to you.'

At that moment the house was shaken by the roar of a train, which passed like lightning so close to the bedroom that its thunderous rumble seemed to traverse the room itself; and he added:

'That's his train, the through train to Paris. He's got off at Barentin, he'll be here in half an hour.'

Neither Jacques nor Séverine spoke further, and a long silence ensued. They pictured the man out in the dark night making his way along the narrow paths. Jacques had begun automatically to pace about the room, as if he were counting the other man's footsteps as each one brought him nearer and nearer. Another, and another: and with the last footstep he would ambush him behind the hall door, he would plant the knife in his neck the moment he entered. Séverine, lying in bed with the sheet still pulled up to her neck, watched him with big, staring eyes as he came and went in the room, her mind lulled by the rhythm of his pacing, which came to her like the echo of those distant footsteps. On they would go, one after another, ceaselessly, nothing now could stop them. When there had been a sufficient number, she would get out of bed and go down, barefoot, without a light, to let him in. 'It's you, darling, come in, I'd gone to bed.' And he would not even reply, he would fall in the darkness, his throat slit.

Once more a train went by, a down train this time, the slow which passed the through train some five minutes before La Croix-de-Maufras. Jacques had stopped in surprise. Only five minutes gone! How long this half-hour wait was going to be! The need to keep moving drove him on, and he began once more to pace up and down the room. He was already having anxious doubts, like those males who find their virility affected by momentary nerves: would he manage it? He was well familiar with the phenomenon and the course it took, having observed its progress a dozen times at least: first came the certainty, an absolute resolve to kill; then a tightness in the chest, and a coldness in the feet and hands; and all at once the collapse, the inability of the will to control muscles which had gone slack. In order to goad himself on by reason, he kept repeating what he had already told himself so many times: the interest he had in eliminating this man, the fortune awaiting him in America, possessing the woman he loved. The worst of it was that when he had found her half-naked just now, he had been sure that it was all going wrong again; for he ceased to be his own man the moment that shuddering of old came back. For an instant he had worried that the temptation was too strong, with her offering herself like that and the knife lying open and to hand. But now he was solidly in control, firm, erect, ready for the effort. He would manage it. And he continued to wait for the man, pacing the room from door to window and each time trying not to look as he passed by the bed.

Lying in this bed where they had made love during the dark, burning hours of the previous night, Séverine still did not move. Her head motionless on the pillow, she followed him with her eyes this way and that, herself anxious too, troubled by the fear that this time, once again, he would not dare. To have done with it and make a fresh start, that was all she wanted, with the unconcern of a woman whose nature is to love, to be the willing helpmeet, totally devoted to the man who now possessed her and unfeeling towards the man whom she had never desired. He was in the way, so you got rid of him; what could be more natural? And she had to reflect consciously before she could feel moved by the abominable nature of the crime: as soon as she stopped picturing the blood and the horrible complications, she reverted to a state of cheerful calm, and her innocent face was filled with tenderness and compliance. And yet, though she thought she knew Jacques well, she was surprised. Here was the round, handsome face, the curly hair, the jet-black moustache, and those brown eyes speckled with gold, but his lower jaw jutted out so far, like some ravening beast's, that it quite disfigured him. Passing by just now, he had looked at her, as though in spite of himself, and the brightness in his eyes had been clouded by a red mist, while his whole body seemed to recoil from her. Why was he avoiding her? Was it, yet again, that his courage was failing him? For some time now, unaware of the continual danger of death which she ran by being in his presence, she had interpreted the baseless, instinctive fear she felt as the presentiment of an imminent break in their relationship. Suddenly she knew for certain that if, in the coming moments he found himself once more unable to strike, he would disappear and never return. So she determined that he *would* kill, that she would succeed in giving him the strength to do it, if the need arose. At that moment another train was passing, an interminable goods train, whose string of wagons seemed to have been rolling past for an eternity in the heavy silence of the room. And, propped up on her elbow, she lay waiting for the blast of this hurricane to fade into the distance, far away in the sleeping countryside.

'Quarter of an hour to go,' Jacques said out loud. 'He's past Bécourt forest by now, halfway here. God, doesn't the time pass slowly!'

But as he was coming back from the window, he found Séverine standing in front of the bed, in her nightdress.

'What about going down with the lamp?' she suggested. 'You could see the actual spot, choose your position, and I could show you how I'll open the door and which way you'll need to strike.'

He was recoiling, trembling.

'No! No! Not with the lamp!'

'But why? We can always hide it afterwards. We should really go and look.'

'No, no. Get back into bed!'

Refusing to obey, she was instead walking towards him, with that invincible, despotic smile of a woman who knows how omnipotent she has been rendered by another's desire. Once she had held him in her arms, he would yield to her flesh, he would do as she wished. And she continued to talk, soothingly, to subdue him.

'But what is it, my darling, what's the matter? Anyone would think you were afraid of me. Whenever I go near you, you seem to avoid me. And if you only knew at this moment how much I need to feel you close, to know that you are there, that we are one together, for ever and ever, don't you see?'

She had finally backed him up against a table: he could flee her no further, and he beheld her in the bright light of the lamp. Never had he seen her like this, with her nightdress open and her hair piled so high that she was completely uncovered, her neck naked, her breasts naked. He was choking, struggling, already gripped, dazed by the blood rushing to his head, by the dreadful shuddering. And he remembered that the knife was there, behind him, on the table: he could sense its presence, all he had to do was to stretch out his hand.

With great effort he still managed to stammer out:

'Get back into bed, I beg you.'

But she was in no doubt: it was the overwhelming strength of his desire for her that was making him tremble like this. It made her feel somehow proud. Why would she have obeyed him, since she wanted to be loved that night as much as he possibly could love her, loved till she went mad with it. Soft and wheedling, she continued to edge closer and closer to him, and now she was upon him.

'Come on, kiss me . . . Kiss me hard, the way you love me. It will give us courage . . . Oh yes, courage, that's what we need. We must love each other differently from other people, more than all the others, to be able to do what we are going to do . . . Kiss me with all your heart, with all your soul.'

Choking for air, he could no longer breathe. A tumultuous din inside his head blocked out all other sound. Behind his ears, it felt as though red-hot teeth were tearing holes in his skull, before attacking his arms and legs, driving him out of his own body even as that other self, the invading beast, rushed headlong in. Soon his hands would cease to be his own, amidst the overwhelming intoxication of this female nudity. The bare breasts crushed against his clothes, the bare neck stretched up, so white and delicate, irresistibly tempting; and the sovereign sway of her sharp, warm scent finally reduced him to a state of wild dizziness, an endless, giddy oscillation, in which his independent will, torn from him and destroyed, was vanishing without trace.

'Kiss me, my darling, while we still have a minute . . . You know he'll be here any moment. Even now he may knock at any second, if he has walked quickly . . . Since you don't want us to go down, just remember: I'll open the door to him, and you'll be behind the door; and don't wait, do it immediately, oh yes, immediately, and get it over with . . . I love you so much, we'll be so happy together! He's just a wicked man who has made me suffer, the one thing that stands in the way of our happiness . . . Kiss me, oh, kiss me hard, hard! Kiss me as if you were devouring me, so there's nothing left of me that's not inside you!'

Without turning round, groping behind him with his right hand, Jacques had taken hold of the knife. And for a moment he remained like that, gripping it tight. Had that thirst of his returned, that thirst to avenge ancient wrongs which he could no longer quite remember, that sense of grievance accumulated from male to male ever since that first betrayal in the depths of some cave? He fixed his crazed eyes upon Séverine and felt only the need to sling her dead body over his shoulder, like a prey snatched away from others. The gates of horror were opening on to the black chasm of sexuality, of love unto death, of destruction as the most complete possession.

'Kiss me, kiss me . . .'

She offered up her submissive face in loving supplication, exposing her bare neck where it rose voluptuously from her bosom. And he, catching sight of this white flesh as though in the sudden flaring of a blaze, raised his fist, armed with the knife. But she had seen the flash of the blade, and recoiled, gaping in astonishment and terror.

'Jacques, Jacques . . . My God! But why me, why?'

His teeth clenched, he said nothing; he went after her. A brief struggle brought her back to the edge of the bed. She shrank back, defenceless, her nightdress ripped, with a wild look in her eyes.

'But why? My God, why?'

He brought his fist down, and the knife pinned the question to her throat. In doing so he had twisted the weapon, as though his hand were satisfying some gruesome need of its own: the same blow that did for President Grandmorin, in the same place, with the same savagery. Had she cried out? He never knew. At that very moment the Paris express was passing, so violently and so rapidly that the floor shook; and she had died as though struck by lightning during the storm.

Jacques now stood motionless, staring down at her as she lay stretched out at his feet in front of the bed. The sound of the train was fading into the distance, and he gazed at her in the heavy silence of the room. Surrounded by the red walls and the red curtains, she lay there with blood pouring from her, a red stream running down between her breasts and spreading out over her belly till it reached the thigh, from which it fell in large drops on to the wooden floor. The nightdress, half-rent in two, was soaked in it. He would never have believed she could have so much blood in her. And what held his gaze, what haunted him, was the expression of appalling terror assumed in death by the face of this pretty, gentle, most docile of women. Her black hair had stood on end, a helmet of horror as dark as the night. The periwinkle eyes, immeasurably wide, were still asking 'Why?', stunned and terrified by the mystery of it all. Why, why had he killed her? And she had just been crushed and borne away in the fateful path of murder, a person whom life had steeped in filth and now in blood without her being really aware of it, so that she remained none the less loving and innocent, never having understood.

But Jacques listened in surprise. He could hear an animal snorting or was it the grunting of a wild boar, the roaring of a lion? Then his mind was set at rest, it was only the sound of his own breathing. At last, at last, he had found satisfaction, he had killed! Yes, he had done that. A burst of frantic joy, an enormous sense of pleasurable relief, bore him up in the full satisfaction of eternal desire. He felt a sudden surge of pride, as though his supremacy as a male had somehow been enhanced. He had killed womankind, and he possessed her now as he had for so long desired to possess her, completely, even unto destruction. She was no more, she would never belong to anyone now. And a vivid memory came to him of that other murder victim, of President Grandmorin's corpse which he had seen on that terrible night five hundred metres from where he now stood. This delicate body, so white, streaked with red, was the same tatter of humanity, the same broken puppet, the same limp rag to which a living creature is reduced by the simple stab of a knife. Yes, this was it. He had killed, and there it was on the ground. She had toppled over just like the other one, but on her back, with her legs apart, her left arm bent under her side, and the right one twisted half out of its socket. Was this not the night when he had sworn, with pounding heart, that he in turn would dare to do it, to do it out of an itch to murder that had turned into a violent lust at the sight of that man who had had his throat slit? Oh, to have the nerve, to satisfy the need, to plunge the knife in! Darkly this need had germinated and grown within him, and for a year now every hour that passed had brought him closer to the inevitable; even in this woman's arms, and as she kissed him, the silent process had continued. And now the two murders had come together. Was not one the logical consequence of the other?

Jacques was roused from his gaping contemplation of the dead woman by a violent sound of collapsing masonry and a shaking floor. Were the doors about to shatter into tiny pieces? Were they coming to arrest him? He looked about him and found only unresponsive solitude. Oh, of course, yet another train! And then there was that man about to knock at the door downstairs, the man he had been meaning to kill! He had forgotten all about him. Though he regretted nothing, already he saw how foolish

he had been. What was this? What had happened? Here was the
woman he loved, and who had passionately loved him, lying on
the floor with her throat slit; while her husband, the obstacle to
his happiness, was still alive and coming towards him, step by
step, through the darkness. He had not been able to wait for the
man whose life he had been sparing for months because of the
scruples born of education, and all the humane notions which
had gradually been acquired and transmitted from one generation to another; and against his own interests he had just been
carried away by the heritage of violence, by that need to kill
which, in primordial forests, had once set beast upon beast. As if
one killed by calculation! A person kills only from an impulse
that springs from his blood and sinews, from the vestiges of
ancient struggles, from the need to live and the joy of being
strong. All Jacques felt now was a sated weariness; and he began
to panic, to try to understand, but he encountered instead, even
at the heart of his satisfied passion, only astonishment and bitter
sadness at what could not be undone. The sight of the poor
woman still gazing at him in terrified enquiry was becoming
unbearable. He tried to look away, and suddenly had the impression that another white shape was standing at the foot of the
bed. Was it the dead woman's double? Then he recognized
Flore. She had come back before, when he had been feverish
after the accident. No doubt she was gloating at finding herself
now avenged. He froze with horror, and began to wonder what
on earth he was doing, still lingering in this room like this. He
had killed, he was gorged, replete, drunk, on the terrible liquor
of crime. Tripping on the knife that still lay on the floor, he made
a run for it, tumbling down the stairs and flinging open the great
hall door as though the smaller door within it were insufficiently
wide; he hurled himself out into the inky blackness of the night,
and tore madly off into the distance. He had not looked back,
and the strange house, standing at an angle to the railway line,
stood open and desolate behind him, in the deserted solitude of
death.

That night as on every other, Cabuche had come through the
hedge and was hanging about beneath Séverine's window. He
knew that Roubaud was expected, and was not surprised at the
light filtering through a chink in one of the shutters. But the

sight of this man leaping down the front steps and galloping off into the countryside like some crazed beast had just brought him up short in astonishment. And since it was already too late to run after the fugitive, the quarryman stood there bewildered, filled with anxiety and uncertainty in front of this door and the great black hole of the hallway on to which it opened. What was going on? Should he go in? The heavy silence, the complete stillness, with that lamp still burning upstairs, made his heart contract with growing anguish.

At length Cabuche made up his mind and began to grope his way upstairs. Outside the bedroom door, which had also been left open, he stopped again. In the soft lamplight he thought he could make out a pile of skirts, lying over beside the bed. Séverine must have undressed. Gently he called to her, in sudden agitation, as his pulse raced. Then he saw the blood, he understood, and rushed forward with a terrible scream that sprang from the depths of his breaking heart. My God, it was her, murdered, just thrown there on to the floor in all her pitiable nakedness. He thought she was still breathing and felt such despair, such agonizing shame, to see her dying like this, completely naked, that he seized her in his arms as a brother might and lifted her on to the bed, folding back the sheet to cover her. But in the course of this embrace, this one moment of intimacy between them, he had got blood all over himself, on his chest and both his hands. He was streaming with her blood. And at that moment he saw Roubaud and Misard standing there. They too, on finding all the doors open, had decided to come up. Roubaud was late, having stopped to chat to the crossing-keeper, who had then accompanied him as they continued their conversation. Both men stood there appalled, staring at Cabuche whose hands were dripping blood like a butcher's.

'Same way as the President,' Misard said eventually, having examined the wound.

Roubaud nodded silently, unable to tear his eyes away from Séverine, from that expression of unspeakable terror, and the black hair standing on end above her forehead, and those blue eyes, opened so immeasurably wide, which were still asking 'Why?'

CHAPTER XII

THREE months later, on a warm June evening, Jacques was driving the Le Havre express, having left Paris at half-past six. He was beginning to get the measure of his new locomotive, No. 608, which had recently entered service (he had taken her virginity, as he put it); and she was proving rather cussed, being restive and temperamental like a young filly that has to be broken in by hard work before she will yield to the harness. He often swore at her, wishing he still had La Lison; he had to keep a close eye on her, and have his hand constantly on the gear-wheel. But on this particular evening the sky was so deliciously serene that he was feeling indulgent, allowing her to run on a little as the fancy took her, thankful himself to be taking great lungfuls of air. He had never felt better, was untroubled by remorse, and seemed to have been relieved of a burden, to be happy and at peace with the world.

He who normally never spoke during a journey now teased Pecqueux, whom they had continued to assign as his fireman.

'What's this, then? Anyone'd think you'd been sticking to water, you look so wide-awake.'

And indeed Pecqueux, contrary to his normal habits, seemed to be both stone-cold sober and deeply despondent. He answered in a harsh tone:

'Best to keep awake if you want to see what's going on.'

Jacques cast him a wary glance, as one whose conscience is far from clear. The previous week he had given in to his workmate's mistress, the incorrigible Philomène, who'd been rubbing herself against him for ages like some scrawny cat on heat. And he had done so without the slightest trace of sexual interest in her. More than anything he had yielded to the desire to experiment: now that he had satisfied his dreadful craving, was he definitively cured? Could he possess the woman without sticking a knife in her throat? He had already had her twice, and felt nothing, no hint of that queer feeling, not the slightest tremor. Though he was not conscious of the fact, his great joy and air of jovial contentment sprang undoubtedly from his delight at now being just a man like any other.

Pecqueux opened the firebox door to shovel in more coal, but Jacques stopped him.

'No, no, don't give her too much, she's doing fine.'

The fireman proceeded to mutter a number of unsavoury remarks.

'Oh, indeed, just fine . . . A little madam she is, a right tart! . . . When I think how we used to give the last one hell, and her so obedient! . . . This little trollop isn't even worth a kick up the arse.'

Rather than have a row, Jacques made no reply. But he was well aware that their threesome of old was no more; for the firm friendship between himself, his workmate, and the engine had ended with the death of La Lison. Now the pair of them quarrelled about the slightest thing, a nut screwed on too tight, a shovelful of coal incorrectly applied. So he promised himself he would be careful as regarded Philomène, not wanting things to reach the point of open hostility here on this narrow moving floor that carried them both along, the driver and the fireman side by side. So long as Pecqueux, out of gratitude for not being chivvied and being allowed to take the occasional nap and finish off the food-baskets, had played the part of his obedient dog, ready to spring at anyone's throat on his behalf, then the two men had lived as brothers, silent partners in their daily peril who had no need of words to understand each other perfectly. But it would be a living hell if they ceased to get on, rattling along together like this, cheek by jowl, but all the time intent on destroying each other. Indeed only the previous week the Company had had to separate the driver and fireman of the Cherbourg express because, having fallen out over a woman, the driver had been bullying the fireman, who had stopped obeying his orders; fisticuffs there had been, actual fights while the engine was under way, with never a thought for the trainload of passengers following along at top speed behind.

Twice more Pecqueux opened the firebox door and threw in some coal, deliberately disobeying Jacques and doubtless wanting to start a quarrel; and Jacques pretended not to notice, seemingly preoccupied with his driving but taking particular care each time to adjust the injector-wheel so as to reduce the pressure. The air was so pleasant, and the cool breeze in their faces felt so good as they sped along on this hot July night!* When the express reached Le Havre at five past eleven, the two men cleaned up the engine together, apparently on as good terms as ever.

But just as they were leaving the station to go and spend the night in the Rue François-Mazeline, a voice called to them:

'Are we in such a hurry, then? Come in for a minute.'

It was Philomène, who must have been watching out for Jacques from the door of her brother's house. She had looked decidedly put out to see Pecqueux; and she only resolved to hail both men for the pleasure of at least being able to talk to her new lover, at the price of having to put up with the presence of the old.

'Leave us be,' muttered Pecqueux. 'Stop pestering us, we both need to get some sleep.'

'What a friendly fellow!' Philomène merrily replied. 'But Monsieur Jacques isn't like you, he'll at least have a little drink with me, won't you, Monsieur Jacques?'

Jacques was about to refuse, to be on the safe side, when suddenly Pecqueux accepted, thinking he could then observe them together and so be absolutely certain. They went into the kitchen and sat down at the table, on which she had placed some glasses and a bottle of brandy. Lowering her voice, she continued:

'Try not to make too much noise, my brother's asleep upstairs, and he's not very keen on me having company.'

Then, as she was serving them, she added immediately:

'Incidentally, did you know old Madame Lebleu snuffed it this morning? . . . Oh, I said so at the time: it will kill her, I said, if they put her in that flat at the back. A proper prison it is. She lasted another four months, though, eating her heart out with nothing to look at but that zinc roof . . . And I'm sure what did for her in the end, once she couldn't leave her chair, was not being able to spy on Mademoiselle Guichon and Monsieur Dabadie any more. It'd been a habit with her. Yes indeed, it drove her mad that she'd never caught them at anything. And that's what killed her.'

Philomène paused to swallow a mouthful of brandy, and then added with a laugh:

'But of course they sleep together. Only they're so cunning! What the eye don't see . . . Though I think little Madame Moulin did spot them one evening. But there's not much danger of that one talking: she's too stupid, and anyway her husband, the assistant manager . . .'

Again she broke off and exclaimed:

'Oh yes, of course, it's next week, isn't it, that the Roubaud case comes up in Rouen?'

Until then Jacques and Pecqueux had listened without intervening. The latter simply thought she was being very chatty: she had never been much of a one for conversation when she was with him. And now he began to watch her closely, growing gradually more jealous as he saw her so animated in the presence of his driver.

'Yes,' Jacques replied with an air of perfect calm, 'I've been summoned to appear.'

Philomène drew closer, glad to brush against him with her elbow.

'Yes, I'm a witness too . . . Oh, Monsieur Jacques, when they questioned me about you—because, as you know, they wanted to find out the real truth about your connection with that poor lady—when they questioned me, I just told the magistrate: "But, Monsieur, he adored her, he can't possibly have done her any harm!" Well, I'd seen you together, hadn't I? I was in a position to know.'

'Oh,' the young man gestured casually, 'I wasn't worried. I was able to give them my movements hour by hour . . . That's why the Company kept me on, there wasn't the slightest thing I could be blamed for.'

Silence fell, and the three of them drank slowly.

'It's creepy, though,' Philomène went on. 'That wild beast, that Cabuche they arrested, still all covered in the poor lady's blood! There must be some stupid men about the place! Think of it, killing a woman just because you fancy her! As if that got them anywhere, with the woman dead and gone! . . . But what I shall never forget, I can tell you, for as long as I live, was Monsieur Cauche turning up on that platform over there and arresting

Monsieur Roubaud too. I was actually there. It was only a week,
you know, since Monsieur Roubaud had gone back to work, as
calm as you please, the day after his wife was buried. And there
was Monsieur Cauche tapping him on the shoulder and telling
him he had a warrant to take him off to prison. Imagine! The pair
of them, never out of each other's company, always gambling
together, for nights on end! But I suppose when you're a police-
man, you'd haul your own mother and father off to the guillo-
tine. It's all part of the job. Not that he cares, that Monsieur
Cauche. I saw him again at the Café du Commerce, just the other
day, and there he was shuffling his cards, no more worried about
his friend than the man in the moon!'

Pecqueux smashed his fist down on the table and said through
clenched teeth:

'God damn it! Oh, if I were Roubaud, if I were in that cuck-
old's shoes, I don't mind telling you . . . You were sleeping with
his wife, someone else goes and kills her, and then they send *him*
for trial! No, it's enough to make your blood boil!'

'But, you great fool,' cried Philomène, 'it's because he's accused of having the other man get rid of his wife for him. Yes, for
the money, or something like that anyway! It seems they found
President Grandmorin's watch at Cabuche's place. You remember, that gentleman that was murdered on the train a year and a
half ago. So they've connected that bad business with this
recent one, quite a saga, you could write a book about it. I can't
remember the ins and outs of it, but it was all in the newspaper,
two columns at least all about it.'

Jacques seemed not even to be listening, his attention elsewhere. He murmured:

'Why worry about it? What's it got to do with us? . . . If the
law doesn't know what it's doing, we're hardly going to do any
better.'

Then he added, his eyes gazing into the distance and his
cheeks suddenly pale:

'And in the end it all comes back to that poor woman . . . Oh,
that poor, poor woman!'

'Well if you ask me,' Pecqueux concluded angrily, 'me that
has a wife, if anyone dared lay a finger on her, I'd strangle the

pair of them for a start. And they could come and chop my head off then if they wanted to, I wouldn't care.'

There was a further silence. Philomène, who was refilling the little glasses, affected to shrug with a sneer. But underneath she was completely nonplussed, and she studied him out of the corner of her eye. Extremely dirty and with his clothes in tatters, he had been letting himself go ever since Mère Victoire had been crippled by her fracture and obliged to give up her job cleaning the lavatories and go into an institution. She was no longer about the place ready to be motherly and understanding, slipping him the odd coin and doing his mending because she did not want the other woman, the one in Le Havre, to accuse her of not looking after their man properly. And Philomène, attracted by the spruce, clean-cut appearance of Jacques, shot him a look of disgust.

'So you'd strangle your Paris wife then, would you?' she taunted. 'Not much danger of anyone taking *her* away from you!'

'Her or another,' he muttered.

But already she was cheerily proposing a toast.

'Your good health! And bring me your dirty clothes so I can wash and mend them, because really, you know, you're a disgrace to the pair of us women . . . And here's to your health too, Monsieur Jacques!'

Jacques gave a start, as though waking from a dream. Despite his complete lack of remorse, and in the midst of the sense of relief and physical well-being in which he had been living since the murder, the thought of Séverine would sometimes occur to him like this, reducing the gentler side of him to tears of pity. And he raised his glass, remarking hurriedly in order to conceal his distress:

'There's going to be war, you know.'

'Surely not!' exclaimed Philomène. 'But who with?'

'With the Prussians, of course . . . It's true, all because of some prince of theirs who wants to be King of Spain.* In Parliament yesterday they talked about nothing else.'

She then began to lament.

'Oh marvellous, that will be fun! As if that crowd in Paris hadn't caused us enough trouble already with their elections and their plebiscite and their riots! . . .* So if there is fighting, does that mean they'll take all the men?'

'Oh, we'll be all right, they can't disrupt the railways . . . Except they'd have us rushing all over the place, transporting troops and supplies! Anyway, if it comes to it, we'll just have to do our duty.'

Thereupon he stood up, conscious that she had slid her leg beneath his and that Pecqueux, who had noticed, was going red in the face and already clenching his fists.

'It's high time we went to bed.'

'Yes, we'd better,' the fireman spluttered.

He had grabbed Philomène by the arm and was squeezing it hard as though he might break it. She stifled a cry of pain, and instead simply whispered in Jacques's ear while the other man was furiously draining his glass:

'Watch out, he's a real brute when he's been drinking.'

But heavy footsteps could be heard coming down the stairs, and she panicked:

'My brother! . . . Quick, go, go on.'

The two men had hardly gone twenty paces from the house when they heard the sound of someone being slapped, followed by screaming. She was getting a terrible thrashing, like a little girl caught with her finger in the jam-pot. Jacques had stopped, ready to go to her rescue. But Pecqueux restrained him.

'What's it got to do with you, eh? . . . The little slut! God, if only he'd finish her off once and for all!'

Back in the Rue François-Mazeline Jacques and Pecqueux went to bed without exchanging another word. The two beds were almost touching in the narrow room; and for a long time they both lay awake, eyes wide open, each listening to the other's breathing.

The hearings in the Roubaud case were due to begin on Monday. The whole business represented a triumph on the part of Denizet, the examining magistrate, for there was no end of praise in legal circles for the way in which he had brought this complex and murky affair to a satisfactory conclusion: a masterpiece of subtle analysis, they said, a logical reconstruction of the truth, in short quite a creation.

The first thing Monsieur Denizet had done as soon as he reached the scene at La Croix-de-Maufras, a few hours after Séverine's murder, was to have Cabuche arrested. Everything quite clearly pointed to him, the blood dripping from him, the incriminating statements of Roubaud and Misard, who reported how they had found him with the body, all alone and distraught. When questioned and pressed to say why and how he had come to be in the room, the quarryman gave a garbled account which the magistrate greeted with a shrug of the shoulders, so much did it seem to be the same old, idiotic story. This tale was just what he'd been expecting, the usual yarn about the imaginary assassin, the fictitious culprit whom the real criminal said he had heard running off into the dark countryside. This werewolf would be miles away by now, wouldn't he, if he were still running? Anyway, when they asked him what he'd been doing hanging round outside the house at that hour of the night, Cabuche became flustered and refused to answer, finally saying that he'd been out for a walk. It was completely childish: how was one supposed to believe this story of a mysterious stranger coming along, killing Séverine, running away, and leaving all the doors open, without disturbing a single piece of furniture or taking so much as a handkerchief? Where was he supposed to have come from? Why would he have killed her? All the same, being aware of the relationship between the victim and Jacques, the magistrate had, from the beginning of the investigation, been concerned about the times of Jacques's movements; but not only had the accused testified to having accompanied Jacques to catch the train at Barentin at 4.14, the innkeeper at Rouen swore by all that was sacred that the young man had gone straight to bed after dinner and had not come out of his room until the following morning at about seven o'clock. And in any case a lover doesn't slit the throat of a mistress he adores without some good reason, especially a mistress with whom he's never had the shadow of a quarrel. It would be quite absurd. No, no, there was only one possible murderer, an obvious murderer, the man with a criminal record who had been caught red-handed at the scene with the knife at his feet, that dumb brute of a man who was telling the law some very tall stories.

But having reached this stage in his deliberations, and despite his own conviction, despite his nose for things, which, he said, told him more than any piece of evidence, Monsieur Denizet had then been given a moment's pause. When they had first searched the accused's hovel in the middle of Bécourt forest, absolutely nothing had been found. Unable therefore to establish a theft, another motive had to be found for the crime. Out of the blue, in the middle of being questioned, Misard put him on the scent by telling him that he had seen Cabuche one night climbing over the wall of the property to go and look through the window of the room where Madame Roubaud was getting ready for bed. Questioned in turn, Jacques calmly told what he knew, about the quarryman's silent worship of Séverine, and the ardour with which he pursued her, always under her feet, ever ready to serve. There could be no further doubt: brutish passion alone had driven him to it. And with this everything fell into place very nicely: the man returning by the door to which he could have had a key, perhaps even leaving it open in the heat of the moment; then the struggle which had led to the murder; and finally the rape, which had only been interrupted by the husband's arrival. However, one last objection presented itself, for it was odd that this fellow, knowing that the other man might arrive at any minute, should have chosen precisely the moment when the husband might catch him in the act. But on reflection this only made the accused's position worse, and indeed clinched the matter, because it showed that he must have acted in a moment of extreme desire, maddened by the thought that if he did not take advantage of Séverine's last moment alone in this isolated house, he would never have her, since she was leaving the next day. From then on the magistrate was utterly and unshakeably convinced.

Pressed by further interrogation, repeatedly caught out by the clever meshing of the questions but heedless of the traps being set for him, Cabuche stuck to his original story. He was passing by on the road and enjoying the cool night air when somebody had suddenly brushed past him, and going at such a rate in the darkness that he could not even tell which way he had gone. Then, concerned, he had looked across at the house and noticed that the front door was wide open. Finally he had decided to go up to the first floor, and there he had found the dead woman, her body still warm, staring at him with her great big eyes; so, meaning to put her on the bed, thinking she was still alive, he had got himself covered in blood. That was all he knew, all he said, and not a single detail changed, as though he were sticking rigidly to a story which he had fixed upon in advance. When they tried to make him depart from his version of events, he would panic and fall silent, as a man of limited intelligence does when he no longer quite understands. The first time Monsieur Denizet had interrogated him about his passion for the victim, he had turned very red, like some young boy being scolded for his first crush; and he had denied it, he had flatly rejected any suggestion that he had dreamt of sleeping with this lady as being something especially dreadful, not to be spoken of, something delicate and mysterious too, buried in the depths of his heart, which he need confess to no one. No, no, he didn't love her, he didn't desire her, nothing would induce him to talk about what seemed to him a profanation now that she was dead. But this stubborn refusal to admit something to which several witnesses attested was also beginning to tell against him. Clearly, given the nature of the charge, it was in his interests to conceal the frenzied desire he felt for the unfortunate woman, whose throat he had had to slit in order that it might be satisfied. And when the magistrate had faced him with all his hypotheses at once in an attempt to extract the truth from him, staking all on accusing him openly of the murder and the rape, Cabuche had flown into a wild rage of protest. Him, kill so he could have her! Him, who worshipped her like a saint! The gendarmes had to be called to restrain him, as he raved about slitting the throats of the whole damn lot of them! A thoroughly nasty piece of work in short, and cunning with it, but his violence gave him away all the same, was itself a confession of the very crimes which he sought to deny.

The investigation had reached this stage, with the accused flying into a rage every time they mentioned the murder and screaming that that other man had done it, the mysterious fugitive, when Monsieur Denizet made a discovery which transformed the whole case and made it suddenly ten times as important. As he said himself, he had a nose for the truth; and so he decided, with a kind of presentiment, to carry out a further search of Cabuche's hovel himself. And there he found, merely concealed behind a beam, a secret hiding-place full of lady's handkerchiefs and gloves, beneath which lay a gold watch. He recognized it at once with a great surge of joy: it was President Grandmorin's watch, for which he had searched so hard the previous time, a large, solid watch with the two interwoven initials, bearing the maker's number 2516 on the inside of the case. It was like a thunderbolt: everything became clear, the past connected with the present, and he was entranced by the happy logic with which the facts fitted together. But the consequences were going to be so serious that he did not mention the watch at first but instead questioned Cabuche about the gloves and the handkerchiefs. For a moment confession hovered on his lips: yes, he adored her, yes he desired her, so much so that he kissed the dresses she had worn, that he went round after her picking up—no, stealing—everything that fell from her person, laces from her stays, hooks, eyes, hairpins. Then a sense of shame, of insuperable modesty, caused him to remain silent. And when the magistrate finally decided to show him the watch, he looked at it in bewilderment. He remembered perfectly: he had been surprised to discover it tied up in a handkerchief which he had taken from under a bolster and carried home in triumph; there it had remained while he racked his brains to think of some way of returning it. But why tell them all that? He'd only have to confess the rest of his pilfering, the stray ribbons, the personal linen that smelt so sweet, the things of which he was so ashamed. Already nobody believed a word of what he said. Moreover he was beginning not quite to understand things himself, everything was getting into a muddle in his simple head, and it was all becoming a nightmare. And he didn't even fly into a rage now when they accused him of the murder; he just sat there in a daze, repeatedly answering every question by saying that he didn't know. Gloves? Handkerchiefs? He didn't know. Watch? He didn't know. These people were getting on his nerves: why couldn't they just leave him alone and have him guillotined straightaway?

The following day Monsieur Denizet had Roubaud arrested. Firm in the knowledge of his wide-ranging powers, he had issued the warrant during one of those inspired moments when he believed in the genius of his own perspicacity, and before he had even prepared an adequate case against the assistant station-master. Although many things were still not clear, he sensed that this man was the pivot, the fountain-head, of this double affair; and his triumph was immediate when he seized the deed of gift, signed before Maître Colin, notary of Le Havre, in which Roubaud and Séverine, a week after entering into possession of La Croix-de-Maufras, had each made over their estate to the surviving spouse. Thereafter the entire story pieced itself together in his head: the sureness of the logic and the strength of the evidence lent such irrefragable solidity to the case he had constructed that the truth itself would have seemed less true, sullied by fantasy and illogicality. Roubaud was a coward who twice, not daring to kill someone himself, had employed the hand of Cabuche, that violent brute. On the first occasion, having been in a hurry to inherit from President Grandmorin, the contents of whose will were known to him, and aware also of the quarryman's grievance against him, he had put a knife in his hand and shoved him into the coupé at Rouen. Then, having shared the ten thousand francs, the two accomplices might never have seen each other again had not murder given rise to further murder. And this was where Denizet had shown that deep insight of his into criminal psychology which was so much admired; for, and he could say it now, he had had Cabuche kept under constant watch, he had been convinced that the first murder would lead mathematically to a second. Eighteen months had been sufficient: the Roubauds' marriage had broken down, the husband had gambled away the five thousand francs, and to take her mind off things the wife had finally taken a lover. She had probably refused to sell La Croix-de-Maufras for fear that her husband would squander the money; perhaps she had even threatened, in the course of their endless quarrels, to tell the police. Whatever the case, numerous witnesses testified to the complete breakdown of the couple's marriage; and thereupon, finally, the first crime had produced its distant consequence: Cabuche reappearing on the scene with his brutish appetites, and the husband lurking in the shadows and again putting the knife in his hand, to be sure once and for all of possessing that accursed house which had already cost one human life. Such was the truth, the blinding truth, everything pointed to it: the watch found at the quarryman's hovel, and above all the two bodies, both stabbed in the throat, in the same way, by the same hand, with the same weapon, with that knife which had been found lying in the bedroom. On this last point, however, the prosecution voiced an element of doubt: the President's wound had apparently been made by a smaller, sharper blade.

At first Roubaud simply replied 'yes' and 'no', with that dull, sleepy air which he now habitually displayed. He seemed to feel no surprise at his arrest, having become indifferent to everything as his moral being slowly disintegrated. To make him talk he had been given a permanent guard, with whom he played cards from morning till night; and he was perfectly content. In any case he was thoroughly convinced that Cabuche was guilty: only he could have murdered her. When questioned about Jacques, he had simply laughed and shrugged his shoulders, thereby intimating that he knew all about the driver's relationship with Séverine. But when Monsieur Denizet, after carefully feeling his way, finally produced his theory about what had happened, prodding him, battering him with the fact of his complicity, thereby trying to extract a confession from him in the moment of shock at seeing himself thus exposed, Roubaud had become very wary. What was all this? It wasn't him any more but the quarryman who had killed the President, just as he had Séverine; and yet nevertheless on both occasions he, Roubaud, had been the guilty party since the other man had been acting on his account and in his stead? This tortuous story left him bewildered and filled with suspicion: there could be no question, they were setting a trap for him, they were making it up so as to force him to confess his part in the crimes, how he had committed the first murder. From the moment of his arrest he had been fairly certain that the earlier business was going to come up. On being confronted with Cabuche, he maintained that he did not know him. But when he kept repeating that he had found him covered in blood and on the point of raping the victim, the quarryman lost his temper, and a violent scene of utter confusion ensued, complicating matters still further. Three days went by, and the magistrate prolonged his questioning in the certain knowledge that the two accomplices were colluding and putting on this show of hostility just to fool him. Now very tired, Roubaud had decided to answer no more questions when all at once, in a moment of exasperation, wanting to have done with the entire thing and yielding to a secret urge which had been gnawing away at him for months, he came out with the truth, the whole truth, and nothing but the truth.

That day, precisely, Monsieur Denizet had been engaged in subtle combat, seated behind his desk, his eyes veiled by those heavy eyelids, his restless lips pursing in the struggle for sagacity. For a whole hour he had been trying ploy after ploy on the accused, this stolid man whose body had run to unwholesome sallow fat, and yet whom he judged to have a shrewd and agile brain beneath the ponderous exterior. And he firmly believed that, step by step, he had finally tracked him down, that he had tied him in knots and trapped him at last, when Roubaud, with the gesture of a man who can stand no more, cried out that he had had enough, that he would rather confess than be tortured any longer. If they were determined he was guilty, then at least let him be guilty of the things he really had done. But as he related the story, how his wife had been abused by Grandmorin as a young girl, his fit of jealous rage when he learnt about such filth, how he had killed him, and why he had taken the ten thousand francs, then the magistrate's eyelids began to rise in a frown of doubt, and a wave of irrepressible incredulity, the incredulity of the professional, twisted his lips into a moue of mocking disbelief. He was smiling quite openly when the accused fell silent. This chap was even cleverer than he'd thought: to accept responsibility for the first crime and turn it into a pure crime of passion, thus clearing himself of any premeditated theft and, above all, of any complicity in the murder of Séverine, well, it was certainly a bold move, indicative of uncommon intelligence and resolve. Only, it wouldn't wash.

'Come, come, Roubaud, we're not children, you know . . . So you claim you were jealous, that it was a fit of jealousy that made you do it?'

'Certainly.'

'And, if we are to believe what you say, you married your wife without knowing anything about her relationship with the

President . . . Is that likely? Indeed everything would seem rather to point the other way in your case, to there having been some deal that was offered, and discussed, and accepted. You get a young woman who has had a good upbringing, she is given a dowry, her protector becomes your protector, you are given to understand that he is leaving her a country house in his will. And yet you claim that you suspected nothing, absolutely nothing! Come now, you knew everything, there's no other possible explanation for your marriage . . . In any event, there's one simple fact which destroys your case. You're not the jealous type, so how can you say you were jealous?'

'I have told you the truth. I killed him in a fit of jealous rage.'

'So, having killed the President because of something or other that went on between them in the past, and which in any case you've invented, kindly explain how you were then able to put up with your wife taking a lover? Yes, I mean that Jacques Lantier fellow, and a fine young man he is too! Everybody has told me about their relationship, and you yourself have made no attempt to conceal from me that you knew about it . . . You left them to it. Why?'

Slumped in his seat and looking dazed, Roubaud stared fixedly into space, unable to find an explanation. Finally he stammered:

'I don't know . . . I did the first one, but I didn't do this one.'

'So you needn't bother telling me you were a jealous man out for revenge, and I suggest you don't repeat such a far-fetched tale to the gentlemen of the jury either. It won't cut much ice with them . . . Take my advice, and change your story. Only the truth can save you.'

Thereafter the more Roubaud insisted on stating the truth, the more he was damned as a liar. Indeed everything was beginning to work against him, to the extent that his replies at the time of the first enquiry, which should have supported his new version of events (since he had then denounced Cabuche), now became proof on the contrary that there had been extraordinarily clever collusion between them. The magistrate continued to probe the psychology of the case with true professional zeal. Never, he said, had he delved so deep into human nature, it was more like divination than observation; for he flattered himself on belonging to that all-seeing school of magistrates who can weave a spell over a man and expose him with a single glance. And moreover there was no shortage of evidence, a whole incriminating pile of it. From now on the investigation could proceed on a firm basis: the certain truth shone out like the bright light of the sun.

And what added still further to Monsieur Denizet's glorious triumph was the fact that he was bringing the two cases to court as one, having all the time been patiently piecing them together in total secret. Ever since the resounding success of the plebiscite, a fever had gripped the nation, rather like the rumblings which precede and foreshadow great natural disasters. As the Empire approached its end, an atmosphere of continual disquiet prevailed throughout society, in political life, and especially in the press, a state of nervous excitement in which joy itself assumed an unhealthily violent form. Thus, when those who had been following the murder of this woman in a remote house at La Croix-de-Maufras learnt how the examining magistrate in Rouen had, by a stroke of genius, dug up the old Grandmorin case and linked it with this latest crime, there was an explosion of triumph in the establishment press. For indeed, from time to time, the opposition papers still occasionally made jokes about the mythical assassin who could not be found, that fiction invented by the police to conceal the turpitude of certain compromised persons in high places. And now there would be a clear answer; the killer and his accomplice had been arrested, President Grandmorin's memory would emerge untainted from the whole business. The old controversies started up afresh, and excitement grew daily, in Rouen and in Paris. Apart from the gruesome story itself, which had captured everyone's imagination, people grew more and more passionately involved at the prospect that this revelation, at last, of the irrefutable truth might restore calm to the body politic. For an entire week the press seemed to carry nothing else.

Summoned to Paris, Monsieur Denizet presented himself in the Rue du Rocher at the personal residence of the Secretary General, Monsieur Camy-Lamotte. He found him standing in the middle of his austere study, now thinner in the face, and looking more tired and drawn; for he was on the wane, filled with the sadness of his scepticism, as if he had already sensed, in the midst of this moment of triumph, the imminent collapse of the régime he served. For two days he had been debating with himself what to do, still not sure in his mind to what use he might put Séverine's letter, which he had kept: it could demolish the prosecution's whole case by offering conclusive evidence in corroboration of Roubaud's story. Nobody else in the whole world knew of its existence, he could destroy it if he chose. But on the previous day the Emperor had told him how this time he was insistent that justice should follow its natural course, free from any interference, and even at the risk of damage to his own government: it had been a simple cry for honesty, born of the superstition perhaps that one single unjust action might, after his recent acclaim by the nation,* alter the entire course of his destiny. And even though the Secretary General for his own part felt no scruples of conscience, having reduced the affairs of this world to a simple question of mechanics, he was troubled by the order which he had received, and wondered whether he should perhaps love his master to the point of disobeying him.

Immediately Monsieur Denizet began to crow.

'Well, my instincts were right, it was indeed that Cabuche fellow who killed the President . . . Mind you, I admit, the other line of enquiry did contain an element of truth, and I thought myself that Roubaud's version didn't quite ring true . . . Anyway, we've got the pair of them now.'

Monsieur Camy-Lamotte stared at him with his pale eyes.

'So, all the facts in the dossier I was sent have been checked, and you are absolutely sure?'

'Absolutely, beyond a shadow of a doubt . . . Everything fits. Indeed, in spite of the apparent complications, I can't remember a case where the crime followed a more logical course or could have been more easily predicted in advance.'

'But Roubaud is protesting his innocence, admitting the first murder but telling some tale about his wife being deflowered and how he, mad with jealousy, killed in a fit of blind rage. The opposition newspapers are all saying the same thing.'

'Oh, they're just repeating the gossip, they wouldn't dream of believing him. Roubaud jealous? When he actually made things easier for his wife and her lover to meet?! Oh, he can repeat that tale in open court if he likes, but it won't bring him any nearer to exposing the scandal they're all after! . . . If he had some proof even! But no, he's got nothing. Yes, he talks about the letter which he claims he forced his wife to write and which ought to have been found among the victim's papers . . . You filed those papers, didn't you, sir? You would have found it, wouldn't you?'

Monsieur Camy-Lamotte did not reply. It was true, the scandal was finally about to be laid to rest thanks to the magistrate's case for the prosecution: no one would believe Roubaud, the President's name would be cleared of those foul allegations, the ringing vindication of one of the Empire's own would bring it nothing but benefit. Besides, since this man Roubaud was admitting his guilt, of what relevance was it to the notion of justice that he should be condemned for one version of events or the other! True, there was Cabuche to think about; but even if he had not been involved in the first murder, he really did seem to be responsible for the second. And anyway, my God, justice! The last great illusion! To want to be just, wasn't that simply a snare, given that truth is always so hedged about? It was better to be sensible and do what he could to prop up this crumbling society that was on the brink of ruin.

'Wouldn't you, sir?' Monsieur Denizet repeated. 'I mean, you didn't find that letter, did you?'

Once more Monsieur Camy-Lamotte looked up at him. Calmly, as sole master of the situation, he took upon his own conscience the remorse which had troubled the Emperor, and replied:

'I found absolutely nothing.'

Then, smiling, at his most affable, he showered the magistrate with praise. Barely a quiver of the lips betrayed his incorrigible irony. Never had an investigation been conducted with greater insight; and soon, it had already been decided in high places, Monsieur Denizet would be called to the bench in Paris, after the recess. With more of the same he showed him out into the hall.

'You were the only one who saw things clearly, it really is quite admirable . . . And the moment truth has spoken, nothing can stop it, neither personal interests nor even reasons of state . . . Proceed, and may the case follow its course, whatever the consequences may be.'

'The judiciary has no other duty,' concluded Monsieur Denizet, who departed, beaming, with a bow.

Left alone, Monsieur Camy-Lamotte first lit a candle; then he went to fetch Séverine's letter from the drawer in which he had filed it. With the candle burning brightly, he unfolded the letter, wanting to read again its two lines; and his memory filled with that dainty criminal with the periwinkle eyes, who had once moved him to such tender sympathy. She was dead now, and he saw her in a new, tragic light. Who else could possibly know the secret which she must have taken with her to the grave? Oh yes, most assuredly: truth, justice, all an illusion! For him there remained of this unknown, charming woman only the moment's passing desire with which she had touched him and which he had not satisfied. And as he brought the letter over the flame and it began to burn, he was filled with enormous sadness, a foreboding of misfortune: why destroy this piece of evidence, why burden his conscience with such an act, if it was the Empire's fate to be swept away, like the pinch of black ash which had now fallen from his fingers?

In less than a week Monsieur Denizet had completed his investigation. He received the fullest co-operation from the Compagnie de l'Ouest; he had all the documents he desired, all the information he needed. For it, too, heartily wished to see an end to the matter, to have done with this deplorable business which involved one of its own employees, and the effect of which had gradually made itself felt all the way up through the various arteries of its corporate body and almost brought down its board of directors. The gangrened limb must be severed at the earliest opportunity. Accordingly the station staff from Le Havre once again paraded through the magistrate's office, Monsieur Dabadie, Moulin, and the others, who gave damning evidence about Roubaud's unsatisfactory conduct; then the station-master from Barentin, Monsieur Bessière, along with several station-workers from Rouen, whose statements were of decisive importance in respect of the first murder; then Monsieur Vandorpe, the station-master in Paris, Misard, the section-post watchman, and the chief guard Henri Dauvergne, these last two strongly confirming the fact of the accused's conjugal complaisance. And Henri, whom Séverine had nursed at La Croix-de-Maufras, even recounted how one evening, when he was still very ill, he thought he had heard the voices of Roubaud and Cabuche plotting together outside his window, something which explained much and would destroy the case put forward by the two accused, who claimed not to know each other. The Company's entire staff was of one accord in its condemnation, and everyone felt for the unfortunate victims, that poor woman for whose lapse there were so many excuses, and that elderly gentleman, such an honourable man, whose name had now been cleared of all the ugly rumours which had been circulating about him.

But the new investigation had stirred up strong feeling among the Grandmorin family in particular, and in that quarter, even if Monsieur Denizet continued to meet with powerful support, he had also to struggle to safeguard the coherence of his case. The Lachesnayes were cock-a-hoop, for in their exasperation and avaricious despair at the bequest of La Croix-de-Maufras they had always asserted Roubaud's guilt. Hence they saw in the renewed interest being taken in the case simply an opportunity to contest the will; and as there was only one way to get the will set aside, namely to have Séverine disqualified as an ungrateful legatee, they partially accepted Roubaud's version of events, how the wife had been an accomplice and helped him to kill, but not in order to avenge some imagined infamy but rather to rob the man. This meant that the magistrate found himself at odds with them, and with Berthe especially, who was very bitter against the murdered woman, her former friend, whom she accused of all manner of things and whom he defended with warmth, anger even, the moment he could see his masterpiece threatened, his great edifice of logic, which had been so well constructed (as he himself proudly declared) that if anyone were to change a single piece of it, the whole thing would come tumbling down. There was a lively debate on this subject in his chambers between the Lachesnayes and Madame Bonnehon. The latter, having previously been on the Roubauds' side, had had to forsake the husband; but she continued to support the wife out of a kind of affectionate complicity, having a particular tolerance for personal charm and affairs of the heart, and being thoroughly upset by this tragic, bloody tale. She made herself quite clear on the matter, filled as she was with disdain for money. Was her niece

not ashamed to be raking up this question of the legacy? If
Séverine were guilty, did that not mean accepting Roubaud's
supposed confession in its entirety and thus blackening the
President's name once more? If the magistrate's investigation
had not so cleverly established the truth, they would have had to
invent it, for the sake of the family's honour. And she spoke with
some bitterness of Rouen society, in which the affair was causing
such a stir, a society over which she no longer reigned now that
the years were catching up with her and she was losing even that
blond, opulent beauty of an ageing goddess. Why only the previous day, at Madame Leboucq's, the judge's wife, the tall,
elegant brunette who was usurping her throne, people had been
whispering risqué stories to each other about that business with
Louisette, and about all the other things that public ill-will had
been able to concoct. At that point, after Monsieur Denizet had
intervened to tell her that Monsieur Leboucq would be sitting as
an assessor at the forthcoming assizes,* the Lachesnayes fell
silent, apparently conceding out of sudden misgivings. But
Madame Bonnehon reassured them that she was confident the
law would do its duty: for the assizes would be presided over by
her old friend Monsieur Desbazeilles, the one whose rheumatism had reduced him to naught but fond memories, and the
other assessor was to be Monsieur Chaumette, the father of the
young deputy prosecutor who was her protégé. Her mind, therefore, was at rest, although a melancholy smile had come to her
lips as she mentioned Monsieur Chaumette: his son's presence
had been noted at Madame Leboucq's for some time, which was
where she herself had sent him so that his prospects should not
be blighted.

When the celebrated trial finally began, the rumours about an
imminent war and the ferment of unrest which was spreading
throughout France detracted considerably from the publicity
given to the proceedings. All the same Rouen spent three days in
a state of high excitement, and at the entrance to the courtroom
there was a continual crush of people trying to get in, the reserved seats having already been taken by the ladies of the town.
Never, since it had been first converted into law courts, had the
former palace of the Dukes of Normandy seen such a crowd. It
was towards the end of June, and the afternoons were warm and

sunny: the bright sunshine lit up the stained glass in the palace's ten windows, pouring in on the oak panelling, and the white stone crucifix that stood out at the far end against the scarlet hangings strewn with bees,* and on the famous ceiling dating from Louis XII's time, with its coffered compartments of carved wood gilded in the softest of old gold. It was already stiflingly hot, even before the court went into session. Women strained to see the table of exhibits: Grandmorin's watch, Séverine's blood-stained nightdress, and the knife which had been used in both murders. Cabuche's defence lawyer, from Paris, was also the object of much attention. Lined up on the jury benches sat twelve men of Rouen, trussed in black frock-coats, stout and solemn. And when the court entered, there was such a shoving and pushing among the standing public that the President of the Court had at once to threaten to clear the courtroom.

At last the proceedings began: the jury was sworn in, and a tremor of curiosity once more ran through the crowd as the witnesses were summoned. At the names of Madame Bonnehon and Monsieur de Lachesnaye, heads swivelled; but it was Jacques who particularly interested the ladies, and their eyes followed him as he entered. After that, once the two accused men were present and each seated between two gendarmes, they were the object of constant scrutiny: and opinions were exchanged. People thought they looked fierce and mean, like a pair of bandits. Roubaud, in his dark jacket and with his tie untidily knotted like that of a gentleman who has gone to seed, surprised people by how old he looked; and his face, fat to bursting, bore a witless air. As for Cabuche, he was just as they had imagined him, dressed in a long, blue smock, the very picture of a murderer, with his enormous fists and great, carnivorous jaws, in short just the kind of person one would not wish to come upon in the middle of a dark wood. His conduct in the witness-box confirmed this unfavourable impression, and some of his replies provoked vociferous mutterings. Each time the President of the Court asked him a question, Cabuche replied that he didn't know: he did not know how the watch came to be on his premises, he did not know why he had let the real murderer get away; and he stuck to his story of this mysterious stranger and how he had heard him dashing off into the night. Then, on being asked about his bestial passion for his unfortunate victim, he had begun to splutter with such sudden and violent anger that the two gendarmes had each seized him by the arm: no, no, he hadn't loved her, he hadn't wanted her, it was all lies, even just wanting her would have made her dirty, her, a lady, whereas he'd done time, he lived rough! Then, having calmed down, he had fallen into a sullen silence, replying only with the occasional monosyllable and quite indifferent to the judgement that might now be passed upon him. Similarly, Roubaud stuck to what the prosecution called his 'system': he related how and why he had killed Grandmorin, and he denied any possible involvement in the murder of his wife. But he said it all in broken, almost incoherent sentences, with sudden lapses of memory, his eyes so dull and his voice so indistinct that he seemed at moments to be trying to make up the details as he went along. And with the President constantly pressing him and pointing out the inconsistencies in his story, he finally shrugged his shoulders and refused to say more: why bother to tell the truth, since it was falsehood that was logical? This attitude of aggressive disdain for the due process of law did him the greatest disservice. People also noticed the complete lack of interest which the two accused showed in each other, which proved that they were in cahoots; it was all part of the cunning plan which had been followed with extraordinary determination. They claimed not to know each other and even accused each other, but it was all done just to deceive the court. By the time they had finished being questioned, the verdict was a foregone conclusion, so skilfully had the President steered the interrogation, with the result that Roubaud and Cabuche, by falling into the traps which had been set, appeared to have condemned themselves. One or two further witnesses, of no importance, were heard that day. By five o'clock the heat had become so unbearable that two ladies fainted.

But on the following day the greatest excitement was reserved for the examination of certain witnesses in particular. Madame Bonnehon achieved a veritable triumph by her tact and good manners. The Company's employees were listened to with interest: Monsieur Vandorpe, Monsieur Bessière, Monsieur Dabadie, and especially Monsieur Cauche, who told them at great length how well he knew Roubaud, having often played cards with him at the Café du Commerce. Henri Dauvergne repeated his damning testimony, his almost total certainty that while feverish and trying to sleep he had heard the two accused plotting together in low voices; and when questioned about Séverine he was discretion itself, intimating that he had loved her but that, knowing her heart to lie elsewhere, he had honourably stood aside. Thus when that someone else, Jacques Lantier, was finally called, a buzz went round the courtroom, people stood up to get a better look, and even among the members of the jury there was a marked quickening of interest. Quite unperturbed, Jacques leant with both hands on the rail of the witnessbox as though he were at work, automatically assuming the pose which he habitually adopted when driving his train. This appearance in court, which should have troubled him deeply, found him in fact with great lucidity of mind, as if none of this were his concern. He would give his evidence as an innocent bystander; for since the crime he had not felt a single tremor, he had never even given the matter a second's thought, his memory had been wiped clean, and his physical being was in a state of perfect equilibrium, of perfect health. Even here, at the rail, he felt neither remorse nor scruple; he was quite without conscience. Immediately his bright, clear eyes had fallen on Roubaud and Cabuche. The former he knew to be guilty, and he nodded to him in discreet recognition, heedless of the fact that today he was standing there as the known lover of this man's wife. Then he smiled at Cabuche, the innocent party, whose place in the dock he himself should have been occupying: a decent creature underneath it all, despite his criminal air, a good man whom he'd watched at his work and whose hand he had shaken. And with total composure he gave his evidence, replying briefly and clearly to the judge who, having asked him endless questions about his relationship with the victim, made him recount his departure from La Croix-de-Maufras, some few hours before the murder, how he had gone to catch the train at Barentin, how he had spent the night at Rouen. Cabuche and Roubaud were listening to him, seeming implicitly to confirm his evidence; and at that moment the three men were joined in a communion of unspeakable sadness. There was deathly silence in the courtroom, and the members of the jury felt a lump in their throats at this sudden wave of emotion which seemed to have sprung from nowhere: they were witnessing the silent passage of the truth. When the President asked him what he thought of the quarryman's statement about a stranger vanishing into the darkness, Jacques simply shook his head, as though he did not want to make matters worse for an accused man. And then something happened which completely overwhelmed those sitting in the courtroom: tears began to well in Jacques's eyes, brimming over and coursing down his cheeks. In just the same way as before, the picture of Séverine had come to him, the picture of that poor, murdered woman as he had last seen her, with her blue eyes open wide, immeasurably wide, and her black hair standing on end above her forehead like a helmet of horror. He still adored her. An enormous feeling of compassion had taken hold of him, and he wept for her, copiously, oblivious to his crime, oblivious to where he was, amidst all these people. Ladies sobbed, overcome by the emotion; and people were deeply moved at the sight of this lover's pain while the husband sat there dry-eyed. The President having asked the defence if they had any questions for the witness, the lawyers thanked him but declined, and the dazed eyes of the two accused followed Jacques as he returned to his seat surrounded by the public's sympathy.

The third day of the case was entirely taken up by the public prosecutor's address and the speeches of various counsel. First, the President had presented a summing-up in which, beneath a veneer of absolute impartiality, the prosecution charges were particularly emphasized. Following that, the state prosecutor seemed not to be in full command of his talents: usually he spoke with more conviction, with a less empty eloquence. This was put down to the heat, which was indeed stifling. On the other hand, Cabuche's defending counsel, the lawyer from Paris, went down very well, though without convincing anyone. Roubaud's defence counsel, a distinguished member of the Rouen bar, tried similarly to extract what advantage he could from his weak case. Quite worn out, the prosecution did not even reply. And when the jury retired to consider its verdict, it was only six o'clock; sunlight was still streaming in through the ten windows, and the last rays fell upon their imposts, decorated with the arms of the towns of Normandy. The sound of noisy chatter rose towards the ancient gilded ceiling, while brief surges of impatience shook the iron railing that separated the reserved seats from the standing public. But a solemn hush fell once more as the jury and the court returned. The verdict accepted the plea of extenuating circumstances, and the bench sentenced the two men to hard labour for life. This came as a considerable surprise, and the courtroom began to empty in uproar, while isolated whistles could be heard, as though this were a theatre.

All over Rouen that evening the sentence was the subject of endless discussion and debate. The general view was that it marked a defeat for Madame Bonnehon and the Lachesnayes. Only the death sentence, it seemed, would have satisfied the family; and quite plainly some influence must have been brought to bear from the other side. Already the name of Madame Leboucq was being quietly mentioned; three or four members of the jury were loyal to her. There had been nothing irregular about her husband's conduct as an assessor, of course; it was just that it did seem as if neither the other assessor, Monsieur Chaumette, nor the President of the Court himself, Monsieur Desbazeilles, had quite felt themselves to be as much in control of the proceedings as they would have wished. Perhaps the jury had simply had scruples, and by accepting the plea of extenuating circumstances had merely yielded to the uncomfortable feeling of doubt which had momentarily run through the courtroom during that silent passage of the melancholy truth. Otherwise the whole affair continued to represent a triumph for the examining magistrate, Monsieur Denizet, since nothing had arisen to detract from his masterly piece of work; for the family itself lost much sympathy when the rumour began to circulate that, in order to recover La Croix-de-Maufras, Monsieur de Lachesnaye, contrary to normal legal practice, was talking of bringing an action to have the bequest revoked, despite the death of the legatee, which was a surprising thing for a magistrate to be doing.

Outside the courthouse Jacques was joined by Philomène, who had stayed on as one of the witnesses; and she refused to leave his side, detaining him in an attempt to spend the night with him in Rouen. He was not due back to work until the following day, and he would gladly let her remain with him for dinner in that inn near the station where he claimed to have slept on the night of the crime; but he would not be spending the night there, he absolutely had to return to Paris by the 12.50 train.

'Incidentally, you'll never guess,' she told him, as she walked on his arm in the direction of the inn. 'I would swear that just now I saw a familiar face . . . Yes, Pecqueux. And there he was telling me again only the other day that no one was going to catch him going to Rouen for the case . . . I turned round for a second, and this man—I only saw his back—disappeared into the crowd . . .'

Jacques interrupted her with a shrug.

'Pecqueux's in Paris, on a drinking spree, and only too happy to be having days off because I've got leave of absence.'

'Maybe . . . Anyway, we'd better be careful, he's a right brute when he's in a temper.'

She pressed closer to him and added with a backward glance: 'And him, the man who's following us. Do you know him?'

'Oh, don't worry . . . He's probably got something to ask me.'

It was Misard, who had indeed been following them at a distance since the Rue des Juifs. He, too, had testified, as though half-asleep; and he had remained behind, prowling round after Jacques without quite making up his mind to ask him the question which he was evidently anxious to put. When the couple had disappeared into the inn, he went in also and ordered a glass of wine.

'Ah, it's you, Misard,' Jacques called out. 'And how are things with that new wife of yours?'

'All right, all right,' growled Misard. 'Oh, that bitch, she fooled me good and proper, she did. Eh? I told you all about it, didn't I, the last time I came here?'

The story tickled Jacques greatly. La Ducloux, the former waitress with a shady past whom Misard had taken on to mind the level-crossing, had soon noticed him rummaging around everywhere and realized that he must be searching for a nest-egg left behind by his late wife; and she had had the brainwave of getting him to marry her by hinting to him, by little nervous giggles and an apparent reluctance to tell, that she had found it herself. At first he had nearly throttled her; then, thinking that

the thousand francs would elude his grasp yet again if he got rid
of her like he'd got rid of the first one before getting his hands on
them, he had become all cajoling, kindness itself; but she rejected
him, didn't even want him to touch her any more: no, no, once
she was his wife, he could have it all, her and the money to boot.
And he had married her, and she had laughed in his face, telling
him how stupid he was, believing anything anyone told him. The
best of it, though, was that once she was in the know, she had
caught the fever herself and now searched as furiously as he. Oh,
they'd track them down one day, those elusive thousand francs,
now that there were two of them! And they searched, and they
searched.

'So, still nothing?' asked Jacques teasingly. 'Isn't she any help
to you, then, La Ducloux?'

Misard stared at him, and finally he said:

'You know where they are, so tell me.'

But Jacques began to lose his temper.

'I know nothing of the sort, Aunt Phasie gave me nothing.
You're not going to accuse me of stealing them, I hope?'

'Oh, so she never gave you anything, eh? Oh no, of course, she
didn't . . . Come on, you can see it's driving me out of my mind.
If you know where they are, just tell me.'

'Look, bugger off. And just you watch yourself, or I might
start saying a thing or two . . . Why don't you go and have a look
in the salt tin, eh? Maybe that's where they are.'

Pale, his eyes blazing, Misard stared at him still. It was as
though he had had a sudden inspiration.

'In the salt tin, yes, of course. There's a place beneath the
drawer where I haven't looked yet.'

And hurriedly he paid for his wine and dashed off to see if he
could still catch the 7.10. Back there in that little house he would
go on searching, for ever.

That evening after dinner, as they waited for the 12.50 train,
Philomène was determined to take Jacques out, along the dark
back streets, into the nearby countryside. It was very close, a real
July night, sultry and moonless, and her bosom rose with heavy
sighs as she wrapped her arms around his neck. Twice she had
turned round, thinking she heard footsteps behind them, but
saw nobody, so thick was the darkness. He was finding this

oppressive night hard to bear. In the midst of his tranquil state of equilibrium and the perfect state of health which he had been enjoying since the murder, he had just now, at table, sensed the return of a distant malaise every time this woman's straying hands had touched him. Tiredness probably, an edginess brought on by the airless atmosphere. And now he could feel the agony of desire starting up again within him, stronger than ever, full of nagging terror, as he held her thus against his body. Yet he was completely cured, he had tried the experiment, possessing her, coolly and calmly, to make sure. His state of arousal became such that the fear of another attack would already have made him break free of their embrace if the surrounding darkness had not reassured him; for he would never, not even in the direst moments of his malady, have struck when he couldn't see. And suddenly, as they passed a grassy bank along a deserted lane, and she pulled him towards her, sinking to the ground, the monstrous urge took hold of him once more, filling him with a raging fury as he groped in the grass for some weapon, a stone, with which to smash her skull. Abruptly he leapt to his feet, and already he was careering off into the distance when he heard a man's voice, a stream of oaths, and a full-scale battle going on.

'Ah, you bitch! I waited till the very last moment, I wanted to be sure.'

'It's not true! Let go of me!'

'Ah, so it isn't true! Oh, he can run away if he wants to, I know who it is, I'll soon find him! . . . Take that, you bitch, and just you try telling me again it's not true!'

Jacques was racing through the night, fleeing not from Pecqueux, whom he had just recognized, but, mad with grief, from himself.

What! So one murder had not been enough? He hadn't had his fill with the blood of Séverine as, even that very morning, he had thought he had? Here he was, at it again. Another woman, and another, and then still another! As soon as he was sated and another few weeks of torpor went by, his dreadful craving would start up again, he would always require the flesh of woman if it was to be satisfied. And now he didn't even need to see the flesh that tempted him: he had only to feel it all warm in his arms, and already he would be yielding to his murderous lust like a rutting beast, like the wild and savage male who rips his females' stomachs open. There was nothing more to live for: all that remained ahead of him was this black night of limitless despair through which he was now fleeing.

A few days went by. Jacques had returned to work, avoiding the other railwaymen and reverting to his previous touchy and unsociable ways. War had just been declared,* after some stormy sessions in Parliament; and already a skirmish had taken place between outposts, which was said to have ended in success. For the past week the transport of troops had left everyone on the railways completely exhausted. Regular services had been disrupted, and unscheduled trains continued to cause severe delays; added to which the best drivers had been commandeered to speed up the process of reuniting various army corps. And this was why in Le Havre one evening Jacques found himself having to drive, instead of his usual express, an enormous train of eighteen wagons crammed with soldiers.

That evening Pecqueux arrived very drunk at the depot. The day after he had caught Philomène and Jacques together, he had climbed aboard engine 608 as Jacques's fireman; and since then he had made no reference to the matter, persistently morose and apparently not daring to look his driver in the face. But Jacques could sense his growing resistance, as he refused to obey and responded with a low grunt every time he gave him an order. In the end they had stopped speaking to each other altogether. This moving sheet of metal, this little bridge that had once borne them along in such harmony, had now become the narrow, perilous strip upon which their rivalry clashed. Their hatred was growing, and they were ready to tear each other to pieces within these few square feet, from which the slightest jolt could have sent them flying as they hurtled along at full speed. So this evening, seeing Pecqueux drunk, Jacques was particularly watchful: for he knew he was too sly to get angry when sober; drink alone unleashed the beast in him.

The train, due to leave at about six, was delayed. It was already dark by the time the soldiers were loaded like sheep into the cattle wagons. Planks had simply been nailed across as seats, and the men were piled in by the squad, loading the wagons beyond capacity, so that they ended up sitting on top of each other, while one or two remained standing, squeezed in so tight that they could not even lift an arm. As soon as they arrived in Paris, another train would be waiting to take them to the Rhine. They were already dropping with exhaustion, dazed by the commotion of departure. But as they had all been issued with a tot of spirits and many of them had also done the rounds of the local bars, they were in a state of coarse and over-excited merriment, their eyes bulging and bloodshot. And the moment the train began to leave the station, they broke into song.

Jacques immediately glanced up at the sky, where a storm-haze hid the stars from view. It was going to be a very dark night, not a breath of wind stirred the stifling air; and the breeze made by the train's movement, usually so cool, seemed warm. On the dark horizon there were no other lights but the bright sparkles of the signal-lamps. He raised the pressure to take the great incline from Harfleur to Saint-Romain. Despite his careful attention over the past few weeks, he was still not master of engine 608: she was still too new, and her moments of caprice and youthful indiscipline continued to take him by surprise. That night particularly he could sense how restive and temperamental she was, ready to bolt the moment she was given a few lumps of coal too many. So, with his hand constantly on the gear-wheel, he kept his eye on the fire, growing more and more uneasy at his fireman's demeanour. The little lamp over the water-gauge bathed the platform in a half-light which was turned a violet blue by the glow from the firebox door, itself red-hot. He could not see Pecqueux clearly, and twice he had felt something brushing against his legs, as though fingers had been trying to grab him. But no doubt these had been no more than the clumsy movements of a drunk, for above the noise of the train he could hear Pecqueux's loud sneering laughter as he broke up the coal with wild blows of his hammer and fought with his shovel. Again and again he kept opening the firebox door and shovelling excessive amounts of fuel on to the grate.

'Enough!' shouted Jacques.

The other man pretended not to understand, and continued to throw on shovel after shovel; and when Jacques grabbed him by the arm, he turned menacingly, having got the fight he had been asking for, in the mounting fury of his drunkenness.

'Get your hands off me, or I'll hit you! . . . I like going fast like this!'

The train was now running at top speed across the plateau which stretches from Bolbec to Motteville. It was due to proceed directly to Paris without stopping, except at the appointed places to take on water. Its enormous mass—eighteen wagons all laden, crammed tight, with human livestock—traversed the dark countryside in one long roll of thunder. And these men being carted off to the slaughter were singing, singing their heads off, and so loudly that it drowned out the noise of the wheels.

Jacques had kicked the firebox door shut. Then, adjusting the injector and still controlling himself, he said:

'The fire's too high . . . Why don't you sleep it off if you're drunk.'

Pecqueux promptly opened the door again and madly shovelled on more coal, as though he wanted the whole engine to explode. This was open revolt, wilful disobedience, a passionate anger that no longer cared about all these human lives. And when Jacques bent down to lower the ashpan rod himself, so as at least to reduce the draught, the fireman suddenly seized him round the body and tried to push him backwards, to throw him out on to the line with one frantic shove.

'You bastard! So that's it? . . . Clever, eh? And then you could say I'd fallen off, you cunning bugger!'

He had saved himself by grabbing on to the edge of the tender, and they both tried to recover their footing as the struggle continued on the little metal bridge, which was violently bouncing up and down. Their teeth clenched, they spoke no further as each tried to push the other out through the narrow opening which was closed off by no more than a single iron bar. But it was not easy, with the engine still hurtling forwards, devouring the track; and as Barentin shot past and the train plunged into the Malaunay tunnel, they were still locked tight in combat, scrabbling in the coal and banging their heads against the water tank, trying to avoid the red-hot door of the firebox, which scorched their legs every time they extended them.

For a moment Jacques thought that if he could just get up, he would shut off the regulator and pull the whistle for help, in the hope that someone might free him from this raging madman, who was crazed with drunkenness and jealousy. Being the smaller of the two he was getting weaker, and he now despaired of finding the strength to throw him off; he was already beaten, and he could feel the terror of his imminent fall rippling through his hair. As he made one last effort and stretched out a groping hand, Pecqueux realized what he was up to, braced his back, and picked Jacques up like a child.

'Ah, so you want to stop, do you? ... But you took my woman ... So here we are, it's time you got what's coming.'

And on the engine raced, onward and onward: the train had just emerged from the tunnel with a great roar, and now it was continuing on its way across the dark, empty countryside. They went through Malaunay station in such a flash that the assistant station-master, who was standing on the platform, did not even see the two men fighting to the death as the thunderbolt carried them off into the distance.

But with one last shove Pecqueux pushed Jacques out; and Jacques, feeling the void beneath him, desperately hung on to Pecqueux's neck, and so tightly that he dragged him down with him. There were two terrible screams, which mingled and then ceased. Falling together, and sucked under the wheels by the sheer speed of the train, they were hacked and chopped to pieces as they clung fast in their terrible embrace, they who had for so long lived as brothers. They were found later, decapitated, their feet severed, two bleeding trunks still locked together as though intent on squeezing the life out of each other.

And on the engine raced, now out of control, onward and onward. At last this restive, temperamental thing could yield to the wild energy of youth, like a young filly, still unbroken, who has slipped the clutches of her groom and gone galloping off across the open plain. There was water in the boiler, and the firebox, which had just been stoked, was all ablaze; and as the pressure rose wildly during the first half hour, so the engine reached a terrifying speed. The chief guard must have succumbed to exhaustion and dropped off to sleep. The soldiers, whose drunkenness was increased by their being thus piled on top of each other, suddenly grew merry at this furious onrush and sang even more loudly. They shot through Maromme like lightning. The whistle no longer sounded as they approached signals or went through stations. It was the forward charge of a beast putting its head down in dumb deliberation and brushing all obstacles aside. And on she raced, ever onward, as though increasingly maddened by the strident shriek of her own breath.

At Rouen they were supposed to take on water; and station onlookers froze in horror to see this lunatic train flashing past in a swirl of smoke and flame, the engine without driver or fireman, and the cattle wagons full of soldier-boys yelling patriotic songs. They were off to war, and all this speed was so they could get there sooner, to the banks of the Rhine. The railway staff had simply stood there open-mouthed, waving their arms. And at once the cry went up: unchecked and left to itself, this train would never have a clear run through Sotteville station, which, like all large depots, was always blocked by shunting and cluttered with rolling-stock. And they rushed to telegraph a warning. As it happened, there was a goods train on the line there which could be backed into a shed. Already, in the distance, they could hear the runaway monster tearing towards them. It had raced through the two tunnels soon after Rouen, and was approaching at a furious speed, like some prodigious, irresistible force that nothing now could stop. And it tore through Sotteville station, slipping unscathed between the obstacles before plunging back into the darkness, where its thunder gradually faded.

But by now every telegraph bell along the line was ringing, and every heart beat faster at the news of this ghost train that had just been seen passing through Rouen and Sotteville. People were afraid: there was an express travelling further up the line, it would surely be caught. Like a wild boar charging through a forest, the train continued on its way, oblivious to red signals and detonators alike. At Oissel it nearly collided with a pilot-engine; it brought terror to Pont-de-l'Arche, for its speed showed no sign of slackening. Once more it vanished, and on it raced, onward and onward into the dark night, bound they knew not where, simply onward.

What did it matter what victims it crushed in its path! Was it not, after all, heading into the future, heedless of the blood that was spilled? And on it sped through the darkness, driverless, like some blind, deaf beast turned loose upon the field of death, onward and onward, laden with its freight of cannon-fodder, with these soldiers, already senseless with exhaustion and drink, still singing away.

EXPLANATORY NOTES

3 *Compagnie de l'Ouest*: from 1855 franchise holders for the railway network of Normandy and Northern Brittany.

Quartier de l'Europe: the area around the Place de l'Europe, later the Pont de l'Europe, where the streets bear the names of European capitals.

the mail and the foot-warmer depots: a foot-warmer was a flat hot-water tin placed on the compartment floor, which provided the only source of heating until, from the 1890s onwards, direct steam heating from the locomotive's boiler became the norm. It had its disadvantages, as C. Hamilton Ellis records in *The Trains We Loved* (London, 1947): 'at one stage in the history of British fashion, boots with gutta-percha soles came into favour. These stuck to the foot-warmers, and left their wearers effectively birdlimed' (p. 138).

the other, smaller sheds of the Argenteuil, Versailles, and Ceinture lines: the local railway services to Argenteuil on the Seine, north-west of Paris, and to Versailles. The Ceinture (literally 'girdle' or 'belt'), begun in 1852, linked different stations in Paris itself: it provides the backdrop to the burial of Claude Lantier at the end of *The Masterpiece*.

7 *the daughter of President Grandmorin*: throughout the novel Grandmorin is referred to as a *Président*: that is, the presiding judge, or magistrate, in a court. Rather than translate the term as 'Judge', 'President' has been preferred in order to preserve Zola's insistence on this term which, for his readers under the Third Republic as today under the Fifth Republic, had and has clear political connotations. The office of President had recently been brought into disrepute by President Grévy who was forced to resign in 1887 after his son-in-law Daniel Wilson was discovered selling decorations and other favours in the presidential gift. On the French legal system in general, see Introduction, pp. xxiv–xxv.

11 *the forthcoming general election*: held in May 1869 at a particularly tense moment in French political history. See Introduction, pp. xxvii–xxviii.

12 *a member of the General Council since 1855*: the General Council of a Département was a board of thirty-six or more elected

councillors (representing individual districts, or cantons) who administered the Département's affairs.

13 *was earning in Le Havre*: Pol Lefèvre (see Introduction, pp. xiii–xiv) had informed Zola that a station-manager aged 45 could earn 3,000 francs per annum. As assistant-manager Roubaud earns 2,000 francs p.a., compared with the 4,000 francs earned by the Pecqueux household and the similar sum earned by Jacques, who earns a basic salary of 2,800 francs, plus 1,200 in bonuses for fuel economies. (Zola appears to have used the salary levels of 1890 even though the novel is set twenty years earlier.) One may compare these sums with the 20,000 francs which Zola was paid by *La Vie populaire* for the serial rights to *La Bête humaine*.

32 *a private coupé*: a private compartment situated at the end of a carriage and in which there was only one bench (facing forwards).

36 *a cousin of his father's, a Lantier*: here Zola 'attaches' the recently created figure of Jacques Lantier to the family tree of the Rougon-Macquart which he had already drawn up in 1878 and appended to *A Page of Love*. Originally he had envisaged Étienne Lantier as his 'murderer', but the character of the man who leads the miners' strike in *Germinal* had evolved during the composition of that novel and was no longer his 'hereditary killer' (even though he commits a murder). The reason for his absence from *L'Assommoir* as the son of Gervaise and Auguste Lantier is here retrospectively 'explained'.

the Paris–Orléans line: this line was run by the Compagnie d'Orléans, which had begun operating in 1838 and been granted the franchise for Southern Brittany in 1855 and for some of central France in 1857. As a 'driver first class' Jacques is qualified to drive the faster locomotives, as opposed to those which hauled stopping trains (*omnibus*) and trains combining passenger coaches and goods wagons (*trains mixtes*).

37 *to ensure the proper running of the trains*: under the 'block system' a signalman or block-section watchman like Misard 'accepts' a train into his section and 'offers' it on to the next section using a telegraphic bell code.

38 *doing the ballast*: working on the construction or maintenance of a railway line by laying broken stone as a bed for the rails.

52 *to cost Gervaise so many tears*: Jacques's father abandons Gervaise at the beginning of *L'Assommoir*. In that novel the alcoholism which runs in the family eventually destroys Gervaise.

65 *the arrival of the Paris express, at* 11.05: in 1869 the 6.30 express
from Paris to Le Havre would have arrived at 11.25.

69 *sorry-looking buildings all covered in cracks*: on his visit to Le Havre
in 1889, Zola sought a first-hand description of the station as it was
in 1869 from a railwayman who had known it. The station had been
renovated in 1884.

90 *Monsieur Denizet, the examining magistrate*: see Introduction,
pp. xxiv–xxvi.

the creation of a municipal council: in March 1869 the powers of
Monsieur de Bourgoing, an equerry to the Emperor, and Monsieur
de Piennes, his Chamberlain, became the subject of parliamentary
controversy; and during debate of a bill relating to the finances of
the City of Paris, Baron Haussmann, Prefect of the Seine region,
was bitterly attacked by the opposition, who demanded (on 6
March) the creation of a municipal council.

91 *the Secretary General, Monsieur Camy-Lamotte*: on the role of a
Secretary General, see Introduction, pp. xxvi–xxvii.

184 *and ran over detonators*: a detonator is a small device which can be
fixed to the rail head by lead clips and is exploded by the wheel of
a locomotive passing over it.

223 *I hadn't pulled . . . the communication cord*: in point of fact the
Compagnie de l'Ouest did not fit alarm systems to their trains until
1882, although there had been calls for them in the press since the
Poinsot affair began in 1860.

336 *on this hot July night!*: given the reference to June at the beginning
of this chapter, this would appear to be a minor slip on Zola's part.

339 *some prince of theirs who wants to be King of Spain*: see Introduction,
p. xxviii.

340 *with their elections and their plebiscite and their riots!*: see Introduction, pp. xxvii–xxviii.

350 *after his recent acclaim by the nation*: in the plebiscite. See Introduction, p. xxviii.

354 *sitting as an assessor at the forthcoming assizes*: in *How France is
Governed* the sometime President of France Raymond Poincaré
describes the assizes thus: 'If you now feel equal to assist at a
lugubrious spectacle, let us go to the Assize Court, where hooli-
gans, assassins, incendiaries, and violent robbers are tried; you will
hear sentence pronounced upon them of death, hard labour, or
imprisonment.—Who is to declare them guilty? The three magistrates who sit yonder facing the public? No: but the twelve citizens

in ordinary clothes who are seated facing the accused. They are the jurors, and together they form the jury.—The three magistrates are three councillors if we are in a town which boasts of a court of appeal. Otherwise the presiding magistrate is a councillor, delegated by a neighbouring court, and the two assessors are judges borrowed from the local court. All these deliberate upon the application of the penalty when the jury has given its verdict of "guilty"' (trans. Bernard Miall (London, 1913), 256–7). See also Introduction, pp. xxiv–xxv.

355 *the scarlet hangings strewn with bees*: a reference to the imperial livery of Napoléon III.

363 *War had just been declared*: on 19 July 1870. See Introduction, p. xxviii.

*The
Oxford
World's
Classics
Website*

www.worldsclassics.co.uk

- Browse the full range of Oxford World's Classics online

- Sign up for our monthly e-alert to receive information on new titles

- Read extracts from the Introductions

- Listen to our editors and translators talk about the world's greatest literature with our Oxford World's Classics audio guides

- Join the conversation, follow us on Twitter at OWC_Oxford

- Teachers and lecturers can order inspection copies quickly and simply via our website

www.worldsclassics.co.uk

American Literature

British and Irish Literature

Children's Literature

Classics and Ancient Literature

Colonial Literature

Eastern Literature

European Literature

Gothic Literature

History

Medieval Literature

Oxford English Drama

Poetry

Philosophy

Politics

Religion

The Oxford Shakespeare

A complete list of Oxford World's Classics, including Authors in Context, Oxford English Drama, and the Oxford Shakespeare, is available in the UK from the Marketing Services Department, Oxford University Press, Great Clarendon Street, Oxford OX2 6DP, or visit the website at www.oup.com/uk/worldsclassics.

In the USA, visit www.oup.com/us/owc for a complete title list.

Oxford World's Classics are available from all good bookshops. In case of difficulty, customers in the UK should contact Oxford University Press Bookshop, 116 High Street, Oxford OX1 4BR.